HIT ME
WITH YOUR
BEST
CHARM

A Note from the Author

Dear Reader,

Hit Me with Your Best Charm is a funny, bittersweet, heartfelt YA novel with paranormal happenings in the woods and kids on a quest with a lot of hope and very little clue about camping or hiking. The story also contains missing (presumed dead) parents, childhood guilt, threats of violence, death that occurs off the page, skeletal remains, and dangers associated with hiking in an isolated location. Readers who may be sensitive to these elements, please take care.

Lillie Vale

Books by Lillie Vale

YA
Small Town Hearts
Beauty and the Besharam

For Adults
The Shaadi Set-Up
The Decoy Girlfriend
Wrapped with a Beau

HIT ME WITH YOUR BEST CHARM

Lillie Vale

VIKING

VIKING
An imprint of Penguin Random House LLC
1745 Broadway, New York, New York 10019

First published in the United States of America by Viking,
an imprint of Penguin Random House LLC, 2025

Visit us online at PenguinRandomHouse.com.

Library of Congress Cataloging-in-Publication Data is available.

ISBN 9780593623916

1 3 5 7 9 10 8 6 4 2

Printed in the United States of America

BVG

Edited by Dana Leydig
Design by Lucia Baez | Text set in Stempel Schneidler Std

The authorized representative in the EU for product safety and compliance is
Penguin Random House Ireland, Morrison Chambers, 32 Nassau Street,
Dublin D02 YH68, Ireland, https://eu-contact.penguin.ie.

Magic is always pushing and drawing and making things out of nothing. Everything is made out of magic, leaves and trees, flowers and birds, badgers and foxes and squirrels and people. So it must be all around us . . . in all the places.

—*The Secret Garden* by Frances Hodgson Burnett

HIT ME
WITH YOUR
BEST
CHARM

Foreword from *The Way of the Wish* chronicling the founding of our town from Henry Prior's journal, published by his descendants in 1999

Dear Reader,

A year before the Revolutionary War would result in American victory, a young Henry Prior, then twenty-two, founded the town of Prior's End. He was the youngest of his family to survive, having lost his older brothers in battle and his younger brother in a swimming accident.

Failing to save his beloved brother from the tragedy of drowning was, perhaps, Henry Prior's earliest regret.

History may have forgotten this young man, the last living Prior, had it not been for his discovery of a mysterious staircase made of ancient stone. These steps are believed by some to be a gateway to a forgotten place long lost to time, where dwindling traces of magic still reside. Others theorize that they're remnants of an ancient, mythical civilization more creature than human. Yet others claim they are an invitation from the spirits of the forest to come seek a hidden treasure . . .

Whatever their origin, the stairs did indeed lead Prior and the company he traveled with to a treasure. His journal reveals the stone stood as high as a grown man's shoulder and was untouched by the passing of time. Curiously, the markings on the stone were in English.

Prior's journal reveals them as a warning disguised as a riddle:

> *For the well to undo*
> *Prior woe for you*
> *A gift you must bring*
> *A coin offering*
> *For only one will you get*
> *To prevent your regret*
> *These woods are the bridge*
> *To all that you wish*
> *Your hurts we will stitch*
> *But should you break faith*
> *Beware the wraiths*
> *Until you are ready for me*
> *To diminish*

Fearing unchecked human greed and exploitation, Prior felt called to protect the miracle from misuse at some point after its discovery in 1782. By the time the war ended with the Treaty of Paris in 1783, town founder Henry Prior had defaced his own notes to obscure the location of the wishing well.

Modern historians take a less noble view of his actions. Eyewitness accounts are subject to memory bias and differ widely among the co-witnesses who accompanied Prior on his journey, with some allegations of threats against those who spoke about what they had seen.

Prior's hand of fate changed swiftly afterward. The woman to whom he once gave offense and who had later rejected his suit in marriage became so lovesick for him that her intended jilted her at the altar in shame. Prior then set aside his *own* betrothed in order to marry her. Debts he incurred to build the town of Prior's End were mysteriously forgiven.

Most strange of all is that none who were present at the discovery of the wishing well survived the decade.

In his later years, letters exchanged between his wife and her family expressed that Prior was tormented by the death of his brother, which he felt was at his hands. It is baffling, then, that he never used the power of the wishing well to undo this regret.

His wife later disappeared, allegedly with a lover, though historical records are unclear on the circumstances. Letters to her brother gave us a glimpse at an unhappy marriage, but they are hearsay only, as the evidence was lost in a fire that killed his wife's brother and his family.

After the mourning period, he married the woman he had once set aside. There was constant enmity between the children from his first and second marriages.

Over the years, Prior was accused of coercion, bribery, intimidation, and murder. He never went to trial and lived to see future generations of his many children and grandchildren. These allegations petered out by the end of the nineteenth century.

Later generations of Priors fought for the Union Army during the American Civil War, became governors of Tennessee, and were inducted in the Baseball Hall of Fame. Today, they are teachers, doctors, and small business owners raising their families in the small but thriving town of Prior's End.

One thing is clear: never has there been a Prior so revered or so reviled as Henry Prior.

History regards both the man and the myth with skepticism. To some he is an adventurer, to others merely an opportunist.

We will, perhaps, never know the truth. This is humanity's eternal quarrel with history.

—The Rose family

PART I
Prior's End

1

*N*ova, if you weren't so good at keeping secrets, you wouldn't be in the dark maw of the forest now.

Certainly not on the heels of dusk, hugging myself against the biting cold and the prickling unease. Definitely not after I'd been forbidden by my last remaining parent. Not once, not twice, but as long as memory. And considering these are the same woods that stole my father from us seven years ago, Mom has good reason.

But she's given up hope, and I never will.

I try to make it out here once a week, try to push myself to go an extra step, then fifty feet, then half a mile. Today I'm the farthest I've ever been, but compared to the impossible vastness of Longing Woods, that's not saying much. Between school, home, volunteering, and friends, I don't get to spend much time here. It's not *nothing*, but at this rate, I'll never find Dad.

And after this long, I'm the only one still looking.

If anyone knew I was doing this, they'd say it was a fool's hope. A desperate daughter plunging headfirst into danger to find a man everyone else believes to be long dead. Maybe they're right, but my heart tells me my dad is alive. And if he is . . . I'm his last hope.

He's been missing exactly seven years to the day. The day of our town's Fall Festival. Today is scarred into us like my parents' initials carved into the bark of the trees I passed a mile back. Losing him isn't something we've gotten over or moved past, as though such a thing should even be possible. One of the people who loved me the most in the world is gone. Nothing about that will ever be okay.

Mom and I have never acknowledged the anniversary of his disappearance, not even once. It hurt and confused me when I was a child, but I get it now. It already tortures Mom enough every other day of the year. The last thing I want is to compound it, but here I am, doing just that.

Is it worth risking Mom's wrath and being grounded for the rest of my junior year?

Without question.

There are thousands of living things merrily going about their business, completely unconcerned with the fading day and the teenage girl in their midst and the fear nipping at her heart. I'm the furthest thing from alone out here, but that's not as comforting as it sounds. Strange noises always follow me wherever I go. Something more than the wind rustling dry leaves or crickets calling to each other.

There! There it is again.

Soft crunches surround me. Whisper soft, like careful foot-falls trying not to give themselves away. My breath catches. I rub away the prickles on the back of my neck, the insides of my wrists. Steady my breathing the way Dad and, later, my therapist taught me.

It could be anything: Gray squirrels scrambling across brittle September leaves, collecting nuts. The huffs and grunts of antlered elk. Plump wild turkeys with their dark plumage foraging for seeds and insects, stalking the odd small reptile, too. I don't mind the frogs and lizards, but the last thing I want is to run across a snake.

Dad's stomach wouldn't be tense with sick dread, but mine definitely is. I might have been raised by a fearless outdoors- man for the first ten years of my life, but I spent the next seven living in the shadow of his disappearance.

I whip around, wild eyes darting.

Nothing there.

And even though I strain my eyes and ears, I can't hear anything except my own shallow breathing, and even that's drummed out by the violent ticking in my ears. Blood rushes to the tips of my fingers, and just like that, I'm not cold anymore.

Somehow, I always expect coming here to be easier, but it still takes all my courage to step beyond the tree line that stands as the gateway between the Tennessee mountain town of Prior's End and the Longing Woods. I'm about two miles in today, according to the last trail marker I passed. The way has been uneven in parts but nowhere near as rocky and rambling as it will get if I go deeper.

As much as I want to, I don't have the gear to keep going.

Hiking and camping equipment is expensive, and besides, I have nowhere to hide it at home.

Can't ask my friends to hang on to it for me, either. Austin and Caroline would rightfully flip out if they knew what I was doing; they wouldn't find it easy to keep my stuff . . . or my secret. And my forays into the woods *have* to be a secret, which means I have to be back before sunset. Before Mom wonders where I am or what I'm doing.

So tonight, this is as far as I go.

Guilt surges in my belly. I was wrong. Two miles is nothing. If Dad was this close to civilization, he would have made it back to us. He would have come across other hikers who could have helped him. Wherever he is, it's nowhere close.

And on my own, I'm no closer to finding him.

Even if it's hopeless, I need answers. I need to know his fate. Not to move on, because that's one thing I will never do. I will love and miss him forever. But I do need to reshape myself around his absence. And I can't do that if I don't know what happened out there.

My father, Jules Marwood, was a wilderness survival specialist. He took groups out for overnight excursions, long weekends, even tailored weeklong corporate training designed to promote team building, problem-solving, and leadership. He and Shane, Austin's dad, practically spent their childhood in the woods. The two best friends knew every stump, stone, and stem. They were the ones who went looking for unprepared folks, not the ones who got lost.

Which is why it's never made sense to me how Austin's dad got swallowed up in the Longing Woods, and so, too, did my dad when he went after him. My rational mind knows that park rangers and volunteer search parties made it deeper than I ever have before they gave up, but my wounded heart fights it like a wild thing in a trap, fierce and doomed.

As I turn back, for a half second, I think I see a dark silhouette moving between the trees.

I don't dare blink, but it's gone anyway. If it was ever there at all.

It doesn't stop me from imagining a flash of a blue backpack, sleeping bag rolled tight and snug at the top. A man's dimple sinking into his beard when he catches sight of me, kind eyes crinkling at the corners. His favorite olive-green belt that had lost so much color over the years. Socks pulled up high against tanned calves. The same weathered down jacket he's had for years, a birthday present from Mom the year they began dating. He's the way I remember him, early thirties and a little scruffy. His smile overtaking his whole face, like he can't believe it's really his little Nova, all grown up.

A Super Nova, he'd joke, or at least I think he would. The passage of time is unforgiving, and memory is dicey. Austin and I didn't have our own phones when we were ten to record goofy videos with our dads, to immortalize the grins and good-natured protests when they'd catch us. Unlike our friend Caroline, all we have are the faded memories that crumble a little more with every year that passes.

What I can be absolutely sure of, however, is that I'm just a girl alone in the woods.

No backup, no true bushcraft supplies. The almost-empty water bottle and trail mix that's more sugar than nutrition would earn me one of Dad's expressive eye rolls, a bad habit I inherited along with, evidently, a penchant for bad ideas. I can almost hear his voice whisper on the wind, *What's the first lesson of wilderness survival that I always tell my students before we head out on the trail, Nova?*

My answer is swift, instinctive:

Trust your team. Your partners are your best rescuers in case of any injury, misfortune, or calamity.

The anger is unexpected and immediate.

It was your *lesson, Dad. Why did you ignore it?*

Silence.

The thorny spikes in my chest snip away one by one. Being pissed at my dad and missing him are the same thing. I can never gauge which emotion will hit me first because it's never considerate enough to face me head-on. It prefers to assault at all angles, burrowing into the soft parts of me that still hope, and stab that same hope right out of me. I can't control it any more than I can control the wetness building behind my eyes. It's nonsensical. It's also normal, according to the grief therapist my mom insisted we go to after that first year of waiting and waiting and waiting.

I do my breathing exercises and wait it out. I'm good at that. After, I survey my surroundings, digging in my pocket for peanut M&M's and dried fruit. It's been long minutes since the last chirp or a squawk. It's an eerie sort of quiet, broken only by the crinkly sounds of my rifling through a Ziploc bag.

Thirty minutes of brisk walking later, I can see a hint of the parking lot peeking through the gaps between tree trunks. The usual rush of relief is dampened by heavy steps crashing through the woods and some annoyed noises that suggest an argument. From the left, four hikers join up with the main trail and are about to overtake me, but then they slow instead. I note that their expressions are grim, lacking the usual triumphant exhilaration hikers wear when they make it out of the Longing Woods.

"Hey," says a girl with flushed cheeks and blond Heidi braids. There's a breathless note of relief in her voice. "Oh my god, you have no idea how good it is to see you."

I don't know her. Confused, I stand there awkwardly.

"You're the first person we've come across," explains the boy she's with, the one holding the map. He's wearing a hoodie with the mascot of our rival high school. No wonder I don't know them.

"Today?" I ask.

He shakes his head. "Since we set out."

The other girl offers me a smile. "At least we didn't miss the carnival. Right, Ahsan?"

She's speaking to a boy who must be her brother. They share the same dark hair and soulful eyes. Where everyone else's gear stands out with stiff newness, Ahsan's is broken in.

I glance at his footwear with approval; his hiking boots are rugged and beat up like Dad's used to be. I subtly check him out, but he seems too sullen to even notice.

My gaze darts to his backpack. It, too, is the same kind as Dad's.

Is this the flash of blue I thought I saw?

Ahsan scowls. "Our turnaround time wasn't scheduled for *days*, Aaliyah. It wouldn't surprise me if you did this on purpose so you wouldn't miss the stupid carnival."

Aaliyah's face pinches. I get the feeling it isn't the first time she's heard that accusation.

Quickly, the other boy asks, "Are we close to the trailhead?"

"Yeah." I point ahead of us, where light pokes through the trees. "Half a mile back to town."

Ahsan stalks past, walking at such a rapid clip that the blond girl has to run after him. With a nod of thanks, the other boy takes off after them.

"Everything okay?" I ask Aaliyah. She's lingering, adjusting the straps of her backpack. "Your group, uh, seems pretty tense."

She looks miserable. "My brother loves hiking, and he finally convinced us all to join him. He wanted to find the wishing well." She glances at me as if making sure I know what she's talking about.

My chest tightens. Of course I do. Every child in Prior's End grows up with the legend of the well where you can wish for any of your regrets to be undone.

If you can find it.

And since our town's founding, so few have. Oh, plenty of locals and visitors alike *claim* the wishes they spoke over the wishing well have come true, and with no one to disprove it, the boasts stand.

In every single group Dad took out, there was at least one person who wanted to try their luck. Mostly novices who thought they were hot stuff, but sometimes even hikers who knew what they were doing tried to coax Dad and Shane to be their guides to the wishing well. Especially when they found out through the independently published guidebook *The Way of the Wish* that Dad descended from Henry Prior himself.

Their tour company's online reviews show plenty of five stars, but the last few are ungenerous. People hate being told no. The most incensed one is from a man who spent five paragraphs ranting that it serves Dad right that he went missing looking for the same miracle that he dissuaded so many others from. Accusing him of wanting the magic all to himself.

Asshole. My dad would never have risked his life for something so stupid, something that probably doesn't even exist. It's that guidebook's fault and that of the Roses who published it.

The Marwoods and the Roses are distant branches of the Prior family tree, each descended from a different wife. By all accounts, our forefather was a controversial figure. Dad and I come from Henry Prior's first wife while my classmate Radhika's grandfather is a Rose by adoption. Radhika's dad never cared about family history as much as his father did, but Radhika cares as much about the Prior lineage as she does her Indian ancestry from her mother's side.

History regards Henry Prior with esteem but also with fear and suspicion, so sure that this legend of a man was driven to paranoia and murder to protect the wishing well from prying eyes. There hasn't been anyone with the Prior last name for the last couple of generations, but nonetheless, his legacy lives on. The legend lures adrenaline junkies and the desperate to our town, and my dad was neither of those things.

"You really chased after that old myth?" I ask.

"Yeah, I know," Aaliyah says, misreading the expression on my face. "Ahsan's too old and too rational to believe in fairy tales, right? That's what I said. I didn't even want to come, but our parents said he had to go with a group, and he said this could count as my birthday present to him. So here I am."

"That's . . . nice of you?"

"Not that nice." At my questioning look, she explains. "We lost our lighter after our first night. My brother had it last, and he swears he zipped it up safe and sound, but I made so much fun of him instead of helping him look. It's just that he's so annoying when he acts like he knows everything! He spent this whole trip showing off, and now he's embarrassed about all the setbacks. We haven't been able to start a fire for the last couple of nights, so everyone's hungry and cranky. I'm so sick of granola bars."

I laugh. "My dad always brought bags of rice and beans. That's all he knew how to cook."

"I'd murder for some rice and beans." She sighs. "It's nice you can do fun things like this with your dad."

"Yeah," I say.

I don't correct her, tell her that he's *gone*. A word so loaded yet so nebulous.

I close my eyes and see Dad hunching over our campfire, stirring taco seasoning into our pot of beans while I suck applesauce through a squeezable pouch and watch him. It's so real I can almost feel the smoked paprika tickle my nostrils, breathe in the scent of his vetiver aftershave and the spruce needles scattered around us and the faintest scent of eco-soap from the rinse in the river.

Aaliyah's voice intrudes on my memory. "My brother was so stoked. He had this trip planned down to the minute, and now he thinks I wrecked it all. Said I didn't pack matches on purpose so we'd have to turn back. And then our lanterns ran out of power in the middle of the night, and nobody could find the spare batteries in the dark. I thought I stashed them in my backpack, but we couldn't find them in the morning. This whole trip sucked, and what's worse is my dumbass brother thinks I sabotaged it on purpose."

We walk in tandem, far enough behind the others that I don't lower my voice to ask, "Did you?"

She shakes her head. "I'm not a total jerk. We just . . . didn't plan it well, I guess."

I don't know what compels me to say it. "He'll forgive you. It wasn't your fault."

It's clearly the right thing to say. She brightens. "Of course he will. Family always does." And then she gives me a conspiratorial little smile, like I'm supposed to know this, too.

We walk farther, spilling out into the dusky pink-and-blue twilight where her friends are loading their things into the back of an SUV. The rest of the gravel parking lot is empty. The blond girl jumps into the driver's seat and shouts, "Aaliyah, hurry up! I want to shower and get all this grime off me!"

"Coming!" She turns to me. "Do you need a ride?"

Her friend honks twice. "That's okay," I say. "My house isn't far."

"See you tonight maybe!" Aaliyah says.

I neither agree nor disagree, and we part ways. Enjoying myself at the Fall Festival feels like a betrayal. How do I mark the day I lost my dad? By gobbling caramel apples and sugared pecans and kettle corn? This is the first year since it happened that I agreed to go with my friends, and I already regret it.

Why are you punishing yourself like this, Nova? the dad of my memory asks. *I don't want this for you.*

Maybe that's so, but it doesn't mean I don't deserve it. If he knew the truth, he'd agree.

Someone laughs. I startle, recognizing the overlapping voices. When I turn over my shoulder, Aaliyah is thrusting her backpack at her brother, who takes it with a grin and pretends to stagger under the weight. Agog, I stare at the obvious affection between them. She's forgiven, then. I didn't expect that.

It's hard not to envy her.

I'm almost out of the parking lot when she calls out, "Hey, I forgot to ask! Were you out there looking for something, too?"

I don't answer. I lift my hand as if I've misheard, as if I'm just saying goodbye.

A moment later, their SUV overtakes me. No hands wave at me from the windows. Their tires spit up gravel, the radio blasting lyrics I can't even hear over the sounds of their chatter.

And then I'm alone. I'm in their rear view, relegated to "that one girl we met that one time we thought it would be fun to go camping." They didn't find what they came to the Longing Woods for.

Neither did I.

Heart heavier than before, I point my feet in the direction of home. At dusk, the carnival that marks the first day of the Fall Festival will begin, and the music and merriment will be so raucous that I won't be surprised if it stretches all the way into the woods. Wild, giddy hope takes flight in my chest. For a second—a half second—I imagine the pipes and strings leading Dad out of the forest. Back home.

Jules Marwood is everywhere my eyes land, my fingers touch, my lungs breathe. Every blade of grass and dirt-caked pebble could be one he trod on first. His presence haunts every step I take, but my dad is nowhere to be found.

2

*L*ong before the bewitching hour descends upon Prior's End, the midnight-velvet sky claims the hamlet first. It arrives swiftly this Wednesday and, as usual, without warning. Exactly at 7:59 p.m. For the span of one breath, the glow from the half-moon is all that illuminates the labyrinthine warren of streets below my kitchen window. Prior's End: 1. Nova Marwood: 0. What else is new?

My reflection gleams back at me, a girl all set for a night out: black leather jacket, peacock-green chrome cat-eye swiped across her lids, and vigilant blue eyes braced for impact. I catch the split-second flicker of disappointment on my round face before it transfigures into familiar resignation.

Why did I expect tonight of all nights to be any different?

The carnival commands the view from my perch in the tallest house on the tallest hill overlooking the town. Below, the cracks spiderwebbed across the concrete in the vast parking lot where the old mall still stands—long abandoned by department stores and possibly haunted—are well concealed with garish tents and attractions promising enchantment and old-fashioned family fun.

But I know better. I haven't forgotten that Dad was taken from us seven years ago to the day.

One by one, the attractions light up with starburst splendor; the Ferris wheel is first, followed by flaring streetlamps and twinkling fairy lights on festive front porches. The shrilling calliope trickles the tune of "Scarborough Fair" all the way up here, the harbinger of the first day of the festival. My inhale is shaky. Dad's favorite folk tune feels like a taunt tonight.

Hands still pruny from washing up the dinner plates, I rub my fingers against the ragged edge of a dish towel before opening the weather app on my phone.

I already know what I'll find. Sundown: 8:23 p.m.

The app is wrong again. Just like dawn. Just like sundown yesterday and the day before and the day before that, too. The town's forecast has never once been accurate. Or even in the vicinity of accurate.

Out-of-nowhere drizzles on good hair days, surprise electric storms that catch pumpkins on fire in the middle of autumn. Snow flurries when there should be spring showers. It's all too strange to be shrugged off as a wonky weather model, almost spiteful in its contrariness.

Prior's End—a place teeming with what the locals call *occasional magic* and mercurial whims of its own—rarely does what's expected and almost never on anyone's schedule except its own.

"You changed your clothes," Mom says from behind me. "Are you going out?"

I turn away from the window to see Mom coming out from her bedroom. She's still in her work clothes but with her lipstick reapplied and her hair in loose waves around her shoulders. My gaze lingers on the inky violet-colored brocade shawl she wears over the black cardigan, gold tassels dancing against her trousers. It's new. I've never seen it before, but I can guess who it's from.

Mom takes in my outfit, too, a confused furrow between her eyebrows, before her eyes flit to the sink. "Oh, Nova, you didn't have to—"

"I don't mind." I really don't, but I can tell she's flustered.

She used to cook for us every day, experimenting with different cuisines that Dad would unfailingly declare were all ten out of ten as he helped himself to seconds and thirds. It's mostly takeout these days or five-ingredient meals that we eat in front of the television. Sometimes I think she keeps herself so busy at work that she doesn't have time to feel anything other than tired.

We don't talk about it, but her zest for cooking fizzled out without Dad around to be her sous chef, doing all the chopping and washing up, badly serenading her with ABBA songs and stealing kisses when he thought I was engrossed with my coloring. The kitchen was the room in our house where everything happened. Now I think it's the place where we're both reminded how much it hurts to love somebody.

"Thanks for taking care of the dishes, sweetheart." Mom pauses and then, with a trace of embarrassment, adds, "And for making dinner. It was delicious. You have your dad's magic touch."

It's a compliment, but her words stab right through me. No magic could revive the too-far-gone brussels sprouts shoved to the back of the crisper. No magic can bring my dad back.

The fact Mom is mentioning him at all sets me on edge. She watches me put the jar of expired fermented black bean sauce and sriracha bottle in the fridge. Her mouth works side to side as I throw out the empty takeout container of leftover white rice.

The way she's acting . . . it's like she doesn't know how to talk to me.

When I've run out of things to do, when my hands do nothing else but fidget against my thighs as I wait her out, she gives me a smile I've never seen before. "I've been talking to Aurora," she says.

Again, my gaze is drawn to her shawl. "Yeah?"

I'm careful not to have any kind of inflection, since the last time Aurora's name came up, apparently I had a *tone* that set Mom off.

"It's been seven years," she says, suddenly finding the kitchen tiles inordinately interesting.

Like I could forget. The second mention of Dad takes me aback.

"Yeah?" I say again.

"I was thinking it's . . . it's time that we talked about . . ." Mom takes a deep breath, still not looking at me. I can only remember one other time in my life that she was this nervous. That wasn't an easy conversation, either. She finally meets my eyes. "About what happens now," she says.

We're the same height. For some reason, my mind blanks, and this is what I focus on. We're the same height. She doesn't have to crouch to deliver bad news this time. Because whatever she says next is something I won't want to hear. I can read it in the set of her mouth, the apology in her eyes.

"It's . . . good that we're moving on." At my flinch, she quickly says, "Moving forward. *Forward*."

My brow furrows. Whatever it is that we've been doing, it feels like the opposite.

"You're going to the carnival." She gestures at my outfit. "Right? With your friends? And I'm . . . putting myself out there again."

My jaw drops. How Mom is friends with this woman is beyond me. Of all the insensitive, batshit . . . Thoroughly jolted, I ask, "Aurora encouraged you to go on a date tonight?"

Mom's face does a complicated, twisty frown. "No! I meant that I'm not going to avoid the festival this year. We used to love it. Don't you remember, Nova?"

I'm helpless against the onslaught of betrayal that makes my pulse quicken, my fingertips tingle. Life is split into a Before and an After. We were whole. The Marwoods did fun things together. Little Nova loved the carnival.

Before.

Now it's my turn to not meet my mother's eyes.

"I made a mistake," she says. "In the beginning, when the therapist suggested we find a way to honor your dad's anniversary." She worries at her lower lip. "I thought since the festival was always his thing with you, maybe it could have been *our* thing. The way we remembered him every year. But you were so against it . . ." Mom's face crumples. Softly, she says, "We were both hurting. I didn't want to push and make it worse."

Emotion lumps in my throat. "I'm glad you didn't."

The silence that falls between us isn't comfortable, but it isn't uncomfortable, either, until she says, "Aurora's going to take a break from her tent to meet me at Chalice for a quick drink."

Chalice is the popular, cozy wine bar that my parents inherited from Dad's favorite aunt. It's strictly twenty-one plus, so I've only poked my head in a few times, and I've never really minded, but now I'm annoyed she's meeting Aurora there.

"She's been good to me since Dad's been gone," Mom says.

Gone. It's the word everyone uses because it's better than that other word.

Four letters but far more final.

Mom's face pleads with me . . . for what? "I wasn't sure . . . but now that you're moving forward, too, I think Aurora was right," she says. "It's the right time. Now that we're both ready."

She's tiptoeing around saying it, and horribly, a part of me wants her to use the words. The other part, the bigger part, wants to cry and tell her that I will never be ready to legally have Dad declared dead.

The vicious talons of torment grip my heart. How is that something I can ever be ready for? Giving up? Resigning myself to a world in which I don't have a dad anymore and never will again? But she's not asking me if I'm okay with it, maybe because she doesn't know what happens if I tell her I'm not.

This is all Aurora's fault. Madame Aurora, the psychic.

She came into our lives seven years ago and never left. She showed up at the house one day—looking like a princess-witch-movie star in embroidered bell sleeves and a half dozen gold necklaces and a flamboyant diamond engagement ring—asking if Rhea Marwood was home. One of Mom's girlfriends at Chalice had made the appointment as a surprise; otherwise, I know Mom would never have sought out the services of a psychic.

Aurora used to live in the area, but now she travels on her own circuit, visiting clients around Tennessee and North Carolina. She always comes back to Prior's End, though, like a bird returning to her roost. I can't fathom what hold this place has over her because she doesn't come here for family or the wishing well, and there's definitely more money to be made in bigger cities like Nashville and Memphis.

Festival time is when Aurora palms off charms and herbal remedies that will inevitably end up squirreled into the nooks and crannies of my home: dried lavender sachets in sock drawers; next to the coffee beans, valerian root tea in shiny tins to help with Mom's sleep and migraines; thick creams crushed with wild mountain roses from the Blue Ridge peaks where Aurora rambles in the summertime, the scent lingering on pulse points, promising to attract a lover.

She's not entirely made of crap, but I have had enough. I won't allow her to do this to me, to my dad. I don't care if she's

Mom's friend. This is *my* family she's interfering with. If Mom is going to make decisions without even consulting me, then I'm going to do something, too.

My impromptu plan is simple, although that alone is enough of an invitation for something to go wrong, especially in Prior's End. I'll go to Madame Aurora's tent, get my fortune told. Entrap the psychic into making a prediction so ludicrous that I can decry it immediately in front of the whole town. It's the only way to make Mom see that Aurora doesn't know best.

"I should go," I say. My voice sounds rough. "Austin and Caroline are waiting for me."

They're the reason I'm going tonight. My best friends are so obviously into each other, but since we've been a trio for so long, neither is making a move. I think it's for my sake, but just because I'm hopelessly single doesn't mean I want them to be.

"Wait." Mom rummages in her purse, which hangs on the back of a kitchen chair. She presses two crumpled twenties and a grimy bunch of ones into my hand. "Do you want to go down together?"

I shake my head. Words are hard right now.

"Okay." She squeezes my fingers. "Have fun, sweetheart. Enjoy cotton candy and carnival games."

"Cotton candy and games, yup." I don't let my forced smile drop until I'm out the door.

I can breathe out here. I gulp cool air into my lungs. My bike leans against the porch, same place I left it after school this afternoon before my hike. It's so noticeable that I never risk taking it with me. I nudge back the kickstand of my bumblebee-yellow bike with the toe of my platform Oxfords.

The ride down to the carnival is bracing, wind nipping at my cheeks and whipping my hair into a spectacle. For most locals, autumn started on the first of September, when Demeter's Drinks switched to a new seasonal coffee menu. But for me, it isn't the cinnamon-maple latte or the white-chocolate pumpkin spice that heralds the season.

It's the taste in the air, like the town has just taken its first bite out of a tart caramel apple. It tingles in the back of my throat, soft and sweet at first and then sharp and satisfying. Just how I like it.

I've never lived anywhere else, but I know that there's nowhere quite like Prior's End.

Tiny tornadoes of leaves scatter around me as I whiz past rain gutters. Everyone's already at the carnival, the town's beating heart, but the streets are far from empty. Sidewalk shadows flicker in the corners of my eyes, coming close enough to snatch at my ankles.

I steel myself and pedal faster. A trick of the light and wind, nothing more.

The shadows grow greedier when I pass the copse of trees where I found old Mrs. Honeywell's best laying hen—well, what remained of her. Mrs. Honeywell had been inconsolable. Overimaginative tourists had found the bloodied white feathers and leaped to satanic rituals in the woods, locals feeding outsiders to some eldritch creature in the pitch black. Of course, the next morning's newspaper headline identified the culprit as a particularly hungry fox, but that version of the story, however true, wasn't the one that spread like wildfire.

Suspicion, superstition, and love of a good story are our otherwise charming town's only flaws.

I slow my speed as I approach the carnival. The thrum of people and music surrounds me as I lock up my bike on the rack farthest away then sidle my way around the perimeter, keeping an eye out. Any other night, I would seek out my friends. But tonight I have a bone to pick.

Madame Aurora's tent is easily spotted, as ostentatious as the psychic herself. A purple so deep it could pass for black, shimmering with gold thread. I expect a crowd waiting their turn in front, but to my disappointment, there's nobody around. Okay, that's fine. I can just go in and wait for an audience.

I take a deep breath then leap inside.

The tent is empty.

I swallow my disappointment. Great, she must have already left to meet Mom at Chalice.

What do I do now? I've worked myself up for embarrassing and exposing Aurora, who has Mom wrapped around her manipulative little finger, and then cotton candy and carnival games with my friends, just like I'd said.

Caroline and Austin would never miss the first day of the Fall Festival. They're probably just a few tents away, Caroline pretending to pout while Austin steals little pieces of her cotton candy for himself, acquitting himself by winning her the biggest, cuddliest stuffed toy while they both ignore their feelings like the dumbasses they are.

I would rather be with them, smushing them together in my self-appointed wingwoman capacity, but nope. Instead, I'm here. The last place I want to be.

"Seriously?" I mutter, pushing aside the gauzy violet fabric that's draped everyfuckingwhere and the glittering baubles suspended so low they could take someone's eye out.

With a frown, I approach the table with two chairs and a crystal ball. Crystals and a well-worn deck of tarot cards rest in velvet-lined boxes and, strangely, a silver trinket tray with a handful of buttons. Nothing special, nothing vintage. They're all different, only one of each, but nondescript and plain like a collection of extra buttons provided by shirt manufacturers. Mom once told me that buttons are Aurora's preferred divination method, but I have zero inkling of how that would even work.

Overlapping carpets in jewel tones are scattered over the floor, worn enough that no one would trip. Reflective beaded curtains shimmer like columns of tiny disco balls. The faintest whiff of rose incense tickles the air. I *guess* I can see why this mystical setup might appeal to people.

I shake my head, squashing whatever bit of unwilling awe stirs in my chest. The magical aesthetic is all part of the con, and I am absolutely *not* falling for it.

Everything here is strategically designed for one purpose and one purpose only—to trick people into believing in Aurora's power enough that they'll part with their cash.

Vulnerable people like my mother. Suckered into thinking Aurora had the answers they so desperately desired. For years she kept Mom dangling with hope that Dad could still be alive, and now she decides to take it all away? No. No way.

Dim lamps cast patterns across the walls and ceiling—no, not patterns, constellations. I can't be sure, but the night sky looks accurate, at least what I remember from my dad's back-yard stargazing before he left, an activity he'd just started to share with me. I can hear his voice so clearly. *Look up, Nova.*

Unbidden, Dad's face flashes in front of me, aged up to match the seven years he's been gone. The memories of his arms around me, the sharp and clean scent of his aftershave, the reverential timbre of his voice when he showed me some-thing new in the telescope . . . it all brings a lump to my throat.

"Hello?" someone calls. "Your away sign has been up a long time. Are you okay to take—"

I barely hear the question. All I hear is "Are you okay?" and so, frantic, I yelp, "Er. Yes." Crap, I sound nothing like Aurora. I try again, hoping whoever's outside won't know the differ-ence. "Yes, fine!"

Then I realize, with dawning horror, that in my panicked hurry, my response might have sounded an awful lot like I was inviting them in. Even worse, the person outside sounds strangely familiar.

"Oh, awesome! We've been waiting for you!"

And then Kiara Mistry bursts in.

3

*K*iara Mistry is—in a word—gorgeous. In two, devastatingly gorgeous.

What's left of my frazzled mind promptly scrambles. Because Kiara is wearing that vexingly dimpled smile that could level a city, and she has Devon Lake on her arm. The same boy whose shoulder I tapped in AP Chem last week to borrow a sheet of notepaper and promptly lost my heart to.

Which brings me to the next thing Kiara is: an obstacle.

I grit my teeth, thankful for the same gauzy swathes of fabric I was cursing a minute ago. Now they shield me from view in the back of the tent while the visitors in front are still brightly spotlighted. Not only is Kiara the last person I want to see, but the inside of a psychic's tent is *not* a place I want to be caught. But it's just like Prior's End to direct its capricious, fickle magic my way, using a generous sprinkling of what the whole town calls *occasional* magic.

Because I definitely don't believe in occasional magic. Or sometimes-if-you-squint-sideways-real-hard magic. Or magic at all. Not really. Not anymore. I simply can't. Because then that would mean—

No, I can't allow myself to think about that.

Before, things like toadstool fairy rings in the woods enchanted me. Even my dad's gentle warning not to mess with nature, to leave things be, that stepping into a circle was considered as unlucky as destroying it. He knew a man who mowed one down in his front yard who was then plagued by a host of other household pests until he finally moved out. Spiders coursing across ceilings in black waves, his vegetable patch torn apart with an unexplainable animosity, birds hitting his roof *thud-thud-thud* in the middle of the night, already dead. You never had to look far for the warnings in his stories.

Dad kept so many tales like that tucked away in his back pocket, pulling them out to share with me whenever he took me for a walk in his cherished woods. I was enthralled with the occasional magic then. Before. How could I not be when he could spin stories with so much wonder and whimsy, cob-webbed with just enough creepiness to appeal to a child's imagination? Especially a child raised by him, spoon-fed won-derment until it spilled out of her. Before.

I don't think I know how to leave things alone anymore.

Everything is tarnished now.

Everything. Including me.

"I told you that you didn't have to come in with me," Kiara mutters, half frowning at her companion.

Devon frowns, too. "Why shouldn't I? I don't have any se-crets from *you*."

Kiara blinks. Her brown eyes are soft and honeyed in the

glow of the tent. Hypnotic. "It's only our first date. You should. That's . . . weird."

"That's commitment. You'll see, babe. I'm the guy in your future."

Ha! Good luck with all that unfounded confidence, dude. You're not the guy for her. I just barely hold back a snort. Which is to say, I absolutely snort then smother it with fake cough.

Kiara cocks her head, long brown hair spilling over a shoulder. For one horrible moment, it's almost as if she has X-ray vision and knows exactly who is hidden behind all this gaudy frippery.

Every single muscle in my body tenses. My heart slingshots into my throat. Panic sweat gathers under my breasts as though my temperature just went up a few degrees. I cast a furtive look around.

Please, please, please don't recognize me. Not here of all places.

Kiara tucks one of her face-framing apricot locks behind her ear. Her earrings glimmer as they catch the light. "I'd like to know what's in my future," she says.

Devon chuckles and puts his arm around her shoulder, looking preemptively proud of himself.

I roll my eyes. *Puh-leese. You* wish *it was you.*

Kiara shrugs him off with an impatient sound, wringing her hands like there's a real question she wants the answer to but doesn't want to ask in front of him.

Like always, Prior's End does its thing, screwing up my plans and putting me at the mercy of a girl who's used to doing the exact same thing. Just like she's doing right here and now with yet another person who I liked first. And just like the others, Crush #5 is totally oblivious to the fact.

It's the Kiara Effect. It's how she is. Not even on purpose. No sooner do I start to crush on someone than they fall for her first. She just has to look at someone for them to fall head over heels for her.

Literally. One smile from her lips sent a boy tripping last year—several girlfriends later, he still hasn't lived it down. And his eyes still trail after Kiara whenever she enters or exits a classroom, which I would find completely pathetic, if it weren't for the fact that I'm kinda maybe *sorta* guilty of the same thing.

Love her or hate her, it's impossible not to be one of Kiara's conquests.

Hating her would be the easy option. Oh, I pretend, of course. Pretend to hate that hopeful, heart-stopping smile. The way Kiara fills the room like she's the only person in it.

How nothing negative ever seems to touch her, not even autumn's sharp teeth. She never dresses for the weather, as though something as mundane as garden-variety cold wouldn't *dare*. Those enviably long bare legs that strut down our high school hallways like she owns them are now neatly tucked into ankle boots.

"Of course," I announce, striving to maintain Aurora's lower, breathier voice. It comes out more sexy than mysterious, but I valiantly keep going, inching toward the back flap and a quick getaway. "Why don't you sit down at the table and think good thoughts while I . . . stay here . . . to better get in touch with . . . um . . . the future . . . which will only work if you're there and I'm here, okay?"

"Are you sure she's legit?" Devon whispers, moving his chair closer to Kiara's. "She sounds kinda spacey. Or drunk. And she didn't even take our tickets."

I bristle but keep my eyes on the prize. A few more feet, and I'm outta here with no one any the wiser. Devon is superfluous and so far in my rearview he's a pinprick. Or maybe just a prick.

I'm already over him.

"*Shhh!*" Kiara hisses. "Don't be rude. Madame Aurora is getting in the zone. She's so talented, it's no wonder she's a little eccentric. I promise you, she's the real deal. There's something I need her to tell me, and you are *not* getting us kicked out."

I actually freeze midstep. Kiara is adamant—surprisingly fierce—voice teetering right into threatening territory. Huh. That's . . . new. She's never sounded so unlike herself. All this time, hidden steel under that sweetness and sunshine. I find myself leaning forward, drawn in like a moth.

With a grumpy *hmph*, Devon crosses his arms. My tense shoulders relax a fraction, but they immediately hike back up again. Kiara believes in the paranormal about as much as everyone else in Prior's End, but her insistence on knowing this mysterious something?

Reluctant intrigue makes me falter when I reach the flap.

Ducking out right now would be so easy. I could do it in a heartbeat. But then I wouldn't discover what Kiara wants to know so badly.

And for some reason, that makes me want to know it, too. Maybe because I didn't get what I wanted in coming here: the petty victory of embarrassing Aurora and making her back off Mom. Maybe because I'm tired of losing to Kiara and pathetically need to know something important to her that she wouldn't want me to know. My breath comes out in short, controlled bursts. I'm unable to leave it alone.

I dig deep, all the way down to the pit in my stomach that's writhing with snakes, and summon a deep breath, fortifying myself for what I'm going to do next.

"I will *happily* give you what you deserve," I announce. Something electric goes through me, something I've only felt once before. Confidence strums my body, the next words already perched on my tongue. My mouth isn't dry anymore. "Place both hands on the crystal ball and close your eyes."

This instruction is immediately obeyed. Part of me wants to see how long the silence will stretch, how long it'll take for Kiara to grow impatient. But it's me who's impatient now.

"Do you see anything?" I prompt, watching Kiara's fingertips clench.

Kiara shakes her head. "Um, my eyes are closed. Shouldn't *you* be the one touching it?"

"She probably means your inner eye," Devon says with a snort.

"You are my conduit," I bluff without batting an eye. That sounds vaguely plausible. It's not like I've ever touched one of those things before. "I'm channeling your energies."

"Babe, I'll catch you outside. This is bullshi—" Devon darts a look at the curtains, a solid five feet from where I'm standing, and seems to think twice about the adjective he was about to use.

Kiara doesn't even wait until he's gone before she mutters, "Sorry about him."

I shrug before remembering that Kiara can't see me. "Do you have a specific question?"

Again, Kiara looks like she's on the verge of saying something, but then she shakes her head rapidly. "No, I . . . There's something I want to happen. Something that should have happened long before now. But it hasn't, even once when I thought she might—" She cuts herself off with another shake of her head. "Anyway," she says.

My pulse jumps. She? But Kiara's not giving anything else away.

"Do you see anything now?" I ask.

She squints. "The crystal ball is still clear. No smoke or anything. Shouldn't it get, I don't know, cloudy and magic-looking?"

"By psychics who pawn off cheap tricks, maybe," I say with a snort.

Kiara laughs. "Right. Sorry. It's just that this is pretty important to me."

"Right," I echo. "This mysterious question you're with-holding."

"For someone who's the real deal, it shouldn't be a problem, right?"

Cheeky. I narrow my eyes. "Never said it was. But if I don't have specifics, I can't control what I see. Be warned, you might encounter a fate you don't like."

Kiara's mouth settles into a determined line, almost a silent *Do your worst.*

And oh, I will. I don't need to know whatever secret my romantic rival is hugging close to her heart. I can simply give a phony prediction, and with one stone, I can annoy two birds. Foresee Kiara's worst nightmare, tarnish Madame Aurora's reputation . . . My original plan didn't work out, but tonight can still work to my advantage. Instead of receiving a prediction from Aurora, *I'll* give one to Kiara.

"What you seek is right in front of you." My chest quakes with the effort to keep from laughing at the poetry of my plan. Who knew being cryptic could be so much fun?

Kiara bites her lip. "But I don't—"

My melodramatic gasp cuts her off. "Then it is as I feared."

"Um, what do you—"

"I must have silence! It's coming to me!" I inject a warble into my already theatrical performance, trying not to laugh as I work my way up to the climax. "Oh no . . . it is much, much worse." I draw the moment out, counting Mississippis until Kiara finally blinks. *"In your future, I see"*—It's petty, it's probably inadvisable, and it's definitely going to prick at my conscience later—"*many, many days of bad luck ahead, Kiara Mistry. Your good fortune has come to an end.*"

Kiara recoils so hard that her chair scrapes. Her lip-glossed mouth drops into ugly, furious disbelief. It's clear that out of everything she expected to hear, a prophecy of her downfall didn't make the cut.

I carry on, the intonation coming easier now. "The closer you get to what you want, the worse off you will be. You, who have only known fate's favor all these years, will finally know what it is to suffer. However, you can still turn from this path. If you have the will and fortitude to give up your heart's desire."

Kiara jerks her head in a horrified *No, no, no.*

"Are you sure? Even if it spells your own disaster? Your doom?" I prod. Getting into the theatrics of my performance now, I pronounce, "Here is what you have to look forward to, then. All the good fortune you've hoarded these many years is turning to ash. Bad luck will plague your footsteps. Anything you think is a sure thing will slip out of your fingers like mist. The very ground you tread will turn treacherous. You will suffer this reversal of fortune until you summon the strength to sacrifice what you want most. We're talking a *lot* of suffering, by the way."

"This *can't* be right." Kiara stares. "I haven't done anything to deserve this. You have to help me! Please. This isn't what I wanted."

"The future doesn't lie," I say tartly. "It is pitiless and un-caring of mortal affairs."

"Wait, but that's only one interpretation, right? The future is malleable. It can change."

"Perhaps," I chirp, watching Kiara's face brighten with hope. "But at this point, not very likely."

Kiara's shoulders slump. "There has to be something I can—"

"Nope. Nothing. Never before have I perceived such ill tidings."

"But—you—can't just—" Kiara starts to sputter.

"I told you that you might not like your future," I remind her. Strange, pulling this off didn't make me feel the way I thought I would. My heart pinches with—

No, it's not sympathy. It's not pesky, inconvenient guilt pricking at my conscience. She got a bad fortune, so what? Kiara can deal with one night of shitty news, of worry that wrecks her beauty sleep, of something not going her way. And tomorrow everything will go back to normal for both of us, her to her perfectly charmed life and me to . . . well. The point being, no harm done.

"I want you to do my reading again," Kiara demands. "You said something about sacrifice?"

"Can't fight fate!" I dive for the tent flap. "Good luck with the impending doom! Don't forget to leave a review!"

4

"You did *what* last night?" Austin Lyons, my ex-boyfriend and best friend, makes a wonky expression like he's both horrified and amused at the same time. "Nova, please tell me you didn't."

From the laminate floor of the animal rescue shelter's kitchen, I glance up at him. "That would be a lie." I shake more kibble into the bowls then hand the entire steel tray up to Austin.

He takes it, rolling his eyes. "You mean *another* lie. Lies plural."

"Potayto, potahto."

After volunteering here for the last three years, the two of us are perfectly in sync as we deliver breakfast to the kennels, finishing in record time.

Austin shuts the door on one of our sweetest residents, an elderly miniature schnauzer mix. "Now I kind of regret asking you why you were late meeting us last night."

I wink. "Oh yeah, you're totally my accomplice now."

"You joke, but that's what they'll call me," he deadpans.

"As if you minded the extra alone time"—I waggle my eyebrows—"with Caroline."

He blushes. "Neither confirming nor denying."

I smirk. "And thus transparently giving away your feelings."

"Oh, come on." He levels me with a no-nonsense, don't-lie-to-your-best-friend kind of look. "Like your hexing Kiara was in any way subtle. You were jealous."

"A mistaken crush. I'm already over him," I say, pointedly not even using Devon's name.

"Who said I was talking about him?" Now it's Austin's turn to gloat. "Admit it. You've been pining for her ever since you kissed at my party the summer before freshman year."

I grimace. I don't love that reminder. "You and I had just broken up. Although, I guess it wasn't really broken up since we were basically kids and we only went out for a week, and our first and only kiss was so weird, and your chin knocked my teeth so hard I thought I'd need dental work—"

"An exaggeration," Austin cuts in.

"Needless to say, to recover from the horror of it all, I would have kissed anyone with a pulse."

"Flattering," he says dryly.

"You're the one who said we worked better as friends," I point out.

"And you agreed! You said kissing me was like kissing your nonexistent brother."

"My point," I say primly, "is that both kisses are forever filed under Things Never to be Repeated."

At least I can joke about the one I shared with Austin. We were kids playing pretend, more excited about having our first boyfriend and girlfriend than in actually doing anything with each other. In all honesty, I think we were just giving it a shot because being best friends already felt so right.

With Kiara, on the other hand, I had an embarrassingly obvious crush. It felt like we were having a moment, so I went for it. In hindsight, I don't know what possessed me. Surely I had no business being so confident after that clumsy kiss with Austin?

I relive it now in 4K resolution, everything clearer and more detailed. My head tilts, my eyes close, and I am convinced I know exactly what to do. Kiara is hot, so she'll be amazing at kissing, too. Our lips meet. The music doesn't swell, her nose bumps mine hard enough that my eyes fly open, and it's all too . . . wet. I'm way too conscious of my tongue and freaking out about what she's doing with hers.

How is it possible my second kiss is worse than my first? Is she bad at this? Am I bad at this? It has to be me, right? I've seen her kiss before, in hallways and in class behind teachers' backs. I'm the one with no practice and no idea what to do with my hands or my mouth or my eyes, which are still open, actually.

Just as I'm trying to work out how I feel about it and whether enough seconds have passed to detach from this awkward, humiliating exchange, she pulls back for breath. And then goes in for another kiss. Which I promptly dodge, more out of self-preservation than anything else, convinced that *I* was the one to wreck what should have been a magical kiss.

When she flies back to her friends instead of trying again, I'm pretty sure she's convinced I suck, too.

Why is having a crush the most embarrassing thing ever?

Better to dig it out like a weed instead of letting it bloom. Better to conceal how I feel. Dwelling on a mistake only makes things worse. This is how I deal with things now.

"Nova, Nova, Nova." Austin gives me a grin that's one part playful, one part up to something. "One, you're deflecting. Two . . ." His azure eyes fix somewhere beyond my shoulder. "Good luck."

I whirl around to see Kiara enter the shelter cradling a small black ball of fluff against an unbuttoned cardigan and a carnation-pink tee sporting her family's clothing and outdoor recreation store, Bee Outdoors. The shirt knots at the front, showing a strip of midriff but hiding the titanium navel piercing I know she has.

"You deal with this," I hiss at Austin since it's too late to duck under the counter and hide.

"Hi, Kiara," he says loudly. "Nova, why don't you take care of this? I'll get the cats fed."

Before I can protest, he's already disappeared into the back.

Leaving me and Kiara alone. Again. My heart thumps loud enough I'm surprised we can't hear it.

"How can I help you?" I ask, eyeing the kitten cuddled against Kiara's chest. I wouldn't ordinarily be speaking to someone's chest like a horny teenage boy, but with the phantom taste of her lips still on my mind and only a counter separating us, looking into Kiara's eyes feels impossibly intimate.

"Some hikers found this cutie outside of Bee Outdoors." Kiara pries tiny paws from her strawberry-patterned cardigan, looking as reluctant to hand the kitten over as it seems to be handed. "I gave him some water, but I don't have any pets, so I didn't know what he can eat at this age."

"Wet food. Kibble is too hard on their minuscule teeth." I hold out my hands, palms out. "C'mere, little guy." With a look I can only describe as panic, the kitten flails wildly, wriggling back to Kiara. Claws curl into the knit and, as though I'm watching in slow motion, it's too late to stop it from happening.

With a yowl of outrage, the kitten decimates three strawberries at the same time, unraveling the pink wool.

"My favorite sweater!" Kiara cries.

Her dismay tugs at me in a way it shouldn't. "Sorry. Shitty way to start the day."

"If only you knew."

Something in Kiara's tone pulls my gaze to her face. And her horrifically reddish eye.

I suck in a sharp breath, glancing at the kitten. Without thinking twice, I lean far enough over the counter to get right in Kiara's face, peering at her cornea. "Does it hurt when you blink?"

As I hover repulsively close, I wait for her to oblige me with a couple of startled blinks. Maybe to push away from the counter, separating us with a look of annoyance or surprise. She does neither.

Time seems to freeze as she meets my scrutiny without blinking. I start to worry the lack of moisture will aggravate her eye even more. This is the closest we've been since freshman year, and even though the circumstances are totally different, my heart does a traitorous backflip.

I nod toward the redness. The popped blood vessels make it hard to tell, but . . . "It doesn't look like he scratched your cornea. Did you rinse it out right away with a saline solution?"

"What?" Her voice comes out a little strangled, like she's holding her breath.

"It's what you use for your contact lenses."

In middle school, Kiara used to wear hot pink frames that matched the color of her lip gloss, but neither has made a resurgence in years. Probably because they get in the way of all the people she kisses.

Her lips tip up into a bemused smile. "Nice to know you care, Nova."

I scowl, unable to deny it. Nothing about her appearance implies she's been tossing and turning all night, restless with anticipation and dread about all the bad luck in store. Maybe I wasn't dire enough? Maybe after her initial alarm, she laughed it off with her friends and chalked my dire pronouncement down to a tipsy psychic who'd taken it too far. I don't know whether I'm relieved or disappointed at the possibility. Her smile is too distracting.

Wait, has her skin always been this baby smooth and pore-less? It's one of life's great injustices that Kiara Mistry looks as good as she does. This close, I can count every single tiny sun-spot smattered on her face. Her Disney princess nose. The matchy-matchy eyelids, cheeks, and lips in a glowy shade of apricot that suits her skin tone. The way her brown eyes widen as I enter her personal space bubble, holding her breath like it isn't minty fresh and flossed and all those other things that the average teenager lets slide but Kiara would never fail to include in her daily regimen.

"You know, Nova," she says, sounding like she's barely suppressing a giggle, "anyone would think you just wanted an excuse to stare at me."

I'm the one to recoil. "What? You *really* need to get your eyes checked if you think I'm staring longingly at you."

She looks way too smug as she says, "Who said anything about longingly?"

I scoff. "Fine, maybe next time I won't care about your po-tential injuries."

Okay, I would. Because unlike some who go around steal-ing crushes from others, I'm a good human being. I'd give a shit about internal damage to anyone, including shoppers who sneak fifty-plus items into the grocery's twenty-items-or-less self-checkout and people who walk side by side hogging the entire sidewalk and the truly vile: drivers who don't wave thank-you when you let them ahead of you.

And judging by the perceptive look she gives me after my

snippy words, Kiara knows that I'd care, too. "Anyway," she says, "this isn't the floof's fault. My mascara wand got me good this morning."

Her lashes are naturally curled and lush, so unlike the rest of us mere mortals, she doesn't need the extra help. She also doesn't need the ego boost, so I don't tell her the difference is marginal at best.

"Well, thanks for bringing him in," I say. "I've got it from here."

"Are you sure?"

"I've been volunteering here since I was fourteen, so . . ."

Kiara's eyes widen slightly. "I didn't mean you weren't competent!" She takes a breath, not letting go of the kitten. "What's going to happen to him now?"

I try my hardest not to look at the poster on the wall squashed between ADOPT DON'T SHOP and THE IMPORTANCE OF HEARTWORM SCREENING. The boss and vet, Otto Brady, leaves it up as an evergreen reminder to surrender unwanted animals to the shelter instead of abandoning them. This time of year we get an influx of frogs, ferrets, black adders, lizards, tarantulas, and black cats. It involves a small fee and some paperwork, but superstitious people get all worked up over the silliest things.

"Nova?" Kiara's brows pinch.

I waver between giving her the answer she wants and the truth. The truth being it's the first of October, and as cute as he is, he's still a black cat. We're a no-kill shelter that can offer a loving sanctuary, since in Prior's End, adoption is a long shot for any animal of the witch's familiar variety.

Can't tell her that, though. I want to be unaffected by her, but going by the way Kiara's clinging to him . . . I get the feeling she'll be crushed to know the truth.

With the kind of confidence that wins Oscars, I say, "He'll get adopted, no problem."

"You're not just saying that?"

I huff. "Don't sound so suspicious."

"I . . . well . . . okay."

With a torn expression, Kiara finally relinquishes her handful of fluff. "Have you really been volunteering here for three years?" At my nod, she says, "I never knew that about you."

"Why would you?" The kitten's still a bit agitated, so I tuck in his limbs as best I can. "Anyway, you did the right thing bringing him here. I need to get him in back for Otto to do a physical exam, so . . ."

She takes the hint. "Yeah, no, I'll just . . . I'll get out of your hair."

"And maybe get to the ER. Your eye looks pretty gnarly."

"The redness will clear up on its own. Probably." Kiara half frowns. "I've actually never had a mascara wand attack me like that before. I can't explain it. It was almost like—" She tilts her head back and laughs, breathy and disbelieving.

What did she stop herself from voicing? Unease flutters in my stomach like bat wings. "Attack you?"

She backs away toward the door. "Just a figure of speech."

The distance between us is the same as it was last night. Unbidden, my words come back to haunt me.

". . . many, many days of bad luck ahead, Kiara Mistry. Your good fortune has come to an end."

I swallow. Between her eye injury and her cardigan, it's hard not to at least consider it. Anyone would. I mean, it's not even noon, and weird things have already happened to her. But who *hasn't* poked themselves with their mascara wand at least once? So maybe it's nothing?

Kiara swivels to face the door, and just as I've dismissed that niggling little doubt, the handle catches on the loose wool. It barely touches the knit before rows upon rows undo themselves. In a blink, the bottom half of the cardigan comes apart, hanging limp and shredded like the world's worst fringe ever.

Her horrified eyes meet mine. Even the kitten is stunned, going still in my hands and not even trying to bat at me anymore. All three of our mouths are open in horror. There are, quite literally, no words. Even if I wanted to say something, I can't get my vocal cords to work.

Kiara gathers the dangling ends in her hand, stares, then lets them drop. "What . . . what just happened?"

"You're asking me?"

"Don't tell anyone."

At first, I'm indignant. What makes her think that a morning spent in her presence is the stuff that gossip is made of? Then because I can't let it go, I ask, "Why not? Sure, what happened to your cardigan was a little weird, but accidents happen every—"

"No, they don't," she interrupts. "They don't happen to me. My mom and dad think it's because of the meditation and spiritual cleansing we do, and maybe that's part of it, but I've always had good luck. Amazing luck, actually. All the mantras and essential oils and Ayurvedic massages eliminate negative energy, sure, but I've always known that—" She breaks off and looks away.

Curiosity gets the better of me. "What?"

"You'll make fun of me if I tell you."

"Yeah, probably. But you're on a roll. So." I shrug and wave at her to continue.

She fidgets with the loose strands. "Not to sound conceited, but, well, ever since I was a little kid, I've always known that I'm special."

Did she really just say that?

It takes every facial muscle I have not to gape at her. I mean, she's not wrong. Though I itch to be contrary just to annoy her, there's no point in arguing when I have her whole life history as proof positive.

So yes, as much as I hate to agree with her that she is, in fact, special, I totally agree that when the Powers That Be were dealing out good hands in life, she got a royal flush while most of the rest of us landed relative stinkers. It doesn't surprise me that those lucky few go through life with delusions of grandeur, but I guess if everything always went my way as if by magic, I might think the same.

"You're right," I tell her. Catching her look of surprise, I roll my eyes. "Not that you're special. But I do agree that good things seem to go your way a disproportionate amount. I guess if I were you, I wouldn't want people to know I'm only human after all."

She blinks. "I can't tell with you. Is that supposed to be comforting?"

"Uh, since you couldn't tell that was sarcasm, yeah, *totally.*"

Kiara's even prettier when she scowls.

I hate that I notice.

5

"Good work getting him processed, Nova," Otto Brady says cheerfully, giving the kitten a head rub before gently scooching him into the kennel. A hint of a Yorkshire accent slips out on some of his affectionate words, even after three decades in the States. Approaching middle age, he's got the slightest dusting of gray at his temples and plenty of laugh lines around his face when he smiles. "No fleas or ticks, no signs of malnourishment. I'd say Inky here is in reasonable health. He put up with me poking and prodding him on the exam table without any fuss, too."

"Inky?" I ask, watching the kitten explore the padded cat bed, washable fleece blanket, and water dish.

Otto grins as he latches the door. "Well, someone had to name him."

"What was wrong with my suggestions?" Austin asks, sounding indignant but looking like the before picture of a lint roller commercial, dog hair sticking on his black chino shorts and graphic anime tee. After dog grooming, he's always wearing more hair than the brush.

I raise an eyebrow. "You wanted to call him Bagheera? Wednesday? Salem?"

"Kids." Otto's being serious now, which he almost never is. "I know it's tempting, but let's remember that cute names help get our animals adopted."

"Toothless was cute!" I protest. "So was Poe. And Diablo!"

"Isn't that Spanish for devil?" Austin picks at his shirt, gathering hair into his palm.

I shoot him a withering glare that conveys exactly how helpful his comment is.

"Thank you, Austin," says Otto. "Unfair as it is, the names we give strays like Inky create an impression. Our goal is to find their forever homes."

The weekend before Halloween, the shelter organizes a parade down Main Street for our cute costumed canines. It's our chance to show off their leash training and how well socialized they are with other dogs and humans. Each year, without fail, we successfully rehome every dog and most of the cats in the shelter, even the ones that are harder to adopt, like elderly schnauzers whose humans went into assisted living with a no-pets policy, cats with cataracts, and bulldogs with bladder control issues.

I make a face. "Please don't wear your 'I'd shove you in front of a zombie to save my dog' tee to the parade again."

"Hey, it was Otto approved! And it was 'I'd throw you to the zombies to save my dog,' thank you very much. Get it right, Nova."

"Oh, I'm so sorry for not remembering the exact phrasing. Guess I was too busy fixating on the fact that in the event of an apocalypse, my best friend would let the undead chow down on me."

"Hey, it's not *just* you. Anyone."

Our shift over, we say our goodbyes to Otto and head out. I cast my eyes to the sky, to the ominous scowling clouds and the swoop of blackbirds overhead. "Please save me from my best friend's disastrous fashion sense and even worse sense of humor."

Austin grins. "You just haven't met the right graphic tee yet, Little Miss Dark Academia."

"I know you don't mean that as a compliment, but you can't stop me from taking it as one," I say primly, walking faster so he has to break into a jog to catch up.

Can't lie, I do like my thrifted tweed blazers with the shoulder pads and the elbow patches and the silk lining. Pair them with chunky loafers or block-heel boots for some height—perfect. Summer is hell without the comfort of my slouchy sweatshirts and cozy cardigans and pleated miniskirts with black lace-up boots and knee socks. And if all those items tend to skew to a more or less monochrome color palette, what's so wrong with that? When most of your stuff is black, tan, cream, mulberry, or juniper, everything matches, so there's no early-morning rush to dig through my closet for something to wear to school, which gets me a few extra minutes of sleep.

Austin bumps my arm, making sure not to step on a crack in the sidewalk. "All jokes aside, thanks for coming out with us last night. First day of the festival. After so long." He clears his throat. "I'm glad you were there."

I give him a look. "You don't have to thank me for hanging out with my best friends."

"But it was hard for you," he says gently. "I don't want to ignore that."

That's true, and there's little point pretending otherwise, so I just nod.

I didn't want to spoil last night by telling them what Mom was planning to do. Talking about it makes it real. Maybe that's why she hid it from me for so long. But also, I know that Shane is a sore spot for Austin. He'd cheated on their family a year before he disappeared, and while Austin doesn't really remember, his parents never worked through it. His mom started dating again when we were twelve, and he's been more or less okay with it.

Does it make me a bad person that I wouldn't be? I don't want Mom to be alone. I know human beings need companionship. But the idea of that person being anyone other than Dad . . .

Austin must sense I'm ready to change the subject. "I think that's the longest I've ever seen you and Kiara hold a conversation. What was it, twenty minutes?"

"Shut up. No."

He fake gasps. "You mean it was *thirty*?"

"I can't believe I let you eat the rest of my cotton candy last

night," I groan. "For your information, *she* was the chatty one."
I can trust him to be honest to a fault, so I know he'll give it to
me straight when I ask, casually as I can, "Have you ever heard
of, um, bad luck hounding a person?"

His grandma runs the most popular apothecary in town
and is a font of local folklore and superstitious stories that all
happened to someone she knows, or—in the event of their
death thanks to aforementioned superstition—*knew*. Austin is
less superstitious than most in Prior's End, but he doesn't dismiss it, either.

"Hounding?" His brows furrow. "I guess we've all had
those days when everything seems to go wrong. Like you forget to set your alarm for school on Monday, you sleep in, then
you hit every red light on the drive over, and just when you
think you're going to make it to first period on time, you get
busted for running in the hall by the vice principal. Like that?"

I blink. "Uh . . . not exactly."

I fill him in on what's happened to Kiara since last night. I
keep it short since I'll have to repeat it again when we get to
Caroline's house for lunch.

She loves food that resembles other food, like fried egg
gummies and zucchini noodles, and we're heading over to her
place now for her latest obsession, garlic bread pizza. My
stomach gives a hungry lurch. I'm so distracted by thoughts of
crusty bread and gooey cheese that I almost miss Austin's grin.

"And now you're worried about her?" He makes an obnoxious *awwwww* noise. Seeing my grumpy frown, he takes pity

on me, his face softening. "I doubt your bullshit had anything to do with it, Nova. But even if it did, Grandma says bad luck comes in threes, so it's probably run its course already."

"How do you figure?"

As we turn onto Caroline's street, her house coming into view, he counts off on his fingers. "One, the bizarre incident with her cardigan coming apart. Two, poking herself with the mascara wand. Three . . ."

"There is no three!"

"What do you call a black cat crossing her path?"

"He didn't, though. Hikers found him."

Austin laughs. "Don't be so literal. I don't think bad luck is that picky. It takes what it gets."

"So as long as nothing else bad happens, I'm off the hook?"

"I mean, it's not like I have a PhD on the subject, but—hey, why are you so concerned anyway? I thought you didn't really believe in superstition."

Flustered, I frown. "I didn't. I don't. It was just weird, okay? I've never seen her be anything less than fully put together, and I think if she spent even five more minutes in my presence, she'd have, like, erupted in fiery red zits or something, it was that weird."

He doesn't look like he believes me, but he nods. "Well, there you go. Three events. Kiara's run of bad luck is over. Everything will go back to normal now."

6

I want to believe Austin, but as we gobble down pizza while watching *Bewitched* reruns and fill Caroline in on what happened with the animal shelter's newest resident, all I can think is *What if he's wrong?* The thing about bad luck happening in threes is that if it happens once, twice, three times, what's to stop it from happening for a fourth? Anxiety drapes over me like a cloak for the rest of the day.

Because Prior's End, even at the best of times, isn't just unpredictable, it's frustrating and downright weird.

More than anything else, without my dad, our town is the thing that I hate admitting exists: magic.

Not the talking animal kind or the sort that spurts out of a wand. Definitely not the kind that requires potions or incantations, pointy hats or mysterious ingredients. It can't be wielded or relied upon; it's just something that *is*. And it's infuriating, the way that it just happens *to* you, usually when you never intended it. Neither cruel nor kind, it just *is*.

Austin's grandma, Petra, thinks it's because Prior's End is alive. In the roots, in the soil. Cryptic. Inscrutable. Sentient. Like an Ent. Part of the natural world, yes, but also part of the supernatural one.

Which is why I keep a close eye on Kiara tonight at the Cauldron, a pub that prides itself on its year-round spooky-season fare. She's here with her friends, who all happen to be her ridiculously attractive exes: Tayla Holloway, Radhika Rose, and Evan Venables. When I came in to order, I saw them sequestered in a corner booth, whispering and casting furtive glances at me. An enormous pizza lay untouched on the table.

I've been trying to ignore them—trying . . . and failing. They're the most gorgeous group in here. Radhika always crops her glossy brown waves to her shoulders every summer, and it's just starting to grow out. Absently, Kiara tucks it behind her ear while they all listen, enraptured, to whatever Tayla's saying. The gesture annoys me, and I pointedly look away. It's none of my business who she's being affectionate with. The last thing I need is for her to catch me looking over and tease me for staring at her. Again.

I shuffle my feet as I wait at the bar for the food and drinks, wincing when I can feel the stickiness under my soles. Austin and Caroline are out front holding down a table since in here is full and there's barely any standing room even for me. Festival week is as busy as Mother's Day and Christmas for restaurants around here. Kinda regretting not taking Austin up on his offer to brave the crowds, but I was hoping the alone time might be good for them.

While I wait for the mozzarella sticks and fried pickles, I squeeze my arms tight to my sides, trying to minimize myself as large groups elbow their way around in what, admittedly, suddenly feels like a coffin-sized amount of space. Kiara's back is to me, but every so often she runs her fingers through her hair in an agitated manner, which is the first thing that strikes me as odd. She never plays with her hair so her blowout looks fresh for longer.

Once after gym, sometime during sophomore year, I caught her in the changing room with her head down, brown hair flipped over almost to the floor. It still looked great like that, not sweaty and limp like mine. She was aggressively spraying dry shampoo at her roots. "You're so lucky your scalp doesn't get as oily as mine," she'd said with a rueful smile when the toes of my tennis shoes came into her eyeline.

I'd babbled something about how she could always cut her hair if she wanted something fuss free. She'd just laughed, not meanly but like it should have been obvious she wasn't actually inviting an opinion and there was no way she was ever going to touch the length. And I get it; if I had the swishy, waterfall locks that only Kiara, Jonathan Van Ness, and models in TV ads have, I'd be against cutting it, too.

Evan, the only one in the group I actually like, grabs Kiara's hand and tugs it down to the table. Whatever they whisper seems to calm Kiara down. The booth is too far away for me to eavesdrop, and it's not like I can see Kiara anyway, so staring at her is pointless. It's not like I can just look at her and *know* if any other strange incidents have befallen her.

With my luck, she'll feel my eyes on her and catch me staring like a weirdo or, worse, a moony, lovesick sap gazing at her from afar, which is the last thing I want to be mistaken for. But I must have crappier luck than even I thought, because it isn't Kiara who catches me. It's someone way, *way* worse.

From where she sits opposite from Kiara, her best friend, Tayla, turns her head about thirty degrees and aims the full force of her resting bitch face at me. It actually isn't too different from her actual face.

Even though she's a glorious redhead, she has that effortless, powerful vibe of raven-haired Neve Campbell in *The Craft*. One of her eyebrows lifts in a silent question and dismissal. The other muscles in her face don't move, which is doubly terrifying. I break eye contact first.

When our order is ready, I scurry out as fast as I can, feeling her unnerving hydrangea-blue eyes on my back as I weave through packed bodies like an eel. Outside, my friends occupy the last of the outdoor seating, Caroline Chen's legs propped up on the black wrought-iron chair. Across the leaping flames of the firepit, her defiant face dares anyone to ask if the seat is free.

She swings her legs aside, smoothing a nonexistent ruffle in her plaid skirt. Her black eyebrows draw together. "What's wrong? You look kinda panicked."

I sink into the seat she saved me. The table wobbles when I put the tray down, like one of its three legs is short. "Tayla's stink eye."

Caroline shudders, though it's probably more from the cold. Austin almost knocks our drinks off the rickety table when he whips off his jacket to drape over her shoulders.

Subtle, I mouth.

He glowers.

"Thank you," Caroline says, snuggling deeper into the sherpa-lined denim jacket. She probably doesn't even realize that she's seeking out Austin's body warmth.

I wish I could just grab them both by the back of their necks and smash their heads together, demanding that they *just kiss already!* the way Caroline and I howl at the TV when we watch rom-coms. It's not even like they hide it all that well. They're so painfully into each other that it's more uncomfortable watching them walk on eggshells around me instead of just admitting they're deeply In Like.

"I have to tell you something," Caroline says now after exchanging a glance with Austin so laden with meaning that my heart skips a beat.

Is this it? Are they going to finally stop denying what's been obvious to me for weeks? Did my plan to leave them alone work? Meddling and matchmaking isn't my calling. Too much stress and not enough progress. Nowhere as fun as the movies make it out to be.

Austin gives a little shake of his head before shoving his hand through his styled blond hair, lips pursed unhappily around his straw. Whatever Caroline wants to share, he's not on board.

Which makes me want to know even more.

I can just about bear the mysteries of Prior's End but not my best friends keeping secrets from me. When she bites her lip, he mimics the action like he doesn't even know he's doing it.

I glance between them, swishing the straw in my mock-tail, a gory purple muddle of pomegranate and acai juice and lychee syrup. All three lychees bob about, stuffed with a plump blueberry in their cavity, the juice staining the white flesh to look like strained, bloodshot eyes. "Well?" I ask.

Caroline leans in and drops her voice to a whisper, even though I can barely hear her over the conversations surrounding us. "You know how Kiara drives her mom's old Mini Cooper?"

I nod, scooting my chair closer. The legs shriek as they scrape against the stone.

Caroline darts her eyes carefully around us the way you only would if you're about to impart something secret. "Well," she says, "after you two left, I heard my parents talking. My dad was at the garage for a routine maintenance check this morning when he overheard Kiara's dad having an argument. Apparently one of the mechanics must have had a utility knife in his back pocket or something when he sat in the driver's seat because there's a huge rip in the leather. The service writer and mechanic both claimed the car came in like that, so Mr. Mistry refused to pay the bill for service, Kiara was in tears, and now both *my* dads want to take our cars to a new place. It's a whole thing."

At the conclusion of the tale, Austin sighs. "Care, I told you, that's not bad luck. That's an accident, a couple of shady employees who wouldn't own up, and shitty customer service."

I pop a lychee in my mouth whole, teeth tearing through tender flesh. "Weren't you the one who told me bad luck isn't picky? That it takes what it can get?"

"But this is normal bad luck," he insists. "Listen. A few months ago my mom took her car to the same garage, and the next day she heard this horrible clanking in the engine. When she investigated, she found a screwdriver knocking around in there and a half-eaten tuna sandwich."

"Gross," says Caroline, wrinkling her nose.

"Dangerous," I say at the same time, knowing absolutely nothing about cars but pretty sure having an extra piece of metal and hot, rancid fish does an engine no favors.

Austin steeples his fingers together. "And what does this tell us?"

I snort. "That the people of Prior's End need to find a new garage."

Caroline giggles and reaches for a mozzarella stick, sighing happily at her first bite.

"My point is, these things happen." Austin drains his witch's brew, a menacing neon concoction that's mostly lime soda and sports drink, then goes for the cherry garnish resting across the rim on a toothpick.

"Or," I counter, "it's a pattern."

"Or these are very normal, very regular things that happen in real life."

"*Or* her bad luck is turning into worse luck."

Austin calmly grabs the fried pickles. "Nova, do you *want* it to be bad luck?"

My mouth drops open. "What? Why would I—That's not even—Care, help a girl out?"

"I don't know, I think I'm with Austin on this one." She bites her lip, not looking at me. Instead, she seems transfixed by her candy corn drink. "You seem pretty convinced this is your fault."

My toes scrunch in my Mary Janes, cheap dupes for the ones I really wanted. "I have *never* said—"

"We're your best friends," she interrupts. "We know you. It's obvious that you're feeling guilty. You're doing that thing where you're trying to act too casual and unbothered about it."

"And your voice gets all false, and that vein in your forehead throbs," Austin adds. "You have tells."

"But I also *do* believe in bad luck," Caroline says. "So I'm not ruling out this Kiara thing. Come on, right after Nova pretends to be the psychic and hexes Kiara, all this weird stuff starts happening? The timing is suspicious. Even you have to admit it."

He groans.

We're not going to agree on this, so I decide to swing the conversation to something else. Literally anything will work: the two-page history essay Mrs. Branson assigned on our favorite festival tradition, whether anyone wants to order more food, or maybe "You know me, but I know you just as much, and I know you're both into each other, so just it admit it already!"

There's no tactful way to address the unsubtle glances they keep peeking at each other, so I'm about to say it exactly how I'm thinking it when there's a commotion behind us. Someone's chair topples over, and everyone rushes to the pub's open doorway.

"Is there a doctor here?" a familiar voice yells. "She's choking!"

I startle. "Is that Radhika?"

Without waiting for an answer, I shove past the adults crowding the threshold. My friends are right behind me. The air is heavy with greasy fried food and unmistakable panic.

People have leaped away from their seating, leaving space for two girls, one choking, the other performing the Heimlich. There's a ring of customers packed shoulder to shoulder, all frozen in place, not knowing what to do but unable to look away.

"Oh my god," Caroline whispers behind me, so close that her breath tickles my ear. "Nova, do you think it could be—" She cuts herself off when my eyes fly to her in warning.

"Not here," says Austin, clearly of the same mind as me. "Hey, man, could you . . . ?" A solid head taller than us, he taps at a teenager's shoulder to get him to budge up a bit so Caroline and I can better see what's going on.

"Sure," the boy says without turning. With a start, I realize it's Devon Lake, there with his swim team buddies, only decent-human-being concerned and not *that's my girlfriend* out of his mind with worry.

Kiara's face is red, brown eyes bulging, hands clawing at her throat. If she was agitated before, it's nothing to what she's feeling now.

How is Devon not rushing to her side? Hell, I have no idea how to do the Heimlich, and I *still* want to do something. And *I* wasn't the one draped all over her last night, hinting that I was her happily ever after.

"It's okay, I've got you," pants Tayla. Her arms are wrapped tight around Kiara's middle, and her straight hair is slipping from its high ponytail, several strands plastered wetly to her forehead. She's such a pale white that emotions and exertions alike have her flushing like she's run a mile.

Everything about Tayla screams scared but determined. Credit where it's due—I'd be too terrified of making it worse to press my fist just above Kiara's belly button and give her abdomen swift, hard thrusts.

Kiara finally coughs up a roundish black lump coated with saliva. Looking at it makes her gag, and Radhika throws a frankly wasteful amount of paper napkins from another table onto Kiara's hand. If it's possible, Radhika looks even more repulsed. She turns away and grimaces into her shoulder.

Evidently made of sterner stuff, Evan rolls their eyes at Radhika and rubs soothing circles on Kiara's back, but it must have had the opposite effect from the way she shakes them off. She gestures between the clump of napkins in her hand and the half-eaten pizza back at their booth.

I can't hear her over the claps and shouts of praise, but from the patchy red of her cheeks and the angry jut of her finger and the way her mouth forms the same handful of words over and over, she seems insistent and angry. *I told you, I told you, I told you.*

Following her finger, I get a good look at the pizza for the first time. There's only a couple of slices left, but it's unmistakably the Cauldron's specialty: spiderweb pizza. The Romano-Parmesan-mozzarella cheese blend decoration is delicate enough for the webbing, but not so thin as to burn in the pizza oven. The usual black-olive spider with slivers for legs is noticeably absent.

"I'm so sorry," the manager says, wringing her hands. "Our olives are all pitted. I don't know what happened. The machine must have missed punching this one out. Of course, we'll comp your bill."

"It's okay, I'm fine," says Kiara. Her voice is a hoarse croak. "Accidents happen."

The manager looks even more distressed.

As I watch, Kiara blinks back her watery eyes and summons up a yearbook smile. "Really, don't worry about it." She puts a hand on the manager's arm, sweet and placating. "It wasn't your fault."

The chatter all around me turns into white noise, a faint drone of nothingness that makes it all too easy to zero in on Kiara's face. It's been minutes, and her cheeks are still a stark, vivid pink against the fairness of her skin. Her eyes are impossibly large, her smile false, like she wants to give the impression she's okay.

And I'd maybe buy it if her hands weren't in fists at her side, her shoulders hunched up to her ears. It's the worst posture she's ever exhibited in front of me. She's never appeared this horribly vulnerable, not even when she so earnestly wanted to hear something good about her future and I didn't give it to her.

A terrible pressure builds in the back of my throat. I glance once more to the abandoned pizza.

"Let's go." Caroline tugs my hand when the crowd starts

to dissipate back to their tables, crisis averted. Kiara keeps assuring the manager there's no harm done. "Kiara doesn't need us gawking at her."

"*We* aren't the ones gawking," says Austin. Despite the fact that everything's fine and no one's dead, his body is rigid and tense next to mine. He nods toward Kiara's exes.

Evan, Radhika, and Tayla have me in their sights: brown eyes, brown eyes, blue eyes.

Evan's expression betrays nothing when their eyes slide away from mine. Unease strikes me hard and fast. My belly squirms. Evan's never *avoided* me before.

Radhika watches me with a disquieting, probing intensity. She scrunches up her whole face like she's trying to remember my name, which is just plain insulting, then whispers something to the redhead at her side.

To my surprise, Tayla isn't preening under the glowing attention of saving her best friend's life. While the whole crowd is looking at her, commending her quick action, her eyes skewer me. It's rather disconcerting, considering she's looked at me more tonight than she has all year so far. She reaches back to tighten her ponytail and brush some stragglers away from her temples. Without breaking eye contact, she says something in that usual dispassionate way she has that makes Radhika nod.

Both girls look determined.

Foreboding wiggles its way between my shoulder blades, sharp and prickling.

Caroline slips her hand into mind and holds tight. "Tree house?"

Relief whooshes through me. I nod, tearing my gaze away from the trio of exes. "Tree house."

"I'll grab our food," says Austin. In a low voice, he asks me, "What's up with Tayla?"

"You mean Darth Barbie? She's been giving me the creeps all night."

Without meaning to, my eyes flick to Kiara. She's repeated she's okay a dozen times by now, and yet all I want is to hear her say it again for nothing more than my own peace of mind.

She catches me looking. She tilts her head, almost like she's waiting for me to go over and say something. Me, not Devon. The boy sitting at a table with his friends, laughing and stuffing his face with jalapeño poppers. He doesn't spare Kiara a glance or vice versa. I don't get it; how has their whole relationship changed so drastically in one day?

I swallow. To be fair, all it takes is one sentence to change a life. I should know.

A waitress is cleaning Kiara's booth, whisking away all evidence of the pizza. Suddenly, I realize Kiara is still holding the clump of napkins and the almost fatal olive pit. My stomach twists.

When Caroline pulls me away, I force my feet to move in the opposite direction of where I really want to be.

I don't look back.

7

We haven't been to the tree house, all three of us, in forever. Well, I say forever, but I know exactly how long it's been. After what happened to our fathers, the tree house was no longer a sanctuary for Austin. In high school, he retreated to indoor activities, finding the solace in creativity that I find in the woods, where I can be closest to my dad. Austin became one of the other cool guys who toted their guitars around and looked hot and mournful in their beanies, like they were nursing a broken heart and a slipping GPA.

Caroline hung on a little longer, but in the end, her own interests eclipsed the time she was willing to spend schlepping out to the tree house in the woods, crunching over twigs and unmarked paths to find our way to our special spot. Even now, she's pouting about how the soles of her new shoes are going to be "so gross."

I did once consider using the tree house as a place to store hiking equipment, but it was too big a risk. When my friends hang here now, it's always a surprise pop in:

When Austin wants to test his latest lyrics (I'm easily pleased, but Caroline is quick to call something out for being too cringe or too cheesy) or complain about how the latest guy his mom is dating feels the need to bond with a football or unsolicited girl advice. When we're studying for exams and Caroline's dads arm us with plenty of prawn crackers and Pocky. When I need to bitch about Kiara enchanting yet another person I liked first, and Austin draws Kiara's face, Caroline brings darts, and we pockmark that paper until I feel better.

"I haven't been back here since summer," Austin says with some surprise, loping alongside me on patchy grass and pebbles. He turns over his shoulder to address Caroline. "You?"

She shakes her head. "Same. It's fine in summer, but autumn is different. Creepier."

They both know better than to ask when I was last here; it's my home away from home. It's sequestered in the woods, not deep enough in for parents to worry but far enough from the town proper to feel remote.

"Yeah, with good reason," Austin says, somber. He yanks up the hood of his navy pullover.

I stiffen but don't say anything. He's not *wrong*. And the two of us would know better than most.

The rest of our journey passes in silence. It's hard to keep up a conversation with the thrash of the October wind. I shove my fists deep in my pockets until I feel the bite of nails. Caroline huddles in Austin's jacket, subconsciously angling her steps until their shoulders brush.

According to Prior's End lore—if you believe *The Way of the Wish*, the guidebook Radhika's family self-published before we were born—no one knows who built the tree house, and it's been around basically forever, but it hasn't stopped anyone from adding on to it. Mostly for safety but sometimes for aesthetic, adding their own mark to the place.

Even my dad, along with Austin's mom and Caroline's dads, replaced some boards the summer before he left and added a platform encircling the loft. It's technically open to everyone, but for the last seven years, it's been me replacing the dollar-store paper garlands whenever they fade, the string lights when they pop, the chalk artwork on the platform.

When we reach the rope ladder, Caroline lifts her feet to examine the muddy soles of her Converse and sighs. I don't take it to heart; nature isn't her thing anymore. She's all about fashion and makeup these days. Anytime we go remotely near the woods, she gets jumpy and anxious. It's hard to imagine she'd once been stoked to join me, Austin, and our dads on a possible camping trip in the Blue Ridge Mountains.

Warblers trill nearby, wind whispering through the trees. I'm the first to scramble up, then Austin, then Caroline. Our feet scuff over the faded remains of my chalk wildflowers, swept away with the rain.

"You okay, Nova?" asks Caroline as I turn on the star-shaped LED ceiling lights. We plop on the floor cushions, which are comfortable and squashy with age. "You've barely said a word. Is it being here?" She looks around with sad eyes. "It's gotta bring up some . . . stuff."

That's one way of putting it. My laugh teeters on the edge

of bitter. "I can't stop thinking about the last thing I said to him. I was a fucking brat."

Austin gives me a quizzical look. "What could you have said that was so bad? You were just ten."

"A brat," I repeat.

What else can I call a girl who had everything—*a dad who loved her*—and still, with one damning sentence, exiled him forever?

I know I promised to take you to the festival tonight, Nova, but I know why Shane did this foolish, foolish thing. I have to go after him.

Why does it have to be you?

The woods are in my blood. Shane is my best friend, my brother. Like you and Austin. You'll understand when you're older what it means to be responsible for someone. I'll bring Shane back before the week is over, and then I'll take you to the festival every single night. I promise, Nova.

Fine! Go, then! If you love the woods so much, stay there forever! I hope you never come back!

I don't remember what he said after that.

What I do remember: his disappointed eyes. My sullen silence when he told me, *I love you, be good for your mother, I'll be back*. The way I didn't return his hug even when he held on extra long, waiting for me to forgive him. How I knew I was in the wrong even while I was withholding it.

If I could do it all again, I would never say those things. I would squeeze every last moment of that hug like I could put a stopper in time, bottle his love because it was so, so precious.

The walls of the tree house make my secrets seem much bigger. Unwieldy. Like they're too much for just me. My friends' faces are unguarded. I could tell them. I could do it right now. I could tell them about seven years ago.

Shame fills me like smoke. Scours my throat. No. I can't.

"Aurora's been whispering in Mom's ear about 'moving forward,'" I say instead. My voice is as scathing as I can make it. "It's code. They want the court to declare Dad legally dead. Mom wants to."

Wants isn't the right word. But she's going to do it anyway, isn't she?

Austin's mouth twists. "Aurora will be gone soon. She never stays past Halloween."

"Doesn't she have a partner she needs to get back to?" asks Caroline. A little wistfully, she says, "The cut and clarity of her diamond engagement ring is superb."

Trust Caroline to notice. "Not," I point out, "that we've ever heard of a wedding or a spouse in the last seven years."

Austin hums thoughtfully. "Think she knows what you did last night?"

I snort, reaching for the fried pickle he hands me. It's cold and limp now, but I still chew it. "I think if she had half the powers she claims she does, she would have seen it coming."

Caroline crosses her legs and leans forward with her elbows on her knees. "We need to talk about what happened tonight."

"We don't," says Austin, doling out the food three ways. "We've been over this already."

I stare at the paper napkin I'm using as a plate. I'm a terrible person for not losing my appetite after what we just witnessed.

No. It's not my fault. It's just an accident, like Kiara said. It could have happened to anyone. Commercial pitting machines aren't perfect. People don't always chew as much as they should.

See? Perfectly reasonable, plausible explanations. It's nothing like what happened to Dad.

"Austin, you can't seriously wave this off as another 'very normal, very regular thing.' Kiara almost *died*," Caroline says, eyes wide. "If Tayla hadn't known how to do the Heimlich maneuver . . ."

Great, even the mozzarella stick is terrible. With a greasy, rubbery taste coating my tongue, it's not easy to say my next words, much less believe them. But I have to pose the hypothesis and run all the angles. "Maybe all this has nothing to do with me and more to do with the black cat that crossed her path. If you think about it, that's when all her trouble actually got started."

"Except she said her mascara wand attacked her," says Caroline. "So she would already have gotten dressed and done her makeup *before* working her shift at Bee Outdoors when the hikers found Inky."

"Inky," I say under my breath. "More like Lucifer."

Austin laughs and chows down on another pickle because his stomach is an undiscerning bottomless pit.

"*Guys*," Caroline says, face scrunched with frustration. "You might not want it to be true, but that doesn't mean it's not. Whatever's happening to Kiara is real."

"I agree," declares a new voice.

All three of us startle.

Radhika's head hovers above the platform, the rest of her presumably swaying on the rope ladder below. We must not have heard the creaks over our conversation.

Shit. How much did she hear?

"What are you doing here?" I ask, not caring how rude it sounds. My voice makes it clear that the tree house is *our* place. As far as I know, this is the first time she's ever visited, and she sure looks it from the way she's visibly taking it all in, like she doesn't want to miss a thing.

About nine generations ago, our families shared a common ancestor, Henry Prior, which is as good as being strangers, honestly. Dad used to be more sentimental about the other branch on our family tree, especially since Radhika and I are the only two of our generation. But we're so distant that her parents never even expressed their sympathies when we lost Dad, and if it wasn't for a handful of group projects over the years, I wouldn't even have Radhika's phone number.

As I suspect, she doesn't take my tone to heart. Radhika rolls her eyes. "The tree house is public property. Also, I followed you."

"What the hell?" Austin says at the same time I demand, "Why?"

She gives us a Tayla-worthy look of disbelief. "You're kidding me, right? You were all there." With that, she clambers up the rest of the way into our tree house, settling herself on a paisley cushion and helping herself to a mozzarella stick from my napkin.

I don't even want it, but *still*.

"How's Kiara?" Caroline asks, shooting me a disapproving look.

Around a gob of cheese, Radhika evasively says, "I called Keiffer. He was helping his mom sell her jewelry at the festival, but he's dropping everyone home."

Keiffer is her boyfriend. He's also Kiara's ex-boyfriend and one of the guys I crushed on before she got to him first. And as a rule, I've never gone for anyone after she's dumped them, which left the field open for Radhika to swoop in and bond with him over their crushed hearts. It's all very evolved.

"That's good," says Caroline. "I hope Kiara will be okay. We were all pretty scared for her."

Radhika licks her fingers clean. "Which is why I'm here. We need your help." She looks at me, lips pursed, as if it's the last thing she wants to admit. Up close, she looks exhausted, the corners of her eyes drooping like she could just curl up here and go to sleep.

"We?" asks Austin.

"Tayla, Evan, and me." She grimaces. "The psychic at the festival totally messed with Kiara. Hexed her or something. Freaky stuff has been happening, like earlier today when Kiara found a spider swimming in her butterscotch soda, and later, she almost face-planted on the sidewalk when she stumbled over a crack. But when we stopped by Aurora's tent earlier, she denied everything. And those things were fairly harmless compared to what we just witnessed! If things get worse . . ." Her brown eyes, winged with sharp, dramatic lines, punch through my brain fuzz. "But you . . . you can help."

Guilt coils in my gut like a heavy snake. "You already talked to Aurora?"

She gives the tree house a quick skim. "Your dad used to run tours into the forest, right?"

Guess that explains why they think I can help. "Yeah," I say tightly. "So about Aurora—"

"Did he ever, you know, find it?"

She doesn't need to clarify what she's talking about. We all know: the wishing well.

"*That's* why you need my help?" I scoff. I need to head this off, stat. "Sorry, wrong girl."

"But—"

"The wishing well is just a rumor, Radhika. Only kids, cranks, and tourists believe."

Her voice rises. "That's not true, and you know it." She leans in earnestly. "Your dad—"

"Don't talk about my dad. He wasn't like everyone else! He wouldn't go looking for it!"

"Nova's right." Austin's voice shoulders a hard edge. He glares at Radhika. "You really think that if the legend was true, someone wouldn't have found it by now?"

"Someone *did*," she shoots back. "My great-great-great-great-great-great-great-grandfather."

I bristle. "*Our* great-great-great—yeah, I'm not saying all that—grandfather."

"And yet you don't believe in his discovery? Some descendant you are." Condescension drips from every word. "The wishing well can undo any curse. That's not rumor, that's fact. That's our town history, which you should know since we devote a whole festival to it every fall." She quotes directly from our history textbook. "'Upon his discovery of the wishing well in 1782, Henry Prior founded the town of Prior's End, where everything prior could be undone if one only asked for it.'"

Shaking my head, I say, "Right, and it had absolutely nothing to do with the fact that his last name was Prior." When she opens her mouth to argue, I hasten to add, "Look, it makes for a nice origin story, which is fine. Whatever. And upholding the legend gives us a quirky little hook to draw the tourists in, and your guidebook plays it up, but you should know better than to believe in your own con."

"Are you kidding me with this bullshit, Nova? You know your dad believed it was real, don't you? Why else would his aunt have fallen out with my grandparents over publishing the book?"

Invoking my dad, acting like she knew him, is too far. Gritting my teeth, I say, "Yeah? What exactly did the great Henry Prior discover? A crumbling ruin in the middle of a forest? And then suddenly his woes were ended and he lived happily ever after, blah, blah, blah. All hail ye olde pile of rocks."

"Henry died of syphilis, so not exactly a HEA," Caroline mutters.

We all stare.

She blinks. "What, did none of you read to the end of the chapter?"

Radhika isn't distracted for long. "The well has powers—" she starts to say, but Austin cuts her off.

"That people have *died* looking for."

The emphasis he places on that one simple word changes everything, reminds her what he's lost. What I've lost. What all those adventure seekers come here to find. It's jarring, hearing him say that he thinks our dads are dead. Whenever people talk about Dad, they use the word *gone*. But if Mom's going to do what she said she wants to, then I have to get used to hearing the other word, too. Caroline lays her hand on top of Austin's knuckles, not squeezing. Just enough pressure to let him know she's there.

Stricken, and with enough sense to know she's overstepped, Radhika falls silent.

"You should leave," Caroline says firmly.

Radhika crawls to the rope ladder and swings one leg over the side until she locates a rung. "Things are going to get worse, Nova. Even if you don't believe, can you at least accept that Kiara does? That she's going to the wishing well whether you help her or not?"

"This is not my problem," I tell her.

I really, really try to believe it.

8

I don't have time to wonder about Kiara's bad luck the next day and if it's worse, like Radhika seemed so sure it would be. After checking how Inky's doing, today is a full day of avoiding Mom by doing my history essay at the library, even though I have the whole week off from school for the festival to get it done. I run every imaginable errand just to keep out of the house so Mom doesn't ask how I'm *feeling*.

I'm in front of the grocery store, teetering precariously on the seat of my bike as I balance both canvas bags on the handlebars. Just as I'm about to push off, the shrill tinkle of a bell peals out, and a familiar figure comes out of Demeter's Drinks. Madame Aurora wears a long violet dress that accentuates her towering height and a black jacket that looks like a cloak. The silver charms on her bracelets, worn halfway up her forearm, catch the last of the morning light as she tosses something in the air, only to snatch it a second later.

I bite my lip. Against my better judgment, I pedal across the street. "Aurora!"

If she's surprised I'm willingly acknowledging her, she doesn't show it. "Hello, Nova."

Up close, it's obvious the small object in her palm is a button, small and powder pink. I know where I've seen it before. My eyes shoot to Aurora's startling green ones. "What are you doing with that?"

She seems bemused. "Your mother has surely told you."

"Well, yeah. But what are you doing with hers? I mean, with that one specifically?"

Aurora hums. "You've never been interested in my work before."

"I . . ." Faltering, I can't come up with a single reason for my nosiness. "I recognize it. It's a . . . friend's."

She cocks her head. "Kiara Mistry is your friend?"

"She's my . . . yes. Yes, we're friends." I brave letting go of the handlebars to cross my arms, annoyed with the tiny smile playing on her lips and the obnoxious hum that implies she doesn't believe me. Okay, so friends might not be *exactly* what Kiara and I are, but now that I've said it, it doesn't sound so bad.

In fact, it doesn't sound bad at all.

"Your friend"—here Aurora pauses, checks my expression— "scheduled a consultation with me. She brought several of her friends with her as what I can only assume was backup, and the poor girl was most insistent that we meet in a public place." The corners of her mouth tic up. "I've never had a frightening reputation before. It's oddly flattering. Though . . ." She turns shrewd. "I *suspect* it's someone else's doing."

I hear what she leaves unsaid. It's obvious that she knows precisely who that someone is. It's irritating to have to look up at her, an indignity that I'm sure she's aware of, cutting as imposing a figure as she does.

"Come," she says imperiously. "We must speak."

She leads us to the gazebo in the town square. Just a few weeks ago, the trees surrounding the diamond-shaped patch of grass were bright green, clover and dandelions clumped under the canopy of lush branches. Now the grass is shorn low, dry and brown. Most of the leaves are gone, too. White sheets sway ominously on skeletal branches, given ghostly shape with balloons and wire. Suspended aloft, their arms join as if they're playing ring-around-the-rosy.

I walk my bike over to the side of the gazebo where the white paint is recoiling in peeling curls. Inside the covered gazebo are benches engraved with names of the lost, and my gut tells me Aurora's chosen the one with my dad's name on it. When I join her, I'm proven correct.

"You shouldn't mess with magic you don't understand," she says, far more gently than I would expect.

She knows, then. Everything, probably. It's a relief in a way. "Did the spirits tell you?" I ask, half-morose, half jesting.

"Yes." At the look on my face, she laughs. "No. And don't joke about the spirits."

The wooden bench is uncomfortable beneath me, and the proximity to Aurora doesn't help. My stomach squirms as chattering golden leaves, clinging obstinately to the topmost branches, flutter overhead. They aren't swept away, not yet. Like everything else in Prior's End, they'll pick their moment.

"Crystal ball?" I ask dubiously.

"Hmm, no again." Her voice lilts in singsong, pleased and mischievous.

She's playing with me. I cross and uncross my ankles, working my jaw. "Tea leaves?"

"Your guesses amuse me, incorrect as they are." Aurora waves a hand, as if she's a benevolent monarch bestowing her favor on an undeserving peasant. "You may continue."

I hold back a *hmph*. Just barely. "You could just tell me."

"I could," she agrees with a flash of white teeth.

But she won't.

My skin burns. With a touch of scorn, I ask, "Did the tarot cards tell you the future?"

She sighs. "Now you're just being silly."

"I was going for sarcastic." Actually, I was aiming for plain disrespectful. I would never speak to an adult this way, but Aurora has one of those faces that doesn't look much older than mine, coy and unlined. Unlike Mom, who's been collecting worries in every crease ever since Dad left.

Aurora doesn't even bat an eye. "You know perfectly well that the cards do not predict anything. They are a tool that tell us stories of all the possible things that *could* happen, and it's our responsibility to read them and make of the outcomes what we will."

What's most annoying is that thanks to Mom, I *do* know that.

"Ugh. Fine. Whatever. I give up."

For all the appearance of youth on her side, the look she

gives me is undiluted Disappointed Adult. I shove my hands in my pockets. I've gotten away with all the rudeness I'm comfortable with, and now I'm oddly deflated.

Over the years, I've never quite managed to get a rise out of her, not even at our second meeting when I was an angry eleven-year-old who was full of big emotions during the one-year anniversary of my father's disappearance when she told me not to blame myself and, in outrage, I blew out every single one of her candles and stormed out of her tent. That was six festivals ago.

Aurora wants Mom to declare Dad dead but still looks at me like she cares. I can't reconcile that.

"That's your problem," she says now. Her pointer finger twitches like she wants to cross the distance and lay it on top of mine, but I flinch. She sighs. "You hold on to your fire yet forfeit other things too easily."

You're my problem, I want to say, but I've used up my quota of insolence as quickly as I ran through last month's 2 GB of data on my phone plan.

She arches a dark brow, threaded bold and sharp like one of Kiara's, as if she heard it anyway. "Security cam footage," she says calmly.

"What?"

"I caught you hexing Kiara Mistry on video."

It's the last thing I expected to come out of her mouth. It's also strangely anticlimactic and humiliating that I credited her abilities instead of thinking of the most obvious answer.

"You . . . you . . ." I sputter. "Is that even legal?"

Aurora hums. "I have a lot of valuables in my tent. There are other . . . ways I have of dissuading would-be thieves, of course, but law enforcement gets very twitchy about . . . well, let's just say I've learned the hard way that they'd much prefer proof that comes from technology and not . . . other things."

Okay, there are *so* many cryptic pauses in that sentence that my interest is piqued despite myself. I open my mouth to ask, but Aurora holds up a hand.

"No, I will not elaborate," she says, as if that is that.

"But—"

"Don't give me that look," she scolds. "The more important question you should be asking me is what to do about the mess you've created with your"—keen peridot eyes peer into mine—"*friend*."

The hypocrisy isn't lost on me that yesterday I was low-key fretting about my part in this, and today, faced with Aurora's claim that I am, in fact, at fault, I want nothing more than to abdicate responsibility.

Summoning every scrap of conviction I have, I say, "Kiara will be fine. If you saw what happened, then you'll also know there's no way that it was my fault. I just, like, spouted some bullshit. It wasn't that serious."

Aurora tilts her head. "You think the power of your words isn't serious?"

I can't stand to look at her a second longer. It's not a real question; she sounds like a teacher trying to lead me to the answer she wants to hear, when the truth is that the likeliest place I'll end up if I listen to her drivel is *astray* and with a severe case of brain rot.

Turning away, I collect myself. "I didn't do this."

She tucks a glossy brown curl behind her ear. "That's too bad, then. Because the person who invoked the hex would be the likeliest person to remedy the consequences, however unintended. From what Kiara told me, her misfortunes are escalating. And during this time of year, too . . ." She sighs.

"What does *that* mean?"

Somberly, she says, "The full moon is four days from now."

Ah. Everything slots into place. While every phase of the moon has some influence on mortal matters, it's undeniably the full moon that's most potent. Anyone who is even slightly spiritual prepares for its arrival in a frenzy of activity. Full moons are a time of endings, which makes it the perfect time to shed things weighing you down, holding you back.

Caroline's parents air out the house, decluttering and donating what they can. I once overheard Kiara telling Evan that she only gets her hair trimmed on a full moon because an astrologer once told her Indian grandmother that it helps hair grow quicker, thicker, and stronger. But another had given the exact opposite advice, claiming ill omens if you acted against the full moon's abundance.

It's also a convenient time to release any unwanted habits or people, too. It's not unheard of for Prior's End couples to time their breakups at the zenith of the full moon, which people swear helps make the parting more amicable. The only person I've ever broken up with is Austin, so I'll take their word for it.

But the night of a full moon is also ripe for embracing fresh starts and setting new intentions. Everything is amplified, which means harnessing the energy of the moon powers up pretty much anything you set your mind to.

A case could be made either way. Basically, it's all balderdash. Mysticism dressed in flowy skirts and doused in stinking patchouli.

My dad believed in the occasional magic of our town. He would have believed in this, too. And for just a moment, I yearn for his conviction to flow in my veins.

Aurora holds her hand up to her face and examines the gunmetal polish on her nails as though she's utterly unaffected. Her honking big diamond engagement ring twinkles. "So you see, Nova," she says, "if Kiara gets through this full moon unscathed without anything *too* dire befalling her, she should survive. But if not . . ."

Survive? For the span of several seconds, I hope I've misheard.

My pulse thuds loudly in my ears. "If not?"

Aurora quotes me back to me, "Then good luck with the impending doom."

9

It starts at sundown—with a girl, a cat, and a squash. Rather, the entirety of a RAM 3500's truck bed heaped high with pumpkins and acorn squash, and they don't *stay* there so much as they spill out the back of the truck, cascading over the cherry-red siding like water overflowing a glass.

And it's with this one event that I can no longer pretend Kiara's fate is not my problem. Because as the teenage driver of the pickup flirts out the open window with the pretty girl setting up the caramel apple stall at the festival, oblivious to the road ahead riddled with potholes, Kiara and Inky are about to get, well, squashed. No pun intended.

When it comes to Kiara, I seem to do things without thinking, and tackling her to safety is no different.

My body crashes into hers, sending us both sprawling on the sidewalk. I don't know why I expected it to be like the movies, where the love interest heroically rescues the main character, and then they both right themselves, still looking fresh as daisies, not a hair out of place. Real life is nothing like that.

There's a low groan and then a quiet "Fuck."

It takes me a beat to realize I'm not the one who cursed out loud. Kiara props herself up on one elbow, still cupping Inky snug in her hands. He lets out a plaintive meow and bats at her fingers. She's absolutely disheveled, side braid loose and the black silk hair scarf dusty with sidewalk grit. The apricot locks of hair framing her face are more frizz than curl, a far cry from the spirals they were a second ago.

"You saved me," she says with awe and a morsel of confusion. "From . . . an onslaught of squash?"

"Looks that way." I hiss, gingerly pressing my fingertips against my shoulder. I knocked my knee on my bike when I hopped off in a panicked frenzy, hit the sidewalk when I bowled her over, and now I feel like I'm going to vomit.

The wheels of my fallen bike are still spinning, and a few people in the midst of setting up their booths for the festival are looking over in concern. Honestly, I'm surprised I was able to blur across the street so fast. If I hadn't been on my way to Austin's grandmother for a second opinion on Aurora's diagnosis of certain doom, if I hadn't been looking at Kiara right when it happened, she might not have been as lucky.

Perched cozily on a street sign next to us, two magpies look at us inquisitively. The rhyme comes back to me: one for sorrow, two for joy. In more superstitious times, the number of magpies spotted together was used to forecast the future. As I watch, one of the magpies flutters off.

Great. More bad luck.

"What are you doing with Inky?" I ask, heart still lodged in my throat.

Kiara switches to a one-hand hold on Inky to rotate her other elbow ninety degrees. "You mean Loki?"

I still think Inky is a pretty milquetoast name for a black cat, but I dig my heels in. Or I would anyway, if I was upright. "No, I mean Inky."

Her smile is impish. "I spotted *Loki* in the road and had to get to him before something bad happened."

"Technically, something bad did happen."

"Technically," says Kiara, "you stopped something bad from happening. My heroine."

The laugh bursts out of me, shrill and jarring. Heroine? More like her wicked witch. No, I don't want to be *her* anything. I tell myself that until I believe it.

"Nova?" She reaches out to touch my wrist, her eyes soft. "I promise I'm okay. You saved me."

I swallow, tamping down the fluttering in my belly. Sure, disaster was averted this time . . . I pull away from her, rubbing my shoulders, but tingles from her touch continue shooting up to my elbow. I shove all dire and distracting thoughts aside and focus. "What? Are you serious? He was just wandering?"

She smirks. "See why I called our little escape artist Loki now?" My tummy does a funny flip when she says *our*. "I called the shelter," she continues, "and Otto said one of the new volunteers had taken him out to play and got distracted. I was just about to bring him back."

Probably another newbie who thought volunteering was

just about the fun stuff and would ghost us out of embarrassment instead of learning from their mistake.

Inky makes the kitten equivalent of a grumble. Kiara gives in to the demand and scratches the top of his head. "Anyway," she says, "I came here early to meet someone before the festival went full swing."

I shouldn't care, but a part of me wants to know if it's Devon she's meeting. I'm completely over him, but it's the principle of the thing. And really, *Devon?* After his unaffected behavior at the Cauldron when Kiara was literally choking? Snippily, I say, "I can do that. You don't want to be late for your date."

Kiara's brow furrows. "I never said it was a—"

"Are you two okay?" The teenage driver hurries over, phone out. "Do I need to call for an ambulance? Shit. I literally *just* got my license. My dad's going to kill me." He pauses for breath just long enough to take stock of the spillage, blinking rapidly. "I just took my eye off the road for a second, I swear."

There's an indignant squawk behind me, and then bony fingers are digging into my armpits, hauling me up without so much as a hello. "It was long enough for you to get the name of the apple seller!"

I twist my neck around—ugh, *mistake*—but the glance is worth it because it reveals a seething Petra Lyons at my back. Austin's grandmother is a bit north of sixty, with a proud mane of short golden curls and homemade peacock-feather earrings that graze her petite shoulders.

She rakes her gaze over both me and Kiara, verifying we're

unharmed. I'm used to seeing her fun-loving and casual, so the blue fire in her eyes is a bit terrifying. In that moment, I see why some people rudely call her the witch behind the apothecary counter.

"Do you drive your grandmother to her hospital appointments like this?" she demands.

The boy blushes. "No, ma'am."

"If I ever hear you driving so irresponsibly again," she starts to warn.

"You won't!" he yelps. "I promise!"

She glares, wholly unimpressed.

"She's never going to give me her number now," he says miserably as the apple seller flirts with one of the photographer's assistants arranging pumpkins on hay bales for photoshoots.

I scoff. "Gotta say, dude, you're getting no sympathy from me."

"Hot girls don't like bad drivers," Kiara chimes in. She gets up and flips her braid over her shoulder.

Faced with three angry women, he babbles something that's a cross between "I'm so sorry" and "Please don't tell my dad" and flees back to his truck, abandoning the pumpkins and acorn squashes on the road.

Kiara rolls her eyes after him then tentatively approaches me with an outstretched arm, like I'm a snarling hellhound and she's flinging me a piece of kibble. She's not offering me the kitten but her free hand. There's something tender in her gaze that so far I've only seen aimed at her friends and small, helpless animals and *me* that one time. "Thanks, Nova. I owe you one."

I stick mine out, too, in a way I'm about to immediately regret. "You don't," I say, giving her a brisk shake just as she gives me a gentle squeeze. We're so blatantly out of sync that she laughs, and I yank the offending body part back. Her skin was cool while I was hot all over. Even after we're no longer in contact, the tingles don't stop racing up my arm, making my scalp tickle and tighten.

Oh. My cheeks burn. It's possible I misread her intentions, and she doesn't see me as the hellhound in this scenario. Did I really just shake her hand like she's a stranger at a meeting? God, I'm so embarrassed.

"Here." She transfers Inky to my arms. "I should go." She gives Petra a brief smile and Inky a wave.

When Kiara takes off, she doesn't meet up with Devon. She's heading in the direction of Aurora's tent, where, if I squint, I can make out Tayla, Evan, Keiffer, and Radhika waiting for her. Seriously, do they just travel everywhere in a pack?

My belly cramps as I imagine how this latest accident is going to convince the others that Kiara's life is in serious jeopardy. And if Aurora drops the word *survival* around them, all four of their pretty little heads will explode, brain goo going splat everywhere inside her tent.

I sigh. My way forward is clear now.

It *is* my problem. I don't want to say I trust Aurora, exactly, but I get the distinct impression she'd rather I help Kiara on my own instead of forcing me into it, so my secret is safe for now.

"I know your secret," says Petra, bringing me close for a hug. A swift bolt of panic lances through me before melting away, the swirling scents of lavender, peppermint, and rosemary immediately taking its place. Petra, like me, is a headache sufferer, and while injections and medication can help, she relies mostly on folk remedies like daubs of aromatherapy oil on her temples. "You like her," she imparts.

"Just because I saved her life doesn't mean I like her."

She laughs and taps my chin. "Don't look so mutinous."

"Misunderstood, not mutinous."

"You never looked at my grandson like that," she points out.

"Austin has the good sense not to stand in the middle of the street," I counter.

"Mm-hmm." Petra's blue eyes sparkle down at me. "What if I told you how she was looking at you?"

I avert my gaze and mutter, "I'd be entirely uninterested."

She makes a doubtful sound at the back of her throat but doesn't contradict me. "Now, why don't you come in for a nice cup of tea and tell me what's so mysterious that you had to meet me after close."

The wooden sign flapping above the door reads MORTAR & THISTLE in gold Gothic lettering. It's an unassuming sort of place, a narrow storefront with dark tinted windows to limit sun exposure to the potions inside. There's floor-to-ceiling cabinetry and creaky floors in ancient and weathered teak.

The shelves are well stocked with colorful glass vials and vintage perfume bottles, all filled with natural, clean, ethically sourced ingredients.

Petra's wife, Daniela, is sanitizing and tidying up the testers. The bottles make tiny clinks as she puts them back in place. When they married five years ago, Petra introduced her as her third spouse, second wife, and first soulmate.

To a twelve-year-old girl on the cusp of her bisexual awakening, Petra was my hero.

"Joining us for dinner, love?" Daniela chirps, chucking me under the chin. She smiles with her whole face, revealing deep dimples in her brown cheeks.

"It's vegan tonight," says Petra. "We always have room for one more!"

Austin's mom works long hours as an emergency room doctor at our local hospital, especially after her promotion and throwing herself into work after her husband left, so Austin's more or less been raised by Petra. He grew up eating chicken nuggets, tangelos, and frozen meals until Petra met Daniela at a crystal conference, where they fell in love when they reached for the same pink topaz—once they were done arguing over who got to take it home. They wound up leaving with each other instead, and Daniela proposed to Petra with it a year later.

"Thanks, but I can't tonight," I tell the older women. "I need your help, actually."

Spider plants, sword ferns, and weeping figs dangle from

the exposed beams, purifying the air. They rustle as we pass underneath, almost like they're talking to each other. Much like the flora, the owners communicate with wordless glances, probably running through everything that can happen to a teenage girl.

"I know just the tea," says Petra.

Dani gives her an apologetic look. "I'll stick to my coffee."

Mortar & Thistle is a narrow shop, made narrower by the slim tables splitting the store down the middle, and it's in some disarray from shoppers browsing all day, but Petra and Dani put everything back in place without breaking stride as we walk.

There are velvet trays of precious stones and gemstone bracelets, pink soap loaves generously sprinkled with crushed rose petals that look good enough to eat, the lavender and sage sugar scrubs I buy for my dry winter skin that are almost sold out, and in the back, jars of teas and a weighing station so people can make their own custom blends.

Petra plucks hyssop, the purple buds immediately perfuming the air with the scent of licorice, then goes for golden-yellow chamomile flowers and lemon peel, finishing it off with a kiss of honey. After pouring two steaming teacups, she gestures for me to join her in the window seat.

Dani has disappeared, but the delicious smell of dinner cooking wafts from their upstairs flat. She's taken Inky with her for cuddles. Something tells me he's found his forever home.

"Now," says Petra, a touch sternly. "Tell me what's on your mind."

I inhale the spirals of steam and just blurt it out like ripping off a Band-Aid. "I think I hurt someone. Kiara. That girl I saved from the whole squash thing. I didn't mean to, but horrible things have been happening to her ever since I, um, said some things on the first day of the festival. Bad luck. The real kind, Petra. And it's getting worse."

She takes a long, slow sip then waits for me to do the same. "What exactly did you say, Nova?"

I recap for her, hunching myself behind my drawn knees until I'm pressed against the corner of the window seat. The tea's cooled enough to drink, and I gulp it down, wishing it was that easy to just take back everything I said to Kiara so it never happened at all and her life wasn't in jeopardy thanks to me.

This isn't me. It *can't* be me. Not after Dad. My emotions wouldn't rule me, I'd promised myself. Recklessness came with risks. Once, Dad was the one I'd run to when I made a mistake, and I always knew he would make things okay again. Without him to guide me, it's harder to see a way forward. There are some sorrows that time cannot mend. Some wrongs that go too deep.

His voice is nothing more than a faded memory. *Whatever you've done, nothing is so bad that you can't tell me. You are not alone. I am always with you. You tell me, Nova girl, and I'll help you.*

Where do I run to now when his safe, protective arms are gone?

"Oh, Nova," says Petra when I'm done with both the tale and the tea.

Weakly, I ask, "You didn't, like, put any truth serum in this, did you?"

"Ha!" Petra seems tickled with the notion as she whisks the empty cups away. "So it seems to me that you only have two options. Fix your mistake, or let Kiara's bad luck play out to whatever end."

That's what I like best about her, other than the fact she's a totally cool gay grandma—she takes everything in stride with levity and a no-nonsense attitude.

"So you put stock in the idea of a made-up hex?" I trust Petra. If she says yes, I'll do whatever I have to do to fix my mistake. And maybe it won't be the only thing I put right along the way.

"The universe is always listening, Nova. Intentions have power. You said the words and meant every one of them," she says, gentle but grave at the same time. "Does that sound made up to you?"

"Well, no," I admit, heart shriveling. "I guess not when you put it like that. I was just . . . mad. Wanted to mess with her. Freak her out, not actually hurt her." I wince. I sound annoying and defensive even to my own ears, but I can't stop. "It was a harmless prank. I didn't mean to, like, manifest it into existence. I mean, there's so many other things that I said, that other people said . . . things that never manifested. Why now? Why me? Why me *again*?"

"You know our town history. The magic is unpredictable. Prior's End has played its part in more endings than not." The twist of her mouth is faintly sad. "It will always seek to destroy what came before. That is its nature."

I think about my dad. Austin's dad. All those others who lost their way and lost their lives looking for a wishing well that maybe no one's even seen in generations. After all, there's no photographic evidence, only hearsay that's dubious at best. But when winter gives way to spring, the tourists descend like clockwork to chase after a legend. *The Way of the Wish* stokes people's imaginations to a boiling point; the potential reward far outweighs the risk.

"But," Petra adds, "a full moon is also a chance for bright new beginnings to come out of those unhappy endings."

My stomach clenches like a fist. A moment ago, I could have discarded everything Aurora said. Now I know I can't. "You know, Petra, you're not the first person to say that to me recently."

Is a moon just a moon? Or . . . is this my opportunity to finally have a partner to join me? We can have each other's backs as we trek through the Longing Woods to find the wishing well. I'll finally have someone to journey with. This is what I've been waiting for. Kiara can undo her bad luck, and I . . .

I can wish for my dad back.

I'm not the same little girl who so easily believed in magic, who marveled at the majesty of the woods and hung on to my dad's stories as if he draped the very stars in the sky. I see the woods as something to fear, to mistrust. As a place that takes and doesn't give back. Day by day, year by year, the wonder has waned until only the barest sliver remains. It's precious, but it hurts, too, like a bruise I can't help but press.

Petra raises her arm to examine the column of bracelets. Carefully, she selects one with smooth green stone beads, sliding the elastic over her narrow wrist. "Here, for you. If you're going to go traipsing around in the woods, I'd feel better if you had this."

I slip it on, admiring the shimmer from all angles. "It's beautiful. What is it supposed to do?"

"Do?" Her forehead creases. "It's a bracelet, my dear. It doesn't *do* anything."

Deflated, I sink against the window seat cushions. So even if I did want to go on a wild goose chase for the fabled wishing well, this isn't the magical tool from my wise mentor that will help me do it.

Petra fondly rolls her eyes. Leaning forward, she taps the bracelet. "Don't be so dramatic. I didn't say the beads were useless."

I perk up. "They're not?"

"Green aventurine," she explains. "Among other things, it's considered to be the crystal of good fortune and personal growth. Maybe the luckiest of all crystals. Some call it the stone of opportunity."

"And if I give this to Kiara, she'll be okay?"

Petra clucks her tongue. "It's not for her. It's for you. Charms may keep the negative energy at bay for a while, but all it takes is another pothole, another boy too distracted to pay attention, another truckload of squash . . ."

"No, you're right. I bet the other squash families really have it out for her."

Petra's blue eyes turn flinty.

"I was kidding! Sorry, sorry."

"It's not me to whom you owe the apology," she says mildly.

Ugh. She's right. But there's no way I'm confessing anything to Kiara. What purpose would it serve? I'm going to help her regardless. I may not see the world the way I once did, but I am still my father's daughter. He wouldn't abandon a friend in trouble, and neither will I.

For the second time in my life, my words have caused real, true harm. And despite what I told Radhika, Kiara *is* my problem. But.

Helping her also helps me.

She never needs to know it was me that night who hexed her, not Aurora. Besides the fact that her friends would come for me with flaming pitchforks, I don't want her to know. I mean, I want her to trust me, and that's going to be categorically more difficult if she knows I have it out for her. Had. *Had* it out for her. Past tense.

Turns out Kiara was right after all. Because from this moment onward, I am 100 percent going to be Kiara Mistry's heroine.

10

Mom stands in the kitchen, on hold with our insurance company, phone in one hand and a steaming cup of coffee in the other. The sun's just starting to come up, casting Mom in a golden glow that just barely glamours the dark half-moons under her eyes. She exhales as though all her patience is spent. It makes me wonder exactly how long she's been up, which cup of coffee this is.

"When did you tell me about this?" she asks, more furious about the packed backpack and sleeping bag at my feet than the automated voice in her ear telling her she's thirty-eighth in line to speak to a real person and her business is very important to them.

"Last week?" I know she's spotted a chink in my armor when my words come out like a question.

"Nova, you did not breathe a word about this camping trip," she snaps.

"I swear I did."

I didn't, but considering that I only had last night to hastily pull everything together, it's easier to let her think she's just forgotten. My thumb lightly rubs the green beads on my wrist.

Last night, after returning Inky and a quick stop at Bee

Outdoors to grab hiking boots, I used my so-called feminine wiles—something I'm pretty sure I've never had—on Kiara—who has them in spades—to convince her that finding the wishing well was in her best interest. To my surprise, she didn't seem that keen on going into the woods despite Radhika's claims at the tree house. It turned out that Radhika was the one who was trying to talk Kiara into it. Which, weird?

But Kiara has me to help her now. Whatever wiles I managed to employ were hard won, and even though she seemed deeply distrusting at first, she's going to meet me at the edge of the woods at 8:00 a.m. on the dot.

I can't be late, and if Mom holds me up much longer, I will be.

The obstinate jut of Mom's chin mirrors mine. "Don't lie to me, Nova."

I inch toward the door, but the look on her face stops me in my tracks. "I didn't think you'd mind. We're just going to hang out," I try.

"And if I hadn't been up, would you have sneaked out?"

That does kind of offend me. "Of course not!" I exclaim. "That's shitty. I would have woken you up."

She rubs her eyes and sighs. "The woods are dangerous. And you've never been camping without your dad. And who did you say you're doing this with? Austin and Caroline? Do either of them know what to do if you encounter a bear? Has Austin even *been* in the woods since—"

"I'm ninety-nine percent sure my best friend wouldn't let me get mauled by a bear."

"Camping is still dangerous," she says stubbornly.

"Plenty of people do it, and nothing terrible happens."

Mom tugs her fingers through her unbrushed hair and yanks harder when the tangles resist. "To *them*. Do you know how many people go missing in national parks and forests every year? I watched a docuseries about it! That couple new to town who just lost their baby? They've been telling horror stories all over town about how they got so turned around in there that they nearly didn't make it out! That DUI driver trying to undo the death he caused didn't make it out at all! And everyone at Chalice has been talking about that handsome Australian hiker who stopped in for a drink before he headed into the woods. He's retired from the army and hiked all over the Outback, and he *still* hasn't returned yet. I'm sure he also thought nothing would happen to him."

"That's exactly why I'm not going alone!"

"His wife and children were on the news, Nova. Heartbroken. Wanting answers they don't have."

Like us, I think but don't say. But I need to push this. It's my only chance to find out what happened to Dad. Does she really think I don't know why she's up early in the morning to talk to our insurance company? Does she think I've forgotten that she's going to declare him legally dead?

"Mom, I just turned seventeen. You can trust me."

And she can. I don't drink, don't party, don't stay out late and make her worry. Even when I go into the woods for Dad, everything is perfectly timed so she's never scared about where I am.

"You want to talk about trust?" She actually hangs up the phone, losing her place in the queue. "You think being old enough to lie to your mother makes you old enough to go camping by yourself? This is just like that damn field trip."

"*Mom.*"

"Nova."

Mom takes a deep breath that does nothing to steady the hysterical edge in her voice then says, "Do you know that your father proposed to me in those woods, Nova? He got down on one knee in the violets and butterfly weed and promised he'd love me forever. Forever. We barely got a decade."

I feel like an asshole, and then I don't. She kept this story to herself all this time and only shares it to guilt me?

"Do you think I want Jules declared dead?" she demands. "Do you think I don't hate myself for it? But you're going to college in a couple of years, and maybe, just *maybe*, if we do this, the insurance bastards will finally pay out on your dad's policy after years of telling me death by misadventure or hazardous activity isn't covered. But now here you are, wanting to go off and do exactly the same thing."

Looking into her watery eyes—the eyes she gave me—I almost want to call everything off.

Text Kiara back and tell her I'm out, I can't help, she's on her own.

Except I'm terrified of what will happen to her if I do.

Even if it's too late for Dad, if I give up on her now . . .

I can't I can't do it. Dad would be so disappointed in me. *I* would be disappointed in me, too.

I'd been prepared to lie to my mom, told myself the duplicity was a necessary sacrifice. But I wasn't prepared for how much it would hurt her. Hurt both of us. My throat is tight, scraped raw with lies.

"Austin's and Caroline's parents said yes," I say, which isn't a lie but not the whole truth, either.

Her fingers twitch like she wants a cigarette. Has she taken it up again? She hasn't had one since she found out she was pregnant with me. It was a resolution she and Dad made together on a full moon, and they stuck to it.

It's the story he liked telling the most, even more than how they met (Fall Festival caramel apple stand and love at first sight) or how I was braver at age six than some adults when we camped under the stars together for the first time (I wasn't, but I liked that he thought so). Dad's stories were like that—less about the events that happened and more to do with how the stories of those events made him feel.

Once we knew you existed, our whole lives became about you, he would tell me, showing me the nautical star tattoo on his wrist that he'd gotten when I was born. *We have to take good care of ourselves so we can always be here to take care of you, my little North Star.*

Mom presses her palms together, exhales, and then opens the kitchen drawer behind her. She digs under a mess of coupons and appointment cards and pulls out a battered pack of cigarettes. I stare. She always said if it wasn't for Dad's will-power, she would never have managed to kick the bad habit. She'd say it with an arm around his shoulders, her lips pressed to his cheek, so close to the corner of his mouth that I used to groan and pretend to close my eyes. It was revoltingly cute how they'd kiss each other so deeply, as though they'd never get enough, not those quick little parent pecks I'd seen other adults do.

But as annoying as it was that my parents had been smok-ers in the first place, it isn't nearly as heartbreaking as the re-alization that Mom wasn't exaggerating Dad's role in her going cold turkey. I drag my gaze away from the cigarettes and search her misty eyes for the woman she used to be. The ache in my chest reminds me that we could fill the Longing Woods with all the things we've never been able to say to each other.

If I was his North Star, he was hers, and without him, she's lost and adrift.

"How long?" I ask. I have a sudden vision of her sticking her head out the window at night to smoke so the smell doesn't reach me, religiously swishing mouthwash so I can't catch it on her breath.

"It's not mine. It's your dad's from before you were born. It comforts me."

She doesn't do anything but hold it. Doesn't pluck one out or reach for a lighter. The rubber band around my chest eases a bit.

"I don't care *whose* parents said they could go," she says, still clutching the pack. "*I'm* your mother, Nova, and I do not give you permission." She huffs, shaking her blond waves behind her shoulders. "I hate calling my kid a liar, but unless you give me a good reason, you are not walking out that door."

"Mom, it's all planned," I protest. "They're all going to be waiting for me, and if I don't show up—"

She frowns, still unconvinced. "Who's 'all'? It's not just Austin and Caroline?"

Oops, I didn't mean to let that slip. I hesitate then say, "Kiara Mistry is coming, too."

Both of Mom's eyebrows jump, that little tidbit clearly taking her by surprise. I've certainly bitched about Kiara stealing my crushes often enough. "I thought you didn't like her," she says.

"I don't *dislike* her." Again, not exactly a lie. "Actually, I'm . . . trying to get to know her better."

Mom's face relaxes a fraction. "Are you two . . . ?"

It takes a second for her meaning to click. My face feels as hot as the bottom of the cast-iron skillet I use for blistering brussels sprouts. "Oh my god, no. It's not like that. I just have to do this one thing with her, and then—"

"And you *want* to go camping with her?"

"Y-yes?"

"Oh, I knew it!" she crows, as though I've given something away. "I don't appreciate your lying to me about having okayed this trip, Nova, but I understand how it feels when you have a crush on someone. Especially someone you've liked for such a long time."

This is mortifying. I can't believe she thinks—

Ugh. But at least she doesn't seem pissed anymore. Her pinched look relaxes, almost like she wants to laugh at herself for thinking it could be anything else, like she could be dealing with a full-blown teenage rebellion. Relief blooms across her face like the petals of a morning glory at its first peek at dawn.

What did she imagine? That I'd caught what she called his *treesickness*, the solace that came over him when he was with the towering trees, the ancient sentinels of the forest?

Unbidden, a memory of my parents swoops into my mind:

Dad double-checking the contents of his blue backpack while I wait by the door, whining for him to hurry. Breakfast is over, my bag is packed, my jacket is zipped. Check, check, and check. *Dad, let's gooooo.*

The rumble of his chuckle. The dimple peeking through the scruff on his cheek. *Austin and Shane won't start the hike without us. Have a little patience, Nova. The forest isn't going anywhere.*

Mom chimes in, all teasing words and soft eyes. *Listen to your father. He knows what he's talking about. You know this man is 90 percent sap and bark?*

For you, I am 100 percent sap.

Then the sound of a lot of kissing. In the memory, I avert my eyes and dive for the doorknob.

I think that now I would have wanted that kiss to go on forever. The forever they thought they'd have.

"You wouldn't believe how many college sports I had to sit through while I was dating your dad," Mom says. I think the comment surprises her, too, because she stares at the phone and lets it drop on the back of the sofa, where eventually it'll slink behind the pillows, and she'll forget where she left it.

"I like it when you mention him," I say. "I know you probably don't mean for it to slip out, but it's nice to know how he was—how you both were—before."

Maybe it's the honesty that does it. The wrinkle between her brows softens. "You should have told me, Nova. I . . . I don't like it, but I understand that you're trying to share her interests."

Yes, I am interested in keeping her alive, I think. *I am interested in getting Dad back. I am interested in you being happy again.*

Mom's cautious excitement hovers on the precipice of saying I have her permission to go. With a whirlpool of guilt churning my stomach, I nod. "Yeah, and the Mistrys own Bee Outdoors, so Kiara isn't, like, a damsel in distress or anything. She knows her way around camping stuff. I'm in safe hands with her."

"Well, I'm not thrilled with how you went about this, but . . ." She sighs. "I remember what it was like being seventeen and crushing on someone. Everything's so life and death."

Guilt worms its way through my ribs. *More than she can possibly know.*

Mom's smile is crooked, wistful. "I promise I'll do better. I'll talk about him more and not just when it comes to insurance bullshit."

"I'd like that."

"But this? The lying? That stops now. I want your word, Nova. It's just the two of us now." There's a note of urgency in her voice when she says, "We can't *be* like this."

"We won't be. Everything will be better when I'm back, I promise." I mean it so much my heart aches.

"That assumes you're going." She shakes her head. "I should have known I can't stop you any more than I could stop Jules. He always said the woods were in your blood."

"Does that mean you're saying I can go . . . ?"

"Very reluctantly." She levels me with a look of fraying patience. "But stay close to town, and I want you to check in with a text every—No, *twice* a day. At least. Morning and night. I'm serious about this, Nova."

The tension leaves me in a *whoosh*. "Done," I say.

Luckily, I'd had the foresight—the regular kind, not the Aurora kind—to anticipate that everyone's parents wouldn't want their kids totally off the grid. It's why Austin and Caroline won't be coming with us at all. They'll set up camp as close to town as possible and send out texts and pictures at regular intervals from our phones to pacify the parents.

"Thank you, thank you, thank you!" I say, throwing myself at her.

"Twice a day," Mom says firmly, wrapping her arms around me. She drops a kiss on my crown. I can't remember the last time we were this close. The corner of the cigarette pack pokes me in the back, but I don't move away. "And I want you to stick with Austin and Caroline," she says. "No wandering by yourself. Your dad always said—"

"'Things in the forest will lead you astray if you let them.' I remember." I pull back from her embrace and offer her my pinkie. "I promise I'll be safe."

She cocks her head then twines her pinkie around mine, giving it a firm shake. "You are so like Jules sometimes." She says it with a smile, and her delivery is light, but it doesn't land like a compliment.

"Wildly good-looking?"

Mom snorts and gives me another squeeze. "Try willful and pigheaded."

I fish the phone from behind the sofa cushions and come up with the television remote, her lost hair tie, and one of the many lip balms she misplaces. "I also get that from you."

"I tell you that you can go for a flirty camping trip with Kiara Mistry and your friends, and you give me this kind of backtalk?" She pretends to scowl, but she can't stop her lips from twitching. "Go, before I change my mind. And remember, I want proof of life. Pics of you two would be nice."

"You've got it. And, um, Mom? Will you make me a promise, too?" She looks surprised but nods. "Don't smoke it." I look at the pack then back at her. "There are better ways to remember Dad."

"When did you become such an adult?" She smiles, but she hears me. Maybe. She doesn't throw it away, but she does shove it back in the drawer, out of sight but possibly not out of mind. "I promise. Have fun with Kiara." Her eyes sparkle as she says it. "I always knew there was something between you two."

A checkered past? A giant secret? Simmering resentment?

"Something magical," she adds.

I find myself unwilling to dim her excitement. "Yeah, magic is definitely the word for it," I say.

After kissing her cheek, I heft my backpack over my shoulder, take the filled thermos of coffee and packaged cake she hands me, and walk out the door. She waves at me through the window, and elation buzzes under my skin when she doesn't call me back to say she's changed her mind.

I wonder which of us will break our promise first.

Who am I kidding? It's totally going to be me.

But if I come back with Dad, it won't matter, I tell myself. *I've got this.*

Fixing my mistake will fix my family. Finding Dad will fix everything.

PART II
The Fellowship of the Fling

11

It takes me precisely ten minutes of sprinting with thirty pounds on my back to come to the conclusion that I so don't got this. In addition to layers of clothing, food, and camping equipment, I have a handful of charms from Petra that, with any luck, will buy Kiara some time, including a fresh four-leaf clover that hasn't yet started to wilt secured safely in the pocket of my fleece jacket.

Panting, I come to a standstill and point at the figures standing at the tree line—all of Kiara's exes, casually sipping from their own thermoses and decked out in camping gear. "What are *they* doing here?"

"That's what I said!" Austin throws up his hands and matches my scowl. "They were here when we got here, and you're late, by the way, and also why are you so red?"

"I had to run part of the way," I say with a huff, dumping my backpack on the grass and passing my thermos to Caroline to hold. "There's no way they think they're, like, joining us, right?"

"Considering they're standing there like a special forces unit, I'd say that's definitely what they're thinking," Caroline says.

Yeah, there's no way. After the squash avalanche and my chat with Petra, I had texted Kiara about Radhika's tree house ambush and that I could, after all, help her. But it was imperative that we keep our trip a secret. If any adults found out we wouldn't just be camping but actually hiking into the Blue Ridge Mountains to find the wishing well, the plan would be screwed.

All three of us stomp over to where Kiara's waiting with her friends. Tayla's cool gaze travels from the top of my head to the tips of my brand-new hiking boots, looking supremely unimpressed. A yawning Radhika and Keiffer are studiously scrolling her phone, but he looks up and offers me a small smile of welcome. Evan studies me with curious brown eyes from under the brim of their sage-green cap.

"Hi, Nova," they say, taking the cap off to run their hand over their freshly shaved head. Devoid of their usual teeny afro, their new look shows off their amazing bone structure. "Kiara was just about to text you."

I stare. "What are you all doing here?"

"Well, we're coming with you," says Tayla. *"Obviously."*

"The more the merrier!" Keiffer takes the pulse of the group then sighs. "Or not. I can tell this trip is going to be *real* fun."

"It's not supposed to be fun," I say, frowning. "It's not a vacation."

With an embarrassed little scratch of his nose, he agrees, "Yeah, you're right."

Oof, now I'm the one who feels like a jerk.

Despite Keiffer being a handsome jock, I've never witnessed him do anything mean, like shove a kid into a locker or start a nasty rumor about a girl, and he started an antihazing campaign when some seniors on the football team took it too far with a new guy. He actually got them suspended, and he's been everyone's hero ever since.

He's the kind of nice that puts a Disney princess to shame, but c'mon, his whole life is a party. There's a rumor he's getting straight Cs in everything except biology. He barely scrapes by with the grades to stay on the football team because he studies with Radhika, and as a freshman, he earned the nickname "Kegger Keif" after throwing a party that was supposedly so legendary most of us didn't hear about it until school on Monday. The only thing you can even fault him for is that weird little fuzz above his upper lip, like he's trying to grow a stache, but that's kind of a reach since he still looks hot.

The burning pinpricks on my forehead is probably Radhika noticing me noticing him.

She curls into his side, jostling him a bit to accommodate her. "Well, since it was my idea in the first place to ask Nova to join our journey to the wishing well," she says, "I get to decide who comes."

"We're not in school this week, babe," Keiffer says, smiling as he turns just enough to brush a kiss on her temple. "You don't need to claim the credit."

Evan's shoulders shake with laughter as they pour tea into

their thermos cup, amber liquid sloshing. Of all of them, I like Evan the best, followed by Keiffer, but that doesn't mean I want to be responsible for the well-being of so many other unprepared camping virgins. They all have so much *stuff* with them.

I nod to their gear. "We don't have time for this. Kiara and I already went over the packing list. We don't have the supplies for four more."

"Don't worry about us. We came prepared." Tayla narrows her eyes at Austin and Caroline.

Austin tugs two walkie-talkies out of his backpack and brandishes them. "So did we."

"See?" I can't keep the annoyance out of my voice. "You don't need to come. We've got this."

"No way," says Keiffer. "I respect that you know what you're doing, Nova, but only two of you alone in the woods? That's dangerous as shit. And before you say anything, it has nothing to do with you being girls." He casts an uneasy look over his shoulder. The woods look innocuous in the daylight, but he still says, "People of all ages and experience levels have—well—*you know.*"

"Like we'd let the two of you fuck off in the woods together," says Tayla. "Alone."

Oh my god, this girl is so annoying. She makes it sound like I *want* to be here. Like it's my sole purpose in life to engineer creepy first-date situations with a girl who spurned me and then spent the next two years blithely stealing crushes and turning them into her best friends.

There are easier ways to get the girl. If, you know, I wanted that. Which I don't.

"Actually, guys, Nova's in the woods solo all the time," says Radhika.

Everything screeches to a standstill. I stare at her. "What?"

"What," says Austin.

"I've seen her," Radhika says. "Sorry, did you not want people to know?"

Austin spins toward me. Worry makes his voice higher than normal. "Why would you—"

"My . . . I . . . I thought that maybe I could . . ." My brain catches up to my mouth. This isn't how I wanted it to come out. More to the point, I don't have to explain myself in front of everyone just because someone outed me. I glare at Radhika. "Seriously? You were spying on me?"

"Hardly." She holds herself a little straighter. "I was in the area."

"Doing *what*?" I spit. "There's nothing there except an empty parking lot where people go for hand jobs."

"We're losing daylight," says Evan, in what's possibly an attempt to get us back on track and head off this fight. They turn to me and say, "Kiara sent us the packing list you gave her. We have everything we need."

"And then some, it looks like," Austin mumbles.

"Nova, they're my best friends." Kiara throws out both arms to include all four of her exes. "It can't hurt to have backup. Like, a proper team. We may not have your knowledge, but together we can do this."

When I speak, it's with Dad's words: "The more you know, the less you have to carry."

"Don't worry about us," Tayla snaps. "You can quit it with the superiority, by the way. All the knowledge in the world couldn't save your—"

"Hey," says Kiara. "No. Don't do that."

"Fuck you," I say. My blood feels like it could spew out of me, hot and itchy.

"Don't you dare say a word about our dads," says Austin. I've never seen him so furious.

The rest of Kiara's exes are just as disgusted. The looks on their faces make Tayla flush, staring down at her hiking boots. There's a reason I call her Machete Mouth in my head, a nickname that I accidentally let slip after she hacked apart some poor kid in speech and debate, an English elective we'd both taken last year. It caught on, though nobody knew where to attribute the source, and I wouldn't put it past her to have spent every day since homing in on the culprit. It would certainly explain those looks she gives me.

Tayla doesn't apologize.

"Do whatever you want," I say, the words clipped. I can't even look at her.

If it gets us moving faster, I'm not going to waste precious daylight hours arguing that Keiffer doesn't take anything seriously except football plays, Radhika's an annoying know-it-all, and Evan is dreamy enough to go off the path chasing butterflies. Which actually, now that I think about it, is actually a thing they did on a middle school field trip to the Longing Woods that got all other field trips canceled for the rest of the semester.

"Thanks for the permission," Tayla says. Her words have lost most of their bite, but there's still an edge of sarcasm that makes Kiara frown and me seethe. "And what about them? I see that you brought *your* friends," Tayla continues. "Unless Austin and Caroline are just standing there for decoration."

Austin ignores her, but Caroline looks like she's not sure if she's just been called pretty or not.

"That's why we have walkie-talkies. My friends are base camp." I hesitate, raking my teeth over my lip. "Um, I looked up phone coverage in this area, and we're going to lose it, like, twenty miles in."

Keiffer visibly gulps, looking back at the woods. "What if one of my buddies sends me a message?"

"What if our parents want to get a hold of us?" asks Evan, a worried scrunch to their face.

"Yeah, mine will flip if they can't get in touch," says Radhika.

Austin shuffles his feet. "Yeah, my mom wasn't thrilled about it, either, but my grandmas convinced her. They all insisted Nova and I take the walkies just in case we run into trouble or get split up."

"Bet your mom has seen some weird hiking shit in the ER," Keiffer says to Austin, now looking even more worried. "I heard on the news this morning that some kids from the next town over haven't been seen or heard from since the first night of the festival."

I bite my lip, hoping it wasn't Aaliyah and her friends making a second attempt. Hopefully they've had enough of the woods. "Do you know who it was?"

He shakes his head.

"Okay," says Kiara, "there's no way we're doing this. I can't believe I let myself get talked into this mission-quest-*thing*. My bad luck will go away on its own. If we just give it time—"

"It's not hiccups," I point out a little more harshly than I intend.

I'm antsy to set off, and so far all we've done is stand around squabbling, squandering daylight. Even at the last minute, I had the forethought to plan this trip and account for parental worries, while Kiara's exes have contributed nothing constructive so far. Too many opinions, too little action. I see no upside to holding their hands the whole way when Kiara and I can do this on our own. Honestly, their presence is a complication we could do without.

"I don't want anyone risking their life for me," Kiara says stubbornly.

"No way, we have to." Radhika reaches for the pocket of her lightweight gray Patagonia jacket, where a thin paperback sticks out.

Sour recognition hits me when I see the glimpse of the tan cover, the blue ombré of our little corner of the Blue Ridge forests. I've never read the book, but years before I was born, Dad bought a copy when her grandparents published it. Dad was always baffled that they never saw eye to eye on the dangers of exploiting something so precious. As far as he was concerned, Henry Prior was a questionable individual with a suspicious, checkered past, but he'd had the right idea about obscuring the location of the wishing well. The legend of the well should fade, same as the man. Footnotes of history.

"I know I can get us there," Radhika says. She meets my gaze, and she raises her chin, almost as if she's daring me to contradict her. Seeing her smugness, I hope Dad used that book as kindling. "Maybe the tourists didn't make it because they didn't have the inside track like we do."

"Um, just to be clear," says Evan. "By 'make it,' do you mean make it to the wishing well or make it out alive? Because that kinda sounds like a deciding factor we should be aware of."

Tayla elbows them in the side.

Radhika seems to lose some confidence when she says, "My point is, none of them had a descendant of Henry Prior. And we have *two*."

Oh, she's *definitely* lost confidence if she thinks admitting my connection to the great Henry is going to boost anyone's spirits. Maybe Radhika fangirls over the family history, but I have a strong aversion to romanticizing anything about the Prior lineage. Uncomfortable with the way everyone's eyes cut to me, I clear my throat. "Look, we all know the risks. Whatever you decide to do, you need to do it quickly because we're losing daylight."

"What are you talking about?" Radhika uses the book to gesture at the sky. "Bright and sunny."

I frown. "It gets darker inside. Doesn't your guidebook have anything in there about that?"

She crosses her arms and doesn't respond.

"And shouldn't *you* have known about not having phone coverage in there?" Caroline asks. "Oh great descendant of Henry Prior?"

"Never thought I'd say this," says Tayla, "but Nova is right. Madame Aurora was super clear about this: if we don't make it, Kiara's bad luck will last forever. So all of you shut up and make your choice."

"Again, a pretty opaque definition of what 'make it' means," grumbles Evan.

This time, Keiffer is the one who elbows them.

"We can stand around arguing, or we can get moving," I snap. "We've established that we've all got people who will freak out if they can't reach us, and since we're going to lose connection in there anyway, I suggest we all leave our phones with my friends so they can respond to messages on our behalf."

The commotion is instantaneous.

"You've got to be kidding. She's kidding, right? Right?"

"WHAT? I don't want any of you reading my messages!"

"Fuck off, I'm not giving up my phone."

"I'm not going in there without a connection to the outside world!"

And then one voice breaks through the din. Tayla, the last person I would ever dream would be my supporter (again), says calmly, "I truly hate to say it, but Nova's right. Our parents all think we're just camping, and if we want any chance of pulling this off, we need them to keep believing that. Our phones are going to be useless once we get deeper into the forest, so leaving them behind is the only way the cat stays in the proverbial bag. Unless anyone has a better idea?"

They don't.

I'm momentarily bugged by the fact that she's essentially repeated my exact plan of action, just more authoritatively. Her get-shit-done attitude was one of the reasons I once had a crush on her, but thankfully I snapped out of it before I could do something truly heinous, like tell her.

"Great," Tayla says. She smiles at Kiara with more warmth than I've seen her give anyone. It's a bit surreal to see the softness on her normally aloof features. "Solved."

"Maybe all of you don't have to come," Kiara starts to say, but Tayla cuts her off. "Of course we do. We all want to be by your side the whole way. Where you go, we go."

Kiara loops her arm through Tayla's and lays her head on the redhead's shoulder. "Love you."

"I love you, too."

Did Tayla just sniff her hair? I blink. WTF. Evan looks equally gobsmacked, but when I meet their brown eyes, they lightly shake their head. A warning, maybe, that I should pretend I didn't see anything.

The two girls look good together, which makes it all the more sickening. Jealousy rears its ugly head. It's hard to fake my nonchalance toward Kiara with Tayla throwing herself at her. I see zero to like or love about Tayla. The fact I once had a crush on her feels like a lifetime ago. Like, what was I even thinking? This girl is cutthroat, and she was just such a bitch to me, and Kiara's acting like . . . Tears of frustration pool in my eyes. *Do not cry, Nova. Do not cry.*

"Now that we all love each other, can we go . . . ?" asks Radhika. She waves her book again.

Keiffer's wearing his game-day face, all decisive and projecting conviction. "I'm ready."

"I said I would go, so I will," Evan says simply when their friends all turn to them. "You're my friends, and I love you, but you have zero survival skills. Besides, have any of *you* been camping before?"

Keiffer cocks his head. "And you have? Wait a second, I thought you said it was a family vacation in a rented RV at a national campground that had showers and toilets? Not exactly roughing it."

Evan smiles enigmatically and sips their tea. Keiffer huffs.

When it's my turn, I have my answer ready. "Of course I'm with you. If I was already ready to risk bodily injury to save Kiara from a gourd avalanche, might as well risk more life and limb, right?"

"Oh, goody," says Tayla. She turns to my friends. "Looks like you two are surplus to questing requirements. Austin, you better know how to work that radio. Caroline, I'm trusting you with my phone. If you open or read or mess with anything you shouldn't, believe me, I will know."

"What she means is," Kiara says hastily, "that we really appreciate you hanging back to look out for us. The fact you're even here means so much to me, I can't even tell you." Her eyes are watery, like she's really moved by their presence. "Are you sure you're both okay with setting up base camp . . . ?"

"Okay with it?" Austin's smile is grim. "I'd prefer it. I'm very much an indoor cat."

Caroline nods emphatically.

Even though this split-up was always the plan, every inch of me wants to balk. From a two-person trip of just me and Kiara, it's now ballooned to her entire friend group. Just me, Kiara, and four people who love her. Including one who seems to hate me. Terrific. If there's ever a bear eating or mauling situation, I can imagine who else Tayla would determine is *surplus to requirements*.

But on the other hand, maybe the alone time will get Austin and Caroline to actually go for it instead of tiptoeing around me. Truly, how much more obvious can I make it that I'd love for my two best friends to get together? They're perfect for each other, but their pesky internal friend code is clearly a blockade.

"So that's settled," I say with a forced cheerfulness.

Finally. They really suck at falling in line.

Caroline grabs my hand and tugs me to the side. "Are you sure about this?" Her gaze flits over my shoulder. "It's five of them and only one of you."

"Just because I'm not a member of Kiara's entourage doesn't mean they're going to leave me for dead in the forest somewhere with just the squirrels and birds to keep me company." Probably not anyway.

She huffs. "I didn't mean it in a murder-y true-crime documentary way, Nova."

"Whew."

"Quit being sarcastic. Are *you* going to be okay is what I'm asking." She lowers her voice, but it occurs to me that we're not standing far enough away for true secrecy. With those furtive little glances over my shoulder, she's not exactly subtle. "They're all a little, well, protective of her, aren't they?" The delicate way Caroline pauses leaves no doubt that what she really means is possessive. Lower still, she says, "And Tayla . . ." She trails off, biting her lip.

"Is right there," I point out. "It's pretty obvious we're talking about them, Care."

"You don't have to go."

I sigh. "Yes, I do. You know why."

There's nothing she can say to that, and she knows it.

12

We've been in the woods for less than two hours, and I'm already over it. Frankly, I've already spent two hours more than I wanted to in Tayla's presence.

When we found a clearing for our base camp a while back, she'd taken charge of setting up Austin and Caroline's tent—a fact that bugged Austin more than he wanted to let on—and explained what a bear bag was and why it was important, even though he had brought one. It's obvious all her knowledge comes from YouTube rather than lived experience, and what makes it even more insufferable is that she knows she's still the best prepared out of her entire friend group. Every time she opens her mouth, I'm livid all over again, and I don't know how I'm going to get through the next few days without my friends by my side. Our two-way walkies, bulky and old-school, are our dads' spares—much like Austin's old red tent—and ever since Tayla said she had room in her backpack to hold on to my radio, I've carried it with a death grip.

"I'm sorry about earlier. I promise Tayla isn't usually so . . . Tayla," says Kiara, falling back to where I'm straggling. "Hey, you okay? You look a little winded."

"I'm fine," I say automatically, unwilling to admit to weakness. I thought it would at least be day two before the walking wore me out, but evidently I don't even have the stamina for that.

"You hate gym, and now you're in the forest with Tayla. You can admit you're not fine."

"How do you know I hate gym?"

"You come out of the girl's locker room after everyone else. It's a delay tactic, right?"

I shrug, wincing as the straps on my backpack dig into my shoulder. "It works out on the days Mr. Cole forgets to take attendance."

"What, you mean you just *stay* in the locker room the whole time?"

"Haven't been caught yet."

On the rare occasions that Mr. Cole doesn't assign her as a team captain, she's first pick in team selection. The only reason I can get away with being a no-show is I'm always in the bottom four anyway.

"Maybe next time I'll hang out with you," she says with a grin.

"But you actually like gym."

"Maybe I'd like loitering around with you, too."

The idea of Kiara Mistry disappearing for fifty minutes of gym to spend time with me, with no one any the wiser, is so implausible my tummy actually lurches, all fluttery and twisty. Just me and her. No exes lurking over her shoulder, suspicious and hostile. But I could do without inhaling the overpowering locker room odors of sweat, wet swimsuits, and obscene amounts of body spray.

No, if we're hanging out, I'd like to be somewhere nicer. Not the Cauldron—I want a place that she associates with me, not with her near-death experience. Maybe Demeter's Drinks. A cozy little booth where we'd have to sit so close together our thighs touch, and Kiara's subtle coconut scent sticks to me even hours afterward. I want it to linger the way we'll linger long after we slurp the last of our drinks, maybe even order the same again. I'll get the maple latte, and I think she'll choose something sweeter with a cherry and lots of whipped cream. Maybe she'll offer me a lick. My tongue feels like sandpaper all of a sudden. *Stop thinking about food, Nova*, I chide myself. *Stay on mission. You don't want anything else.*

"Think they're making all that noise to ward off the hypothetical bears?" When I jolt, Kiara uses her chin to nod at her friends up ahead, loudly gabbing away about the latest episode of some fantasy show they're all watching.

"Or to stay awake," I say. "I think I caught Radhika yawning about ten times so far."

"Yeah, I was so anxious about this that I couldn't fall asleep until almost six in the morning," Kiara admits.

I glance at her profile. "You can't tell."

She giggles. "Trying to say I'm pretty?"

Good job, Nova, you really walked right into that one. I tear my gaze away and mutter, "You really need me to tell you that?"

"Need it? No. But maybe I'd like it."

"You're making fun of me," I say. I can't put my finger on why the teasing bothers me so much.

Kiara's smile dips, and then she says, "Is it weird that we sell all kinds of camping stuff, and yet I've never been camping in here before?"

"Not really. The woods can get weird sometimes."

"I don't want you to think I'm a coward."

"I don't." I really don't. "Anyway, sometimes being scared is a good thing. It means you have self-preservation instincts."

"If I wasn't hexed, I probably wouldn't have ever stepped foot in here. That one time our class came here when we were in eighth grade, do you remember? We couldn't find Evan for hours. I remember the teacher had to hold my hand because I wouldn't stop crying. Evan and I had just broken up, and I was so mad I wasn't with them. I thought that somehow my being with them would make a difference. I told myself then and there that it didn't matter if our relationship was over; I would always keep the people I love in my life." She gives me a quick sidelong glance. "Did you know the school board forbade any more field trips to the Longing Woods after that?"

Shaking my head, I say, "Not just because of Evan. They found out I forged my mom's signature on the permission slip in order to go."

The laugh startles out of Kiara like a flock of birds fleeing a tree. "What?"

"Don't you remember my mom barging into class to shout at our science teacher?" I ask.

"Oh . . . oh, right."

Mom had raged for ten minutes straight about how nobody had the right to take her daughter into those woods, how she'd never signed the field trip liability waiver, *how dare they how dare they how dare they*. I can still remember my horror and humiliation, the teacher's stammering confusion, the entire room's stunned silence, and, somewhere in the back of my mind, the fleeting feel of Kiara's hand squeezing my shoulder from the row behind me, bringing the scent of her strawberry shampoo with her. Her gentle comfort had lingered then, too, like a friendly ghost. And if I'd leaned into her touch, well, that's just another ghost of the past. Something we don't talk about. Not even Austin and Caroline—who had both chosen to visit the school library instead of going on the field trip—know.

"Do you make a habit of lying to your mother?" Kiara asks.

I almost stumble over an uneven patch in the path we're following. Kiara steadies me. Her hands are warm on my arm even through all my layers. Or maybe I'm imagining it. "You, Mom, everyone."

Her eyes widen. "Nova . . . ?" she says.

Her voice sounds small, baffled. She didn't expect my flippant words. Hell, *I* didn't expect my flippant words. Regret bites hard and ravenous. I cast around wildly for something to say and land on a truth I had no intention of sharing. "You heard Radhika," I blurt out. "She . . . she was right. I do walk in the woods. Nobody knows. If people found out, they'd try to stop me."

"Why do it, then?" Kiara's fingers lightly dig into my arm.

"Sorry," I say, flustered. "I don't know why I'm telling you this."

She looks at me askance but doesn't press the bruise I've inadvertently revealed. She lets go of my arm and puts a bit more distance between us but not as much as there was before.

By the third hour, we're deep enough in the trees that we only get dregs of pallid sunlight. I'm officially the farthest into the forest I've ever been, every step from now on taking me farther away from home. From the corner of my eye, I spot the stopping point from a few weeks ago, a giant flat rock big enough to use as a seat while I guzzled water. The others don't give it any notice, but to me, going beyond the rock is an achievement. Hope floats in my chest, airy with possibility, thrusting me with enough forward momentum that I feel like I could walk another three hours without stopping.

The trunks are packed more densely here, branches tangling up with each other to create a canopy overhead, gnarled roots grasping for the path like hungry limbs. Twice so far, someone's mistaken a root for a snake, which put everyone on edge, considering I'm with people who turned green dissecting frogs and owl pellets in biology.

The air is strange, still and silent, like nothing and no one has passed by to disturb it. I itch to ask Radhika if this is normal since evidently she's been one with nature, but she's not exactly forthcoming with information, hoarding her book like it's as rare and precious as Leonardo da Vinci's *Codex Leicester*.

Now that I think of it, when was the last time I heard the

chitter-chatter of squirrels and birds? It must have been when we'd parted ways with my friends, leaving them at the threshold of the forest.

The lack of sound is disconcerting, especially since it's getting darker and Keiffer's already got his flashlight on. Did he bring so many batteries that he can afford to waste them?

I frown. If he runs out, I certainly don't have enough to share. I'd scooped a ripped-open box of Dad's old batteries from the junk drawer to power the walkie-talkies, and as much as I want to check in with my friends, I have to remember one of Dad's favorite maxims: *Be prepared, not scared.* I hold on to his words as hard as I clutch the radio.

I jog to catch up to Keiffer, bypassing Evan, who's listening to something on a super old iPod, the kind that wouldn't be worth anything now, too obsolete yet not retro. Tayla's walk is militant, not breaking stride and not stumbling over anything, unlike me. She spares me a glance as we march shoulder to shoulder.

"Thanks for having my back earlier," I offer, holding out the olive branch.

"You're welcome." And then she figuratively grabs that olive branch with both hands, smiles, and breaks it in two with an almighty *crack*. "Don't get used to it. I don't like you."

My eyebrows shoot up. Okay, this is not how I thought our convo would go. "That's it?"

"Did you expect an apology? I meant what I said, and I didn't say anything about your dad that wasn't true. The others seem to think we need you, but your usefulness remains to be proven."

My arms alight with blazing pinpricks. I'm kicking myself for even bothering to reach a truce with her. Clearly, her bad attitude is not going be cured by reaching a truce with *me*.

What am I even doing out here? Why did I even think we could pull off this stupid, stupid quest?

Kiara has all her exes out here, and my missing dad only has me. I can't afford to get distracted by anyone, can't afford to let them in or show them the most secret parts of myself. Not even to the one person I want to the most. I get why Kiara wants to stay besties with her exes, but this whole package-deal situation makes me want to tear out my hair in frustration. Or better yet, Tayla's long, silky red hair.

"We're only on the same side as long as saving Kiara is your number-one priority," Tayla says.

I bristle. "What is *that* supposed to mean?"

"No distractions." She snorts. "No flirting."

Ugh, I'm over her cryptic bullshit. I'm here, aren't I? I'm not even one of the group, one of the exes.

"I'm taking this just as seriously as you," I spit.

Before she can say anything else to get my blood pressure up, I increase my pace, dried leaves and twigs crunching under my boots. They're so stiff that even though they're the right size, they still feel a half size too small. I stomp right past Kiara, zero intention of even looking at her while Tayla's so close.

"Nova, hold up a second." Fingers circle my wrist then release just as quickly. Her skin is warm, and a starburst of tingles explode in the spot she touched me.

Kiara flashes me a smile as she finishes unwrapping her Tootsie Pop then offers me another one. It's chocolate, which comes second only to cherry. "Helps with the dry mouth. Mine's terrible when it gets cold."

"Thanks," I say, nearly dropping the lollipop when our fingers brush.

She folds her red wrapper into a neat, tiny square before sticking it in the pocket of her hot pink hoodie. It's a small gesture, but I like that she didn't just drop it underfoot and keep walking like littering isn't a big deal. "I should be thanking you," she says. "For doing this."

"You already did. If you want to do it again, though, save me a cherry Tootsie next time."

She laughs—a delighted little sound that I just know will get Tayla's hackles up—and pulls her lollipop out with a *pop*. I watch the string of saliva trailing between the candy and her mouth with gross fascination. "You've got it," Kiara says.

Her lip gloss is shiny, the same color as the candy. It clings to the white stick, to her pout. She must have touched it up sometime in the half hour after we had our walking lunch of Pringles and Clif Bars. Lip balm, okay, I'm wearing it, too. But gloss? Shiny, sticky, megawatt crimson? It's impractical for a hike.

Which of her crushes is she trying to impress?

The thought is so distracting that I almost forget to slip her the four-leaf clover. Almost. I've been waiting for an opportunity all morning, and I can't chicken out now. I take a deep breath. "Hey, one of your compartments isn't zipped up all the way. Mind if I . . . ?"

"Oh my gosh, yes, please." Kiara stops and twists so her backpack is toward me.

Okay, gotta move fast. It needs to be somewhere she isn't constantly opening and closing, so the clover won't fall out. Somewhere inconspicuous that she won't use to jam a wad of trash. Good thing I already picked out the zip I'm going for.

"All good," I announce.

She whips around to give me one of her perfect, dazzling smiles. We're close enough that I can't stop staring at her glossy mouth. "Thanks, Nova."

"I'm just gonna go, uh, see what's going on up ahead," I say awkwardly when she keeps smiling at me. "Him using up our batteries this early is making me nervous."

I speed walk to Keiffer, who's at the front of the pack with Radhika, swinging the flashlight to and fro so the light shines on the path.

"I saw a snake," he explains, accidentally aiming the flashlight at my face. "Ah, sorry."

"Copperhead?"

"Uhhh . . . is that a rattlesnake?"

I grin. "No, a copperhead is a copperhead. You have no idea what one looks like, do you?"

He releases a rueful laugh. "Yeah, 'fraid not. Guessing they're the color of copper?"

"Yeah. With darker hourglass-shaped markings."

"Oh, no, this one was . . . I wanna say greenish?" He looks sheepish. "And it had a friendly face?"

"Friendly for a snake," Radhika adds. "Because that really needs a caveat."

"Like, it would definitely bite me, but it would look cute doing it," he says. He zips up his Carhartt jacket and scans the ground with the kind of intensity I've only seen him wear on the field.

"If it was green and didn't have a scary *rawr* face, then my guess is it was just a regular old garden snake. They're not venomous nor aggressive, either, so it's unlikely they'd bite."

Keiffer looks marginally less wary. He even switches off the flashlight.

"Same with the copperhead?" asks Evan. They've overtaken Tayla and Kiara, brown cheeks rosy with the wind and headphones hanging around their neck.

I wait for Radhika to chime in, but she's oddly quiet, nose buried in the guidebook. I would have thought she'd use this as her moment to shine, but instead, it's Dad's lessons coming in handy.

After another beat, I tell them both, "The copperhead *is* a venomous pit viper. Even the babies hatch with fully functional fangs that are just as toxic as an adult's."

"And here I thought you were about to say something comforting." A curl tugs at the corner of Keiffer's mouth. "And you come out with *fangs*."

"Uhhh . . . well, here's something comforting. A copperhead bite isn't fatal." I pause. "Usually."

Keiffer's jaw drops. The flashlight flicks back on.

"*That* is your idea of comforting?" Evan looks like they don't know whether to laugh or run screaming.

Okay, maybe not the best tidbit to share. But in my defense, fun facts are meant to be educational, not actually fun. "You'll be fine! Just don't provoke them."

"Yeah, because that was really high up on my priority list," they say. "How do you know so much about snakes?"

"Science project in eighth grade. The environmental impact on shedding snakeskin. Otto at the animal rescue helped. Even let me handle a couple before we released them back into the wild. That's how I started volunteering there."

"Whoa," they say. "That's pretty cool. I mean, mostly still terrifying. But you know what I mean."

Hoping to put both Evan and Keiffer at ease, I say, "Just be observant, watch where you're walking. Check logs before you step over them. Be careful about the roots or vines, too, make sure they don't have eyes or patterns."

Keiffer makes a gulping, panicked sound then pivots to an unsure laugh.

"Watch out for the rattlesnakes, too," I say. "A bite can turn nasty if they envenomate you."

Faintly, he says, "Let me guess, rattlesnake bites are fatal?"

"If you don't get help in time, yeah."

"Is there anything in this forest that doesn't want to kill us?" asks Evan.

"Butterflies," I say. "Try not to follow any this time, please."

They groan. "One time, Nova. One time."

"So glad none of us have our phones on us to call 911," Keiffer drawls. "Super not regretting going off half-cocked on this adventure in a forest where literally everything is more dangerous than us."

"Keif, if you're going to be a baby, can you do it more quietly?" Tayla calls up to us.

Keiffer rolls his eyes, though he does it when I'm the only one who can see. I guess it's good to know she isn't solely singling me out with her sharp tongue—apparently anyone who isn't Kiara is fair game.

"Shut up, Tayla," Radhika calls over her shoulder.

For her bravery, she goes up half a notch in my grudging respect.

Then to Keiffer she says, "And we are *not* going off half-cocked. I bought flares and an antivenom kit at Bee Outdoors. *I* paid attention to Nova's list."

She squints down at the book and blinks a few times like her eyes are irritated from all the reading while walking. "Okay, so according to this, there are signs all around us that can point us in the direction of the wishing well. 'Signs of wonderment,' Henry calls it. Flora and fauna naturally gravitate toward sources of magic like the well."

"Does that include the lethal ones trying to kill us?" Keiffer asks.

"*Baby,*" someone fake coughs. My money's on Tayla.

"Any examples?" I ask. "In case it's escaped your notice, flora and fauna are everywhere."

Kiara and Tayla join us, and we all examine our immediate area. I wonder how they see the world, if there's a sparkle that Dad's eyes always caught. My wonder is gone, and I don't know how to get it back.

But then—

The wind carries a whisper of Dad's voice with it: *In every blade of grass, in every bug crawling on a mushroom cap, in every broken stick fallen in the dirt, in every budding flower, in every bird that's ever been born, is the story of the earth. They* want *to tell you their secrets.*

Look closely at everything with your own eyes, Nova girl, because when you find something that makes you question, that makes you change perspective, that's when you know you've found a sign of wonder.

I close my eyes and tip my head to the sky, inhaling deep. It should be no surprise that Dad's voice is clearer in this place, the woods he loved so deeply, so terribly. And yet. Being here, the past is excavated, my heart eviscerated. His lessons are embedded into what remains, fossilized and half forgotten.

"Well, of course Henry wouldn't write it down for just anyone to find," Radhika says at last.

She's using his first name like she's personally acquainted. I resist the overpowering urge to roll my eyes. "*Henry* didn't. His notes were private. He probably never thought his descendants would publish his trail journal. How do you even know all this crap isn't embellished to sell copies?"

Radhika looks furious for a second before her expression

frosts over. "I'm literally not even going to dignify that with a response, Nova. You're talking about my grandparents."

"So, to clarify, Henry didn't specify what any of these supposed signs are."

"Oh my god, you're not letting this go. Fine, no, he didn't. But if you'd just keep an open mind—"

"I'm just saying that something as generic, vague, and open ended as a 'sign' is like looking for a leaf in"—I gesture all around us, narrowly avoiding whacking Keiffer in the chest—"yep, you guessed it! Seventy thousand square acres of forest."

Radhika looks like she wants to scream. I almost feel bad. Almost. Am I really the bad guy here for pointing out that as noble as our quest is, without more information, it's the equivalent of a wild goose chase?

I hold my hand out. "Can I take a look at the book?"

"You two look for signs, I'll keep watch for snakes," says Keiffer. "Hey, Nova, they can't pierce our shoes, right?"

"We're all wearing hiking boots, so we should be good. Ugh, these are killing me, by the way."

"They're new," Evan observes. "Why didn't you break them in first?"

"Didn't exactly have a lot of time between last night and this morning," I explain. "Always used my tennis shoes before so my mom didn't wonder what I needed hiking boots for." What I don't explain is that buying supplies for this trip has wiped out the little bit of money I'd been saving and that I was incredibly lucky Petra generously let me have the charms for free.

Radhika hums. "What made you change your mind about helping Kiara? You never said."

Oh, *clever* of her to slip that in so casually. With a bright smile, I say, "Nope, I didn't."

She frowns and begins to part her lips.

"Does it matter?" Keiffer asks. He shrugs. "Everyone has their reason for coming, don't they?"

I'm getting a little sick of the mistrust, honestly, but considering the reason for this trip in the first place, I keep my mouth shut. The knot of guilt in my stomach tightens, and I brace myself for Radhika's response.

She doesn't look like she's happy about it in the slightest, but for some reason, Radhika drops it. A muscle tenses in her jaw.

I throw him a smile of gratitude. *Bless you, kind footballer.*

That's not something I ever thought I'd say, but I never thought I'd be trekking through the Blue Ridge Mountains to find the wishing well, either. Not without Dad anyway. But at the end of this, if I get Dad back, it will all be worth it.

"Kind of like *The Lord of the Rings*," I say. "If you think about it, that's us. Trying to save Middle-earth, but in our case, it's Kiara. Doing the right thing. Trying to help a friend. Except we're . . . oh, I've got it." I wait until they're all looking my way before pronouncing with unmitigated glee, "We're the Fellowship of the Fling."

Keiffer whoops. Kiara groans.

I walk on, whistling.

13

By the time we break for dinner, my calves are screaming foul obscenities at me for being so out of shape. I'm used to walking, but not this much and not this long. And certainly not while lugging enough supplies to last a week. Not to mention the backpack straps that I'm convinced have permanently disfigured my shoulders and the fear that when I attempt to peel my socks off, they'll have crusted to my heels with blood.

My friends would tell me not to be melodramatic when my whining inevitably got too much, but they're not here. I know they'd get a kick about my nickname for our little quest. Who knew Keiffer was a *LOTR* geek like me? Or that the name would pull a reluctant smile from Tayla that I'm 100 percent sure she'd deny if someone called her on it? So far I'd reached for my nonexistent phone no less than five times to shoot off a pithy message to Austin and Caroline, only to belatedly remember it wasn't there.

At least I'm not the only one patting down my pockets—I've caught Tayla once and Kiara twice and, combined, Radhika and Keiffer make nine. The only one who seems unbothered by being totally cut off from civilization—and, frankly, toilets—is Evan.

So instead, I go analog and tell my thoughts to the forest.

Hey, creepy tree that looks like it has a face. Squatting to pee is an indignity that makes me so tense that I swear the urine traveled back up my urethra. Also, if you do, in fact, have a face, don't look, 'kay?

Random bag of potato chips stuck on that swinging tree branch, you might find this funny since Pringles are basically a cousin of yours. Keiffer had pizza-flavored Pringles and asked to swap me for my sour cream and onion, which is obviously *the superior flavor. Can you believe he polished off my entire can? Ugh, boys.*

Decayed remnants of a bird, you're dead so you don't care, but which one of her exes do you think Kiara wants to get back with? And should she really *be thinking about romance at a time like this? I mean, her life hangs in the balance, as everyone keeps telling me. Maybe Tayla should tell her 'no distractions.'*

"I'm so hungry I could even go for that horrible fiber granola bar Evan was eating earlier!" Keiffer exclaims as we find a good place to stop for the night, lowering his backpack on the grass. "I'm ravenous."

"Even after all those Pringles?"

My pack joins his far less gracefully, since I stagger with the sudden change in my center of gravity. Sensation rushes to my shoulders with the backpack straps' removal, a specific misery that people who wear bras would know but ten times worse. I almost want to check my shoulders for indents.

Keiffer blushes. "Sorry about that. I don't eat a lot of junk food usually. Gotta stay in shape."

I eye his lean physique. Defined, sturdy muscles. Powerful

legs capable of tackling and running across fields. Except for the baby stache, which is very much not my thing, he's still the same boy I was into in ninth grade: hot, kind, funny, unashamed to be vulnerable. And unlike me, he doesn't seem tired at all, which I envy, but he also willingly denies himself chips, so now I'm less envious.

"I can pitch the tents," says Kiara, "since I can't cook to save my life." She either ignores or doesn't see Tayla's visible flinch at the reminder that her life is, in fact, in need of saving. "Bee Outdoors's customers sometimes want us to show them how to use the equipment, so I can do it in my sleep," she explains.

Tayla takes the last swig of her water and shakes a couple of drops into her mouth. "I'll take the bottles and see if I can find a water source."

In addition to everything else we needed, we all have pricey water bottles from Bee Outdoors that will purify our drinking water. They work much like a French press, flushing out sediments and contaminants from fresh water, and the activated carbon cartridges neutralize flavor and odor.

"Radhika and I will collect firewood," says Keiffer. "I can slap together a sandwich at home, but I haven't spent a lot of time cooking, so I'll contribute in other ways. I do have powdered eggs and six cans of baked beans in my pack, though, if anyone wants to whip something up?"

"You were carrying cans on your back all day?" I'm horrified. Or impressed. It's hard to tell.

He shrugs. "I had to bring enough for everyone. Besides, we need the protein."

"And beans *were* on the list you sent, Nova," says Tayla, a tad snidely.

"When I thought it was just me and Kiara carrying one can each," I bite out. "If I'd known *you* were coming, I would have added antacid to the list."

"Ouch." Her tone is mocking. "Do you always have to be in control, Nova?"

"Do you always act like a jealous girlfriend, *Tayla*?"

"Stop flirting," says Radhika, once again showing a surprising amount of fearlessness. Tayla and I both recoil. "Kiara, put a thirty-minute timer on your watch? I will, too. If we're not back by then—"

"Start a search party and possibly get lost ourselves?" Evan smiles beatifically. "Of course we would. Leave no member of the Fellowship behind. Good idea on the name, Nova. Every quest needs a name."

Oh, this is a sweet moment. I'm tired and cranky but now oddly touched, too.

"I mean, preferably don't get lost," says Radhika. "Actually, maybe don't come looking for us. I don't think I trust any of you to mount a rescue."

Not such a sweet moment after all. Sadly, this makes more sense.

"Finally someone says something sensible." Tayla laughs, sounding genuinely amused. She and Radhika grin like they're sharing the joke. The camaraderie is such a foreign look on Tayla that I blink, once again wishing for my phone so I can commit it to my camera roll for posterity.

"And I've already got my best chance for protection and rescue with me." Radhika clings to Keiffer's arm, looking up at him with heart eyes.

"Aw, babe." He beams. "Back at ya. No one else I'd rather be stranded with."

Blink, blink, blink. "You're aware he's a giant scaredy-cat, right?" I ask.

I'm not even trying to be rude, it's just . . . come on. It's Keiffer. The boy jumped in the literal air when we heard the piercing shriek of a peregrine falcon a mile back, and don't even get me started on his petrified expression when Tayla asked him how he felt about wolves and bears and foxes.

He shoots me a dejected look.

I flash my palms at him in pseudo apology. "Sorry, dude, just calling it like I see it."

"We might encounter a black bear, but I know what to do," says Radhika. "Look nonthreatening, hold our ground, and make a lot of noise to scare them off. I'll probably, like, hop on Keif's shoulders since I'm a shrimp compared to this stud." She flutters her lashes at him. Blech. Then she raises her arms over her head and waves, showing us how she'll scare off the bear. It looks a little like the cheerleading routine she led in the pep rally last week.

"A-plus plus!" says Kiara. "And don't forget the bear spray."

Tayla makes a face. "*Must* you fawn over him, Radhika?"

"What should Evan and I do?" I hurriedly ask before they can continue talking about bear protocol.

"You can help Kiara with the tents?" suggests Evan. "I'll start dinner prep."

"Great, everyone has their job," says Tayla, and then she officiously claps her hands together. "Get a move on, people!"

It sets my teeth on edge. Instinctively I want to rebel against her leadership but don't have a good reason to. It doesn't help that everyone jumps to do what she says.

As half our group scatters, Kiara tilts her head, beckoning me to follow.

Part of the reason we chose this place to stop is the ground is level enough to set up all our tents, and Kiara and I get to work clearing away rock and twig debris. After a day of walking, the bending hurts our backs, but then we're upright again, checking the trees for damaged branches so nothing falls on our unsuspecting tents during the night. The clearing is a little ways off the path, but we can find our way back easily enough.

Not for the first time, my fingers roll over the smooth green aventurine bracelet Petra gave me. So far, the four-leaf clover has done its job. Nothing awful befell Kiara today. It's a win.

"Your exes are all kind of shitheads, aren't they?" I ask conversationally as she drops to her knees to unzip our packs. "Like, it's just *mean* to tease poor Keiffer."

"Pot, meet kettle." She looks up at me through her lashes. "You totally got a kick out of it just now."

"I didn't!"

A knowing look.

"Okay, fine," I relent. "I did, but not that much."

"I mean, if you think about it, it's no wonder we some-times have friction," Kiara says, ripping things out of plastic with a pink pocket knife she's taken off a keychain. It's been swinging off her backpack all day, cute and lethal, the exact shade of cotton candy.

I'm content to watch her. "Because they all dated you?"

The knife stops. "What? No. Because their personalities are so different. You must have noticed."

"Hard not to," I quip. "If we were in a teen movie, a voiceover by probably, like, Kristen Bell, would spend the first five minutes explaining how you, Tayla, and Radhika are the preppy cool girls who rule our high school with benevolent but iron fists, Keiffer's the hottest athlete to ever athlete, and Evan is the floater who gets along with everyone because they're artistic and have that indeterminate je ne sais quoi."

She scrunches her face. "Uh, Nova. Aren't the queen bees in those movies always really mean?"

I flush. Or I would if my face wasn't already undoubtedly red. I sit cross-legged next to her, accepting some bendy plastic rods she hands me and hoping she doesn't expect me to know what to do with them. "I don't see you as a stereotypical mean girl, though. For what it's worth."

"Oh, so I *am* a mean girl, just not a stereotypical one." Her eyes crinkle with mirth. "Got it."

I huff. "That's not what I meant, and you know it."

She taps her chin. "Hmm, do I, though? You're not exactly easy to read, Nova."

"Hey, I'm practically an open book compared to some people."

"So if I ask you a question, you'd answer honestly?"

"Y-yes?" I clear my throat.

"What's your problem with me?"

She sounds genuinely curious, but I'm automatically defensive. "I don't have one," I tell her.

"Nova," she admonishes. "We communicate almost entirely in glances."

There's an involuntary jump in my chest that makes the hair on my arms prickle. Well, yes, I suppose I do steal glances at her now and then, but am I so transparent that she noticed? Ugh, FML. There's something acutely humiliating about being called out like this. My skin itches uncontrollably. I want to peel off my jacket and throw it far, far away. Or just hold it in front of my face like a shield and pretend she can't see me. Oh my god, I'm so pathetic. It's getting harder to hide my feelings from her.

"Daggered glances," Kiara says, "in your case."

Oh. *Those* kinds of glances.

A lump of something that feels an awful lot like disappointment gathers in the pit of my stomach. This is good, right? That she is totally oblivious to any other looks? That she's never caught me? But if my secret is safe, then why does it feel so . . . bad?

"Maybe I'm just obsessed with you," I say flippantly. "Ever think about that?"

"Yes. All the time."

My eyes fly to hers, but her gaze is down, smoothing the torn plastic wrapping into neat little squares to put away. She's so meticulous that for a long moment, I can do nothing else but watch her. It's adorable how much she cares about those straight edges and crisp folds. Kiara Mistry is tidy. Nova Marwood is mess incarnate. What a weird, irrelevant, totally random thing to muse.

"You should see my bedroom," I find myself saying before I can think it through. "I don't think I've properly made my bed since I was a kid."

"You mean if I should ever find myself so lucky as to be in your bedroom, you're going to put me to work?" asks Kiara.

My entire brain slips into slow motion. Kiara. Mistry. In. My. Bedroom.

She laughs. Actually *laughs*.

The sting of humiliation hits me, and I hold absolutely still, willing myself not to show how much her amusement hurts my feelings. "Got a problem with earning the privilege, Mistry?" I snark, thoroughly embarrassed. "With something not delivered to you on a silver platter?"

I imagine Kiara as the lady of a grand estate, seated at the head of a long dining table, servers presenting Radhika, Kei-ffer, Evan, and Tayla like courses of a lavish meal. She gets everyone she wants without even having to try. Fine, she's everyone's uncontested dream girl, but how unappealing am I, exactly, that not one of her friends ever even considered me? Kiara's the one who kissed me, and even she never made that mistake twice. The spiky humiliation descends into full-blown rejection. Logically, I know she didn't reject me, but it *feels* like she did.

Kiara is lucky in life, period. Her parents are still together, happily married. She's gorgeous and thoughtful and the kind of friend-slash-ex that inspires her other friends-slash-exes to go on a literal *quest* for her sake. She's the textbook definition of good luck. Unlike me, she's gone through life unscathed. Or at least that's how it looks.

Kiara fixes me with an indecipherable look. "You're no open book, Nova Marwood. You're hard fucking work."

"Relax." I bestow her with my evilest smile. "You're not invited to my bedroom."

She smiles back. "Don't want me to see the giant 'I Heart Kiara' posters you have up?"

I think about the crappy drawing of Kiara we once threw darts at in the tree house. It was in the wake of Keiffer and Kiara getting together and my ensuing pity-slash-petty party. "My only problem with you is you always get there first."

Her smile wavers. "Get where?"

Kiara's confusion only makes it worse.

Pushing past my discomfort, I brandish the poles at her. "Let's just do this."

"There you go, trying to put me to work again."

I snort. "Don't try to be cute."

"Nova, I don't have to *try*," she says with exaggerated slowness.

"Go on, then." I gesture. "Impress me."

The way Kiara leaps into action is both an art form and an Olympic sport, if I'm being honest. I watch her fingers fly with nothing short of awe. Kiara Mistry being good with her hands is brand-new information, and how did I not know this?

With a catlike fluidity and grace, she rolls out the juniper-green tent and ground pad, secures the stakes, and attaches the rain fly to the rods and then the thicker canvas-type of cloth on top. I just hand her things and do what she tells me, which, for some reason, isn't anywhere near as irritating as when Tayla does it. Her competence is actually really attractive, and that's not even the *most* attractive thing about her.

I can't believe I find myself thinking this, but I can't even stay mad at her. Luckily, she doesn't seem to hold my prickliness against me, either.

"How's the tension?" Kiara asks.

"Nonexistent," I tell her honestly. When it's just me and her—none of her exes around as a reminder—it's easy to find her funny and smart and kind and forget that she's dated everyone I liked before I could. And now that I'm spending more time with all of them than I ever did before, I can't even remember why losing to her bugged me so much. Not even a little bit begrudgingly, I say, "It's a lot better than I thought it would be."

Her smile is awkward, unsure. "What do you mean? I told you I was good at this."

"Good at relieving tension . . . ?"

She gives me a weird look. "Without tension, the tent would have collapsed by now. Are you paying attention, Nova?"

Oh, *that* kind of tension.

"I, uh . . ." I give the tent a cursory look. It's still upright, so I'm assuming the tension is fine?

"I'm going to start on the next tent," Kiara says. "Can you check the tension on this one? There are Velcro straps in the corners. Just cinch them around the poles extra snug. It'll help strengthen and stabilize. It's not windy enough to need the guylines, so you can ignore the loops on the rain fly."

Do I tell her I have no idea how to do that and look even more useless? I mean, I theoretically understand everything she just did, and I know what tension means, but the rest of it is just random words.

I'm a little embarrassed by how little I know, but I'd been so young when I'd gone camping with my dad that I hadn't been able to do much more than pout and make half-hearted attempts at putting the tent up, despite his encouragement. Finally, he'd just done it himself, expecting I'd watch him and learn, like an intrepid little sponge.

Kiara managed to put shelter together far more efficiently

than I could have, matching Dad's speed, and even though she's looking to me to double-check her work, it's probably fine, right? I mean, she could do this in her sleep. I'd rather bite off my tongue than tell her I've never had to do this on my own before.

"Sure," I say. I walk around the perimeter of the tent, nudging at the stakes, making sure the fabric is stretched taut, the tension even on each pole. The Velcro straps are easy to attach to the poles, and I'm reasonably sure the tent will stand up to a gust of wind.

Working efficiently, we get all three tents up and still have ten minutes to spare before Tayla, Radhika, and Keiffer are supposed to be back. Each tent will fit two people, and since Kiara provided them for us, I assume she's going to hand out the sleeping assignments, too.

"Where should I . . . ?" I gesture at the tents.

"You can share with me!" she says cheerfully, bending over to brush some dirt off her knees. "Come on, this one." She tugs at my hand until I follow her inside with our bags. It's cozy, warm from proximity to her body heat. I can't imagine how much cozier it will be when we roll out our sleeping bags for the night.

"Me?" I try to sound cool and unaffected, but I can't control the surprise in my voice any more than I can control the sudden quiver in my belly.

Kiara seems to take my agreement as a given because she nods and says, "Radhika and Keiffer will be together, of course, so I'm all yours. Do you mind just hanging around outside for a bit? I want to change out of my clothes and use one of our biodegradable body wipes. I'm all grimy." As if to prove her point, she rubs the back of her hand over her cheek, leaving a streak behind.

I scramble to my feet. The tent has turned into an inexplicable vortex, and if I stay here for a minute longer, I might be tempted to . . . I don't even know what. But being within arm's reach of Kiara—joking about my *bedroom*, of all things, let alone tonight's sleeping arrangements—makes the ground shift, my axis tilt. And doing anything about it is out of the question, obviously.

"Yeah, of course," I babble. "I'll go see what Evan's up to."

I take the walkie-talkie with me as I step into the dimming purple twilight.

14

Outside, Evan's been as productive as we have. They've cleared away the dead grass, dug a hole several inches deep, and made a circular mound of the loose dirt to create a firewall. Rocks have been arranged on the outer edge of the wall as reinforcement. They've got a fire going, flames licking at the wood and brush until it curls and withers, blackening to a crisp. They've even managed to intrepidly rig together a stick contraption to suspend a pot of water over the fire.

Evan sits on a camo folding chair they've brought, which leaves me to sit on the log that's tipped over and worn smooth, as though it's seated hundreds of people over the years, a thought that makes the back of my neck prickle. I inhale, a sharp, ragged thing. Then I turn over my shoulder.

Nothing. No one.

"Nova, you look so stunned! Or is that your impressed face? What, did you really think I'd be sitting here idle?" Evan laughs, obviously pleased to have proved me wrong.

I mumble a sheepish "Well . . ."

They roll their eyes. "Tayla better get back with water soon. I had to use the last of my drinking water for this." Carefully, they lower the metal pot to the ground using the same stick that kept it suspended. Then they add a few tablespoons of dried hibiscus flowers to a stainless-steel mesh infuser and let it steep in the pot. While it steeps, they dismantle their stick contraption and set it aside, hunting for larger branches that will hold the weight of our dinner.

I shake off the uncomfortable sensation of being watched. It's too early for the others to be back, and I'm probably just tired and a little on edge after Kiara definitely flirted with me. That's all it is.

"How did you learn how to build a fire from scratch anyway?" I ask. "Keiffer mentioned something about an RV campground? Wouldn't an RV have a kitchenette?"

"It did." Evan juts their chin to the left. The sanitation trowel—which, to everyone's utter mortification, is intended to dig holes to bury our poop—is crusted with dirt and off to the side next to a box of matches. "I just watch a lot of YouTube."

"Nice," I say appreciatively. "I only use it for makeup."

"Well, it always looks nice. Even Tayla's said so."

That's not just hard to believe, it's mind-boggling. "What, really?"

"She's not so bad. Tayla's tough but fair."

"Evan, you can say that about a hard-ass teacher, not a teen girl. Besides, all I've seen from her so far is either utter loathing or cool indifference. There's literally no middle ground with her. Whatever good qualities you all see in her, I have zero evidence of it."

"*Yet.*" They give me a bright smile. "Before this quest is over, you will."

I envy their confidence.

When the tea is ready, Evan transfers some of the piping hot liquid into a thermos for the others and splits what remains between us in two camp mugs. I want to point out that between Keiffer's cans and Evan's folding chair, we've been lugging around way more than we need, but when that first sip of tea sinks into me, I could kiss Evan for bringing enough to share.

I let the rising steam warm my face. The sweetness of the honey mingles with the tart, cranberry-like flavor of the hibiscus flowers. "This hits the spot."

"Kiara! Get your butt out here if you want tea!" Evan calls.

"Almost done!"

The timer goes off on the old generic smartwatch that Kiara borrowed from her mom, pealing out obnoxiously in the otherwise eerily silent clearing. "They're still not back," I say.

I run my fingers over the buttons of my radio and peer between the densely packed tree trunks and shrubbery. I can't see anyone. It's an amorphous green-black vastness out there, void of sight or sound. Even squinting doesn't help. It's almost like we wouldn't see them until they crept up on us.

Which means *anyone* could find our camp, and we wouldn't know until they were already here.

But, my mind reasons, *you haven't passed a single soul out here all day. If someone was in the woods, wouldn't you know?*

Would we, though?

"We should start dinner," Evan says, as though I didn't say anything of concern. "I hope he brought cans with a pop tab because I didn't bring a can opener."

"You want to eat his beans when he's missing?"

I mean, I don't want to call it bad manners, but you don't just touch a man's beans.

Or a woman's Pringles. Fuck it, let's go for those beans.

"So dramatic," Evan teases, grinning. "They're not even a full minute late. And they'll be hungry when they come back, so we should start before it gets dark. We're already losing the light."

I throw a glance back to the juniper-colored tent from which Kiara has yet to emerge, even though she turned off the timer. She let it go on longer than I would have expected. Maybe she's worried for them, too. They wouldn't be the first to go missing here. Maybe she thought the sound would be like a Marco Polo cry to help them find their way back to us.

Evan follows my gaze. "You don't have to feel like the odd one out, you know."

"Because I'm the only one among us who Kiara never dated?"

They hum. "You could look at it that way."

I'm skeptical, but I still ask, "What other way is there?"

"That you're the only one of us who Kiara never dumped."

Evan was her first, when we were in eighth grade, then Radhika and Keiffer in ninth, and most recently, Tayla, who she was with sophomore year from Christmas break all the way through summer. Everyone thought maybe Tayla was the One. Hell, even *Tayla* probably thought Tayla was the One.

But by the time junior year began, Kiara was single again. It's why I dubbed us the Fellowship of the Fling; no relationship has lasted longer than Tayla's eight months.

"So it was always Kiara's decision to end the relationship? With all of you?" I ask.

"Mm-hmm."

"Why?"

Evan gives me a weird look. "Kind of personal, no?"

"I don't mean specific details. It's just . . . it's weird, right? How things are always on her terms?"

"Not always." Evan shrugs. "And not really."

Right. The bad luck that brought us out here in the first place. My eyes flick back to the tent, where Kiara is still cloistered. "I hope it stays good."

"The tent? Or whatever's going on between you two?" they ask wryly.

I wonder how much, if anything, Evan overheard. "Is it that obvious?"

They take a languid sip of their tea. "I'm observant."

"Trying to say you stare at me?" I joke.

"Sometimes. You're really pretty."

I choke out a laugh. "Evan!"

"What? It's true." Unperturbed, they set their cup aside and rifle through Keiffer's bag for provisions.

"Is the subtext of your casual flirting that you're not here to get Kiara back?"

"Nah," they say easily. "I love her as my best friend, and she'll always be a big part of my life. But she's not the one for me, and I'm not the one for her. That's okay, though. It doesn't make me sad."

I think on that, poking at the fire while they gleefully crow over the pop tabs, peeling back the lids.

"Nova?" Evan waits until I *mm-hmm* before asking, "If we're the Fellowship of the Fling, does that make Kiara basically Aragorn, then? Since everyone wanted his D."

"Evan!" I pretend to be scandalized, clutching my invisible pearls.

"What? That scene when he throws open the doors of King Théoden's fortress and walks in all wet and majestic after everyone thought that awful orc dragged him off the cliff? Don't tell me that didn't do it for you." They sigh just thinking about it.

"You're full of surprises," I tell them, smiling.

"I think," says Evan, airy as cotton candy, "I'm not the only one."

My smile drops. What do they think they know?

Standing abruptly, I blurt out, "I think I'll, um, radio in. See how Austin and Caroline are." Without waiting for a response, I bolt for one of the empty tents.

15

When the other half of our Fellowship finally makes it back, they're almost an hour late. My imagination had been quick to conjure up all sorts of awful things that could have befallen them, so their return releases some of the tension in my twisted-up body. Sore shoulders unhunching, I manage to summon up a smile. Radhika and Keiffer offer small ones back, but their faces are drawn, shadowed by something I can't name.

But other than that little detail, none of them look particularly worse for wear, which sets Kiara's temper flaring.

"What happened? Did you get lost? Weren't you keeping track of the time?" she shrieks. She's changed into cozy clothing and is fresh faced, ready for winding down for the night, but the relief at seeing them back safe and unharmed has given way to anger. "We were worried sick!"

Evan stirs the beans to keep them from sticking, looking supremely unworried.

Again, I wonder what they know that the rest of us don't.

Tayla's face is contrite. There's a leaf crumbled in her hair, which is tousled and a little frizzy in its high ponytail. "It took me a while to find a stream," she explains, rubbing her neck. "The water was cool and clear, but I went ahead and started decontaminating everyone's so we could rehydrate ASAP."

"And we ran into T on our way back," says Radhika, shivering as she approaches the fire. "Oh my god, I'm *so* hungry. Can we eat?"

"And what were you two doing?" Kiara gestures at Radhika's and Keiffer's arms. They're not empty-handed, but the amount of firewood they've collected is, well, pitiful.

"The two of them were making out," Evan says without looking up.

At the same time:

"We were not," Radhika says hotly.

"Yeah," Keiffer says with a goofy grin.

Tayla sighs loudly, rolling her eyes into the next dimension, and starts handing out our water bottles. "None of the bottles were marked, so I had to draw things on them so we knew whose was whose."

I stare at mine. "Um, I think I got the wrong one."

Everyone looks at the metallic-silver symbols drawn on the side of their own bottles. Mine's a heart, which means when Tayla drew it, it was either subconsciously or consciously meant for Kiara.

"Nope, that's yours," says Tayla.

I don't trust her smile. I tilt the bottle closer to the fire.

Evan can't hold back their laugh, almost dropping the pouch of just-add-water powdered eggs.

Yeah, this is definitely mine. "Thanks a lot, Tayla," I grit out.

She's drawn a freaking butt. I guess she or someone very corrupt could argue it was a heart, just a bit of a lumpy, mis-shapen one—an *accident*, really. Tough but fair, huh? Yeah right.

"You were saying?" I whisper, raising an eyebrow at Evan.

"We actually ran into some people," says Keiffer, dumping the firewood too close to the fire. I nudge it safely away. "They were looking for the well, too, but they'd given up."

"Anyone from the news?" I ask. "Or school?"

He shakes his head. "Nah, don't think so. Just some bros in their thirties, maybe? Thought it would be funny to come here for a bachelor party."

"What the fuck?" four of us say at once.

"Yeah, it was messed up," says Keiffer. "They didn't really seem all that friendly. Or *too* friendly, depending."

Radhika frowns. "I told them there was no way they should be walking around in here in the dark, but they didn't want to listen. They asked us to come back to their campground with them, offered us a couple beers, but . . ." She and Keiffer exchange a look, one of those wordless ones that couples have when there's something they don't know if they should share.

Questionable heart-butt forgotten but not forgiven, I point at Radhika's face. "Wait, what was that expression?"

"I guess they just creeped me out," she says. "They didn't like that I was telling them what to do."

Keiffer pulls his lips into his mouth and nods. "Yeah, it was uncomfortable. With so many of them and only two of us, there was no way I was going to just, like, stroll into their camp with my girlfriend."

"Assholes," spits Tayla, voicing what all of us are undoubtedly thinking.

"I was glad to see the back of them, to be honest," he continues. "The way they laughed at us for saying no to drinking with them . . . like jackals." He shudders. Then he sniffs the air, turning into a puppy the second he recognizes what's for dinner. "Is that beans? Evan! Beans!"

On two stout branches hanging low over the embers of the fire as a makeshift grate, Evan's got a pot of sweet and spicy beans simmering. The liquid bubbles as they ladle out generous portions into our stainless-steel camping plates and top it with a hunk of fried bread and the powdered eggs they'd quickly scrambled up in the skillet when the Fellowship was back together again. Soft and fluffy, the perfect doneness with a sprinkle of black pepper and sea salt.

"I wish we had real eggs," says Tayla, poking at hers.

"Evan, ignore her," says Kiara. "Everything tastes amazing."

"Next time," Evan says pleasantly, "if you want real eggs so very much, I suggest you store them in your cheeks like a squirrel."

I laugh. "How about 'Next time, everyone carries their own chicken.'"

"Nova," says Keiffer, "the chickens are perfectly capable of walking."

Kiara catches my eye, lips twitching.

"The fuck are you all talking about?" says Radhika. "We are never doing this again."

A second later, everyone but Radhika and Tayla bursts into uncontrollable laughter.

It feels good to laugh after the day we've had. Evan swipes at their eyes, and even Tayla reluctantly smiles and admits the eggs aren't *that* bad. Keiffer, still laughing, wraps his arm around Radhika's waist and tucks her into his side, erasing her pout.

In that moment, I can see exactly what attracted me to all of them. They might get cranky, but they forgive each other just as easily, and camaraderie sweeps over us once again. Even my shoulders feel lighter.

Though we've long lost the light, sunshine seems to beam from Kiara's smile, casting us all in its perfect glow. It's not just me who's affected; the entire Fellowship of the Fling falls under her spell.

We circle around the fire, which has burned down considerably, so Evan feeds it the extra wood Keiffer and Radhika brought back. If Tayla's peeved that Kiara sat between me and Evan, I can only imagine how she's going to seethe when she realizes she's not the one bunking with Kiara, either. I hide my smile just thinking about it.

Kiara sighs as she scoops beans onto her bread, a blissful

little sound that makes my stomach feel funny. Must be hungrier than I thought. I should get this food down me before those tummy rumbles get worse. Fingers clenching tight around my spoon, I attack my eggs, shoveling in a bigger-than-usual bite.

God, this is good. Incredibly good. And not just because I get to enjoy a meal that I didn't have to cook myself. Evan's YouTube cooking skills are definitely not just theoretical. Everyone else looks satisfied, too, like we'd all moan around every mouthful if we weren't conscious of the others' presence. Even Tayla shuts up and eats everything on her plate without another complaint. Is there anything better than a tasty meal after an excruciatingly long day?

"Delicious," Radhika proclaims, sopping up the last of her beans with her crust. "Thanks, Evan."

"And thanks also go to Keiffer for being the superhero who carried the most preposterous ingredients on his back for a whole day," I say, raising my water bottle to him. The heart-butt comes into my eye line, and I twist it away from me. I can't believe I bought this brand new and it's already defaced. "The only thing I needed more than a good night's sleep was a hot dinner. So." I clear my throat. "Thanks, dude."

Keiffer acknowledges my toast with a bashful grin but ducks his head when everyone else chimes in with their own appreciation. He scratches the back of his neck, and I just *know* the flush on his cheeks is from embarrassment, not the warmth of the fire. His thoughtfulness aside, his shyness is even more endearing.

"It was worth it," he says, staring at his empty plate rather than at us. "Anyone mind if I wipe the pot clean with that last slice of bread?"

No one does, so while he reaches for the insulated handle to start mopping up all the saucy bits, Kiara and I get to cleaning the plates and utensils. We do it far enough away from our sleeping area just in case any lingering smells draw the wildlife but not so far that we can't still see the others. There's just enough firelight to see by, and as we fall into a rhythm my skin tingles with every plate she hands me to dry.

"After that story Radhika and Keiffer told us, I wanted to throw ash on the fire. Douse it," I murmur.

Kiara's eyes fly to mine. "Oh my god, you too? I had the same impulse, but I thought maybe I was overreacting." She absently swirls the sponge, sudsy with just a drop or two of biodegradable dish soap, over the back of a spoon, biting her bottom lip. As if she's about to tell me a secret, she leans closer. "I watch a lot of horror movies that I probably shouldn't."

"Yeah, I get pretty jumpy after a slasher, too." I dunk the last plate into the collapsible camping sink Kiara brought. With limited water, it's a pain to rotate the plate all over until its good and wet. Once soaked, I press a microfiber cloth against the plate, letting it absorb the water.

"It's even worse when I'm alone at night because my parents are at work," she says after we get through all the utensils, the ladle, and, finally, the collapsible pot Keiffer brings over.

"Why do you do it, then?"

"Sometimes I like being scared. But in a safe way, when I'm on the couch, and all the doors are locked, and I've checked in the closets and under the beds. Sometimes I even pull out my old teddy, even though half his stuffing's fallen out." She cracks a grin. "I know that sounds totally contradictory."

"No, I get it. Being in the house at night can be creepy for me, too. Mom works long hours at Chalice, and she usually tries to be home before I go to bed. But there's nothing worse than hearing weird creaks and wishing there was an adult around."

I don't say this part, but Mom puts in way more hours now. When I was a kid and Dad had overnight trips in the Longing Woods, she'd cozy up in bed with a book long after I'd fallen asleep. I always knew he'd be safe out there, and we'd be safe at home. Now I can't sleep until I know she's there.

Tonight, I can't help but wonder if she's in bed already, if she's texted me goodnight. If she can sleep knowing I'm out here. If, two Marwoods down, our house feels less like a home.

I wonder what Kiara thinks about when her brown eyes flit away, almost black now that they don't reflect the leaping flames.

"I wish—" She stops herself.

"We'll be okay," I say. "*You'll* be okay."

My words don't reassure her at all. Kiara's brows draw together, two dark slashes on a wan face.

"I'm not worried for *me*, Nova. Do you get how much it sucks that you—that you're all here risking your lives for me?

Before this, nothing bad has ever happened to me. Like, I bombed the PSATs, and my dad's parents in India passed away, and while those things *felt* like the end of the world at the time, I was essentially going to be okay, eventually. But this . . . this hex? This is something bad happening to me, but worse, it's happening to the people I care about *because* of me. I feel like shit." She rubs at her nose, pressing her lips tight. "If anything happens to any of you . . ."

My heart slams against my rib cage, and for the space of one heartbeat, I want to tell her. I want to tell her that it's not on her, that her guilt is actually mine. That I'd gladly take it from her if I could.

But she's not done. She picks up speed, whisper-hissing the words at me, too low for anyone else, but they crash like cymbals in my ears.

"When Radhika, Keiffer, and Tayla didn't come back on time, all I could think about was every horror movie I've ever seen and all the ways they could be hurt or . . . or worse in the woods. And the whole time, I'm not thinking about me at all. I'm thinking about what we're going to do and what we're going to tell their parents if they don't make it back. And that if anything happens to any of you out here, it's my fault." Her voice catches. "I feel guilty—*so fucking guilty*—all the time. You have no idea what that's like."

I hear her, my heart going one hundred miles an hour. Kiara's words are a little too sharp, a little too close to home.

"I say this politely: get over yourself. I know you think you're *oh so special*, but you're not the only person who feels—" I can't get the rest out, not without wanting to vomit beans and bile. "Whatever. Forget it."

I'm not enough of a jerk to leave her to carry everything, so I haul the pot away with me, leaving her to safely dispose of the dirty dishwater and carry back the plates and utensils.

Tayla's gazing into the fire when I return, toying with the collar of her zip-up hoodie while Evan's body is sprawled half in, half out of their tent. Maybe the flames have hypnotized Tayla because her expression doesn't even flicker when I approach, lumbering with the cooking pot. Radhika and Keiffer are snuggled up, sharing a buffalo check blanket.

Evan gives me a sleepy smile before calling out, "Hey, Radhika, can I borrow your book?"

"It's in my tent."

It's not a no, but it's hardly a yes, either. Radhika doesn't volunteer to go get it, and after a few beats of expectant waiting, Evan gives up. Their lips tic upward, and the firelight casts them in an impish, eerie orange glow. "Wanna tell ghost stories?"

"No," Keiffer says quickly.

"Scared?" asks Evan. It's not a challenge, only curiosity.

"It's been a weird night," says Radhika. She and Keiffer glance at each other before she continues. "Plus we have a long walk again tomorrow. We don't need to be up all night scared of shadows and strange noises, which hello, we're outdoors, so of course there will be."

Keiffer rises when he sees me. "I'm gonna go take a leak," he announces, grabbing his flashlight. "Nova, do you mind sitting with Radhika until I get back?"

"Yeah, sure." I'm about to sit opposite her when she holds the blanket open for me to join her.

After my outburst with Kiara, my skin bristles with guilt, and my face feels hot. Getting under the heavy flannel sounds miserable, but I'm not about to ignore Radhika's gesture, either. If this is an olive branch, I'll grab it with both hands.

"Keif!" Radhika calls. When he turns, she says, "Don't go too far."

"You two looked cozy," I say as I settle in next to her, resting the pot on my lap.

She smiles, all soft and tender. "He's a cutie. Thanks for joining me. It's so embarrassing that he thinks I need to be taken care of, but I enjoy it." She peeks at me from the side, like she's waiting for me to judge her or something.

"I would too," I say honestly, earning another smile, but this one is meant for me. "It's been a while since someone took care of me."

I'm thinking of my mom and dad, but Radhika's face creases as she says, "Who were you dating?"

"What? Oh . . . um. The only person I've dated is Austin. It wasn't really anything, and there hasn't been anyone since. Guess I've been having my own run of bad luck."

Radhika makes a face, which at first I think is because I casually dropped *bad luck* in a sentence, but then I realize is an expression of sympathy. Validation thrums through me. It sounds silly, but that face she made makes me feel seen. I might have been a bit tragic just now, but I was also being honest with someone I wouldn't have trusted a day ago. Even a few hours ago.

What's changed? My worry for her? Is this trip going to be one of those things where we'll all come back besties?

"You'll break your curse," says Radhika. "After helping us with Kiara's, yours will be a cinch. Especially when you look like you."

"Can't be any more dangerous than this," I agree. "And . . . thanks?"

Romance isn't everything—it isn't even the most important thing—but I still want it. Not only because Kiara's taken it from me but because I know what it can look like when it's good. It can be a true north.

A twig cracks. It's close, too. Evan squeaks and Radhika goes stiff and Tayla half rises, but when we see it's Keiffer and Kiara, all of us breathe a collective sigh of relief.

"My eyes sting," says Evan, gesturing to the flames and then rubbing at the delicate skin under their eyes with a fist. Radhika winces. "I'm going to bed. Goodnight!" And with that, they roll into their tent.

"I'm going to turn in, too," says Tayla. She turns questioningly to Kiara.

"Oh," says Kiara. "You're with Evan."

Tayla hides her scowl. Barely. "I took care of all our scented items," she says, not quite masking the petulance in her tone. She aims her flashlight straight at my face then slides it to the trees about a hundred feet away, spotlighting the suspended bear bags full of our food, toiletries, and garbage. "We should put the fire out. We're almost down to the embers anyway."

Keiffer regards the dwindling flames. Either we all underestimated how quickly we'd go through the wood, or . . . No. What else could it be? "What about protection from wild animals?" he asks finally.

"They're hopefully far enough away by now," says Radhika, and the way she says it, I don't think she's only talking about bears.

"You'll take care of it?" Tayla waits until Radhika nods confirmation before she, too, tucks herself away in her tent for the night. Delegating as usual.

"I'll help you pack the cooking equipment away," says Keiffer, clicking on his flashlight, shining it at Kiara's tent. "Lead the way." Then to us, he says, "Don't waste your drinking water. Throw dirt on the flames to smother it out. We don't want to risk a forest fire."

I note that he's being logical about conserving water, which is a far cry from the way he was using up his flashlight batteries willy-nilly earlier. Tonight has made him take this more seriously.

Kiara approaches and scoops the pot from my lap without

making eye contact. It sparks something in my belly—regret and frustration that in her eyes, I'm the bad guy.

Okay, maybe I *am* a little bit.

"Did you two fight?" Radhika asks, voice low and gossipy as we watch Kiara go.

"Depends. If we did, are you going to tell Tayla?"

She rolls her eyes then seems to realize I'm being serious, so she gives me the most long-suffering sigh I've ever heard in my life and sticks out a pinkie.

I curl my own around hers and give it a solemn shake. "No, we didn't fight. I don't think I've ever seen her fight with anyone. She just . . . I guess I lost patience with her carrying so much guilt about this quest. We're all here because we want to be. It's not *her* fault."

"You say that like there *is* someone to blame."

I freeze, my tongue pressing against the back of my teeth, praying my expression doesn't give anything away. "What do you mean?"

"Aurora looked into Kiara's future and saw dark omens. She didn't *give* Kiara bad luck, just relayed it. A shitty message, but it's not the messenger's fault."

Letting Aurora off the hook is galling. Haltingly, I say, "I . . . I guess."

Would Radhika's understanding extend to me if she knew? Or would this fragile truce between us snap like spider silk? This is the most we've ever talked. And that isn't hyperbole. This is all Aurora's fault. If I wasn't so pissed at her for getting in Mom's head about Dad, a man she's never even met and has no right to erase, I would never have been in her tent in the first place.

"I kinda don't want to douse the last of the flames," says Radhika, the toe of her boot ready to kick some dirt over it. "Oh, don't give me that look. I didn't say I wouldn't. I just feel like it's at least some protection, you know? Like if anything happens, we'd see it coming." Her expression darkens. "But light also gives us away."

"Those guys are probably stumbling around drunk and getting themselves lost. You said it yourself. They're nowhere near here."

"Nova, I didn't even tell you guys the worst part."

My stomach clenches into a fist as I wait for her to continue.

"I didn't want to scare anyone," she whispers. "I told Keiffer we should keep it to ourselves."

"Okay, now you're actually scaring me a little," I say with a nervous laugh.

"When we told those guys we couldn't drink with them, they wouldn't take no for an answer. They kept badgering us, telling us not to be pussies." She frowns at the word. It sounds wrong and coarse coming from her. "Finally, to get them to back off, we said we couldn't because we had our group waiting for us."

That makes sense. I nod at her to continue.

"I think Keiffer thought they'd drop it if they knew we weren't alone. Like, as far as they knew, there could be a whole football team of high school jocks out here who'd come looking.

Basically, it was like a warning not to keep messing with us. They didn't get close enough to touch or anything, but it was there. The threat that something *could* happen."

She doesn't need to convince me. One girl surrounded by all those men with only Keiffer for protection. I mean, they'd put up a fight, but it's still only two of them against however many others.

"Sure," I say, trying to put her mind at rest about any perceived danger she thought they dumped us in. "It was a scary situation, and they were drunk. They were more than old enough to know that harassing you two was peak scumbag behavior. I'm sure all of us would have done the exact same thing as Keiffer."

She keeps going like she hasn't heard me. "But the thing is, Nova, it didn't put them off at all. If anything, they got even more curious about us. They asked if they could come chill with us at our camp."

"What the fuck?"

Radhika swallows. "By the time we got away, we were already late, but it took us even longer to make our way back because Keiffer took all these twists and turns trying to lose them. Just in case they were following. I don't think he really knew what he was doing. He said he learned from watching a lot of spy thrillers. I was looking over my shoulder the entire time." She rubs her neck like it aches, and it probably does. "And he's scared of the dark, too. Didn't turn on his flashlight once. Was too afraid of us leading them back to you all."

Keiffer's heading back to the tent he's sharing with Radhika. A light glows inside. His blurry shadow moves around, rolling out the bedding. I watch him work, my fingers seeking the comfort of my bracelet.

"Jeez, Rads." My tongue is woolly and thick, dry and sticking. I attempt a laugh, but it comes out as a hacking cough. "And here I thought we weren't going to do the cliché campfire ghost story."

"We'll be fine." She uses her front teeth to drag her lower lip into her mouth. "Also, I don't like nicknames. It's a full-time job preventing Rads from sticking, believe me."

"I'm sorry. My dad gave me so many nicknames that sometimes I forget not everyone is a fan."

"I love my full name," Radhika says. "My dad's side is a whole lot of things—Jewish and Polish and Danish—but my mom's Indian, and she named me after a Hindu goddess. I don't care for it to be shortened to something ugly."

I didn't know that, but now I do. "Won't do it again," I promise. "It's a beautiful name."

"Thanks." She smiles, and for a second, it's like we both forget every other worry. "How about you? What's the story behind yours?"

"Nova? My dad picked it. My mom wanted something else, but I was a grumpy little thing and didn't smile once at any the names they tried on me until I heard Nova."

Sharing isn't as bittersweet as I thought it would be. Maybe because I'm here in the forest where my dad disappeared.

Seven years later and closer to him now than I've been in all these years.

"It's pretty and punchy," Radhika offers. "Nova. It suits you."

A supernova is brilliant only once in its life.

When it's at its most destructive.

Just like that, the worries come rushing back. "I hope not," I mutter. Before she can ask me why, I kick the rest of the dirt over the glowing embers. The darkness swallows her soft gasp, and the air around me shifts as her body jerks, dragging the blanket off my shoulders entirely. "Night, Radhika."

Her voice is tremulous as she whispers back, "Night, Nova."

Neither of us, I suspect, is going to get much sleep tonight.

16

"You look like shit," Kiara says the second I wake up.

I grunt and roll so my head is crammed under the jacket I used as a pillow. "Wow, thanks."

"I thought you'd want to talk last night." When that doesn't get a reaction, she adds, "After our fight?"

I raise my head, aware that the fleece has made my hair all staticky. I blow a clump of straggly bedhead out of my face. "If you wanted pillow talk, maybe you shouldn't have pretended to be asleep when I came in. You even sighed a little and *snored* to sell it. If anyone was avoiding anyone, it wasn't me."

Her brows snap together as she scowls. "I wasn't pret— Okay, fine, I was, but you were supposed to tap me awake so we didn't go to bed mad."

"You *just* said you weren't asleep. And we're not an old married couple." I match her scowl.

Maybe making up before bed is how Kiara's parents handle arguments, but I remember Mom and Dad whisper-fighting behind closed doors long after bedtime. She'd never liked him leading tours in the forest with Austin's dad, liked him going alone even less, and she was right, in the end.

Kiara's mouth opens and closes, a wild strawberry flush

climbing up her cheeks. How does she look this human first thing in the morning? Meanwhile I have eye crusties, noxious morning breath, a tangle of hair around my face, greasy roots, and if that wasn't bad enough, I spent the whole night wondering what would be worse: if intruders invaded our camp or if I accidentally farted in my sleep after all those beans.

I shift inside my sleeping bag, unable to get comfortable. Every muscle rebels as I twist around. At least I was warm enough. My discarded outer layers are balled up next to me, whereas Kiara's are folded and on top of her rolled-up sleeping bag. She's been up for at least a few minutes longer than me, then.

I wet my dry lips, running my tongue over fuzzy, unbrushed teeth. Major ew. "Look, I'll just say it first because I don't want this to be a thing. I'm sorry for—"

"Yelling," says Kiara. Her mouth mutinously twists. "You yelled."

After instinctively gritting my teeth, I force my jaw to relax. "I didn't *yell*. But I am sorry for snapping. You were trying to tell me that you were worried about everyone, and I should have been more sensitive." Her teeth dig into her bottom lip. Waiting. "I'm sorry for being a jerk. It wasn't my inten—"

But it *had* been my intention. Shame sours in my stomach. The memory of her stricken face is still fresh, maybe even more so in the light of day. I don't *want* to argue with her. It's not like I enjoy it. But sometimes, I can't stop myself. I clear my throat, swallow. "You hit a nerve, is all."

I glance to the mouth of our tent, blinking back the last remnants of sleep. She must have already slipped out to take care of business because the zip is open a few inches, just enough to see the anemic hints of what passes for sunrise in here. Another day of graying pallor hanging over us. Lovely. I catch the wafting aroma of coffee, a little on the burned side, and something sweet and cloying.

"It's a little past 7:30 a.m.," says Kiara. "Tayla took charge of breakfast."

"Why doesn't that surprise me?" I say under my breath.

She makes a sound that could be a laugh, but when my eyes dart to her, Kiara is suspiciously smooth-faced. And against my will, I observe more useless, inconsequential facts about her: she doesn't wear a bra to sleep, her unbrushed hair is still artfully tousled and fluffy except for the face-framing apricot locks that she's tucked behind her ears, and her cheeks still bloom with color, like she's as embarrassed to see me first thing in the morning as I am to *be* seen.

"Do you want to talk about it?" Kiara asks, fiddling with her earring even though it's perfectly secure.

I prop myself up on my elbows. "About what?"

She stares like it's obvious. "Why you look so . . ." She seems to search for the right word. "Rattled."

I tear my gaze away. "Don't know what you're talking about."

"Nova."

"Kiara."

She makes a sound of frustration that mimics a growling baby bear and is exactly that adorable.

With a crooked smile, I ask, "Is it honestly that hard to guess why being here is weird and difficult?"

Sympathy softens her. "Then I won't ask if you're okay because I don't want to hear you lie to me."

"What makes you so sure I'd lie?"

"I mean, does anyone ever answer that question honestly?"

I tear my gaze away and sit up all the way. My head feels heavy. There's a dull, persistent throbbing between my eyes and all over my forehead. Thankfully not a migraine, but the tension headaches I've been getting the last couple of years suck, too. The specialist Mom took me to said he's seen it often in people with trauma, stress, and anxiety. I mean, tick, tick, tick.

Closing my eyes, I bring my hands to the sides of my head and squeeze, but the relief only lasts a couple of seconds before the pressure is back with a vengeance.

"Are you okay?"

Prying one eye open, I give her a look. "Didn't we just have this conversation?"

She regards me with a furrowed brow. "What are you looking for?"

I pause in scrounging through my backpack for the amber vial I bought from Mortar & Thistle. I'll remember to put it in my bear bag in the future. "Didn't sleep well," I mumble.

Every nighttime sound was a possible threat, making my

brain overthink and fret. Even when I did manage to nod off, a hoot or a chirp or the hiss of the wind forced me awake. Whenever I'm sleep deprived, physically overexerted, or stressed, my body decides to be extra vicious. I feel like a zombie. A zombie that's been mowed down by a Hummer, a Ford F-450, and a succession of military trucks.

"Radhika has headache relief if you need Advil, Tylenol, or whatever," Kiara says.

"I brought my own 'whatever.'" I dangle the vial between two fingers. "Petra's essential oils are more effective for me than medication."

"Okay. Come here." She holds out a hand, palm up.

I stare at her life and love lines, curling my fingers around the vial. "Um, why?"

Before I can even finish the question, she tucks herself behind me and tugs at my shoulders until my head is in her lap. "So suspicious," she says, voice light with teasing.

Is this a dream? Is this a nightmare? Has to be a nightmare. I look and feel too gross for this to be anything but. Then again, my head is between her thighs, so . . .

I'm not exactly sure what's appropriate here, so I lie stiff, staring up at the ceiling of our juniper polyester tent. When Kiara's fingers fight mine for the bottle, I relinquish it purely because of the bewildered shock of assuming—incorrectly, as it turns out—that she was trying to hold my hand.

"Um." My tongue feels thick and gross in my mouth. "Why

are you . . . um." My cheeks burn at my lack of coherence. But if I ask her why she's touching me, maybe she'll take that as a cue to stop.

"Because we have a long day of walking ahead of us, and I don't want you hurting. So I am going to massage every bad thing out of that head of yours, Nova Marwood."

Coming from her lips, my name sounds like a caress. I repress a shiver as she readjusts me exactly how she wants me. "Can I keep going?" Kiara asks.

Half my brain acknowledges the question and appreciates her asking for consent. The other half literally cannot think straight when she's this close to me, warm and soft and smelling like strawberries.

I blink. "I . . . yes?"

"Good," she whispers, brushing her knuckles down my temples. I inhale sharply, keeping my eyes focused on the tent, the way I can see just a smudge of light at the top from a gap in the trees. It's the only sign that there's a world outside of our bubble.

Her hands touch me like they know me. Each brush feels like a reminder. She does that a couple of times, either to get me used to her or to gather her own courage. The idea of gorgeous, confident Kiara being nervous around a girl, even if that girl is me, makes me laugh.

"Does that tickle?" she asks.

"No, it just feels different when someone else does it."

She hums and unstoppers the vial. "Good different?"

The familiar blend of lavender, sweet orange, and lemongrass fills the tent and suffuses my senses. I jerk my head in a nod, still not looking at her. Kiara takes a moment to warm a couple drops between her fingers and then glides her oil-slicked fingers over my skin.

If the oil is sunshine in a bottle, she's the sunbeam who delivers the immediate soothing relief. Citrus bursts all around me, tickling my nose as her fingertips massage slow circles all over my hairline, her thumb working out the tension between my eyes and above my brows. It should be no surprise that she's as adept at this as she is at everything else.

"Good different," I murmur. "Definitely good different."

Kiara laughs, and this time it doesn't bother me. Her fingers keep working their magic, lulling me into a pleasantly drowsy state. "Gonna tell me now?" she asks.

Opening my eyes is too much work. "Hmm?"

"What's got you all squirrelly, Nova?"

Denial is on the tip of my tongue. I lean into her touch, eyelids fluttering. It feels so good to be taken care of, to know I'm safe in someone else's hands. It makes me wonder what else could be safe, too . . .

Maybe my guard is down because I answer before thinking it through. "Do you think something good can come from a bad beginning?"

The pads of her fingertips graze my cheekbones before returning to my temples and resuming gentle circles across my hairline and browbone. "What are we talking about here?"

"My dad. The last time I saw him, I . . . I said . . . things I didn't mean." It's easier to tell her with my eyes shut. I swallow hard and say in barely a whisper, "I couldn't know that . . . that they would be the last words I'd ever speak to him. That he'd ever hear."

In the contemplative silence that follows, I hear the echoes of my words as though they're traveling yawning distances of space and time:

Fine! Go, then! If you love the woods so much, stay there forever! I hope you never come back!

Kiara remains quiet, but her fingers don't falter. I inhale the sweet, bright scent of the oil that clings to her skin and mine. I'm already feeling much better; even my spirits are lifted.

"The day of the Fall Festival," I say, "I met a girl in the woods. She wanted to know why I was there. She and her brother went looking for the wishing well with their friends, but it didn't work out. He thought she sabotaged their trip by messing with their supplies. But he forgave her?"

I make a soft noise that's part disbelief, part envy. Even now, I think about her certainty with wonder. About the way they'd laughed and clambered in the car. Aaliyah's brother bore her no grudge. Everything forgiven and forgotten. The exact opposite of my life.

"And she said that's what family does," I tell Kiara. "I haven't been able to stop wondering what that would be like."

"To be forgiven?" Kiara asks. I don't have to see her face to hear the confusion in her voice.

"Yes."

"Your dad knows you didn't mean it. Whatever it was that you said."

Hot tears prick at my eyes. I screw them shut even tighter. "But I'll never know for sure."

"That's why you wander around in the woods? For absolution?"

"No. I'm going to get him back." I hear how it sounds and quicky add, "I mean, I'm going to try. If I can. If he's still . . ."

My breath catches. I hadn't meant to say that. The words hang between us.

To my surprise, her hands move farther down my face to cup my jaw. Her thumbs settle at the corners of my mouth. I open my eyes, but this only means that I can see her face hovering scant inches above mine. Was she always this close? I can practically count her every eyelash. What is she doing? What is she waiting for? Can she smell my morning breath?

My thoughts frantically rattle, so I take a deep inhale and hold it until my chest starts to burn, which only makes the butterflies swooping in my belly flap their wings even harder. Kiara doesn't look sad, exactly, but it's not a happy expression, either.

"Can't save everyone, Nova," she says.

To her credit, she doesn't say that finding my dad is impossible, that rescuers far savvier than me have tried and failed, that it's so, so futile to expect anything more than bones.

"I will save you both," I say fiercely.

Now she does smile. "It's not your job to save me."

"Oh, quit it, Kiara." I roll my eyes and lift myself from her lap, turning so I'm on my knees in the V of her crossed legs. "I lied to my mom in order to be here, so I'm not giving up on you."

Her expressive brown eyes flick to my lips. We're close enough to kiss. It's such an unhelpful thought, but my heart does a silly little backflip anyway. Actually, it does about a dozen consecutive backflips. No, I think dizzily. A hundred.

If I leaned in, if I tilted my head just right, if my mouth landed on hers . . . would we be in sync?

Or would it be a disastrous repeat of our first and only kiss?

"Do you want to hear something funny, Nova?"

I'm too preoccupied staring at her lush lower lip to manage more than a distracted "Mm-hmm."

"When I went to Madame Aurora's tent, there was a question I wanted to know the answer to."

My stomach leapfrogs. Feigning nonchalance, I say, "Oh?"

"There's a girl I like," says Kiara. "That I've liked for a really long time. The thing is, though, she's pretty hard work. Can never get a read on what's going through her head, let alone her heart."

I swallow hard. "Doesn't seem worth the effort, honestly."

One corner of her mouth tips up more than the other. "Except," Kiara says softly, "as inscrutable as her heart might be, I know it's a good one."

The impulse to shake my head, to deny it, is overwhelming. I wish I had never opened my eyes. Never saw her as more than the one who got away. It was so much easier when I could pretend that, if I thought of her at all, it was with annoyance. I can't go back to the Before when I could pretend not to care. Her stare pins me like a butterfly in a corkboard.

In the quiet, I am aware that we are caught in the now, a fleeting moment where there is no Before or After. Only what happens now.

A choice. And it's mine.

"Nova," she says. My name curls around her tongue, sends shivery anticipation licking down my spine.

I close the gap between us, stroking a finger down her cheek. "I want to kiss you."

Her smile tells me she wants the same thing, but Kiara voices it a second later. "You can."

There's nothing in my vision except her. Leaning in, I press the softest of close-lipped kisses against the corner of her mouth. She makes a soft noise of disappointment, angling to catch my lips, but I already foresaw the move. Our first kiss was awkward enough; the last thing I want is for my stale, un-brushed breath to ruin our second. With regret, I tell her, "My teeth are all furry."

"Yeah, and my leg stubble has grown back, and it fucking itches." Kiara rolls her eyes. "So what?"

I hide my smile behind my hand and rock back on my heels, putting a solid foot of space between us. "So . . . maybe we wait?"

"I've waited long enough."

There's a roughness to her voice that makes me look at her more closely. This isn't a girl pouting because she didn't get a kiss. There's a note of bitterness, a trace of frustration, a flare to her nostrils that wasn't there before. "Not really," I say. "Even *I* didn't know I wanted to kiss you until a minute ago."

She looks away. "It's been a lot longer than that, Nova."

"Okay, well . . . how long?"

"Forget it. Forget I said anything. It's fine."

I don't need to be a relationship expert to know it's most certainly not fine, but from the determined look on her face, this is all I'm going to get out of her. It occurs to me that she feels rejected, when really, it was just a *not right now*.

"Kiara, can you look at me? Please?" When she does, I say, "You remember our first kiss, right? It wasn't . . . great. I mean, it was memorable, but for all the wrong reasons. I kept replaying it in my mind for *days* after that, analyzing it from all angles, working out the ideal kiss conditions."

I blush, ducking my head. My earnestness is mortifying, but it's out there now, so I may as well continue. Unable to look at her while I say the next part, I mumble, "I've spent every day since then wishing that you knew what it was like to be as obsessed with someone as I am with you. So you'd know for even a minute how it felt to be the one chasing instead of the one being chased. Pardon me if I want everything to be perfect, and lying on the cold, hard ground in a stuffy, cramped tent isn't it."

"Got what you wanted," she says. "Me obsessed with you."

I snort. "And what happens after?"

"I know it's been a while since we first kissed, but typically, you'd kiss me back." She darts for the corner of my mouth and presses a kiss there, warm and firm and tingly.

"Kiara!" I yelp. I clap my hand against my lips and pull back just a little. She looks totally pleased with herself, but there's also a question in her eyes, a silent *Was that okay?*

I mean, yes, it was okay. Better than okay. My entire body feels like honey, the tension softening, and the headache soothing, and the hungry wanting in my belly momentarily sated. I have an overwhelming desire to simply slump into a puddle on the sleeping bags and throw an arm around her warm waist to bring her with me. I want to touch every inch of her: the fabric of her ribbed white tank top, the collarbones peeking out, the smooth tan skin below. Through my haze, I almost forget that she misunderstood my question.

I *meant* what happens after we get back home. When Tayla inevitably wins her back, where does that leave me?

"Fine, fine," Kiara says with an exaggerated, long-suffering sigh. "Whenever you're ready."

"Thank you," I mutter.

"Nova Marwood is a romantic," says Kiara. She smiles, everything forgiven. "Who knew."

I scoff, but a weight is lifted. "My mother. She was convinced the camping trip was just an excuse to get closer to you."

Kiara's dimples are out in full force. "Oh yeah, you hexed me just so I'd need you to escort me to the wishing well. Good plan, Nova. A-plus for effort. F for execution." She laughs and doesn't seem to notice that I don't.

The crushing weight is back with all the force of a boulder. I push my tongue against the back of my teeth, trying desperately hard to keep my expression from betraying me. Do I laugh at her joke? Roll my eyes? I've been in this body for seventeen years, and I can't remember what would naturally come next. Kiara's good at knowing my guilty, squirrelly face, apparently, and I've already taken too long to respond.

Clawing anxiety scrapes my heart. The tent closes in around me, sucking out all the oxygen. I taste the film on my tongue and want to vomit.

This is it. It's over. It's all in the Before. There's never going to be a kiss in our After, is there? No more touches and teasing. She knows.

"Do you think you could be my good luck charm?" she asks, breaking our stare-off.

I choke out a laugh. *"What?"*

"Just saying, think about it. Whenever you're around, things don't seem quite so bad."

Relief pounds through my body. "Stop flirting with me. I already said I'm not going to kiss you right now," I say, more to annoy her than anything else, but I only succeed in making myself cranky.

Because when she smiles like that, so carefree and dimpled, I can see why all four of her exes out there fell for her so fucking hard. Why they're here when they could be home, still snuggled up fast asleep in their nice, warm beds and not sore and stiff from the cold, hard ground.

Kiara's smile wavers. "What? I'm being serious. Why are you giving me that look?"

Because I know she would never have said that to me if we were back in Prior's End. If she'd never burst into Aurora's tent at the exact wrong moment, at the most catastrophic timing. If my four-leaf clover wasn't still squished in her smallest zippered pocket. Her compliment compounds my guilt, and *I hate it*.

I hate the way she makes me feel. How I try so hard to pretend I don't care when caring seems to be all I do when it comes to Kiara Mistry. I can't pull off fake nonchalance even when I try because apparently my willpower has all the strength of a Twizzler.

I've never felt closer to my dad than now, in this place of magic and superstition and legends.

What would he make of a petty hex and a pretty girl and a perilous quest to save her?

I might never know. What I do know is that I am here. For *her* sake. I might have started this journey with my own agenda, desperate for a partner to go with me into the woods to find my dad, but it's no longer just about him. In my world of neat and tidy boxes, all appropriately labeled and shelved, Kiara is the wildfire that's scorching through everything I believe in, one devastating smile at a time.

My perfectly ordered little world is ablaze for her. The worst thing is that she's worth it.

"No one's ever called me their lucky charm before," I say finally. "I'm not so sure it's true. I'm more like the last desperate sandbag standing up to your wave of bad luck. It's not the same thing as being your good luck charm."

"You're so down on yourself. You shouldn't be. You're a good person. I don't know anyone else who would agree to come on a—let's be frank—pretty dubious trip with a bunch of people they hate."

"I don't *hate* them."

Kiara snorts.

I scowl. "Not three-fourths of them anyway," I say.

She leans forward so her brown hair spills over the thin straps of her white tank top. "What about me?"

I study her face like it's a trap. "What about you?"

"I know you want to kiss me. But other than that, how do you feel about me?"

Now I *know* it's a trap. And I'm not about to walk into it when I still feel so discombobulated. I need to . . . recombobulate? I shake away the errant thought.

"Ask me later," I say. "First, I need to brush my teeth and drink about a gallon of coffee so I don't look and feel like a total zombie. Do you have any toothpaste I can borrow?"

I couldn't find it last night, even though I remember packing it in my toiletries case, squished between the SPF and bug spray. But I was in such a rush, maybe it's still at home.

With a disappointed tilt to her lips, she reaches for her backpack and tugs at a zip.

Alarm bells peal through my head. No, not that pocket!

Kiara pulls out a tiny clear baggy of chewable toothpaste tabs. They're small and round like mints. Clinging to the bottom of the baggy is my clover. Without a second thought, she uses her nail to flick it away. It's dried up, shriveled, the edges curling in. More brown than green.

She offers me the baggy. She must have misread the dismay on my face because she explains, "Oh, it's not hard. You just pop it in, take a swig of water, crush it all up until it starts to fizz into toothpaste. When you're done brushing, spit it out. Don't eat it."

"I know how to—"

Before I can finish my sentence, the tent collapses. Not in a gentle flutter, either, or the slumpy sag of one corner, but every single pole gives out at the exact same time in one giant *whoosh*, as though we simply breathed wrong.

I can't help the undignified shriek.

As the heavy canvas pins us to the ground, Kiara winds up on top of me, toothpaste tabs crushed against my chest between us. Even through our clothing, I can feel her softness and warmth. I bring my hand up to brush her hair over her shoulder. My thumb grazes the strap of her tank, the curve of her shoulder.

"I promise this isn't me sabotaging the tent to try and get that kiss," she whispers into the crook of my neck. Her lips curve into a smile against my skin.

I don't know whether to laugh or shiver. In the end, I settle for both.

Kiara retreats but only a little. She hovers a space above my mouth. Neither of us blink. Our chests graze, and my breath hitches when her loose hair falls in a curtain around us. Her hair smells like the sweet summery juiciness of her strawberry shampoo, the same scent I've inhaled when she tosses her hair in front of me in class. I've never really thought about it before, but she does seem to be seated in front or behind me quite a lot.

It takes everything I have not to pull her even closer and bury my face in the crook of her neck and inhale the alluring scent I've come to associate with her and only her. Nova Marwood, Queen of Restraint. Who knew?

"See? My lucky charm after all," Kiara says, bringing her hand to my cheek. "Cushioning my fall." Soft as butterfly wings, knuckles graze my skin. The bubble of laughter in my throat pops, and my entire body turns into one giant goose bump. She doesn't linger, but the ghost of her touch remains even after her fingers fall away. "I know the truth, Nova Marwood," she says quietly.

My breath catches, *strangles*. I stare at her, not trusting myself to speak.

"You," says Kiara, minty breath floating across my face, "are secretly really, really—to a ridiculous degree—into me, even though you give a *great* impression otherwise. But I see you."

Too stunned to refute that bold assertion, I owlishly blink at her as she hoists herself up.

Just in time, too, since Tayla's head pops under the tent as though she's pressed herself to the ground. "What happened? Are you okay?"

She's only looking at Kiara, not me, but I answer anyway. "We're both fine."

Kiara nods.

Tayla's gaze sweeps the tent. "Didn't you check the tension before going to bed?"

"It's not a big deal," says Kiara. "It could happen to anyone."

"Wait. You let *her* do it?" Somehow Tayla's head roving around a foot above the ground is no less scary than Tayla at her full height. To me, she asks, "Have you ever even put up a tent before? Without your dad's help? You're lucky the tent collapsed in the morning and not in the middle of the night!"

"It was my fault," Kiara says quickly. "My bad luck strikes again."

I squelch down the spike of guilt that her covering for me elicits. If I was braver, maybe I would have said, *No, Tayla's right. I didn't know what to do, and I was too embarrassed to ask.*

But I'm not brave. I've never been brave enough. I'm still so afraid to admit when I'm responsible for something bad happening.

"Right," says Tayla, clearly disbelieving. "Well, the others just woke up, so we should eat and get a move on." Her head disappears but not without one last look of disapproval aimed at me.

There's a pit of certainty in my belly that this is not a simple case of my pride; this is the hex rearing its ugly head once again. I throw a despairing glance in the direction of the four-leaf clover. Whatever protective properties it had are long used up. It only lasted a day. Less than I'd anticipated. It didn't help that Kiara flicked it away the second she saw it. Either way, whether the tent collapse was due to my inexperience or the wilted magic or her discarding the clover . . . the fault for hexing her, ultimately, still lies squarely on my shoulders.

I kind of wish I hadn't rejected the horseshoe for being too unwieldy or the rabbit foot too icky. On the fly, I could always find a ladybug or a dotted red-and-white toadstool. But my chances of finding cute little beetles? In this weather? They're probably sneaking into the cracks of people's houses to hole up and hibernate for the winter. Then there's the red-capped mushroom . . .

Even though it's adorable and fairy-tale charming, the *Amanita muscaria* is a hallucinogenic, highly poisonous mushroom. Still, coming across one is considered pretty lucky. While the species can be found here in Tennessee, usually flourishing under a pine tree, my dad only saw them rarely, and I haven't spotted any so far.

Ugh, who am I kidding? I would make a terrible partner for Kiara. Clearly, I suck at hunting and gathering, if I can't get over my own squeamishness to touch a rabbit's foot or keep a lookout for bright red mushrooms.

Quit it, Nova. This is not *the time to catastrophize.*

Dad would want me to change my perspective. A lot of his

lessons and sayings were inherited from his aunt, who brought him up after his parents died in a car accident. My great-aunt Eloise lost her fiancé to the wishing well. She never married or loved anyone else the rest of her days. *A broken heart that never healed*, I overheard Dad telling Mom, even though that wasn't the official cause. Everyone said Eloise hung on long enough to see Dad happy and settled and her wine bar in good hands.

She died before my third birthday, and my memories of her are fragmented, mostly stitched together through half recollections and the stories my parents told to keep her alive. Dad's favorite story was the one about how Eloise, always so forgetful, developed inventive ways to recollect important things. *I'd forget my own name if it was possible*, she always said with a laugh that sounded like a secret.

Dad wrote six letters on a sheet of paper. *ELOISE*. I was nine and enamored with the idea of proving how clever I could be, too. *Can you figure out her trick in remembering her PIN, Nova?*

I could not. Suddenly, nine seemed very small.

His smile took the sting away. He turned the paper upside down so I couldn't read the letters anymore. Only now I could! Excitedly, I told him they were numbers! *35/073*.

In the face of seemingly insurmountable challenges, North Star, it always helps to look at your problem in a different way. Change your perspective, and you'll find everything *changes.*

Okay, time to put his lesson into practice. So what do I have left? I still have an antique brass skeleton key, rumored to be spelled by a shunned witch who lived in Prior's End long ago to bring good luck to thieves. She apparently had little love for her neighbors, and no wonder.

There are also the tarot cards that belonged to Petra's mother, who started the tradition of offering divination to the Mortar & Thistle clients. I have the Sun, the Wheel of Fortune, and the Six of Cups. I don't know much about tarot, but from what Petra told me during our reading, these cards symbolize fate, good fortune, and wishes coming true. In other words, luck is supposedly on my side.

But I'm also the person who hexed Kiara. My own reckless words boomerang into my brain.

Bad luck will plague your footsteps . . . The very ground you tread will turn treacherous . . . You will suffer this reversal of fortune until you summon the strength to sacrifice what you want most.

Kiara's confession changes everything.

When I went to Madame Aurora's tent, there was a question I wanted to know the answer to. There's a girl I like. That I've liked for a really long time.

With this context, what if it was our closeness that collapsed the tent? Our attraction?

What if I'm making things worse? After all, I'd also said . . .

The closer you get to what you want, the worse off you will be.

My body physically hurts at the thought of *me* being the unluckiest charm of all.

I can't risk it. Can't be selfish. I need to take a step back. Like, a lot of steps back.

I roll my thumb over one of the green beads on my bracelet and blink back tears. It definitely doesn't feel like luck is on my side.

"I'm sorry," I say as we both crawl out, bringing our belongings with us. And then helplessly, because I can't apologize for what I really want to, I repeat again, "I'm sorry."

As I flee with my toothbrush and a tab clenched in my fist, I hear an amused Keiffer—a bright red brush sticking out of the side of his mouth—shout, "Spit, don't swallow!"

17

*L*uck must be on my side for once because I successfully manage to avoid Kiara as we go about the business of getting dressed and ready. I dive behind tents and trees to dodge her soft, inquisitive eyes. After our almost kisses, I don't trust myself alone with her, don't trust that my willpower will win out over my wanton heart.

Half an hour later, after drinking Tayla's valiant attempt at brewing coffee, I'm not sure my teeth are any cleaner than they were when I woke up. But the brown sugar oatmeal was good, especially with the diced apple, and spiced with a motley of cinnamon, nutmeg, and clove. Tomorrow is my turn to make oatmeal, and I have nuts and chocolate chips, plus Evan's promised me some of their dried cherries as a mix-in.

Now camp is all packed up, we've made our way back to the path, and Radhika is again intently studying her guidebook as though she'll be able to crack the secret code that no other hiker ever has. Her ambition to be the best, the most knowledgeable person in any given room was why I first admired her, but it's also why she was easy to get over. She and Tayla are driven in a way I'm not and never have been.

A couple of hours later, we come to a fork in the trail, and on the right is a row of trash and recycling containers with cleverly designed handles so animals can't get into them. Kiara and Keiffer get to work offloading our collected trash, including the cans he'd brought without thinking.

On the left of the fork is a massive board with a map of the Blue Ridge Mountains, plus notices of which areas are off-limits due to increased bear activity, storm damage, and ongoing trail maintenance. It's ridiculous, but I catch myself scanning the map for a clue to the wishing well, even though I know full well it's hardly going to be marked. With a little laugh, I return to perusing the board.

There are directions to the nearest ranger's station, which is nowhere close, and reminders not to feed the wildlife. Next to that is a sign, yellowed with age, warning hikers to watch out for thieves. In scratchy ballpoint, someone's sketched the fork in the road then drawn a big *X* over the trail on the right. Underneath they've scribbled *Avoid! Our camp got completely cleaned out. Even took our half-finished soda!!!*

"That's kind of funny," says Evan, pointing to the note. They wrinkle their nose, making their tiny diamond nose stud pop against their brown skin. "I mean, who drinks someone else's gross old soda?"

"Same person who eats someone else's chips?" I point to another set of handwriting that says *Don't worry, only trash bandits out here!* accompanied by a crude but frankly adorable drawing of a raccoon pawing at a bag of potato chips. Remembering his fondness for Pringles, I joke, "Hey, you think Keiffer could be the culprit?"

"Ha ha," he says, squirting some sanitizer on his hands after lowering the container lid. Evan, having skipped Tayla's somewhat burned coffee, laughs and takes a sip of tea from their thermos and passes it to Keiffer when he holds out a hand for a drink.

"Hey," Kiara says, sidling up to me. Her hand grazes mine, and she gives me a secret smile.

I try not to be obvious that I'm putting distance between us when I put my leg up on a rock and pretend to tighten my laces.

"Careful," she says when I wobble a little. She braces her hand against my pack to counter the weight. I swear I can feel the heat of her hand through the fabric and the rest of my backpack's contents. "You're carrying a lot," she says with a soft laugh. "Don't want to fall on your back like a turtle."

I laugh, too, and it's without doubt the single most insincere sound I've heard in my life. "Yeah, thanks."

She shoots me a weird look. "You good?"

"Yep!" Good. I am trying to be good. If I tell myself this often enough, maybe I'll believe it. "Hey, Radhika, find any answers in that book yet?"

"If not, give someone else a shot," says Tayla. She winces, adjusting her backpack straps around her shoulders and torso. "We're all just standing around slowly sinking into the earth."

"Need me to take some of the weight?" Keiffer offers.

Tayla gives him a genuine smile. "You're the best, but no. It's mine to carry. I'm no weakling."

"T," says Kiara in a tone that suggests they've had a conversation about this before. "It's not weakness to accept help. Right, Nova?" The pressure of her hand increases, or maybe it just feels like it does when she's standing this close, heat radiating off her. A line of sweat gathers in the band of my bra.

"Kiara, maybe you should offer to take something of Nova's," says Evan.

When Kiara turns to look at me with a question in her eyes, Evan forms a heart with their hands then points to me and grins meaningfully. I give a swift, abortive shake of my head. I adore Evan, and they have many wonderful qualities, but subtlety is *not* one of them.

"Not necessary," I say quickly. My cheeks feel as hot as stewed tomatoes.

Keiffer pulls his mouth to the side, forming a wordless *Yikes*.

Tayla narrows her eyes at Evan, which only makes them laugh, unbothered.

"*Shhh!* It would help if you'd all be quiet for two seconds," says Radhika, forehead pinched with irritation and concentration.

"Everyone, be quiet," Keiffer says, folding his arms across his chest and doing his best stern impression. "Let her do her thing."

"Thanks, baby." She squints at the page, flips back and forth a bit, and sucks her teeth, all while we watch. I'm starting to think I should have read up myself before we left. Surely, on one of the bookshelves scattered around the house, I would have found Dad's marked-up copy of *The Way of the Wish*.

I can see him dangled over our lumpy, sagging couch with a red pen in hand, muttering and tsking under his breath as he reads. Mom calls us to dinner, serving pan-seared trout to join the mustardy bacon green beans and colorful sliced heirloom tomato salad on our plates. It's our favorite family meal, and child-me is especially proud of how I ripped up all the fragrant basil and sprinkled it over the tomatoes. In my memory, I can still smell the sweet herbs on my warm palms. Hear the irritated huffs from my father, the way he turned the timeworn pages like each one had personally offended him.

Jules, come on! It's getting cold!

His voice, distracted, saying, *I'm so close to the end of the chapter, Rhea! One more minute!*

Is it even his voice? Or just some generic masculine conglomeration that lives in my head?

Missing my dad is so fucking inconvenient.

I can't even enjoy the memories that fade a little more every year without feeling ambushed. Like any number of random things—a delicate leaf fluttering down to land at my feet, a squirrel chittering angrily from the treetops, the guttural croak of a bullfrog before it dives into the stream—these scenes from my childhood catch me unawares. Which makes me sad, then angry, and then incandescent with directionless fury.

Because while my head might pretend that seven years is long enough to not feel grief slicing into me at all angles, the body remembers. There is no magical amount of time in which I will stop missing him. For Mom, maybe she's told herself that seven years is the right time to move forward. I can forgive her, but I'll never be able to forgive myself.

One more minute! I hear him call.

I would trade years of my life to have that one extra minute where I could run after him that night he left to go into the Longing Woods to find Shane. One minute would be enough to throw my arms around his middle, to tell him I didn't mean what I said. To tell him to come home safe. That I loved him.

I will forever be haunted that I didn't.

I need to be good now. Good like my dad. Not bad like me.

"'According to legend, in order to find the path to the wishing well, all one has to do is follow the signs of wonderment,'" Radhika reads out, sighing.

Keiffer purses his lips. "I'm assuming wonderment is not typically found on the clearly marked path."

We all follow his gaze to the overgrown trails veering off the packed dirt beneath our boots where hundreds, if not thousands, of people have already trekked.

Evan clears their throat. "'Two roads diverged in a yellow wood and I—I took the one less traveled by, and that has made all the difference.'" They wait a beat, letting the words sink in before adding, "Robert Frost."

I smile. "Nice." They beam back.

Kiara walks a few steps ahead, peering into the undergrowth. It's a tangle of untamed shrubs, gnarled roots, grasping vines. The trees stretch on and on and on in the eerie infinite, an endless gray-green murk where if you stare too long, you can't unsee it for several seconds even after you swivel your gaze.

Tayla startles. "Did you see—"

"See what?" Radhika hurriedly shuts the book, using her thumb to mark the page.

"I . . . never mind. It was probably nothing."

"Probably nothing or definitely nothing?" muses Evan.

Keiffer's jaw tenses. It's obvious where his worry lies.

"Fellowship of the Fling, day two. Yippee," Radhika says flatly.

"We've been staring at the same scenery for the last half hour," huffs Tayla. "My eyes are playing tricks on me, that's all."

"Even so, new safety rule: none of us should go anywhere alone," I declare. "Not even to pee." At everyone's solemn nods, I say, "Good. Buddy system it is."

Despite insisting she didn't see anything, Tayla doesn't argue against the edict. As we all square our shoulders to venture off the path, she falls in step next to me, bringing up the rear. "So you must have done this a lot, then?" she asks. "Hiking. Camping. With your dad."

I can tell she's trying to sound friendly, but the question is so abrupt, so deliberately casual that it has the exact opposite effect. She's trying to gauge something about me, but what?

My toes curl in my hiking boots. "Never this deep into the forest."

"Scary for a kid," Tayla comments. "Fuck, scary now, too."

Ahead, Keiffer and Radhika take turns holding branches aside for each other while Evan sails right through them, and Kiara does her best to sidestep. She turns around and makes a face, as if to say, *Well,* this *sucks.* Truly, the unmarked paths are too narrow and unwieldy for us to walk two abreast.

Several long strides pass in silence until Tayla finally says, "When Dad got sick, my mom asked your dad to take her to the wishing well. She was going to wish his cancer away, make him better. That was right around the time that those spring break girls from Middle Tennessee got lost. Remember?"

At my "Mm-hmm," she continues. "The ringleader was trying to impress some boy and convinced all her friends that this would be a great photo op for Instagram. All they needed was a high ponytail, a few White Claws, and makeup that wouldn't give them an oily T-zone."

"That was some next-level 'Not like other girls' shit," I mutter, remembering the incident well, even though it was almost a decade ago. The search and rescue had been all over Prior's End news, probably because of our proximity to the university in Murfreesboro and the fact that the missing foursome were all photogenic middle-class white girls.

Tayla snorts in disgust. "All those rangers and cops swarming the woods trying to find them. They'd cordoned everything off, they weren't even letting volunteers in to search. Even if Mom did somehow convince your dad, there's no way they would have managed to sneak in. He advised her to trust the prognosis, that we were lucky the doctors caught it in time. And he was right. Dad pulled through."

As she talks, she keeps touching the thin gold chain around her neck, which I only notice now is actually a pendant of Saint Anthony, patron saint of lost items—and lost people and souls, for that matter.

"I had no idea. I'm glad your dad is okay now."

But I don't know why she's telling me this. I'm the last person on this luck-forsaken trip she'd want to have a heart-to-heart with. Maybe we're having a moment? Sharing things, being real?

"Thanks," she says curtly. She slips the pendant inside her collar. "So it goes without saying that only the reckless, the desperate, the glory seekers, and the sheep think it's a good idea to come here. Which one are you?"

. . . *not a moment, then.* I scoff.

"Tayla, what the actual fuck."

"See, I don't think you're adventurous enough to seek glory, and I don't think you're reckless enough to put your mom through this again unless you have a really, really good reason."

I angrily swat away the vegetation, but the recoil is too fast, and it whips back on me. There must be a thorn because whatever it is stings, leaving a long, thin scratch on the back of my hand.

Tayla studies me like a scientist would a particularly intriguing insect. "Radhika, glory. She prides herself on being a Prior descendant. Probably thinks finding the wishing well is in her DNA, implausible though it is. Keiffer's here for her, so, sheep.

Evan's more of a question mark, but sometimes I get the feeling they think they're invincible because they can see the future in their tea leaves, so I'll go with reckless. Then there's you."

"Maybe I'm just a good person," I say, hearing Kiara's voice in my head and almost believing it.

Heatedly, she says, "You don't even know how to put up a tent—"

"That could just have been Kiara's bad luck!" I snap.

"And you don't have a fucking clue about signs of wonderment," she hisses. "So what good is Nova Marwood, really? I mean you're nice to look at, I suppose, but I can't for the life of me figure out what it is exactly that Kiara sees in you. You're not even competent and *nowhere* near good enough for her."

Gritting my teeth, I rub at my hand. She's impossible. I rue ever thinking Machete Mouth wanted to have a moment with me. The only moments she wants are the ones in which she gets to play inquisition.

My silence doesn't deter her.

"Which leaves . . . *desperate*."

It's so obvious, the way she lands on it like it's what she was aiming for all along, crowing and self-satisfied that she's told me something about myself she's sure will rattle me. And it does, but not as much as she thinks. Because everything she's told me I already know is the truth: I am not good enough.

"Don't project your reason for being here onto me," I snarl, not bothering to match her low tones. I don't care if anyone overhears, if Kiara knows we're fighting over her like jealous lovers. Suddenly, my own words land at the forefront of my mind. *That's* what this is all about. *Of course.*

"You're not just here to save her life," I realize out loud, narrowing my eyes. "You want her back."

Her sharp inhale gives her away. When she doesn't deny it, I shake my head. "I don't care why any of you are here, Tayla. And that trip down memory lane you just told me about those college girls? The glory seeker and her sheep? You are just like her. She came out here to impress someone, too, didn't she?"

With that, I walk briskly ahead, intent on leaving both Tayla and this conversation in the past.

The other four are crouched around the thick trunk of an enormous tree, something ancient enough to have been here even in Henry Prior's time.

"I'm telling you, they've debunked that myth," Keiffer says patiently.

I stoop, squeezing myself between his shoulder and Evan's. My thighs rebel, muscles screaming their agony. My most supple, buttery jeans, comfortable to wear for a whole day at school, feel a size too small. I can't see what's so interesting about this tree out of all the other trees here. "What are we talking about?"

Evan looks at me over their shoulder. "The moss. It's growing on the wrong side of the tree."

"What's the wrong side? How can you tell?"

I hate to ask. It only proves Tayla's accusations. But the difference between this and what happened with the tent collapse is that now I am unashamed of my ignorance. Or rather,

I am unashamed to admit that someone else has knowledge and skills that I lack. If I never admit to what I don't know, how will I learn? After all, if I'd been here by myself, I wouldn't have even known about the moss, but Keiffer and Evan obviously do. Not for the first time, I am inordinately grateful for the Fellowship of the Fling.

"Moss doesn't like sunlight," says Evan. "See how this one is facing in the opposite direction from the others? And look at the trunk right behind it, same thing. And the one after that and the one after that."

"Y-yes?"

"These trees are all in a line, kind of like they've been marked. And the moss is growing *toward* the sun, not away from it."

"Signs of wonderment."

They nod. "Exactly."

"Except," says Keiffer, "the reality is that moss can grow just about anywhere."

"He knows what he's talking about," says Radhika.

"Isn't he averaging, like, a C?" This, naturally, comes from Tayla, who doesn't deign to stoop like we do. She crosses her arms, distinctly unimpressed, looking down on all of us like we're a bad smell.

Kiara shakes her head in disapproval, but Keiffer ignores the jab. "Back in the day, the old wisdom was that moss faces north, so people used it as nature's compass to navigate their way through the forest. But really, all it means is trees have moisture, and moss thrives in the damp and the dark. This whole forest is *covered* in shade. Without even a hint of sun, the moss is pretty much spoiled for choice. Like I said, it can grow anywhere just fine." His eyes, a slate gray, cut to Tayla. "And I have an A in biology."

She flashes her palms at him, actually managing to look contrite. "I stand corrected."

"Just saying, I don't think moss is the sign we're looking for," says Keiffer. "Honestly, guys, who's to say that people don't get lost *because* they followed this line of thinking?"

"But we have to follow something. Otherwise, what are we doing here?" Tayla's face is grim with determination. "Think about it. If the wishing well could be found on the trail, it would hardly be a secret, would it? Anyone could find it just by putting one foot in front of the other." She smiles at Radhika, knowing just what to say. "Only a select few are worthy of Henry Prior's legacy."

That's all it takes to get Radhika on board. She holds her chin a little higher. "I think it's worth the risk. I mean, it's for Kiara. Go big or go home."

Disappointment sinks into Keiffer's face.

Glory, I think, stomach twisting.

Tayla's eyes glitter with victory. "Kiara?"

"I . . . I don't know. If Keiffer thinks—"

"You're the reason we're here." Tayla implores the Fellowship, "Let Kiara decide."

Kiara looks like she's about to be sick. "We should take a vote."

"But there's six of us," interjects Evan. "What if it's a tie?"

"This isn't a democracy." Tayla takes a deep breath then appeals directly to Kiara. "Do you trust me?"

Maybe I should be flattered that Kiara looks at me first, tries to gauge my expression.

I want to save her, but I'm Team Keiffer on this. If he's right about the moss, then we could be putting ourselves in more danger by following the wrong signs. Tayla and Radhika want progress, so of course they're interpreting the presence of the moss on the wrong side of the tree to be a significant clue.

Isn't this exactly what Aurora said about tarot readings? Nothing is conclusive. It's up to us to interpret their meaning.

On the other hand, Tayla's desperation makes sense. It seems unlikely that the way to the wishing well would be so easy. If I'd paid more attention to what Dad was doing when we were in the woods, maybe I wouldn't be so useless. Maybe I would be able to stand up to Tayla and convince everyone to follow me.

But the cool, logical mind I've relied upon all my life has deserted me. Running through the pros and cons of both choices in my mind doesn't clarify the situation, only confuses it further.

There are as many reasons to side with Keiffer as there are to side with Tayla. Playing devil's advocate is a good way to look at a mystery from all angles, but my mind is a pinball machine, all sharp corners and whizzing balls, a dozen going at a time, picking up speed, only to crash and rebound before I can get my bearings.

"Maybe we should split up," says Evan.

Radhika's eyebrows hike up to her hairline. "E, that is an appalling suggestion."

"I've watched enough horror movies to know splitting up is *never* a good idea," says Kiara.

Tayla taps her chin. "It's not a bad compromise, though. We'd cover more ground. And whoever finds the well first sends up a smoke signal. Unless, Nova, you happen to have another walkie on you?"

I shake my head. "Just the one."

"Are you kidding me? We're not splitting up." Kiara's eyes flare wide. "No way."

"Then my way it is." Tayla doesn't waste a second, looping her elbow around Kiara's.

She all but drags Kiara away with her, Evan scrambling to keep up. Kiara throws a frazzled look over her shoulder as if to make sure we're following, and after an apologetic look at her boyfriend, Radhika falls in line, too. "Safety in numbers," she says, already walking away. "We're better sticking together."

"This is a huge mistake," Keiffer mutters, but everything about his body language shouts that he's giving in. He doesn't seem to expect a response.

In the distance, something howls its agreement.

Everyone stiffens. But no one asks what animal could have possibly made that sound, like ignoring it will erase the mournful, haunting note from our collective memory. The others march on.

"Yeah," I tell him hoarsely, swallowing past the panic in my throat. "I think it's a mistake, too."

"Oh, I was meaning to ask you when you got back from brushing your teeth." Keiffer lowers his voice. "Did you happen to borrow some batteries last night? Only there's some missing."

"What? No. I'd ask first."

"I didn't really think it was you." He gives me a rueful smile. "But no one else fessed up to it, either. It's not a big deal. I don't care, it's whatever, but it's just that there's not many left, and I *know* it was almost full earlier. And we might need them, so we should know how many we have for the journey home."

"Yeah, no, one hundred percent," I say. "It wasn't me."

"Okay."

"Maybe they just rolled out somewhere. Double-check your backpack pockets."

He frowns like I'm stating the obvious and *of course* he's already done this, but he just nods. "For sure. Just wanted to ask. And, um, were you wandering around last night?"

Both my eyebrows shoot up. "In the dark?"

"We couldn't sleep for ages. Thought we heard . . . never mind." His cheeks turn pink. "Probably just a trick of the wind. Regular old outdoor nighttime noises."

Cold slinks down my spine. "Keiffer, I don't remember there being that much wind last night."

We stare at each other. Neither of us know what to say.

At the next howl, we both break into a run.

18

It all starts with the butterflies.

As the day trudges on with dragging heels and resentful silences, black wings dance over our heads. Just one or two at first, small and dainty enough to dart out of sight before any of us can get a close look, and then more join in, fluttering low enough that Evan cries out, "Look, butterflies!"

"Are they usually black?" Radhika asks, presumably to Keiffer, but he either didn't hear or is pretending not to hear.

"Monarchs are," I say. "Mostly orange and black, with just a bit of white." It's nice to be able to offer some knowledge, even though I can't imagine what use it will have.

"This one is full black." Tayla tilts her head, studying one of the butterflies as it swoops over Kiara's head, grazing her ear. With a yelp, Kiara swats at it, mistaking it for something that could sting.

"Huh," says Evan, then shrugs. "I like the blue ones."

"Me too," I say. "Must be nice in here." At Evan's sideways look, I clarify, "For them, I mean. No pesticides, no people to threaten their environment. It's like . . . a sanctuary."

They hum in agreement. "A safe haven."

"Safe? This one seems weirdly attached to me," Kiara

complains, ducking to avoid the butterfly that seems to have a preoccupation with her face or, to be more accurate, with flying directly into it.

"Are you wearing any perfume? Makeup? Something it's attracted to?" asks Radhika.

Kiara shakes her head, the butterflies moving with her. It's obvious she's barefaced. There's no sticky red lip gloss today; all of us are sticking to sunscreen, moisturizer, and lip balm to keep our skin from dryness and cracking. "Maybe it's my natural stink," she says. "The wipes are okay, but this is my second day unwashed, and I'm pretty sure I can smell myself."

Tayla laughs. "Babe, we don't call it 'stink.'"

Keiffer raises an arm to sniff his armpit. "I do."

"It is *odeur naturelle*," Tayla says with a dramatic air, rolling all her *R*'s to make us laugh.

"*Ewwwww,*" Radhika squeals, but when Keiffer holds his arm out to her, she snuggles into his side.

I can see why they work as a couple. They're both super cuddly and into physical touch. Not that I'm one of those people who thinks love languages are the end all and be all, but Kiara seems more like an acts of service gal. This line of thinking leads me to what my love language could be, but thinking about love and Kiara in the span of two seconds makes my head hurt. Maybe my heart a little, too.

All I know is that I was right about what I felt at the carnival. As much as I love spending time with Kiara, after all this is over, we'll both return to our respective lives, which might occasionally intersect, Venn-diagram style, but eventually Tayla will win her over. Especially if her natural leadership (a.k.a. bossiness) is a turn-on to Kiara. For all I know, it's why they got together. Mom's friends from Chalice are always talking about how real competence kink is, so . . . that tracks.

Kiara huffs as another butterfly joins the fun, then another. "Okay, but this is getting ridiculous."

"Just ignore them and they'll go away," says Tayla.

"They're wild animals, not bullies."

"Is there really a difference?"

"And she'd know," I say under my breath, not quite low enough to escape detection.

Tayla's voice is sweet as she says, "Didn't quite catch that."

"Nothing," I chirp.

"Hmm."

The butterflies are fascinated with Kiara, with more joining her entourage as we pick our way across the forest floor, following the moss. Where they were shy and skittish before, hovering out of range and hiding when they felt too many eyes on them, now they're daring enough to fly in circles around Kiara's head like she's a cartoon character who's just bumped her head hard enough to see stars.

"Are you still here?" asks Austin. His voice makes me jump.

"Yeah, I am," I say, still a little distracted by the butterflies' peculiar pattern. I had radioed in to let them know which path we took, so they're aware of our general vicinity in case we need rescue. "We seem to have caught the interest of a swarm of butterflies. They've been following us for a little while, and they're fascinated with Kiara. Dancing around her but never quite landing on her. They're kinda obsessed."

Austin masks his words under a cough.

Suspicious, I ask, "What was that?"

"Oh, nothing."

"And it's a *flutter* of butterflies, not a swarm," Caroline pipes up. "If they're being so delicate about it. If they were being disorderly, the collective noun is rabble. And kaleidoscope if it's a big varied bunch of colors."

I blink. "How do you even know that, Care?"

"I read. Open a book sometime, Nova!"

"I read plenty," I protest.

Just not *The Way of the Wish*. Something that I'm now regretting. I mean, what if there's something in there that only I will understand? Some hidden meaning that makes sense only to me?

Oof. I sound like Radhika now. I'm not special. Being a Prior descendant has never made me feel special. It's only brought my family misery. Our lineage is a kind of curse all on its own.

As we say our goodbyes, Tayla is attempting to shoo more of the butterflies away. She catches my eye, the flash of worry there and gone again before I can stow the radio in the side pocket of my backpack.

"They're not dangerous," Evan says calmly, but neither Tayla nor Kiara respond except to continue waving their hands around themselves.

Even Keiffer makes a few brushing motions to startle the butterflies away, but they ignore everyone who isn't Kiara, never straying far. How they haven't exhausted themselves with all that flapping is beyond me, but they keep pace with us with single-minded perseverance.

"I see you can't stay mad for long," I murmur to Keiffer once Radhika's pulled her book out again, falling a few steps behind to furiously turn pages as though she hasn't already read it cover to cover—multiple times, judging by the soft, rounded edges of the paperback and the couple dozen dog-ears, not to mention the handwritten notes in the margins with her familiar half-print, half-cursive penmanship. At the uncertainty on his face, I add, "Don't get me wrong, it's an endearing quality. I mean, *I'm* still a little peeved that everyone unilaterally decided the moss option was a sign of wonderment. You made good points."

He smiles. "Duly noted. I can't hold a grudge to save my life. Wouldn't want to, even if I could."

"That's . . . healthy."

"You sound like you mean something else."

"No, I really do mean it!" I clear my throat, try to go for light and jokey and breezy. "Can't catch me being that mature, though."

"I don't know about that. You set aside your grudge to help Kiara, didn't you?"

Anxiety swells like a sudden wave. "How did you know I had a—"

"Chill. I'm not going to tell anyone." His smile is amused then not. "I'm not Tayla. I don't want to ferret out your secrets."

"I don't have secrets," I say, immediately defensive.

He rolls his eyes. "We all have secrets, Nova."

"Even you?"

He shrugs, all hot and mysterious, and for one tiny little tickle of a second, I remember why I liked him so much. He's sweet and protective and speaks his mind, not the follower Tayla made him out to be.

"Nah," he says cheerfully. "I'm too boring. WYSIWYG."

I parse through all the slang I know. "Visivig?"

"What you see is what you get." He pulls his backpack forward, rummages, then yells, "Second breakfast!"

Maybe he's missing sports and throwing balls around because he insists on lobbing our apples to us even though Evan has zero hand-eye coordination, Radhika's nose is still buried in her book, and Tayla threatens that if hers falls on the ground, she would make *him* eat it.

Nevertheless, we all lurch to snatch our apples out of the air, rewarded by his undaunted smile. As we munch, we keep walking. No one wants their fruit to brown, so only the chorus of crisp sounds of biting and chewing fill the air. Now that we've made it through the first day and night unscathed, there's actually a moment to appreciate the majesty of the forest.

The resplendent yellows, golds, and oranges cling to the birch trees, dousing us in a warm, glowing filter. Papery bits of their slender trunks curl underfoot along with the rocks and roots that mar the path. They flit harmlessly around our feet, rolling closer and scurrying away at the wind's mercy.

Henry Prior's notes might obscure the location of the wishing well, but at least he was clear that it's at the lowest elevation, which is lucky because none of us—except maybe Keiffer—are sturdy enough to go uphill. Even luckier that it's not summer, when bug bites and humidity would undoubtedly plague us.

Mom will be glad to know this trip has made one thing obvious: I am the opposite of outdoorsy.

"They're still obsessed with me," Kiara murmurs. She doesn't need to point to the black butterflies still trailing us for me to know exactly what she's talking about. Her resigned air is a dead giveaway.

"Isn't everyone?"

She side-eyes me. "I can't tell if you're joking or not."

I shrug. I can't help but be more mesmerized with what's happening *above* us than *between* us.

The butterflies aren't just circling her anymore, they're . . . Well, the best way I can describe it is that they're crowning her.

Do I tell her? No, I can't. It sounds so silly. And if they *are* a sign of wonder, then I'm the last person who would be able to see them. Unless, somehow, my sense of wonder is returning? Would I even be aware of it if it was? I don't *feel* any different. I peer at the butterflies. Their numbers have grown at least double what they were before, and now they're almost militant in their devotion.

Kiara makes a sound of frustration. "I don't get you sometimes, Nova."

"What's to get?"

"Are you being for real right now?" Her temper flares. "I thought we had a moment this morning."

Denying it feels like the coward's way out. But I can't let myself talk about my feelings because who knows what might come out of my mouth? What I could be tempted to say? Instead, I push the feelings away to a bottomless pit where they won't do any damage.

"I don't know how nobody else has said anything, but have they actually gotten into some kind of a formation?" I blurt out. "They're not even scared of us anymore. They're, like, claiming you."

Horror settles over her face then erases like an Etch A Sketch.

My brow wrinkles. "What was that?"

"Nothing."

"Kiara," I say in exasperation.

"You're avoiding things, well, so am I," she says. She waves her arms, being careful not to hit any of her little interlopers, and jams on a hat.

A hat I'd seen Tayla wearing yesterday.

Annoyance settles under my skin, hot and prickly. I open my mouth to tell her I don't even know what, but Keiffer's bellow of "Elevenses!" cuts me off.

"You know we're not actually hobbits, right?" But Radhika grins as she says it.

This time, when he throws me a chocolate chip granola bar, I don't catch it so much as get in its way.

"Shit!" Keiffer yelps. "Sorry, Nova! I thought you were paying attention!"

"It's fine. Not like you got me in the face or anything," I say dryly.

Kiara rips into hers and chews determinedly, as though she's prepared to ignore both me and the butterflies for as long as it takes. *I* might be content to let us sulk in silence, but the insects crowning her have no such scruples. By the time she's finished eating, enough of their brethren have joined that she's close to tears, and not even Tayla can coax a smile out of her.

Evan, also at a loss, starts picking off chocolate chips for her, but Kiara clutches them so tight that they melt in her palm, and she has to lick it clean. Seconds later, Evan and I exchange matching looks of concern when a bold butterfly lands on Kiara's sticky finger. With a frustrated shriek, she throws her arm out, all *shoo*, *shoo*, and crumples up on the ground like an old discarded scrunchie.

Tayla looks like she'd like nothing better than to go to her. "We have to keep moving," she says firmly, though not unkindly.

There's a wobble in Kiara's voice when she says, face buried under her arms, "I want to go home."

Keiffer and Radhika walk back to us. "We're probably nearer to the well than we are to town," says Radhika. "We can't turn back now, not when we're this close. We're—she's better off staying the course."

Damn Henry Prior for discovering the wishing well and not keeping his mouth shut about it. Damn the wannabe adventurers for setting off to find it, too, either giving up or getting lost before they do. Damn every single person who doesn't believe the cautionary tales and has the ego to think they'll be the exception.

Most of all, damn us for being here. Because of Kiara.

Because of me.

"Hey," I say.

While everyone else stands around helplessly, I have a move up my sleeve. Well, in my back pocket, but same thing. I reach back and pull out an acorn. It's warm from my body heat—or my butt, to be more exact, which is a little embarrassing as I offer it to Kiara.

"I found this on the ground a while back and thought of you. Acorns are supposed to be lucky, right?"

She takes it.

The second it's between her fingers, the butterflies scatter, fleeing in every direction. With open mouths, we all stare, following their flight until there isn't a single one left hovering around Kiara's head.

"*Wow.*" Evan's eyes are glazed over. "Shit, Nova. You fixed it."

Radhika blinks. "What just happened?"

"Nova happened," Keiffer says admiringly. "I haven't even seen a single acorn here. Figured the squirrels got them all. How did you know that thing about the acorns being lucky?"

"I . . . I must have heard it from Petra. Austin's grandmother."

Tayla meets and holds my gaze. "Pretty lucky you knew what to look for and happened to find one right when we needed it."

"She's my good luck charm," says Kiara. She rises with Tayla's help, teetering under the weight of her backpack. Her smile is the brightest thing I've seen since we entered this accursed place. "Told you, Nova."

"You certainly are full of surprises," Evan agrees but in a way that hints that there's something else they're not saying. It makes me wonder what they know or think they know.

"I mean, Keif's right. It's surprising a squirrel didn't already find it, add it to its winter hoard," says Tayla. "Since it was just on the ground like that. Guess you really are lucky."

"Why are you being so weird?" Kiara sounds incredulous. "The butterflies are gone thanks to her quick thinking. That's a *result*."

Latching on to her support, I quickly say, "I'm just glad I could help."

The last thing I need is for anyone to analyze what Tayla said. If anyone picks at that thread, thinks my finding the acorn is odd, what's to stop them from taking it further? From finding the assortment of charms in my pack? I mean, I could always tell them that I did all this in preparation. Just in case.

Dad was a big proponent of preparedness. *Be prepared, not scared.* But I can't stop my fingers from sliding between my wrist and the aventurine bracelet, the itch to let it snap against my skin. But fidgeting will make me look even more guilty, so I force myself to leave it alone.

Nobody knows about my hex. I'm just being paranoid.

Tayla smiles, but I don't trust it. "Yes, thanks, Nova. I know I speak for all of us when I say we're glad you're here. Being so . . . *helpful*."

As we troop forward, spirits buoyed by the successful banishment of the butterflies, unease drips down the back of my neck. Someone's boring holes in my back, someone's breath is too close as they stand over my shoulder. I turn, half expecting to see Tayla there, suspicious and grim-faced.

But no, she's ahead of me, walking with Kiara and Evan, who keeps up a steady stream of chatter as they point out mossy trees. Thank god for them having the knack of knowing the usefulness of a distraction.

I peek over my shoulder, hoping for a glimpse of *something* through the dense infinity of foliage.

I don't expect to see the eyes glowing back at me.

Not just a pair, but several, too many to count. I nearly trip over a root. The breath catches in my throat, and I swerve my gaze, too panicked to let them catch me looking. Throughout the morning, it had been all too easy to attribute that skin-crawling sensation to the butterflies, knowing they were lurking just out of sight. Easy to imagine that odd little insects were all we had to worry about.

Furtively, I squint back at the trees. I can hardly see anything from under my lashes, can't even tell if I *want* my suspicions confirmed or not. This is a first for me: half praying to be wrong for once.

I force my eyes fully open. Cast my gaze wider. *Don't blink, don't blink, don't blink.*

There's nothing there.

But instead of being relieved, my heart thrums with unease. Just because I can't see the eyes doesn't mean the eyes aren't on me, tracking me—*tracking all of us*—as we go deeper and deeper into the forest's dark throat. Gulping us down in one single swallow.

By some unspoken agreement we all fall silent, even Evan, who never seems deterred by anything. The nothingness is haunting, a warning all on its own. Can silence be loud? Be oppressive? My heart trips over itself like a Slinky going down a steep flight of stairs; I will it to stop.

I almost miss the butterflies, the muffled ferocity of their wings, their faithful presence. When we entered the forest, the silence had been cacophonous. I'd been afraid we were the only ones there. Now I'm afraid we *aren't*.

An abruptly cut off shriek shatters my thoughts.

Immediately, I do a headcount of the Fellowship.

Radhika and I come to the same conclusion at the same time. "Where's Kiara?" she asks.

Tayla's head swings all around, almost comical in the way she thinks a whole person could just vanish into thin air. Except . . . a whole person just did. "She was just here," she stammers. "I only took my eyes off her for a second. Just to tighten my laces."

Evan points to the disturbed ground, where roots stout as arms have reared up. "*They* took her."

19

"Don't be ridiculous, Evan. Those roots have always been there. They're as thick as Keiffer's bicep." Tayla cups her hands around her mouth and shouts, "Kiara?"

"No, they definitely weren't here a minute ago," I say, crouching to get a better look at them. "The ground is disturbed. Here, look. See how the dirt is crumbling in my fingers? All loose?"

"That . . . that doesn't mean anything," says Tayla, but she sounds less convinced. "Evan's just being dramatic and cryptic as usual."

"Why are you so unwilling to believe me?" they ask. "You know I'm not a liar."

"Because . . . because . . . look at where we are!" Tayla throws her hands in the air. "I've been seeing some weird things, too, and every time I think it's real, it turns out to be something totally ordinary."

"Like what?" I ask.

"Footsteps," she says flatly. "Shapes moving in the trees. Something rustling behind a bush. It was a deer once and Keiffer twice. Most of the time, just birds. Wild turkeys look ugly as fuck, but other than a couple of jump scares, they're harmless."

I can't tell whether she actually believes it or she's just trying to keep the Fellowship calm.

"Um. Now that we're having this conversation, has anyone heard, like, static? Radio static, maybe?" asks Keiffer. The question is for everyone, but he's looking at me.

"No, I keep my radio off to conserve power," I say. "Austin leaves his on all the time in case we need to radio in, but he's too far away for us to pick up any feedback or however that works."

"It's probably tinnitus," Radhika mumbles. "Keiffer gets it sometimes."

I'm not sure we should dismiss it so easily, but Keiffer doesn't seem inclined to pursue it. Anyway, now that I know I'm not the only one seeing discomfiting strangeness, I'm about to mention the eyes watching us from the darkness, but then my gaze snags on something familiar, small and polished smooth.

"Hey, I found something!"

The acorn is nestled in the ground between two crumbly rust-colored leaves, surrounded by the stamp of a hiking boot. Did Kiara drop it when she got snatched, or was she snatched because she dropped it?

"So much for luck," Tayla mutters, toeing aside the dead leaves.

"*Not helpful.*" A muscle twitches in Keiffer's jaw, like he's straining to hold back his fear.

Radhika looks like she might hyperventilate if Evan lets go of her. She leans into their side and does some complicated breathing exercise that involves counting and holding her breath.

"Did anyone other than Evan see what actually happened?" I ask, picking up the acorn. It's pitifully small in my palm.

Everyone shakes their head. The roots, if they'd played any part, are now dormant and lifeless.

Specks of dirt cling to the nut. Worrying it between thumb and forefinger, I hesitantly take a step to the left. When nothing happens, I take another. This time, the ground feels different. Less solid. I test it with another step, not trusting to give it my full weight.

When my stomach pitches into my rib cage, that's the first sign I've made a mistake.

The front half of my boot meets air, and I flounder, the backpack tipping me forward just enough to make me realize I'm on the precipice of what's clearly a hidden ledge. Frantic, I try to stumble back, my fist squeezing the acorn tight.

Then the ground gives way.

"Nova!" A hand wraps around my upper arm and yanks me back.

I crash into Tayla's body. It's a reflex to hug me, her front flush against my back. One of her hands digs into my bicep while the other is snug around my abdomen. She releases me just as quickly.

It takes what feels like minutes to recalibrate, but it must only be seconds. "Thanks. I could have—" I can't make my tongue form the word. Don't even want to think it. The depth of the trees was duplicitous, made us think we were shrouded on all sides when there was a stealthy drop-off here all this time. The terrain in this part of the forest does have some ups and downs, but this is way more *down* than I expected.

"But you didn't die. You were lucky." Tayla shoves her hands in her pockets.

I stare at the acorn then shove it into the front pocket of my jeans.

"And now," she says grimly, "we know what must have happened to Kiara."

"It must be erosion," I say, heart still beating erratically. My voice sounds simultaneously booming and distant, like it doesn't belong to me at all. "Explains why we're seeing more exposed roots. Plus, we're all loosening the soil as we walk. Who knows when this was last maintained by the forest services?"

Tayla and Evan are the slightest, so it makes most sense for them to look over the edge with the rest of us ready to grab them just in case. We divest ourselves of our packs, leaving them scattered on the ground behind us.

"Kiara!" Evan shouts.

Tayla repeats the call, hers more of a scream.

We all wait, hearts in our throats.

Nothing.

Evan tries again, hands cupped around their mouth to amplify calling Kiara's name a dozen more times before giving up. "I can't see anything down there," they admit. They pick at their chapped bottom lip until Radhika swats their hand away and offers up a tube of lip balm.

"I can't, either," says Tayla. She rubs her face, but it's not to mask her tears. Her cornflower-blue eyes zigzag with angry red lines. She blinks in quick succession. Frustration roughens her voice as she grits out, "If I even try to focus on one place for too long, the trees drown my vision. My eyeballs burn."

Everyone has their own ideas on what we should do next.

Keiffer thinks he should climb down. Radhika disagrees. *It's too dangerous, you don't know how far down it is, you've never free-climbed before, we don't have any rope.* She's right. It's not a good idea. None of us have the upper-body strength to haul him back up, and we'd probably pull our shoulders out of our sockets if we tried.

Evan's willing to keep moving, see if there's a better place to descend, but Tayla nips that in the bud. *What if you get lost and then we have to rescue both of you, what if something happens to you and we don't know where you ended up, what if what if what if—*

I squeeze the acorn so hard I'd be surprised if there isn't a small crater in my palm. "What if Kiara got hurt in the fall? The longer we stand here arguing, the longer she's all alone, scared and maybe injured."

The question crashes over the overlapping voices, smothering the squabbling.

The question has stunned them. Or maybe it's the fact that it's *me* doing the practical asking.

While the others gnaw their lips and look shamefaced, Tayla eyes with me with new respect.

"I'm going to go after her," I announce. "Who's coming with me? We're sticking to the buddy system. No one should go anywhere by themselves."

"Then I'll go," says Tayla before anyone else can volunteer. "It should be me." She nods decisively. "Keiffer, you're in charge while I'm gone."

Radhika's jaw drops. "Um, excuse me? Who elected you head bitch?"

"It's self-appointed," Evan says blithely.

Keiffer pinches the bridge of his nose between two fingers and releases a long breath. "No one is 'in charge' of the others." He gestures to Radhika and Evan. "We make decisions as a group."

If it wasn't for time being of the essence, I get the impression Tayla would have loved to argue against it, but she presses her lips together and gives a stiff shrug.

We quickly redistribute the food and medical supplies, mostly some gauze to wrap a sprain, antibiotic ointment, and over-the-counter painkillers. Even though I already have a flashlight, Keiffer gives me his along with a ripped-open pack of batteries.

"What about you?" I ask, hesitating to accept them.

"The others have a few batteries. And the flashlight, well, it never hurts to carry a spare. The next time you or Tayla think you see something moving in the trees, shine a light on it. Get confirmation."

"Keif, if I think I see something, I'm going to pretend it doesn't exist so hopefully *it* doesn't realize *I* exist." As an afterthought, I add, "And hopefully it's a vegetarian."

While he snorts with nervous laughter, Radhika gives

Tayla one of the two flares she slipped into her backpack "just in case." Honestly, Radhika Rose never ceases to surprise me. All of Kiara's exes have way more substance than I ever knew.

"Hmm, that's strange. I could have sworn I packed my poncho," Evan says distractedly as they zip up their pack. They rock back on their heels, puzzled. "I wanted you to have it."

I glance at what little we can see of the sky. "Doesn't look like it's going to rain."

"The weather forecast said there was a chance of drizzles all week."

Despite the crappy situation, their blasé comment startles a laugh out of me. *"And you believed it?"*

Evan shakes their head like they're sweeping away cobwebs. "I'm glad you're here," they murmur as they stuff trail mix in my pack. "You cut through the noise and told us what we needed to hear. The four of us don't always . . . let's just say we don't have cooperative personalities."

I remember what Kiara told me about their friction. "Someone would have eventually."

"That someone was you." They give me a serene smile. "There, all done."

"Both aspirin and ibuprofen are pain relivers, fever reducers, and anti-inflammatories," Radhika says, launching into a crash course on dosage. For once, Tayla doesn't think she's the smartest person in the group and listens intently instead of insisting she can just read the labels on the bottles.

"Between you and Keiffer, you've got the whole STEM

power couple thing down pat," I say, impressed despite our urgency. "I'm not even going to ask why you have enough to clean out a Walgreens."

She manages a weak smile. "I get terrible periods and headaches."

"Me, too," Evan grumbles, making a face.

I make a sympathetic sound. I'm lucky my cycle finished the week before the Fall Festival. I would be miserable being this physically active while cramping and worrying about leaks, let alone the question of how we'd even dispose of the soiled sanitary products. Burying them with the trowel doesn't feel very much like leaving no trace.

Radhika pats her bulging backpack, which now holds most of my clothes, a mini candy bar stash, and a couple of squashed clementines. "I've got all the period-havers covered. Tampons, pads, a couple heat packs. Even some condoms if, you know, anyone needs them."

Admiringly, I say, "You really *did* clean out a Walgreens."

Evan laughs and fishes a Twix from the bag, ripping into it. "She's practicing for the apocalypse."

Belatedly, Radhika's words register, and I gawk. "Wait, condoms? Uh, you do realize that you and Keiffer are the only couple here! Did you think we were going to pick up random camper dudes in the woods? One, unsafe. Two . . . *Ew, Radhika!*"

She exaggerates a haughty sniff. "I may not have been in the scouts, but I believe in being prepared."

Swallowing a mouthful of candy bar, Evan says, "I'm with Nova. Zero percent likelihood of any of us hooking up with a sketchy someone we come across. I don't want twigs and bugs in weird places, thank you very much."

I shoot them a smile of solidarity as they wander over to join Keiffer.

"Good job on the flares, though," I tell Radhika. "Thanks for even thinking to bring them, by the way. I don't know if any rangers will see it, but hopefully if we run into any trouble, someone will."

"Nova, I . . ." She seems to struggle. "You know I'd come looking, right?"

"It's okay. Tayla and I already decided we'd go."

"No, I mean, if you set off the flare. I know our branches of the family tree never really got along, and I know your dad's aunt opposed my dad's parents publishing *The Way of the Wish*. And I also know we don't share any DNA, considering that my dad's father was adopted, and my mom's family emigrated from India when she was a teenager, but . . ."

"Radhika, you're rambling."

She huffs. "Nova, I'm trying to say we're family. Kind of. In spirit. So I'd come help you."

My heart crunches at the unexpectedly sweet sentiment. Other than Dad's aunt, who left him Chalice, I've never had extended family. Mom and Dad were only children who had only one child, me. Radhika, on the other hand, is the youngest of the Rose brood and has family on this continent and several others. She doesn't share any blood with me, but she still claims me as family. Even if it's only kind of, in spirit.

It's more than I've ever had before.

"And also because you know if you abandoned us, Tayla's ghost would totally be up for some vengeful haunting," I say.

Radhika grins. "Also that."

The goodbyes are quick, and when Keiffer releases me from his one-armed hug, he turns away to swipe at his eyes. "Be safe," he says for the tenth time.

"Don't kill each other," Evan adds for the eighth.

"Give that book another once-over," I say to Radhika. "Maybe you'll have it all figured out by the time we're back with Kiara." It's supposed to encourage her, but instead, a shadow crosses over her face. "Hey," I say, squeezing her shoulder. "You've got this."

"Nova, about the book . . ." She sucks her teeth. "There's something I've been meaning to tell you."

Finally. I've been waiting for her to admit that the book is basically useless and she's been bullshitting all her authority about it.

But before Radhika can say anything else, Tayla surprises us both by elbowing me aside in order to throw her arms around both Radhika and Evan.

"Take care of each other," she says in as stern a voice as I've ever heard, but she holds on to them like she doesn't want to let go, even when they drop their arms first. "Come on, Nova."

20

When we walk away, our steps drag. And when we go far enough that we round the corner and lose sight of our friends, the whole world seems darker, like all the light is sucked out, leaving the air stale and hopeless. It even smells different now. Less greenery, more . . . what is that odor? Rot? Decay?

Tayla glances up. "Is it just me or . . . ?"

"It's not just you."

"Maybe a sign of wonderment?"

Wonderment? In this place?

Crinkling my nose, I say, "Uhhh, more like nightmarish bad omens."

She cocks her head.

"I mean, just look around us. Barely any sunlight. Poisonous snakes. Stalker butterflies. Roots that maybe come alive? Eyes watching you?" I scoff. "Please, tell me what about the forest screams 'wonderment'? More like 'Here lies some scary shit that will probably definitely kill you, turn around, go home, stay the fuck away.'"

She laughs then bites her lip and guiltily slides her gaze back to the trail. It feels wrong to laugh when Kiara could be in danger, and my own smile dims. I won't make the mistake of thinking I'm sharing a moment with Tayla again. We're never going to be friends.

For several minutes, or maybe more, our walk passes in silence. We don't wear watches, and we don't have our phones, and the nonexistent sun hardly illuminates the passage of time. The trees close in around us, and though we don't see them, every so often, carried over a great distance, come the faint caws of a crow, the battle cry of a falcon. Once, I think I see something streak past us under the cover of the trees, but it's gone so fast that I wonder if I imagined it.

"You really didn't see the roots grab Kiara?" I ask. "It's just, we're all a little on edge, right? It makes sense your mind would seek to rationalize what you saw. And Evan seemed pretty sure."

Her shoulders hike up. At first I think she's going to ignore me, but then she says, somewhat reluctantly, "It happened too fast. I can't trust what I thought I saw."

My breath hitches. "So then you *did* see the roots—"

Tayla cuts me off. "My turn," she says. "Did you *really* find that acorn on the forest floor?"

"Uh, yeah? Where else would it come from?"

"Dunno. Maybe you brought it with you."

I scoff. "Yeah? You see me pull it from my pocket or something?"

She sets her jaw. "No. But the ground is picked clean. Do *you* see any lucky acorns lying around for the taking?"

"They're not 'lucky acorns,' they're just acorns. The nut itself is what makes it lucky."

Her mouth opens to fire back a retort, but I clap my hand over it. "*Shhh!* Did you hear that?"

I'm not wholly convinced she won't bite me, but she shakes her head at my question, eyebrows pinching together. I slowly release her, holding up my palms as I back away. The noise is louder now, almost as if it's approaching us, but I can't pinpoint the exact direction. It's a spinning, whirring sound. Smooth. Like a . . .

"Does that sound like a fan to you?" I whisper. There's nothing that can make that kind of sound out here. Maybe cicadas, but we saw the last of them in late September, and now it's October.

"More like the rotor blades of a helicopter," Tayla says.

My eyes widen. "How do you know that?"

"Before we moved here from California, my dad was an air ambulance pilot. Mom was his flight nurse. That's how they met. Trust me, I know what an aircraft sounds like."

"Think they're medevacing someone? From here?"

"Take a look around. We're surrounded by dense forest. Where exactly is a helicopter going to land?"

She makes a good—if somewhat bitchy—point. "Okay, so what if it's search and rescue? Looking for heat signatures? I don't know. Someone could be in trouble."

"Someone is. *Kiara.*"

"Right, I just meant—"

"Stop jumping at every strange sound and *get a move on*, Nova. I swear, you're worse than Keiffer!"

It's clear I've exhausted her patience by the way she strides forward, her pace brisk to make up for lost time. The way she just *expects* me to follow gets my hackles up. Every second in her presence infuriates me. The way Tayla's personality veers between doting and abrasive makes my head spin. She can be fair, yes, but I'm starting to suspect it's only when it happens to align with her own plans.

Once again I find myself bemoaning that I'd ever crushed on her. Okay, fair, Tayla doesn't get what Kiara sees in me, but what does Kiara see in *her?*

Is she going to get back with Tayla when we return to Prior's End? There's a chill in my blood as I contemplate this. I will be so pissed with myself if she gets back with Tayla before I have a chance to kiss her. *Nova, stop it. It's none of your business. You didn't even kiss Kiara this morning when you had a chance. When she was looking at you with all the longing in the world.*

I know why I didn't. I know why I never told any of my crushes that I liked them in time, before Kiara got to them first. Because deep down I don't think I deserve happiness. Not when I'm responsible for ruining my parents'. Unless I bring Dad back with me, there won't be any graying twilight years for Jules and Rhea, only a snipped thread of fate severed forever.

We walk on and on and on in a ceaseless march. The next sound that breaks the silence is my stomach's sharp complaint. We break only long enough to refill our water bottles with cool spring water and eat salted almonds and dried mango slices. Tayla has black licorice she doesn't offer to share, so I don't offer her my peanut M&M's, either. Then we're on our way again, mindful of the uneven terrain below us and the glaring tension between us.

I miss the others. Their friendly squabbling, the nonstop chatter. It's easier to forget where we are and what else could be lurking out there when I hear Keiffer's rumbling laughter, Evan's witty quips, and Radhika's mutterings as she tries to decipher what the book *isn't* revealing about the wishing well.

I find myself dwelling on what she was going to tell me before Tayla interrupted. Was it that our Prior heritage and her precious book haven't done us any favors? Or something else entirely? Another reason to be annoyed with Tayla. Even when she's not trying, she gets between people.

An insect flies past my cheek, and I swat it on reflex. I'm surrounded by pests, *truly*.

I'm trying to pick what I think is a mango fiber out of my teeth when I hear my name.

Nova . . .

The voice is deep, hoarse, like a voice rusty with disuse. I bite the meat of my inner cheek. I taste blood. "Tayla," I say, tongue thick and feeling far too big for my mouth. "Did you say something?"

She answers without breaking stride. "No? Why?"

I'm about to tell her then decide against it. "Never mind. Can we stop for a minute? I think it would be a good idea to tell my friends that we split up from the others. Just in case."

"Fine, but hurry up. I'll go on ahead and see if I can find a vantage point or something."

I don't want her to leave me, but I want to show weakness even less. I find a trunk to rest against and pull my walkie-talkie from my backpack. Knowing that I'm holding our one link to civilization is both terrifying and comforting at the same time.

Turning it on, I'm relieved that it still has plenty of juice. "Austin? It's me."

I settle against the rough bark and work out some stiffness in my neck. Trying to keep my eyes peeled all the time, swiveling my head here and there, it's no wonder.

Within moments, he's joined me on the channel. "Nova! Good to hear your voice. Wasn't expecting it so soon, though. Everything okay?"

Now that I hear his voice, words fail me. If I tell him what happened to Kiara—the absolute unnatural, unreal confusion of it all—he's going to send help. All of us will be brought back to Prior's End by well-meaning adults who will never, ever let me out of their sight again, and there goes my last chance of finding my dad.

Tayla and I will find Kiara. I truly believe that. Even if rescuers set out this very minute, they'd be two days behind. Right now, we have a head start. I know it's irresponsible, but for all I know, even while I'm having this conversation, Tayla will make headway, be the heroine, and save the day.

"Nova? You there?"

"Yeah, everything's fine. Tayla just heard a chopper overhead, and we wondered if you'd seen one leaving town? Heading for the Longing Woods?"

There's some muffled discussion in the background before Caroline's voice chimes in. "No, we haven't seen or heard one. We did encounter some other folks on their way out, though."

"Yeah? Any of them mention stuff going missing on their hike?"

"A guy thought his car had been broken into," Austin says. "But this was at the trailhead, and it was just some spare cash from the glove compartment. But we didn't really chat."

"Oh, okay. Just asking. We've been losing some things, but I guess it's easy to leave something behind when we're on the move all the time."

"For sure," says Caroline. "How's Kiara?"

"She's . . . hanging in there."

With promises to check in again soon, we say goodbye. They both sounded happy and relaxed, which hopefully means by the time I'm back, they'll have gotten over friend code and finally made a move on each other. The thought is my one sliver of brightness in the otherwise dismal day.

As I zip up my pack, I hear it again. *Nova . . .*

Tayla's too far away, and I don't think she's the type to sneak up and scare me for a laugh. I stand slowly, bringing my backpack with me as a shield. Cautiously, I peer behind the tree trunk. Nothing and no one there. Feeling silly, I wear my backpack properly.

Nova . . . it's me.

My lips part in shock. "D-Dad?"

You . . . go . . . wishing well . . . trouble . . . help . . .

I look down at the radio in confusion. It's still on. The disjointed words scratch their way from the radio. He's in trouble? He wants me to go to the wishing well? Something deep inside me renews.

Raising the radio to my lips, I say, "Dad? How do I get to the well? Help me, please."

I get Caroline instead. "Hey, did you say something? We were, um—"

Austin says something so faint I can't even hear it, but it makes Caroline giggle.

"Oh, sorry," I say. "I didn't mean to interrupt anything."

The slow trickle of hope, dripping from a leaky tap, shuts off. Leaving me with nothing. Less than nothing. Because this is worse than if it never happened at all. It's not Dad on the other end, if it ever was.

"No, it's fine!" Another giggle. "I just thought I heard you say something."

"Yeah, no. Your radio must have just picked up some background noise on my end. I forgot to turn it off. Sorry."

"Stay safe!" Austin shouts, and I promise I will before switching the radio off. For sure this time.

"So stupid," I mutter, stashing it back in my backpack. "Like it's really going to be Dad."

21

I find Tayla more or less where she said she would be. She certainly did find a vantage point. I just didn't expect it to be up a tree.

"See anything?" What I really mean is *Do you see Kiara*, but I can tell from the unhappy tilt of her mouth that she doesn't.

"No luck," Tayla admits. She moves with sinewy, feline grace to reach the ground again, and her palms are dirty and scraped, but she doesn't even seem to notice. "Couldn't get high enough. Haven't climbed a tree since I was ten, but I read something in Radhika's book about changing perspective when you run into a seemingly insurmountable problem, so I thought—"

"What did you just say?"

"I said I thought the height would—"

"No, not that." I flap my hand at her. "The part about the book. Changing perspective."

"Why are you being weird?"

The laugh startles out of me. How do I even begin to explain? Hearing one of my dad's catchphrases coming out of her mouth, of all people, is horribly incongruous and unreal. All along, every step of the way, I thought I was carrying so many of my dad's lessons that they would protect me. Protect all of us. And now it doesn't seem like enough. Doesn't seem like mine anymore. A sense of loss pierces through my possessiveness, and just like that, the illusion of protection between me and the forest irreparably fractures.

"I'm not being weird," I say automatically. Unsteady as I feel, I manage to get out, "What you just said about changing perspective is something my dad used to say. How is it in Radhika's book?"

Tayla looks taken aback. "I . . . I don't know. I did think it was odd at the time. It was one of the notes in the margin, but it wasn't in her handwriting. It was like, why is she using an old used copy?"

When the answer lands, it's with a wallop. "Do you remember the color of the pen?"

She doesn't ask me how I know the notes were in ink, not pencil. "Pink gel," she says. "She uses it for everything. But the other writing was in red."

Shock prevents me from speaking. It's my dad's book. It *has* to be. It's his red ink. Why does Radhika have my dad's book with his notes in red ink? *How* does she have it?

"Hey, Nova. You okay? You've gone the color of skim milk."

I barely register the question. The chopper sound is back, but this time it's buzzing in my ears, loud as the drone of a lawnmower. My thoughts jumble, and my brain auto-plays a highlight reel of every moment I've had with Radhika. The ones I thought were nice that meant we were friends.

I was wrong.

"Shit!" Tayla yelps. "Nova, *move!*"

I see her mouth move, but I don't understand what she wants me to do. Move?

"For fuck's sake!" She yanks my hand and pulls me after her. "Run!"

It takes a second for my legs to move, so I ungainly stumble after her. My neck still hurts, but I turn over my shoulder to see what's got her so spooked.

It's a whole-ass murder of crows. Their shaggy black wings flap furiously, their caws piercing shrieks that punch through the fog in my mind. There are hundreds of them, screeching and soaring right for us.

"Not a chopper!" I yell.

It feels like she's about to pull my arm out of my socket as we scrabble over fallen branches, rocks sticking out of the earth, and tangles of vines and weeds. "Read the forest, Nova! Gloat about me being wrong when we're *not* about to be pecked to death!"

To be honest, I hadn't even thought about that likelihood until she said it. The razor-edged cawing is fierce and nonstop, nothing like the inquisitive and probing caw-caw communication calls that are common around Prior's End. Are the crows fleeing from a predator or do they think *we're* the threat?

They're flying fast, gaining on us. Tayla's legs are longer, and I'm panting as I try to match her pace, but she has us going in a straight line. At this rate, they'll overtake us. We need to get off the path, *now*.

The moment I see a place for us to hide, I yank Tayla's hand. "This way!"

Thankfully, she doesn't dig her heels in when I veer to the right, squeezing her fingers so hard she has no choice but to go with it. I push her under a heavy broken branch of a tree so big that it must have just been a sapling during Henry Prior's time. This tree appears damaged by a storm from a long time ago, creating a stub that sticks out horizontally from the trunk. Now, it provides the perfect hiding place.

My breath comes out hard and fast as we huddle together, waiting out the danger. Tayla's face is bright pink, glowing with a sheen of sweat. She squeezes my thigh. "Do. Not. Make. A. Peep."

"Thanks for stating the obvious," I mutter, though it's quiet enough she doesn't hear me.

The birds whoosh past, their screams boring into my brain. Either we were just in their way, or they still think they're pursuing us. Regardless, we stay frozen for what feels like an eternity.

I scooch out first, back aching as I straighten. The smell of decay is strong here, and it only takes a glimpse of the tree to see why. Enormous clusters of white mushrooms have popped up in the gaping wound left behind by the stub, along with a few other creepy crawlies. If the damage is so forgotten and out of sight here, I shudder to imagine the state of the other trees nearby.

Why haven't the rangers closed this trail and started to

take care of the forest in this area? That being said, it explains the dead smell that greeted us this morning . . .

Was it just this morning? It feels like it's been so much longer than just a couple of hours.

Head still spinning that we came out of this unscathed, I offer Tayla a hand up, and she takes it.

"Signs of nightmarish bad omens, indeed," Tayla says with a slightly hysterical laugh.

"First chance we get, we find a different path," I say. "The trail degradation here is too dangerous, and I don't think we'll find Kiara if we keep going in this direction."

"What makes you say that?"

"Well, crows are scavengers."

I can tell it doesn't compute from the blank look on her face. "You know, they're not picky? Insects, berries, eggs. They'll eat anything, including carrion."

"You'll have to spell this one out for me," she says, pursing her lips as if annoyed.

"Carrion. Dead animals, Tayla. That many crows together? They've probably found dinner." I hesitate. "Or is it lunchtime? Anyway, we should probably go in the opposite direction."

Her eyes widen.

"It's *not* Kiara," I say, seeing where her thoughts went. "Crows will strip a carcass down to the bone, they'll gouge out the soft parts first, like the eyes, but—" Seeing her wan face, I hastily say, "Okay, sorry, forget I said all that. What I meant to say is it hasn't been more than, like, a couple of hours? A body needs way, way, way longer than that to decompose. So trust me, there's no way it's Kiara."

"I hope you're aware that nothing that just came out of your mouth was comforting," says Tayla.

"And yet it put your mind at ease?" I ask hopefully.

"If imagining other dead campers' decomposing bodies is soothing, sure."

"You're impossible. You know that, don't you?"

"Just get my map out," she grouses, turning around so I can open one of her backpack pockets. "We'll figure out another trail that takes us to a lower elevation. Do it fast before the next creature that wants to kill us comes along and I have to save you again."

"Again? What do you mean, *again*?" I pull out the map and rezip her. "I just saved you."

She snatches the map from my hand so fast I get a papercut on my middle finger. "I don't recall it happening that way. We're currently two–nil. If we're keeping score." Then she unfolds the map, straightens it out, and whips it up in front of her face. "Which I am."

While she hems and haws without any input from me, my racing heart tries to make sense of my new knowledge. Was Radhika trying to tell me about having my dad's book before Tayla unceremoniously hustled me away? Another reason to be pissed at her. The list is growing exponentially, it seems.

As we head to a new trail—one that's intended to lead us

to the lowest terrain in the forest short of the underground caves that have long collapsed—I have plenty of time to mentally review all the times someone asked Radhika for her book and the ways she found to avoid handing it over. It just doesn't make sense.

Mom hasn't given away any of his clothes or books. I suspect that will be the next phase of *moving forward*, but for now, his belongings are still stored in large plastic latch boxes in Mom's closet. No, I can't imagine where on earth Radhika would have found it. Short of breaking in, of course, but that's a reach. If she found the book, why wouldn't she return it to me?

Ahead, Tayla's feet start to drag. We're moving slower. She must be as tired as I am if she's given up on that brisk march. I take a swig of my water then clip it back to my backpack. Is the quiet as unsettling to her as it is to me? Never thought I'd say this, but I almost miss hearing weirdness creeping around in the underbrush. This calm makes me feel like something bad is about to happen. It's a feeling I can't shake, and after everything else we've had the misfortune of coming across, I'm trusting my instincts.

Neither of us wants to say it, but finally, I broach, "Do you think we should head back?"

Her finely arched red brows shoot up as if she's surprised by the question. "It's barely been—" She stops, and from the intense concentration furrowing her forehead, I can guess she's attempting to do the math. But it's impossible to get right. "Well, I don't know how long *exactly*, but it's too soon to give up."

"Who said anything about giving up? We regroup, put our heads together, come up with a new plan."

"We've come this far," she says, adding dismissively, "You go back if you want."

Frustration makes me forget myself. "Do you have to make everything a competition?" I snap.

"Coming from you? That's rich."

Setting my jaw, I demand, "What does that even mean?"

"Nova, you *are* the competition."

Oh, this girl is going to make my dentist so pissed. I can practically feel my molars grinding into dust.

"If I let myself like you," she says, "I'll forget that. So. You see our impasse."

"I do not," I hiss. "It doesn't have to *be* like that, Tayla. We don't have to fight over a girl. Kiara will pick who she'll pick. Honestly, we both know who it will be."

She scoffs and eyes me with something like venom. "Yeah, we do."

"What is *that* supposed to mean?"

"Forget it. If you're going to play naive, there's no point."

On longer legs, her strides quicken until I'm forced into an awkward hop just to keep pace. Is she seriously implying that Kiara likes me more than her? Yeah, there's no way.

"Would you just come to your damn senses and talk to me like an actual person, please?" I ask.

"I will *not* come to my damn senses."

"Do you even hear yourself?" I'm about to open my mouth

to insist she elaborate when muffled voices wind their way back to us. Tayla and I freeze.

"I'm telling you, I heard it," a girl insists, sounding breathless.

"You hear something every day." This second speaker is a boy with a deep timbre that doesn't eclipse his mirth. "After all this time, you're still scared of the fauna out here. Remember how you ran from that wild turkey?" His chuckle echoes throughout the forest.

"Shut up, Brian. That was literally forever ago. You know it's not the wildlife I'm afraid of."

"Yeah." A long exhale. "I'm sorry, baby. I'm just . . . tired of this."

The girl doesn't reply right away, and when she does, she ignores the apology and doggedly continues. "It was a girl's scream. We should find her. Before anything else does. It's been ages since we've come across anyone. We *need* to."

"Emily, it's probably nothing. Some first-time hiker saw a snake or something. Even if you did hear someone, it was just the one scream, right? So they're fine. They're already on their way."

"Why are you trying to dissuade me?"

"Did you ever stop to think that maybe *I* don't like—"

Brian's words dwindle into nothing as they come face-to-face with me and Tayla. "Hey," he says slowly, blinking at us both like he's not sure we're real.

Emily sizes us up. "Did one of you scream about an hour ago?"

The fuck? Tayla and I exchange wary glances. We were way off. It's only been an hour? Can't be. It feels like it's almost been a full day. We should be close to sunset. But why would they lie?

"Was it seriously only an hour ago?" Tayla asks.

"Yup," says Emily. She smiles slyly. "We've gotten pretty good at telling the time."

"You don't have a phone or a watch?" Tayla presses.

"Oh yes," Brian says. "We have the new iPhone."

Emily smiles brightly. "The fifteen."

"That's . . . not the newest model," says Tayla.

"Oh, that's right." Emily laughs.

Up close, neither Brian nor Emily look how I expected. I'd imagined them as adults who thought it'd be a fun date to go on a couple's hike and swiftly realized they weren't cut out for it. Cue the grumpiness and arguments. Emily still looks like she's gearing up for one, but in a yappy terrier kind of way.

Her skin is pale white, almost chalky, making the shadows under her wide eyes look even darker. I scan her up and down. Thin, overplucked eyebrows, jeans with an unfashionably low waist, and a silver metallic scarf threaded through the loops. The scarf is dingy and wrinkled, the ends damp, like she just dunked it in a stream and wrung it out hard. Belly button pierced with a pink cubic zirconia stud. She's petite, maybe just a couple inches over five feet, and looks like she's our age.

Brian is a bit older, maybe a high school senior. Brown

skin, luxuriously thick hair with bangs that fall in his eyes. His voice is hoarse and deep, and there's no stubble on his face. He wears a Vanderbilt University sweatshirt, collar and sleeves a bit frayed. It's lumpy, a size too big, giving him the impression of having borrowed his dad's old college duds. It hangs off him, looking like it hasn't been washed in days.

He's handsome but seems utterly unaware of it, which usually makes someone sexier to me, but not this time. I rake my eyes over both of them. How long have they been out here? I know campfires can shoot out sparks that singe clothing, but there's no reason the arms of his sweatshirt should look as grayish and unwashed as they do.

"No," I say, finding my voice first. I glance between Brian and Emily. "That wasn't us, it was our friend. She . . . well, we don't really know what happened."

Mentioning the roots Evan thought they saw sounds . . . well, *I* wouldn't believe me, either.

Brian looks discomfited, but Emily lets out a bark of laughter. "Sounds about right," she says. "I'm sure she'll run into someone."

"Where are you coming from?" I ask.

"Oh, we were camping back there." She juts her thumb over her shoulder. "It's nice to meet you girls. We haven't seen anyone in ages." She grins at Brian. "I was starting to doubt we'd see any signs of life!"

He makes a noncommittal sound. "You should find your friend before it's too late."

Tayla arches a brow and readjusts the straps on her backpack. "You mean before it gets too dark?"

"Isn't that what I said?" he says in a tight voice. "Em, c'mon, we should—"

She cuts him off. "We'll help you look."

The obvious thing to do is thank them and accept their offer, but Tayla hesitates.

"Where are your backpacks?" I ask, suddenly realizing what's wrong with their appearance.

Emily sighs. "You know how treacherous it is in here. We lost ours yesterday in a fall."

Being out here is scary enough, but not having any food or equipment is even worse. Yet other than Brian's obvious discomfort, neither seems overly worried. "Shit. That sucks," I say sympathetically.

"And you didn't go back for your stuff?" Tayla sounds skeptical.

"We tried. It was too dangerous."

"*Em.*" Brian's voice is impatient. "Let them go."

"Do you need any provisions?" I ask, hooking my thumbs under my backpack straps.

Then I remember that our friends aren't too far away and could spare more than we can. Maybe even loan a tent. But something makes me hesitate. It's nothing they've said or done, but . . . something about Emily's story doesn't ring true. Tayla's eyes flash to mine like she knows exactly what I am thinking.

"No, we're good. We know our way around. Thanks, though," he says quickly.

"Hey, wait a second." Tayla gives them an apologetic smile. "I can't believe we forgot to mention this, but there was some bear activity the way we came."

I stiffen but say nothing.

"Thanks for the heads-up." Brian tugs at his girlfriend until she budges. "I hope you find your friend."

"Mm-hmm," I say. "Safe travels."

Emily smiles. "You, too."

Brian catches me staring. "Good luck." Biting his lip, he adds, "And be careful."

"Same," Tayla says. "Keep an eye out for that bear activity."

Her ability to lie so glibly, so cheerfully, makes my stomach tighten. What game is she playing?

"Will do." He looks like he wants to say something else, but his obvious desire to leave wins out, and the two of them disappear down a different path, this one even more unwelcoming than the one plagued by crows we trekked earlier.

I wait until I'm positive they're out of earshot before rounding on Tayla. "What did you do that for? We haven't seen a single bear. Freaky crows, check. Weirdo butterflies, check. Why didn't you ask them if they'd seen those things?"

"Me? *You* were about to offer up our limited resources, and you almost sent them straight to the others." Her glower rubs me the wrong way, like I'm the untrustworthy one.

My mouth falls open. I stare at her in disbelief. "So you decided to get them lost instead?"

"You heard Brian. They didn't need our help."

Her ability to justify her actions is truly something. "But—"

"Look, they creeped me out, okay?" When I don't push back, a satisfied smile curls her lips. "If you felt so strongly about my little lie, you could have spoken up. Why didn't you?"

Her question lands like a sledgehammer. "You just made me responsible for what happens to them!"

"No." Tayla towers over me, a scowl marring her pretty face. "*I told you*," she says, each word punching with emphasis. "No distractions. The only person you're responsible for is Kiara."

Responsible for Kiara. Her words knot in my belly, pulled tight enough to cramp. There's no way she can know . . . right?

"Like I told you when we set out," says Tayla, "you can go back if you want."

As she strides off, it strikes me: if this is a competition to her, then it's obvious that she wants to come out the winner for Kiara's heart.

The only question is . . . do I?

22

Time passes differently in this neck of the woods. Slow, sluggish. And what's most frightening is how my sense of timing was all off—that is, if Emily was right about hearing Kiara's scream only a whole hour ago. It wasn't like this yesterday. I felt every minute of walking. Every ache. Every stone underfoot. Every bump in the trail I almost tripped over. And when twilight fell upon us, I didn't question its arrival. I woke the next morning feeling like shit, but at least I knew it was morning. I could see the sun.

Tayla and I haven't seen the sun since we split from the rest of the Fellowship.

Is time preserved in this area? Is that why the tree we hid under is still strong despite the obvious rot and neglect? Is that even possible? Then again, why am I questioning what's possible when so much that should be impossible has already happened? My head hurts just thinking about it, and I don't have any of my oils with me. Kiara's massage feels like a lifetime ago.

"Did your dad ever lose track of time in the forest?" asks Tayla. It's the first sentence she's spoken since we parted ways with Brian and Emily.

I consider. "He spent a lot of time in here, studying the

ecosystem and stuff, and he was late sometimes, but it was an hour or two, tops. And he usually had Shane with him, so even if my mom was worried, it was regular worried and not *worried* worried."

"That's Austin's dad, right?"

"Mm-hmm."

"Do you think *he* went looking for the wishing well?"

Truthfully, I can't say. My memories of Shane are even muddier than memories of my dad. Shane was a man who found joy in the simplest of things, whose suntanned skin held so many laugh lines it looked like cracked earth. He had endless patience for children's poorly performed magic tricks, taught me how to make my first campfire s'mores, and threw my dad a surprise birthday party every year that we all saw coming a mile away. He was a good man.

But then he cheated on Austin's mom with a woman from one of his tours, and even though Austin and I were too young to really understand, we knew he never quite found his way back to his marriage. And now I think I know what Dad realized the night he left. Why Shane did *this foolish, foolish thing*.

"This one time when we were nine, our dads took us camping," I say. "And Austin and I put on this magic show. It wasn't very good because we weren't allowed to adopt one of those fluffy white bunnies Mrs. Honeywell breeds, and we were both sulky about our act being ruined. But our dads couldn't tell us ghost stories anymore, either, because Austin had nightmares for so long our moms forbid it."

Tayla snorts. "My brothers showed me R-rated horror movies when I was younger than that."

I ignore her. "So magic it was. I was the magician and Austin my long-suffering assistant. We were . . . what's a word that's even worse than 'horrible'?"

"Abysmal," she says without missing a beat.

"Thank you. Well, anyway, at the end of our act, Shane gave us a standing ovation, and he said one day, he and my dad would show us *real* magic. My dad got real quiet then and hustled us off to bed."

The memory is sharper, stronger, more vivid and lifelike than it has ever been before. It allows me a moment to observe the scene as if it's playing out in front of me. I'm picking up details with the clarity of a seventeen-year-old rather than a child. Tayla seems to grasp something momentous is happening because she stays blessedly quiet while I let the past wash over me, sepia soft.

"They must have been out there talking by the fire for hours because when I woke up for water, I could still hear them. I didn't think much of it then, but now I wonder if it was the wishing well that, I don't know, divided them? That's not the right word. They were like brothers. Nothing would ever truly *divide* them. But Dad believed in leaving the wishing well alone, and Shane didn't. I think Shane wanted to use its power to undo the mistake he'd made cheating on his wife. Because that was the only way he could see to make it right."

"He could have just worked through whatever it was," says

Tayla. There's such certainty and disdain in her voice. "My dad, Kiara . . . these are actual life-or-death problems. Shane was a cop-out. You can't just pretend your mistakes never happened."

I press my tongue against one of my canine teeth. "It's not always that simple."

She makes a dismissive sound. "Have you thought about what you'll do if you find Shane's remains?"

Remains is a nice way of saying *body*. And no, I haven't because frankly, the fear of finding the remains of my dad are about all I have energy to agonize about. Maybe that's also what Tayla, in her own way, is trying to get at. That I should be prepared for that eventuality.

"Why don't you ask me the right question, Tayla?"

"Meaning?"

Remembering Jules has unstuck one of his lessons:

When you find something that makes you question, that makes you change perspective, that's when you know you've found a sign of wonder.

"We're walking on eggshells," I say. "By Emily and Brian's reckoning, it's barely afternoon. Don't you question that? Doesn't it feel like we've been walking for a full day? Something is going on, and instead of facing it, we're acting like it's normal. This should be freaking you the fuck out because it sure is me."

"We have enough to freak out about," Tayla mutters. "So no, I'm not questioning it. We probably thought that time was passing a lot quicker than it actually did. It happens. Like the last five minutes before the bell rings and school lets out? Those five minutes feel like forever."

That's her final word on the matter. Frankly, I'm starting to get really resentful of the silence. Why is Tayla so afraid to admit the truth? First she sidestepped me questioning her about the roots and what she saw; now she's deluding herself that we're just *imagining* how long this day has been. It's not lost on me that there have been times I've run from the truth, too, but seeing that trait in someone else hits different.

I just hope her inability to reckon with reality doesn't come back to haunt us.

Every couple of minutes, we shout Kiara's name but never get a response. It's starting to feel a little hopeless, but after all her posturing, I'll be damned if I admit that before Tayla does.

We walk through the trees in the kind of hush that would make a graveyard seem raucous. So when she finally does speak, it's nearly swallowed in the silence. "How are you doing?"

I startle, only catching the end, the way her words lilt up.

"They must be pinching," she says matter-of-factly, nodding to my boots. "New ones always do."

I shrug. "I've gotten used to it." I haven't. But the hiking socks help wick and cushion my feet.

Without looking at me, she says, "If you've got blisters on the back of your heel, there are Band-Aids in the med kit Radhika gave us."

"You're scarier when you're being nice."

"Wasn't being nice. Can't have you slowing me down."

I sigh.

She cranes forward to check the other side of a fallen tree trunk before crossing over. "That sigh was pretty loaded, Nova." She surprises me by holding out her hand.

Eyeing her suspiciously, I take it and let her help me over. "Why do you say everything like it's a fight you're trying to win?"

She blinks. "Because I want to win?"

"That sounds . . . exhausting."

"I have seven siblings."

"What does that have to do with anything?"

"My parents have always encouraged us to be our best selves."

I take a moment to parse that. "You mean they raised you to compete with each other?"

She nods.

It sounds a little fucked up, if I'm being honest. But I suppose that at least they have each other. Solidarity. I imagine seven redheads all refusing to play petty games. "Guess you're pretty close to your siblings, then?" I ask.

She seems genuinely confused when she says, "Why would you think that?"

Riiiiight. We lapse back into silence for who knows how long until we come to a little clearing. It looks like someone's already set up there with a ragged tent that might have once been bright red at a crooked angle, zip abandoned halfway, letting in the elements.

The air on my arms prickles. Something feels off here and not just the kind of off that comes from the tension between me and Tayla. Unease slinks down my spine like a drip of cold water.

I don't want to take a single step closer, but I don't want her to think I'm a chicken, so I trail behind her as she examines the remains of the fire and watch as she rakes a stick through the charred black ash. "Didn't Brian and Emily say they camped out in this general vicinity?" she asks.

She phrases it like an idle question, but I know it's not. I shake my head. "This campsite is old."

"Hmm." Tayla pokes at a rusted pot until it tips onto its side and makes a sound of agreement. "What do you think Emily was so afraid of?"

I scoff. "Look at where we are. Take your pick."

"True." She sighs and throws the stick aside.

"We should have asked them why they were here."

"Obvious, isn't it? The wishing well. You saw his raggedy sweatshirt, right? He's probably hoping to get into Vanderbilt, make his daddy proud. And I bet Emily came to make a wish that she and Brian stay together forever." Tayla makes a face. "Do you know what it's like being that revoltingly into someone?"

Uh, pot, meet kettle? I stare at her a beat too long. "Nooooo."

She's already stopped paying attention to me. She's at the

tent opening now. Tugging at the zip, she scowls when it doesn't give way.

"Tayla, forget it. Let's go. This place gives me the creeps."

She huffs, struggling with the uncooperative zipper. "This entire forest is creepy. What else is new?"

"Think about it. Who just leaves their equipment behind like this?"

"Emily and Brian."

"Okay, besides them." I gesture at the tent, bleached pink by the sun. The caught zip, the old ashes, the rust on the pot. "Someone clearly never came back."

"Ha!" She turns around to give me a victorious grin. "Got it!" she crows, yanking the zipper down.

"Are you even listening to me?"

Suddenly, she turns to me, face screwed up. She presses a hand to her stomach like she's steadying herself, then lets it fly to her mouth as she grunts with disgust. "Fuck, it's foul."

The offending odor wafts out. It doesn't take long to hit me. It's like nothing I've smelled before. Mostly spoiled food and the unpleasant tang of mold and mildew and body odor. Cigarettes spilling out of the pack but no lighter. A broken handheld radio missing its batteries. Dead bugs pool in the corners of the tent, upturned beetles and lady bugs and moths with what look like eyes on their bent wings. Faded packets of colorful Fun Dip scattered at the foot of the sleeping bags, their nylon thoroughly gnawed.

I gag, stumbling backward. Even though the tent wasn't

sealed, the captured smell of decay and disuse lingered for what must have been years. Trapped and festering. The odors should have faded with the airflow, but it's been left stagnant. I can taste the noxiousness in the back of my throat.

"Nothing happened to these people," Tayla says hoarsely. "There weren't any backpacks in there. They just packed up and left. We should keep moving, too."

"Packed up?" I'm incredulous. "This mess they left behind isn't exactly 'Leave No Trace,' Tayla. We should take a look at the expiry dates on the food. It's our only clue to how long the tent's been here."

"This is exactly why I said no distractions!" she snaps. "Whatever happened to them, it was ages ago. We can't help them. Like, I'm pretty sure this predates us being born, Nova. We have one job, just one, and you're chasing all this crap that doesn't even matter!"

"Other people matter," I say stubbornly. "And *you're* the one who starting poking around and investigating here! But the second *I* want to take a closer look, you cut me short!"

"The *only* person we should care about right now is Kiara. Do you even give shit about her?"

"Of course I do! I wouldn't be here if I didn't."

"Then quit chasing ghosts and focus on getting the girl." She stomps past me, kicking the pot into the trees, where it's swallowed up immediately. Without waiting to see if I'm following her, she flings herself back in the direction we were heading.

I scramble after her, terrified she'll disappear like the pot. Shame swells in my chest as I replay Tayla's words. Sure, that campsite freaked me out, but I *did* let myself get distracted by the mystery. By the fear. By nameless, faceless people who might be just fine, thirty years older, sitting cozy at home and laughing about that one time they camped in the forest and were so terrified they fled without packing up.

"*Here!*"

At Tayla's shout, I realize she's found a place where we can clamber down the side. Frankly, it's not ideal. As she starts to descend, the dirt shifts, crumbling away under her boots.

"It's not going to support your weight," I say, thrusting out my hand to haul her back up.

"*I—can—do—this.*"

Her desire to be in charge, to best everyone else, to be the smartest in the room is going to kill us both. I grab her wrist, hoping it won't get dislocated if it has to support her body weight if the slope collapses. To be safe, I grapple with her forearm, wrapping my fingers around it tight. "Just take my hand!"

"I'm not scared! I'm fine! I can do thi—*ahhhhh*!"

"Tayla!" I shriek.

She doesn't fall far. And when she lands more or less safely, even though it's on her ass, we're both embarrassed. She hurriedly makes a show of looking all around, getting her bearings, but I'm pretty sure it has more to do with hiding her pink cheeks from me.

She plants her hands on her hips. "Well, what are you waiting for, Nova?"

I roll my eyes. *Of course* she has to sound like this is what she meant to do all along.

My own descent is less dramatic but no less ungainly.

I brush off where the loose dirt has clung to my jeans, wincing at the state of my nails. The once impeccable black polish, shot through with just a hint of midnight-blue glitter, is starting to chip, specks of dirt lodged so deep under the nail that even picking at them doesn't help.

My whole body is clammy and sticky, and I'd like nothing better than to peel off all my clothes and take a hot, bracing shower. I'd even take a body wipe, but I don't have one, and I'm definitely not wasting my drinking water. I've never felt so gross in all my life, and that's counting the gym days when I actually participate.

I drop my hands to my side before Tayla notices and makes a dig. That's the last thing I need.

"Do you still have that acorn, Nova?"

I feel for it in my pocket, relieved to find the familiar lump. "Yeah, why?"

"Because I think we just got lucky."

I follow the direction of her grin. While we had to make our own way down the rocky slope, from here there are low, flat slabs of stone, worn smooth with the years. "Someone made stairs?"

"Someone made stairs," she says, a silly grin overtaking her entire face. "Mind if I take the lead?"

She does so before I can make so much as a peep.

As far as wins go, our find is a pretty glorious one. The path down isn't totally without pitfalls, but we're riding on an adrenaline high, invincibility coursing through our veins. Finally, we have hope.

"Watch out here," says Tayla, pointing to a dangerous step.

"Thanks."

In some places, the stone has cracked, jagged edges big enough to trip on. The steps are polished, slick with rainfall that never reached us. Moss and weeds choke the stone, brushing our ankles as we pick our way down on nimble feet, careful not to step on the flora or, worse, lose our balance and topple.

The moss is a brilliant green, lush and spongy, and between the snarls of weeds are pretty wildflowers: white mountain laurel; spiky magenta bee balm; charming white-and yellow oxeye daisies; white snakeroot, tall and poisonous, topped with clusters of toothy-looking petals; and beds of tiny, delicate periwinkle bluets. How is this possible? Half this flora shouldn't even be in season.

I pause to catch my breath. "Think the fae made this so pretty?"

She smiles at my joke but answers seriously. "Stonemasons, probably."

"Fae stonemasons," I counter.

Tayla doesn't reply, but I hear the muffled sound of her laugh and feel irrationally pleased with myself.

With each step, the full lesson comes back to me: *In every blade of grass, in every bug crawling on a mushroom cap, in every broken stick fallen in the dirt, in every budding flower, in every bird that's ever been born, is the story of the earth. They want to tell you their secrets. Look closely at everything with your own eyes, Nova girl, because when you find something that makes you question, that makes you change perspective, that's when you know you've found a sign of wonder.*

I almost laugh with realization. The wildflowers thriving even as other trees have changed hues into saffron and persimmon and amber honey. Time preserved as though ensorcelled, suspended forever inside a terrarium. Birds slicing through the air as if to attack us but perhaps maneuvering us in a direction of their choosing all along . . .

Signs of wonder.

I decide to keep this to myself for now. If I'm right, I'm right. If I'm wrong, I don't need Tayla to mock me for it.

When we reach the bottom, she scans the ground like she's magically developed the ability to track. "We should double back that way," she says, pointing. "Hopefully Kiara didn't move from where she fell."

Fell? This again? "Do you still think she *did* fall, though? Evan said—"

"Evan has an overactive imagination."

I stop myself from grinding my teeth in the nick of time. After everything we've been through, she's still denying it? If there's anything this trip has taught me, it's that clinging to my denial and trying to fix my mistakes on my own has only made things worse.

Hiding the truth had felt like the best worst choice back then. How could a daughter confess such a devastating sin to her mother? How could a child of ten even begin to say how sorry she was, how she never meant it, how she'd do anything to undo it? How could that child have known then that the awful guilt of what she'd done to her father would be the only thing that kept him alive in her memories?

I thought I could bury my mistake as a child so Mom never had to know what I'd done to Dad. I'd tried to find him on my own, even though I could never get very far. But then, without thinking, I'd hexed Kiara. And it was impossible to deny my responsibility when it mimicked the same tragedy as before, so I decided to help her find the wishing well so I could save my dad, too.

I *needed* the Fellowship to make it this far. Only in being willing to accept help and work together can we pull off this quest—and that won't happen if Tayla keeps denying what's in front of her. Whether that's the roots, or me and Kiara, or whatever other horrors are lying in wait for us. I just doubt that she's ready to do it.

My grip on courtesy is fraying fast, but I still make an attempt to keep the tone from my voice. "I'm just *saying*. If those roots did snatch her, they're not likely to have just politely left her where we could find her, are they?"

She gives me a disappointed look, like I'm a glass-half-empty person and she's the one brimming over with frothy optimism. But from her lack of cutting rebuttal, I've given her something to think about.

And just like that, the tension returns with a vengeance.

We chew on date squares for lunch, forced to take small sips of our water just to help the oatmeal crust go down. I finish first and fold my wrapper up into a neat square, tuck it in my backpack to properly dispose of later. Tayla complains with every bite that it tastes like sawdust, but she forces herself to finish, mouth screwing up in revulsion. I didn't think it was that bad, but some people are just complainers.

The moment I zip the side pocket up again, a single black butterfly introduces itself, dancing like it's going to land on the tip of my nose then darting down to my boots. It flies from left to right in agitation, not giving up on whatever its mission is. Without its army of butterfly buddies, this one is quite pretty on its own.

"Guess who missed us," I say over the noisy crinkles Tayla makes as she rolls her wrapper up into a thin stick then ties it into a knot. I throw out a hand. "Wait, do you hear that?"

She comes to a standstill, tucking her trash away, and cocks her head quizzically. "Hear what?"

"It sounds like—"

Hssssss!

We both freeze.

The butterfly zooms back up to my face, flapping its wings ferociously, then takes off into the trees.

"Nonononono," Tayla moans as one word. Her shoulders defensively hunch up to her ears, and she squeezes her eyes tightly shut, but the sound comes again, louder, closer.

We can't escape the knowledge of what it is or the horrifying fact that more hisses are joining in, a chorus of serpents slithering through the forest floor right under our feet.

"There's too many," I whisper. "How is this even possible?"

"Maybe we interrupted a snake convention?" Her voice is sarcastic, snippy—or tries to be anyway.

Green, black, bronze. The snakes are quick, too, not staying in one place long enough to count them. It makes zero sense. Snakes are generally pretty shy unless they're provoked. They don't *pursue* people.

I don't know about her, but personally, I'm 100 percent up for digging up Henry Prior just to kill him all over again. Signs of wonderment—what total bullshit.

I'm tired, and I'm cranky, and I'm confused. Obviously my realization coming down the steps was wrong. I'm overthinking everything. If the earth was trying to show me signs of wonder, a forest floor full of snakes is not the way to go about it.

Tayla visibly pales, which is quite a feat considering how fair she is. "Are any of them poisonous?"

"Not that one."

Relief softens the harsh creases in her expression.

"But that one, that one, that one . . ."

Her lithe body scrunches. Fear sprints across her face, and whatever she sees mirrored in mine makes her suck her lips into her mouth and bite down with her teeth like she's trying to prevent sound from escaping.

Telling her to be as calm as she can won't go over well. Since she looks like she could pee herself any second, there's exactly zero point in asking if she knows what to do in this situation. Dad would probably know. But he's not here right now, and I am. Without hesitation, I dive into my memories.

This one is jagged with nostalgia. Revisiting hurts because I'm so young, which means Dad is, too. When I flip through all my memories of Dad, I don't come back to this one often.

But this is the one I need.

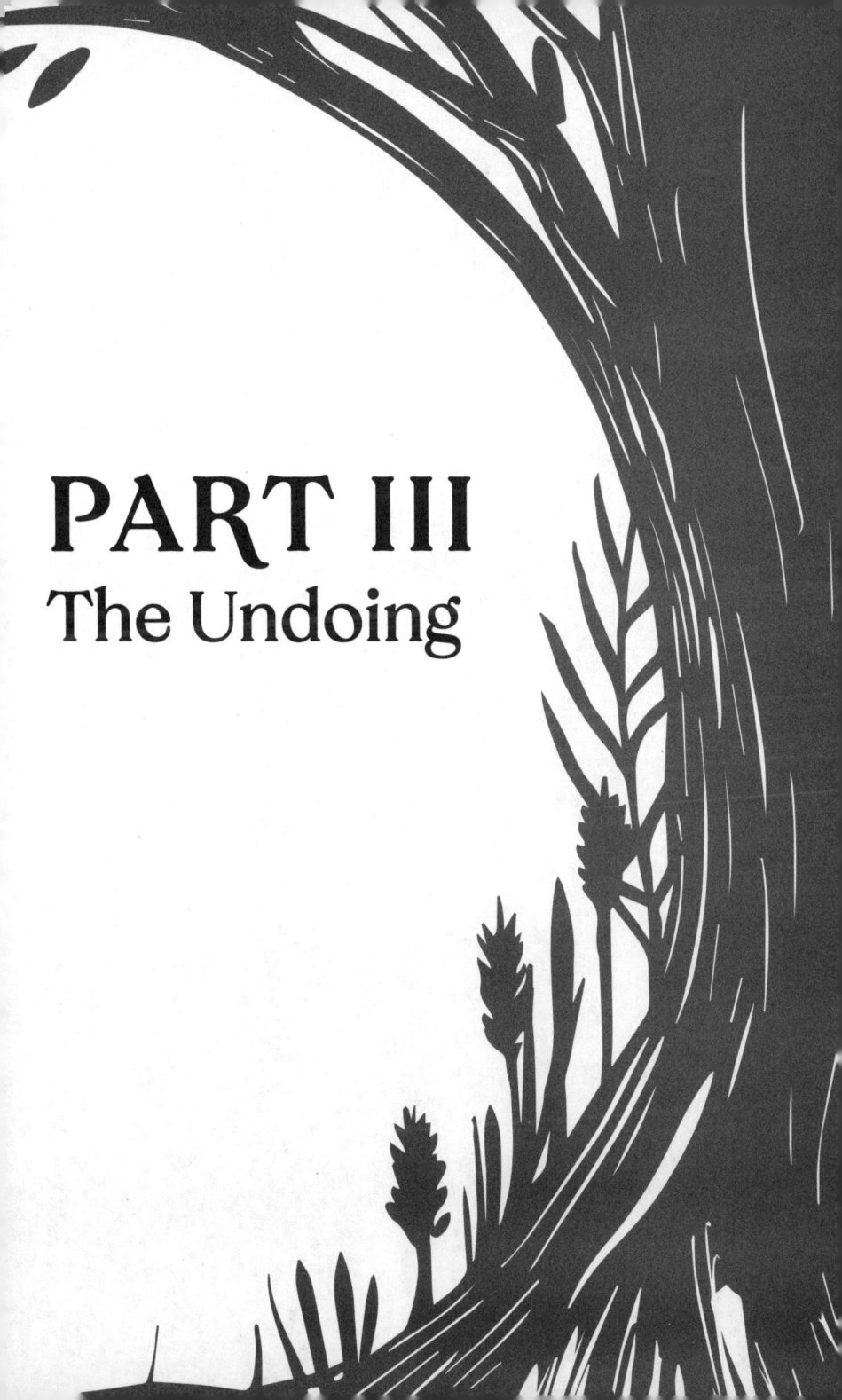

PART III
The Undoing

23

I've newly turned ten, and the double-digit age feels like an enormous milestone. Excitement pulses through me like a heartbeat because Dad's taking me to the Fall Festival. It's always me and Dad since Mom keeps up Aunt Eloise's tradition of extending Chalice's hours until midnight during festival week. I'm wearing hot pink camo leggings, a black zip-up hoodie, and I even learned how to French braid my hair so I can show off my brand-new ear piercings. My lobes still feel hot and uncomfortable, but I want him to notice the gold stars Mom and I chose. I don't know yet that he's about to cancel on me.

Not this time, North Star.

I'd never shouted at him before or since, and recalling the things I said fill me with shame. In my dreams, I always get a do-over to change the last thing I ever told him.

Fine! Go, then! If you love the woods so much, stay there forever! I hope you never come back!

I thought I was so grown up, but that childish tantrum undid everything.

In the days that followed, I thought about running to the forest so many times to try and find him. When I finally did, a month after he went missing, Mom caught up to me first. She caught me in that gravel parking lot, rocked me in her arms like I was a baby again, and cried with me until my throat was so sore I couldn't tell her what I'd done even if I'd wanted to.

There were no more camping trips in the Longing Woods after that. Mom put up with his excursions into the forest because it was his job but, more importantly, the forest was in his blood. But she never wanted the forest to claim me, too.

She let me sulk in those first days of the Fall Festival before she got *worried* worried. She had tried to make the disappointment up to me with all the cotton candy I wanted, funnel cakes and corn dogs for dinner, and sticky taffy that made my teeth hurt. Madame Aurora showed up on our doorstep the next month, a woman who couldn't bring Jules Marwood back but whose support was doing more for Mom than the cops and the forest rangers whose best just wasn't good enough.

Austin had been through this with his dad, but it was too raw for me to let him in. Austin lost Shane; I *made* Jules go. We weren't the same.

Where Mom seemed to need the support of other people more than ever, I retreated. I stayed in my room, crawled into bed, drew the covers over my head, and recited everything Dad had taught me about wilderness survival. Powered through all of it like one of his quizzes.

As a little kid, I had to get every question right before he deemed me ready to accompany him, and going over it again and again anchored me. Made me think that he'd be okay because he taught me everything I knew, which meant he knew it, too.

If you encounter a snake, should you attempt to kill it or move out of its way?

Give the snake right-of-way.

What's the sign that a snake is about to strike?

It'll rear back into an S-shape.

If that happens, should you run or attack it?

Neither. Any sudden movements threaten the snake. I'd back away slowly.

Good job, Nova. I think you're ready.

"We should try to run back to the stairs," says Tayla.

As though they understand what she's saying, the displeased hissing grows tenfold.

"No," I say sharply when she bends her knees as though she's getting ready.

"But—"

"Tayla, trust me."

Even as I say it, I can tell it's not going to come easy. She probably doesn't find me worthy enough to hand trust over. Our eyes meet, and I can't begin to parse the emotions flickering through hers, but then she gives me a tiny, imperceptible nod.

I keep my voice calm and reassuring. "We need to stay really still. Don't. Make. A. Move."

Her eyes widen. "That's your advice?"

"Yes. My dad said—Hey, what are you doing?"

Tayla's twisting her upper body around to look over her shoulder. "Seeing how far back the steps were. I think we can make it."

"What? No!"

"Waiting around to die by a hundred hungry fangs is not how I'm going to go, Nova!"

"Would you just shut up and listen to me?"

She huffs, and I'm not entirely sure she isn't going to take off, so I speak quickly. "Think about it for a second. Why the heck would anyone make a random set of stairs all the way out here? There's no houses, no town. No reason to travel, so no need for infrastructure. So how come it appeared right when we needed it?" Now that I'm saying it out loud, I don't know why it didn't occur to either of us before.

The fight goes out of her. I can literally see the tension dissolving from her shoulders as she slowly relaxes them, relief blooming over her face as her body alleviates some of its strain.

I hesitate. "Also, don't freak out, but I don't even see them there anymore."

I thought it would talk her out of running, but I didn't foresee that Tayla would want to take a look for herself. This time, she forgets to keep her feet planted and twists her whole body in a 180. She realizes her mistake immediately, a strangled gasp escaping from her mouth as she faces a hissing copperhead drawn up to its full height. Granted, it's still way shorter than her, but no matter what, a poisonous snake is still an imposing threat.

Her voice is smaller than I've ever heard it when she ekes out, "Nova?"

"It thinks you're a predator. Seriously, do not move."

"*I'm* the predator?"

There's a hint of sarcasm in her voice, which I choose to take as a positive sign. The day Machete Mouth isn't a smartass is probably, like, a harbinger of the end times or something.

"Yes," I breathe out, careful not to attract any undue attention.

"Next thing you know, you're going to say it's more scared of me than I am of it."

"*Well . . .*"

Her groan trails off into a whimper. "After this, I'm never coming into the forest again."

"Ditto. Now shut up unless you want to die."

I guess that's the threat that gets through to her because she manages to listen and keep her leg quaking to a minimum. It's impossible to tell how long we stand there in limbo. It was hard enough when the trees were robbing our sense of time but interminable when we're achingly aware of each second slipping by, each bead of sweat sliding down our foreheads, dripping off our eyebrows, grazing the corner of our eyes.

Eventually, the snakes lose interest in us. Realizing we pose no threat to them or their habitat, they take off, disappearing into the bramble and undergrowth. Tayla's finally taking this seriously because I don't need to remind her to stay absolutely still until the last one shuffles away.

When at last it's safe to move, her exhale is even bigger than mine. "Let's get out of here," she says.

I doubt they're going to return so soon after dismissing us, but truth be told, I'm hardly in favor of sticking around, either. But when we make it back to where the steps were . . . they're indeed gone.

Tayla appears as though she has to work very hard to school her dismayed expression.

I try to steady my shaky breath. "I told you I didn't see them anymore."

"Yeah, but I thought maybe it just wasn't in your eyeline anymore. Not that they were *gone* gone."

"Well, what do you want to do now?"

She opens her mouth then shuts it. "You're asking me?"

"Y-yes?"

Her frown creates one giant perplexed squiggle. She seems to struggle with her thoughts for a moment before coming to a conclusion. "If we listened to me, we'd both be dead by snakebite right now. You were the one who knew what to do back there. Without you . . ." She swallows with some difficulty.

True enough. But I can't take all the credit.

"I still remember the things Dad taught me," I say quietly. "I haven't had much reason to use any of it until now. I'm glad that it stuck."

"You and me both," she says with a wry smile. "That's why I think you'd make the better leader."

She couldn't have surprised me more if she'd confessed to

harboring secret feelings for me. "We don't need a leader, Tayla. We need teamwork."

"I can do that."

"*Can* you?"

One eyebrow tics, but she passes the first test by not responding with a cutting repartee. "I'll be the best at that," she says decisively. "You'll see."

I level an *Aaaaand there she is* look at her.

Tayla flushes. "Baby steps."

"Okay, well, if I'm right about the steps being given and taken away, then it follows that the forest wants us to go this way. It's leading us. Same as the crows who rerouted us in this direction, too."

She cranes her head in the direction of the snakes and grimaces. "Leading us to where, though? And to what end?"

"That . . . is a question mark," I admit.

"It's a WTF followed by an interrobang and those obnoxious red exclamation point emojis," she declares. "So is the forest, like, a benevolent being? Or does it have it in for us?"

"I don't think it's as binary as benevolent and evil. Petra thinks it's sentient, that it has its own needs. Whims and fancies. Maybe it's amusing to mess with people."

She huffs. "The forest is definitely an asshole, then."

I sputter and frantically wave my hands. *"Shhhhh!"*

"What, you think it can hear us?"

"Wouldn't be the weirdest thing about this day," I mutter. "Treat the forest as a scared, angry snake. Try not to piss it off."

"That analogy would work so much better if the forest wasn't already full of snakes, you know."

"You can't help yourself, can you?"

"Not generally, no."

"Takes an asshole to know an asshole, I guess."

She actually laughs. "Knew I liked you for a reason, Nova Marwood."

I blink. This is Tayla when she likes someone?

"Now, come on," she says, authority back in her voice. "What do we do next?"

She wants a decision, but my mind is racing as fast as my heart. Taking a beat, I observe our surroundings. The steps are gone, but we could attempt to climb up. I was never the best at our school's indoor thirty-six-foot-tall climbing wall, and the difference between us and the trail above is at *least* that high.

The other option would take us through the snarled, straggly bushes and straight into the belly of the forest. Snakes would be the least of what we'd discover there, I'm sure. Biting my lip, I weigh both options in my mind. Neither is great.

Midway through my mull, something catches my eye. A thick, towering oak tree squats just ahead of where the steps once were. Despite its hearty size, the branches are obviously unwell, their bark stripped and peeling to reveal stringy white sapwood.

"Tayla, that wasn't there a minute ago, was it?"

"Can't be sure. All the trees in here kind of look like all the other trees after a point."

I shake my head impatiently. "Yeah, but we'd *remember* this one."

One of the branches stretches out in our direction like an arm, four fingers curling backward and one belligerently jutting out. It isn't crooked like it's beckoning us closer. No, it's more like it's . . .

"It's pointing that way," I realize aloud. Back the way we came. Closer to where Kiara was taken.

"Where the snakes are," Tayla says flatly. "Seriously, Nova? Because a weird tree is being weird?"

I full-body cringe. Apparently these directions are so sketchy that *weird* needed repeating. The guidebook, undoubtedly, would advise following the signs. Generations of Henry's descendants would, too. If Radhika was here, I know what she'd say.

Unfortunately, it's the exact opposite of what my gut is telling me to do.

24

Tayla takes my silence for agreement. "Fucking signs of wonderment," she says with a sigh.

Her words conjure up the image of black butterflies. The insistent ones that stalked Kiara, the lone butterfly fluttering around my boots like it would tug me the other way if it could. "Oh my gosh!" I yelp. "The butterflies! They were trying to warn us!"

She pauses in the middle of winding her long hair into a bun. "Uh . . . what's that now?"

"Tayla, think about it for a second. When did the butter-flies first show up? First, before Kiara was snatched. Then when we ran into the snakes. Any time we were about to be in danger, they tried to avert it. Maybe they thought we'd take them more seriously if they came in huge numbers, but it made us uneasy instead. So then they tried a different tactic and only one single butterfly tried to get my attention."

Tayla scoffs, but her eyebrows draw together like she's giving my theory some credence. "Don't you think you're giving butterflies a little too much credit?"

Unwilling to let doubts enter my line of thought, I rush to say, "We thought they were bad omens because of their color, like how the crows were black, too, but what if we've been wrong about how we've been looking at the signs all this time? Like my dad always said, 'Things in the forest will lead you astray if you let them.'"

"Explain."

"Okay, walk with me."

"*Toward* the big, scary white tree?" For the first time, she's forced to hop-skip along to keep up with me. "Nova, wait up!"

As we walk at a fast clip, I tell her my theory. "The wishing well predates Henry Prior, right? If Petra's right about the forest being, well, *sentient*, then I'd imagine it had some pretty strong feelings about humans suddenly invading its sanctuary. A ton of greedy humans, all looking for the wishing well, trampling the forest underfoot without much care."

By unspoken agreement, we give the white oak a wide berth. I don't take my eyes off the branches for a second. "I'm following," Tayla says as we skirt around it.

"What does something alive do when it's threatened?"

Understanding dawns in her blue eyes. In the glimmer of light refraction, I can visualize the copperhead rearing up in an S-shape, poised to strike. I hear the muted hiss, see the flicking forked tongue.

"They bare their teeth," Tayla breathes. "So this—*all of this*—is the forest fighting back?"

"It's as good an explanation as any."

But even though I shrug and try to play it cool, the way shooting stars are racing across every inch of me means I'm on the right track. I'm so aware of myself and my body, where I am and who I'm with. When I inhale, the air is sweet, refreshing. Nothing like the bracing chill that tasted like the edge of a knife. My ears prick with the rustle of the brittle leaves, the quiet crunch of twigs underneath.

Everything feels sharper, a world in focus after days of walking around with smudged glasses. "Anyone who read the guidebook would follow the signs," I say, picking up steam as I work it out. "I mean, think about the moss. Keiffer *told* us it could grow anywhere, but we still read some kind of meaning into it. That's the whole reason we even *came* this way. The moss led us off the well-marked path and onto frankly dangerous terrain. And the tree is pointing us back toward the snakes because it's trying to lead us away from—" My breath catches. "The wishing well," I breathe. "The forest is protecting the well."

"Where do the butterflies come into it? You said one tried to warn you to turn back before we met up with the snakes. But how can we be sure the butterflies are looking out for us? If they're on our side? I mean, they did scare us before, when they attached themselves to Kiara."

"True," I admit. "But like I said, maybe they wanted to help but simply miscalculated how best to communicate the danger to us. We just attributed all the doom and gloom to them because they weren't a bright, pretty color." I shake my head, peeved with myself for going along with decisions I disagreed with, for jumping to erroneous conclusions like a sheep.

"Correlation is not causation," I say, reminding myself as much as Tayla. The words tumble out faster, my excited heartbeat zinging as I go back to my roots, trusting in *me*. "And that's all superstition is, isn't it? It's so reductive: A happened first, and B happened next, therefore A caused B. When really, there's a million explanations. Like maybe between A and B were a dozen other things that happened, but we missed them, so we fixate only on B, the outcome we saw with our very own eyes. Or maybe A did cause B, but only if X, Y, and Z thing also happened. Or A and B are both caused by C."

The words spill out of me like I'll lose them if I don't share them at the same speed as my racing thoughts. "Do you remember what you said about everyone in the Fellowship being here for their own reasons?"

Tayla's eyes are wide. "Uh-huh."

"Well," I say, "the forest is older, wilier, and more ruthless than all of us put together. Every single thing in this ecosystem has its own agenda. We can't assume that all the butterflies and the crows and the steps and the snakes and the trees are working together. I think *most* things here are working against us. Trying to get hikers lost so they'll never find the wishing well. They don't care if humans live or die. And if you think about it, why would they? It's not like humanity as a whole has done a great job caring about nature. Henry Prior never cared about protecting the well. He just wanted to exploit it for himself, and fuck everyone else."

Not for the first time, I find myself loathing my ancestor.

"So the steps disappeared in order to cut off our escape from the snakes," Tayla realizes aloud.

I nod vigorously until she grabs my shoulders and forces me to stop. "The forest *is* an asshole but only because it's had to be. It's protecting itself, protecting its magic. But I think the butterflies are different. Maybe they've had enough of the missing and the dead. Maybe they don't want this place to be a graveyard."

I finish with a hungry gasp.

"Okay, take a breath, Sherlock." Tayla's words are teasing and light, but the rest of her looks troubled.

I laugh, a little embarrassed at my earnestness, but I can't play it off like nothing.

I'm right. I know it.

"Suppose everything you just said is true," says Tayla. "Does that mean we do the opposite of what the signs are telling us? Is that why we didn't go in the direction the tree was pointing? Do you think this way leads to the wishing well?"

"Yes, exactly! All of that!"

She wets her mouth, frowning when she lifts her hand to touch her chapped lips. "Even if that's one mystery solved, do you think this breakthrough will help us rescue Kiara? It's been . . . god, probably hours by now? And we're moving farther away from the others, too."

"It follows that if the forest *took* Kiara, then it's been doing everything in its power to *prevent* us from finding her. I don't know why it would want to keep her, but . . ."

She sighs. "Considering the other things we've encountered in here so far, the reason can't be good."

"Nature is surprisingly nefarious," I say lightly, sidestepping what looks like the remains of an old, abandoned nest long fallen out of a tree.

"In addition to being an asshole, as the truly nefarious are wont to be," she quips.

"Clearly I've been lied to about the good that going outside will do me."

Tayla snorts, twisting at a dry bit of skin until finally losing patience and ripping it off. A bead of shocking red blood blossoms, and she grimaces at the taste.

"Where's your lip balm?"

"Lost it." She rolls her bloody lip into her mouth. "I don't think I've ever actually finished a tube, actually." After a beat, she adds, "But I've never lost one so fast before."

"Must have fallen out of your pocket."

She shakes her head. "It was in my backpack. Zipped up all safe."

"Maybe someone borrowed it."

"Nope. Evan makes their own vegan rose salve, Radhika is a die-hard Glossier girlie, Kiara uses something tinted and expensive from Sephora, and Keiffer is old school with his cherry ChapStick."

I flash a chubby yellow tube at her, the end squeezed flat. "This is mine. Want some?"

"Please." She uses her finger to swipe off a bit then hands it back to me with a grateful smile.

I tuck it away. The camphor and menthol of Carmex is heady, walking me into memories of Dad unbidden and without warning. It's one of those polarizing scents that people either love or hate, but it's always been comforting to me. He kept one in his car's glove compartment, in his backpack, on the bathroom sink. We were still finding the places he squirreled spares away even a year into his absence.

"You know," I say. "Other stuff's gone missing, too."

She opens her mouth as if to ask what else is missing when the low rumble of male voices makes us both fall silent. Instinct drives us to press our backs against the nearest trees, flattening our bodies.

The first voice is full of scorn. "What makes you think they're the ones?"

"Because no one else has made it this far," says a second, each word laced with patience, as though this isn't the first time they've had this argument. "Not in decades."

"It hasn't been that long." The third voice is deeper than the others, the tone harder to make out.

"Yeah, only feels like it," chimes in a fourth, this one aiming for lightheartedness that doesn't quite land, considering he's the only one to chuckle.

"Putting all our faith in a little girl," says the first. His voice is the most distinctive, maybe because he speaks every word through a sneer. It's a little familiar, too, but I can't be sure amid all the others.

Little girl? mouths Tayla. *Kiara?*

"At least we're at full power now." The fourth guy seems determined to be positive, which makes his next sentence all the more chilling. "Think the pretty boy noticed he's almost out?" he asks with a cackle.

Keiffer's batteries, I mouth back. Tayla's eyes widen with understanding.

"You should have taken them all," snaps the first voice. "I fucking hate the dark. This forest is ours. We shouldn't be forced to stay put at night. Bad enough we're stuck here."

"If I took everything, he would definitely know something was up," argues the fourth guy.

"I agree," says Voice Two. "They're more scared when they wonder what happened."

"We'll get everything eventually anyway," says the third voice, sounding horribly pragmatic. There's a soft *click* when he speaks, then I hear it again and again.

Voice Four laughs. "Remember the last group? Siblings are always fun to fuck with."

My feet are rigid inside my boots, but my toes still curl.

"No one's turned on each other that fast before," agrees Voice Two. "It was good work, boys."

Voice One chuckles. "These new kids will be too easy. They've been at each other's throats from the start. Almost takes the fun out of it."

"We could have beaten our record with those college girls if they hadn't been rescued," sulks Voice Two. "The havoc got to them fucking quick. Too bad the woods were crawling with do-gooders."

"Don't get ahead of yourself," says Voice Three, the most indiscernible. His voice sounds close. Too close. As though he's brushing behind where we've hidden, within grabbing distance. The metallic clicking sound draws closer. "We're not out of the woods yet . . ."

The laughter sounds like it's right in my ear. I squeeze my body tight, imagining a sheet of paper that's been wadded up into a ball. Tayla copies me. Her pin-straight hair is frizzy, strands falling out of her loose bun to frame her fearful face. My mouth forms *We're okay,* and she jerks her chin in acknowledgment, nostrils flaring and chest rapidly rising and falling.

Among his hothead friends, the third man gives the impression of caution, but he could also be the most dangerous and cunning. His next sentence confirms my suspicion when he says, "If they lead us to the wishing well, we won't *need* another group ever again. So no more theft or scares, boys. We need them to keep focused on finding the well. The full moon is almost upon us." *Click, click, click.*

Their conversation peters away—the men talking about the first thing they're going to do when they're out, mostly some disgusting, degrading comments about women—but we stay frozen until I count to one hundred in my head, and even then we stretch the stiffness out of our limbs, stepping gingerly to avoid even the smallest of twigs. Those men sounded like they were hunting us, and the forest is so eerily tranquil that the most inconspicuous of snaps or crunches could easily give away our location.

We both scan the trees, but we don't see anyone. Not even the flash of someone's jacket or hair.

"Sometimes," Tayla says, voice shaky, "I see eyes peering out at us from the dark."

"When? Today?"

She takes a deep breath. "Since the first day."

"The first—!"

"I thought they were birds!" She's careful not to speak above a whisper. "Animals!"

"Why didn't you say something sooner?! Those guys could have been tracking us this entire time," I hiss, absolutely aghast.

She glares. "Yeah, thanks, that did actually just occur to me."

"Do you think they have Kiara? They mentioned a girl. Maybe the roots took her as bait. If they're working in cahoots with those men."

"No," Tayla says thoughtfully. "Remember, they still need us to lead them to the wishing well. If we're looking for her, then we're not doing what they want. I don't think they realize we're looking for anyone at all. And what was up with that creepy-ass clicking?"

I wrap my arms around myself. "I don't even want to know."

"Do you think it was his teeth?"

I glare at Tayla. I absolutely do *not* want to think about that. "We need to warn the others," I say.

"What about Kiara?" she demands. "We can't just turn back."

"Yes, we can. We have to. If we don't, they're sitting ducks. And they've already been in our camp, Tayla. They've gone through our stuff. They've taken Keiffer's batteries and—and probably Evan's poncho, too! Maybe your damn lip balm." My eyes widen. "Shit. They're the same guys Keiffer and Radhika ran into on day one."

Tayla looks nonplussed. "What guys?"

The whole story spills out. I recite everything Radhika told me, word for word, until I can get Tayla to agree that as much as we want to explore further now that we're all the way out here, regrouping is our only option. Split up, we're weaker.

"You said you trusted me," I point out.

"I never said that."

"You wanted me to take charge."

She snorts. "That is *not* the same thing."

"We can argue about it, or we can save our friends, and then we can *all* save Kiara." When she hesitates, I go in with the kill shot. "We have two days left until the full moon. If we don't find the wishing well by the apex, you can kiss Kiara goodbye. And we need Evan and Keiffer and Radhika. Like, they probably don't even have a lookout! Anyone could do *god knows what*. If you really love Kiara, if you know her even a little bit, then you'd know which Kiara would prioritize between her life and those of her friends."

Tayla looks at me for a long moment. What feels like centuries creep past. Finally, she nods.

Even with her grudgingly on board, it takes us the rest of the day to make it back to where the steps once were. We don't encounter any more snakes, but we don't come across any other familiar markers, either. It's like the forest knows what we're up to and is determined to make it as difficult for us as it can.

It's twilight when we finally reach the slope. With the wall collapsed, crumbling in on itself, there's nowhere our feet can find purchase as we struggle to grasp onto roots, hoisting ourselves up. Most of the roots can't support our weight, so we collapse in a heap more times than not.

On what must be the twentieth try, I reach the top. I heave a leg over, throw off my backpack, and then offer a hand to Tayla. She steadfastly ignores it, grunting and gasping. Her entire face is red, muscles straining, but adrenaline helps her the rest of the way. She collapses next to me and makes a pitiful whine, the same one I'd bit back just a minute ago so she wouldn't know how miserable I was.

"We should have left our backpacks down there," she says, voice low and aching, each word spaced out like each one costs her. She tips her water bottle into her mouth, shaking it and cursing when she ends up with just drops. "Damn it. I don't know why I've been so thirsty today. Everything tastes off, and my mouth . . ." She works her jaw. "Maybe I just need to brush my teeth again."

After taking a long swallow of water, I pass her my bottle. "Don't be too proud," I say when I suspect she's about to cut off her nose to spite her face.

"Fine. Thank you."

We take a few minutes to sit in silence, massaging our shoulders and calves until the weird pins-and-needles feeling fades. A breeze stirs, cooling the sweat on my neck. "I'm glad we didn't leave the packs behind," I say, pulling down the quarter zip on my sweatshirt just enough to let air in. "We still need our supplies for the journey home. Would have been easier if this wasn't so high up, though, so we could have tossed the packs over instead of lugging them up on our backs."

Irritably, she says, "Never thought I'd have something in common with Brian and Emily."

"They're long gone. Bear food," I say with a straight face.

She stares at me before cracking a smile. "You're fucking awful sometimes."

I haul myself to my feet, wincing with soreness. "As defending champ, you nervous?"

I give her my hand, and this time, she takes it.

"Shaking in my boots, Nova."

25

irt smudges my cheeks, the sleeves of my fleece-lined thermals. With nothing to do on the walk back, I pick at my nails, flicking away what I can, but in the dark, it's impossible to tell how successful this task is. We don't want to risk a fall, so I flick on Keiffer's flashlight. The glow is anemic, but it's enough to see by. At least at first.

"That's the second time you've smashed the butt," Tayla comments.

My palm still stings from the first time. "Mm-hmm."

"Are you worried?"

Kiara's scream echoes in my mind. "More than I've ever been about anyone."

She sniffs the air like a bloodhound. "We'll see them soon. I can already smell something cooking."

I'm glad it's dark enough that Tayla can't see my flush. I am worried about our friends, too, but when I'd answered her, I was actually thinking of Kiara.

"Good," I say, forcing a smile. "That date bar was so dry, and I hardly had any M&M's."

"You're telling me. I'm still picking plantain chips from my teeth."

"You had plantain chips and didn't share?!"

When we reach camp, I almost want to rush over and put out the fire, but it's such a relief to see their faces that I can't bring myself to plunge us all into darkness again.

"Nova!" Evan is the first to shout.

All three of them jump to their feet from where they'd been huddled around the fire. Radhika looks like she could burst into tears any second. Their voices clamor over each other.

"We were so scared! We heard footsteps coming."

"Did you find her? Where is she? Is Kiara with you?"

"Oh my god, what happened? Are you hurt? Why are you both so dirty?"

Tayla holds up her hands to get them to shut up.

Once everyone hugs it out and sits back down, I quickly launch into everything we've learned.

Radhika looks sick. "You mean they've been watching us this whole time?"

I give her a tense, jerky nod.

Keiffer stiffens, jaw clenching to granite. *"Fuuuuuck."* He clears his throat. "Major serial killer vibes."

Evan is likewise perturbed when I explain my theory that the roving group of men had been hoping to use us to get to the wishing well. "And we still don't know what happened to Kiara," they say, dropping their face into their cupped hands.

No one's happy at the prospect of leaving her out there alone, especially with only two more nights until the full moon, but we don't have a whole lot of other good options available to us. We gnaw at the beef jerky and fruit leathers, sip at the black tea that Evan's brewed up. Dinner is nothing special, but after the day we've had, the instant mashed potatoes topped with packaged fried onions and bacon bits is positively orgasmic.

Tayla doesn't seem to agree, managing only a bite before setting aside her plate.

"Yeah, I know," says Evan, to their credit only sounding a little annoyed. "Would have been better with real potatoes, right?"

"Wasn't going to say that." Tayla tips her plate over mine and scrapes her food into my portion. "I don't have much appetite. Drank too much water, probably. I'm just happy to be back with you all."

Despite eating a double helping of potatoes, I'm still so wolfishly hungry that I make packet ramen with dehydrated veggies, slurping it up at a shocking speed like I've never been taught manners. A stunned Radhika lets me finish her potatoes, and a slightly less agog Evan gives me their half-eaten strawberry Pop-Tart. I can't explain why I'm so ravenous. The hunger hasn't gone away, nor has the pit of terror.

"Are you sure?" I ask around a bite.

"Enjoy," says Evan. "You need it way more than me."

"No wonder you're so ravenous," says Radhika. "We were going to head out at first light to find you."

"You two should get some sleep," says Keiffer, forcing a wooden smile. "I don't know how you both managed to stay upright long enough to walk back."

I'm a little flustered with his praise. Sure, we've had a few dangerous scrapes, and resting does sound amazing, but I can't stop myself from pointing out, a little bemused, "It's been less than a day."

Tayla nods in agreement as she rolls her shoulders and arches her back to work out the stiffness. In the silence, her back pops extra loud.

Keiffer frowns, his brow heavy and brooding. Radhika and Evan, who just finished washing up, wear matching *Oh shit* expressions.

"What?" I ask.

No one responds.

Radhika and Keiffer exchange a look so loaded that Tayla and I share a look of our own.

"What?" Tayla snaps.

"Guys, it's been . . ." Keiffer swallows. "Two days. You've been gone for two days."

"No, that's not—" I begin to stammer while Tayla whispers, "It *can't* be—"

We look at each other.

Radhika holds out her wrist. "My watch doesn't lie," she says softly.

There it is. The date and time. I stare until everything else recedes except the date. The gentle crackle and glow of the campfire dims, our friends blur into the shadowy blue-black trees, and the faint rustles of wind in the brush smooth away.

"But how?" Tayla bursts out at the same time some unintelligible sound emanates from me, a bit of gibberish stammering that makes Evan wrap me in a hug.

Right before my eyes, the time on the generic smartwatch changes to 9:59 p.m. That little twitch of movement breaks the spell and brings me back to myself.

"Time moves . . . funny," says Radhika. She swallows hard. "In here. We've all noticed it."

"Which means," I say, hysteria forcing its way up my throat, "that we don't have two days to get Kiara to the wishing well. We only have one. The full moon is tomorrow night."

The pall that falls over the group is even worse than when I told them about the men and the conversation we'd overheard. Although all of us reel from this new revelation, I know the stark desolation on Tayla's face must be matched only by my own.

"Okay." Keiffer slaps his palms against his thighs. "So this officially takes suck to a whole new undiscovered circle of hell, but it doesn't change the fact that you both need sleep."

"Otherwise you'll be zombies tomorrow," Evan adds sagely. They still hug me close, and I cherish the comfort, even though part of myself hates that I'm not out there right now looking for Kiara. But another part can't even imagine moving.

Now that we know it's been two days of nonstop walking, running, and hiding—all in unimaginably stressful conditions—

the sum of everything I've gone through hits me. I'm all too ready to let sleep claim me. Don't even want to crawl to the tent. I'm good to just slump over right here at the fire and hope someone will lend me their leg or lap as a pillow. Even Tayla's swaying back and forth, eyelids fluttering like she's trying to fight off sleep.

"Bed," says Radhika sternly. "Mean it."

"The three of us were sharing one tent, but we've got the second one up, too," says Keiffer, nodding toward the closest tent.

"Someone should keep watch," I say, glancing at Tayla. She nods, backing me up.

"We'll take care of everything, don't worry," Keiffer says.

"Yeah, we've had it pretty easy hanging back here the last two days. It's our turn to carry the load." Radhika squeezes my hand before hauling me up. I grit my teeth against the small agonies of my muscles rebelling—my calves and thighs feel boneless, and there's an ache in my tailbone that wasn't there before.

Keiffer nods decisively. "I'll take first watch. Babe, any preference? How about you, Evan?"

While the three of them sort out shifts, I make for the tent that Keiffer indicated. To my surprise, Tayla joins me instead of taking the other one. With our backs to each other, we silently wipe off the grime of the day and change into a fresh set of clothing.

There's a camaraderie between us now, and as much as I hate to admit it, I do feel safe with her. You can't go through what we've been through without having each other's back. But trust is fragile and I can't let myself forget that we're both rivals for Kiara's heart. I can be sure that Tayla hasn't forgotten that fact.

The sleeping bags are oddly comfortable, the first soft surface we've encountered all day. Damn it, it's been *two* days. The fresh reminder reawakens my dread, and the fear pisses me off all over again. My back feels like hell, though, so I curl up on my slide so as not to antagonize it further. Tayla mimics the action, sighing deeply when her prostrate form finds the relief we didn't get while on our feet all day.

Days.

"We have way less time than we thought," I whisper.

Tayla nods. "I hate to spend it sleeping."

"Me, too."

"Do you think they're out there even now?" Her voice trembles. "Keeping an eye on us?"

"Can't rule it out."

"Then they'll know Keiffer's up. Know we're onto them."

The thought has occurred to me, too, but what else can we do?

Radhika and Evan will need to feed the fire when they start a new shift, but there's more than enough firewood to see us through the night. Hopefully no one will be able to sneak up on us. And we'd made it back to camp in time; if our friends had tried to go looking for us or Kiara and gotten lost themselves, we would all be in a shittier position.

"Can't be helped," I murmur.

Tayla tosses and turns, clearly dissatisfied with my answer. Finally, she ends up on her back. She laces her fingers together then lays both hands flat across her stomach. "Why do you like Kiara so much?"

I laugh. "What?"

"Don't bullshit, Nova. Not after everything we've been through together."

I scoff, remembering to keep my reaction quiet so the others don't overhear. "You're seriously playing the trauma bonding card after you've made it abundantly clear you don't trust me. Yet you expect *my* absolute trust?"

"It's just a question," she argues. "You're making a mountain out of it."

"It's really not, and I'm really not."

She angrily sets her mouth but is careful not to raise her voice. "I just want to know when you started to have feelings for my girlfriend."

"She's not yours" flies out of my mouth before I can snatch it back.

Tayla looks equally horrified. "Slip of the tongue."

"Yeah, whatever. Let's just go to sleep. I don't want to argue with you." I roll so I face away from her. "And I promise you, I can't like her. I owe her. That's why I'm here, and that's all I'm doing."

"Owe her what?"

My stomach cramps. I hadn't meant to say that. "Human

decency? You do remember what happened with the pizza and the squash, right? Kiara was in trouble, and Radhika thought I could help since Kiara wanted to go looking for the wishing well. I owe her the way I'd owe any person if their life was in danger."

Quietly, so quietly that I don't even think she means for me to hear it, Tayla whispers, "I told you not to lie to me."

I lie there like a lump long after her gentle snores fill the tent. The sleep I was hungering for now evades me, and this tent is suddenly too small, too claustrophobic, too everything.

I'm out of there before I even know what I'm doing.

"Hey," says Keiffer, sounding entirely unsurprised to see me.

I slump next to him, and without a word, he lifts his arm. I burrow in, getting a whiff of citronella biodegradable soap and the jammy scent of strawberry fruit leathers. The former reminds me of Dad and the latter of Kiara. Together, the mingled scents feel like home. Keiffer doesn't tell me he's got this, I should go to sleep, yada yada. Instead, he lets me have silence until I'm ready to break it.

"Do you think we can do this?" I whisper. It's not a question I can bear to ask at my normal volume.

"We're six totally ill-equipped kids wandering around in the woods hoping to find a magical solution to a magical problem." He gives me a gentle squeeze. "What do you think?"

Glumly, I say, "That I can see why your math grades are so mid. There's only five of us."

What a sobering thought. *Only five.*

I can imagine the headlines now: ONLY FIVE SURVIVE

"Do you regret it?" he asks.

For a moment, I want to tell him the truth. That yes, I regret hexing her, however inadvertently. I regret thinking a few charms could make a difference. I regret—

So much.

"Do you wish you hadn't come?" he asks, reframing the question when I'm silent a beat too long.

"No. Do you?"

"Hell no." He rests his head against mine. I can feel his cheek move; instinctively, I know he's smiling. "So there's your answer. Do you think you can fall asleep now?"

I consider. "Honestly? No."

"Well, as long as you're up, mind answering a question that's been nagging at me for days?"

Wariness makes even the slightest desire for sleep flee like a bandit. "Go for it," I tell him.

"Why *did* you come? I don't claim to know you that well, but somehow I don't think it was Radhika visiting your tree house that clinched it for you."

I shoot to my feet. "Keiffer, you know what, I'm pretty wiped after all. Night!"

His soft, knowing laughter follows me as I dive back into the tent.

26

The next morning—our *last* day to make it to the wishing well—gets off to a dismal start. It's drizzling when we wake, no one has a rain cheater, and Radhika's hair poofs in a way I haven't seen since my mom's Polaroids from the nineties. We're all bleary-eyed and stiff, and my calves revolt even walking a little bit away for a pee. Tayla doesn't fare much better; she groans through every minute of her morning stretches.

Breakfast is maple-and-brown-sugar oatmeal ripped out of brown sachets, topped with a handful of walnuts and raisins Evan picks out of the trail mix. Tayla finishes her oatmeal and gnaws on a piece of licorice, offering me the rest of the bag when she sees me using my finger to swipe clean the last of the oatmeal from my bowl.

We hastily pack up camp, none of us willing to waste time beyond what it takes to cram everything back in our packs. While the others take down the tents and douse the fire, I check in with Austin and Caroline. I don't tell them anything about Kiara's disappearance—let alone the dangers Tayla and I encountered in our search for her—just that there are some sketchy dudes in the forest and we're giving them a wide berth. They're not thrilled, but we all know the full moon is tonight.

Whatever happens, the Fellowship of the Fling will be for sure heading back first thing tomorrow. We don't know if we'll find Kiara *or* the well in time, so for now I simultaneously dread the deadline and look forward to all of us going home. Is there a word for that feeling?

There is: foreboding.

"Good luck," Austin says, and I hear his worry and his hope and his love over all these miles separating us. "Be safe."

"Your mom keeps asking for pics of you and Kiara, by the way," says Caroline. "I took one of me and Austin instead and sent it from you. Apparently she was rooting for us?"

So there is an *us* now? This is the best news I've had in days. "Her and me both," I tell them before we say our farewells.

The happiness stays with me for only a few moments before the somber surroundings remind me where I am, what we're doing, and what's at stake. Doom and gloom doesn't hang over everyone's head, though.

"A burger," Keiffer says wistfully.

Tayla blinks. "What?"

"I could really go for a burger right now."

"Keiffer, it's eight a.m."

He continues like he hasn't heard her. "Extra pickles, extra onions, extra mustard, hold the ketchup."

Radhika wrinkles her nose. "Hold the kissing, too, if those are your condiments." She grins to show she doesn't mean it, and they both laugh.

That's the last joyful sound we hear for hours.

Every unexplained noise sends us straight into panic mode. We can't go more than ten minutes without someone asking if the rest of us heard *that*, though what the *that* could be is anybody's guess. At this point, I'm pretty sure all of us would rather cross paths with a bear than whatever else we think is out there, dogging our steps. Human or animal. Friend or foe.

Not that we've met many friends out here. Scratch that, *any* friends.

And Tayla tricked the only two allies we possibly could count on. So.

"This is it here!" she calls out when we reach the drop-off.

Evan peers over the edge. "I thought you said the steps disappeared?"

"Yeah, they—" I break off, jaw dropping in utter disbelief. "Came back?"

"Convenient," Tayla says in a tight voice. "Right when we needed them."

"Radical thought. What if we *don't* do what the forest so obviously wants us to do?" asks Keiffer.

I get the reluctance. I'm not keen to go back down there myself. "I'm with you, Keif, but this place is huge, and we don't even know where to start looking, so it makes the most sense to—"

"Walk through the pit of snakes?" He raises a sardonic brow.

I roll my eyes at his antics. "To go to the last place we *know* she was for certain. Where she fell."

It's the right move, even though the prospect fills all our hearts with dread. The terrain is soft with groundwater, our boots making unhappy wet squelches as we plod our way back to the edge where Kiara was taken. The puddles suck at our feet, and more than once we're forced to stop and shake sopping-wet mud off our boots.

"You don't think there are mud snakes in here, do you?" Tayla asks.

"Well, *now* I do," says Keiffer.

"Hey!" Radhika makes a face as a clump of mud flies free from Evan's boot and onto the knee of her jeans. "Nova, as our resident snake expert, wanna answer that?"

"Honestly? No." My feet sink into a particularly gloopy mess of mud. "I don't think we should dwell on the danger. Who knows, maybe the forest can sense it, feed off our emotions."

"A mind-reading forest is an even scarier notion," says Evan. "Just so you know."

"She does this all the time," Tayla whispers conspiratorially to Keiffer.

"Oh, don't I know it," he says.

Tayla giggles and looks over her shoulder at me. I screw up my face, but that only makes her more amused. *Rats.*

"We knew it from day one," says Evan, gesturing to Keiffer with their thumb. "I don't know if it makes it better or worse that she doesn't do it on purpose."

"Definitely worse," Keiffer says promptly. "Like so much worse."

I scowl at their backs, then unfetter myself from the glop with enough energy to stomp past the three of them, spattering them with mud. Radhika, who looks vindicated that the three of them are as speckled with mud as she is, quickly follows in my wake. "Don't think about it," I command. "Remember, the forest is trying to scare us. Come on, keep moving. It can't be much farther."

Other than the squishes underfoot, I hear a myriad of eerie sounds, too. Small things skittering out of sight. Murky, undefinable noises in the high branches of the trees, and every time I hear a cackle, I look out for crows. Twilight is falling quickly, the hazy Blue Ridge sky suffusing us in indigo and pewter. Once in a while, I catch a silvery shimmer above, a twinkle of something that could be stars, but when I try to peer for them, all I see are branches and branches and more branches.

Finally, we reach the spot we've marked with one of Evan's bandanas tied around an exposed tree root, the red fabric hopefully bright enough for us to see from down here. Luckily, no snakes in sight so far.

"No wonder we couldn't see much over the edge," Radhika says, voice taut as she forces herself to slow, to angle her torso back so she doesn't tip forward. "This incline is steep. Erosion, my ass. This is peak asshole forest behavior."

Evan purses their mouth unhappily, their arm jostling mine. "And the lower we go, the less sun we get." They gesture above, where the canopy is so thick and lush, even in October, that it blots out what little light there is. "It's almost like however far we go, there's still another level to unlock."

"And we're playing in hard mode," I say gloomily.

Keiffer and Tayla both look disheartened, but whatever they're thinking, they keep it to themselves.

"Help! Is anyone out there?"

The cry is so faint, so muffled, that I talk myself out of thinking I heard it at all, but then the voice shouts again, louder, nearer. My heart lurches. "Did you—" I begin to ask.

"I did," Tayla confirms, eyes glinting with hope. She takes off in a sprint before anyone can stop her.

"Tayla!" shrieks Radhika, apparently forgetting we were trying to keep quiet and off the radar. She chases after with another shout of "Wait for me!"

My muscles bunch up. Oh, I'm *so* not going to be left behind.

Evan gives me a conspiratorial smile. They can probably read the determination on my face.

Keiffer turns to me. "Can't even go a day without someone going rogue, right, No—Nova? Nova! Evan? Not you, too!" He groans. *"What are you all doing?"*

"Sorry, Keif," Evan yips. I hear their footsteps behind me, catching up.

I imagine an aggrieved Keiffer in the background, throwing up his arms, bemoaning how no one listens to him. The visual is an amusing one, but the humor turns to horror when I almost crash into Radhika, who's half hiding behind Tayla's shoulder.

The incline has evened out, revealing a verdant glade that could rival any from Snow White's Enchanted Forest. Paper streamers, the kind you'd decorate a birthday party with, billow from low-hanging branches in faded pastel strips. Golden-rod and black-eyed Susans grow rampant on the edges of the clearing, gently dancing away. The forest floor is scattered with an abundance of purple phlox and white bindweed, a plump gray bunny plopped right in the middle. Birds, so absent from the rest of our journey, twitter excitedly from the topmost branches. It's, well . . . in a word? Idyllic. Absolutely perfect.

Until I note the picnic basket nestled into the goldenrod. Yellow powder has disintegrated onto the weave, most of the bottom layers thick and brown. How long has it been here?

And then there's the other stuff. Backpacks ranging in size, running a wide gamut of colors and price points. Some new, some old. A few blue ones, ratty and grimy. Three pairs of binoculars spanning the last fifty or so years going by the dif-ferences between an unwieldy, bulky one and a sleek, compact one. A grandparent, parent, and child? Three generations out here? Seems unlikely.

Evan pops up next to me, not even out of breath. They slide their hand down my forearm to loosely hold my wrist and squeeze. "How does this place exist?" they ask wonderingly.

"Help!"

Tayla's the first one to take off again. Obscured behind the weeds and wildflowers, Kiara struggles against her bonds. She's been lashed to the tree trunk so tightly that she hasn't been able to get free, but it's obvious she's tried hard from the angle of her arm, bent awkwardly behind her. I shudder to think how long she's been forced to hold that position. There's a dingy silver rag hanging from her neck that must have been used to gag her, which explains why she wasn't able to scream for help earlier.

Despite her predicament, relief surges through my belly. She's alive. She's safe.

I glance up at the chalky smudge of the moon peeking between the trees overhead. *For now.*

Tayla grunts as she works the knots out of the rope. She doesn't say a word; she's that intent on the task in front of her. Her singlemindedness has become something I've learned to appreciate about her.

I crouch by Kiara, brushing the hair out of her eyes. "Are you okay? Did you see who did this?"

"Was it the roots?" asks Evan.

"*People* use ropes," Radhika reminds them.

"Something grabbed my ankle. It must have been a root." Kiara nudges her foot in our direction. "It gripped so tight, flung me over the edge. It all happened too fast to know for sure."

"Didn't you hear us yelling your name?" I ask, tucking limp strands behind her ear. Her hair is greasier than I've ever seen it, her skin has an oily sheen, and her eyebrows are wild without her usual painstaking care. And yet despite that . . . My eyes drop to her mouth before flitting away guiltily.

"I think I passed out. When I came to, a guy was there. My ankle was sprained from the fall, and it hurt to put any pressure on it, so he said he'd take me back to his camp then go search for my friends. He seemed to know what he was doing, and he wrapped my ankle and didn't seem like a creep, so I . . ." She looks ashamed. "I went with him."

I cup her jaw and gently ask, "Then what happened?"

"Well, he took forever to come back. And he didn't bring any of you with him. He didn't seem too concerned with getting help, and whenever I tried to push him to go looking, he always had some cagey reason why he couldn't: it was getting dark, he didn't want to leave me alone, it was better for us to stay in one spot so *you* could find *us*."

Tayla intensifies her efforts with the ropes, expression thunderous.

"He snuck away after giving me water and I thought I heard him talking to someone, so I took my chances. I ran. Next thing I know, he's in front of me, looking more scared than I was, and before I could beg him to let me go I got hit from behind. I woke up here. Haven't seen him since. I thought he might come back with food, water . . . but . . ."

Evan reaches out and gently cradles her head. Kiara flinches when their light fingertips find the bump. "I feel it," says Evan. "It's a nasty one."

Kiara laughs weakly. "Yeah. Now can you please hurry up so we can get out of here?"

"Going as fast as I can," says Tayla. Her fingers pick at the last knot with renewed strength.

"At least you got the gag loose," I say. "Without that, we might not have found you."

"I've been trying to get free, but every time I got close, the ropes got even tighter." She worries her lower lip with her teeth. "Couldn't figure out what was going on until I remembered I was hexed." Her laugh is bitter. "A couple of the butterflies returned to keep me company, but the rest kept out of sight."

"They helped us, too," I say quietly.

"Guess we had to run into far scarier shit to realize that the butterflies weren't so bad," Kiara says with a weak smile. "When I was little, my mom told me that black butterflies were angels. The souls of the departed watching over us on their way to the afterlife. Nothing to be scared of. But my dad's family believes it's a premonition of death if black butterflies enter your house. I like my mom's version better. I didn't remember any of that until I thought I would die here and never see them again."

"They also represent rebirth and change," says Evan. "Courage, tenacity, and hope."

"Uh, hold up. If you knew that, why didn't you say?" I ask sharply.

They shrug. "It didn't seem relevant."

"It didn't seem—!" My eyes bug out. "Evan, couldn't you see how freaked we were?"

"Nova, it's fine." Kiara wiggles against her bonds until she can place her hand over mine, a placating gesture I'd seen Dad give Mom whenever he had to go back into the forest. It has the intended effect even now. My annoyance zaps out of me like a fly hitting a lightbulb. My arm tingles all the way up to my elbow with the aftereffects.

Flustered, I look up. It's easier than looking into her eyes. Above, the trees have grown thick and close together, but they've left enough space for moonlight to shower part of the glade in a pearly glow. I swallow back a gasp. Suddenly, I realize that I can make out what evaded me earlier this evening.

The branches have grown in such a way that their outstretched limbs create a luminous outline in the shape of a bird, wingspan unfurled to its limits. The space within is gleaming silver, like one of the signs of wonderment Dad would believe in a heartbeat. It *can't* be real. It can't. I blink, but it's still there.

The tip of the bird's beak is an arrow pointing the way, pure starlight.

"There!" Tayla lets the ropes fall to the ground with a satisfied expression, like she's just barely holding herself back from saying *Ta-da!* with an air of pomp. It promptly sours when she sees Kiara's hand atop mine.

"Thank you." Kiara tries to rise, but her legs don't cooperate.

"Let me," I say quietly.

Trying not to dwell on how intimate it is, I massage the upper thigh closest to me, working my way down to her calves. Evan does the same while Radhika tugs off Kiara's boots to examine the bandage that's been wrapped right around her ankle.

"He did an okay job with this," says Radhika. "I mean, from what I can tell."

"She needs a hospital," says Keiffer, who's finally made his way over. "Fuck, look at her wrists."

We do. The ropes have broken skin, leaving behind ugly circles, red and raw.

Kiara glances down at her ankle. "How am I going to make it back to town like this, though?"

Nobody has the answer to that, so with a sigh, she puts her boots back on and hobbles upright, using the tree and my shoulder for balance. A whimper later, it's obvious it hurts too much to walk on.

"Did you find the well?" she asks, blinking past the pain.

This time, everyone knows the answer, but nobody wants to say it.

It should be me, I realize. If it wasn't for me, none of us would be here. This is all my fault.

Just like how seven years ago was my fault, too.

It all comes back to me.

"I'm sorry. We tried," I say, and the others all nod.

"Oh." She looks dejected for a moment, then she squares her shoulders and looks me in the eye. "We've come all this way, and we still have a couple of hours until midnight. We can't give up yet."

"Who said anything about giving up?" slinks a voice from the darkness. It's the first voice from the night before. His manner of speaking is unmistakable.

A man steps out from behind a barricade of trees. Strangely enough, he wears a suit. The pants show wear and tear, but some effort has gone into mending the jacket. Shiny black patches have been sewn on with red thread in childish, uneven lines.

Evan sucks in a breath. "Nova, that's my poncho."

I wait for Kiara to tell us he's the one who found her, but other than her tense face, she gives nothing away. Well, maybe it was one of his friends. God knows he had plenty of them.

Click, click, click. Now the others emerge, eerie smiles on their otherwise young, handsome faces. They're all dressed exactly alike, from the fraying, yellowed collars of their once-white shirts to the scuffed dustiness of their black leather shoes. Like everything else in the glade, they look pristine and decayed at the same time. The unsettling realization sinks deep into my bones.

"There some backwoods black-tie event going on here?" snarks Tayla.

Instead of it raising his hackles, the man laughs like he finds her amusing, like he wants to put us at ease. "Something like that. Looks like you found our hideout, kids."

Kids sends a shiver down my spine. They're not *that* much older than us.

"You're still here?" asks Keiffer, stepping protectively closer to Radhika.

My knees are quaking, so I'm proud that *his* voice doesn't wobble, too. Proud that Tayla didn't think twice about mouthing off, even though she's gotta be as scared shitless as the rest of us.

I can finally put my finger on what the glade reminds me of. A yard sale full of things that were once sparkly and senti-mental but are now just junk, all the shine long gone. Everything here is old. Though their skin is firm and unlined, the look in the men's' eyes is as though they've lived lifetimes.

"We're always here," says the man, the only one who's opened his mouth so far. "Now, I know you and your pretty girlfriend remember us, but let me introduce myself to the rest of your party." He looks at each of us in turn, a genial smile curling his lips. "I'm Jeremy. And my buddies here are Colin, Gary, and Kyle."

"Don't forget Mickey," Colin pipes up. Voice Four.

"Right. Of course, we could never forget Mickey." Jeremy seems to find this funny. "Why don't you kids introduce yourself to Mickey? He's right behind that tree."

None of us move. If this creep wants us to do something, it can't be for any good reason.

He gives an exaggerated sigh. "No? Well, all right." He lunges, hands outstretched.

Keiffer makes a sound like a wounded animal. Radhika moans and buries her face in his chest.

But the rest of us can't look away.

Because Jeremy is holding what looks like a human skeleton.

Next to me, Tayla's breathing is raspy and harsh, and Evan trembles. At first, I don't understand what I'm seeing. Plastic from a party supply store, maybe. I can't make sense of it. And then it sinks in, like rainfall in parched, cracked, desperate earth. Realization floods, waking me from my stupor.

The bones are dull, but there's still withered flesh clinging to the eye sockets. It's wearing the same suit, but it hangs off the bones in only marginally better condition than the other four men's. Around its neck is a white sash, similarly discolored, that reads GROOM in curling black script. The wrists and ankles are tied with thick rope. More rope around his waist, looped over and over until it's a coil.

"See, this clown thought he was better than us," Jeremy says pleasantly. "The only one to get out of our shithole town, make something of himself. Real college boy, ladies' man. Thought that all he had to do was snap his fingers, and just like that, the whole world would fall at his feet."

He snaps his fingers to make a point, and we all flinch.

His friends bray with jackass laughter.

Malice seeps from Jeremy's smile. "Met himself a pretty little psychic, proposed to her with a big-ass diamond ring he bought with his fancy job money, didn't he?"

Everything feels hot.

Aurora. Her engagement ring that was never joined by a wedding band. Why she keeps coming back to Prior's End . . .

She's just like me. She's waiting for someone she loves to come home.

I want Jeremy to stop talking. He does not.

"Invited us to his bachelor party. Didn't want strippers and liquor, did he? No, he wanted to do something fun. Something unforgettable." His grin stretches slow and sickening across his face. "We gave him that, right, boys? He wasn't laughing when we tied him up and told him we were leaving him here, was he? Too bad his fiancée didn't see that coming, hmm?"

When his friends' whoops and hollers die down, Jeremy's face loses all trace of fake friendliness, the mask of humanity slipping off to reveal the monster underneath. "Except we couldn't find our way out after that. Which is where you come in." He nods at us. "You're going to take us to the wishing well."

"W-what?" Kiara's voice cracks. "I don't know how to—"

"I wasn't speaking to *you*, stupid girl." Jeremy scowls. He points at me. "She's going to do it. The blond. *His* daughter."

"Dad?" Without meaning to, my gaze lands on the back-packs. The blue ones. One of them could be his. "You're talking about Jules Marwood? Is he here?"

Jeremy laughs and pulls his tattered jacket aside to reveal a radio tucked into the ragged waistband of his once-formal trousers. It's bright orange with nicks across the surface, but it still works perfectly fine when he pulls it free and speaks into it.

In a voice that sounds nothing at all like I imagine my dad, he croons, "Nova, it's me. Help me, Nova. Go to the wishing well, I'm in trouble!"

Sick horror bubbles up in my gut. It was never my dad at all.

"It was you!" I burst out. "You tried to trick me!"

"It usually works a charm. Terror comes easy out here. You probably know that by now. If people take a little longer to abandon their campsite and their shit . . . we lure them away with these." He dangles the radio in front of him, smirking. "We place them all over the forest. I used to work at one of those haunted houses when I was in high school, so my sound knowledge came in handy. Though you wouldn't believe how many batteries we run through."

Any dwindling hope of finding Dad turns to mist. It was never him reaching out to me. It was someone's caricature of him, traveling on a frequency and snaking through the trees from some distant radio, all set to the same channel.

Even though I always knew this was a long shot, at least I had *hope* in that long shot. There's now only a dull hollowness where that hope used to be. Every time the forest made me feel closer to Dad's spirit or whatever, it was a lie. And I, that desperate ten-year-old daughter who missed her father, fell for it.

Jeremy throws a disgusted glance at Kiara. "And it would have worked on you, too. But instead, we have to chase you all over the forest looking for this one."

"If I messed up your plan so badly, then why am I even here?" Kiara cries. "Why did you and your evil roots and your . . . your *goon* kidnap me?"

He casts her an irritated look and doesn't deign to respond. "One of you is injured, and except for the stud over there, none of you stand a chance against us. Now, we can work together or . . ." His smile is sinister. "We can show you how well we treat our friends."

27

Kiara's breathing is labored as she staggers along with her arm looped around Keiffer's waist. His arm wraps around her hips, hugging her to him so he can take the brunt of her weight. She shouldn't be walking with that sprained ankle, but we don't have a choice. No one's coming to help us.

You tell me, Nova girl, and I'll help you. I might never find my father, but his voice will always be with me:

In the face of seemingly insurmountable challenges, North Star, it always helps to look at your problem in a different way. Change your perspective, and you'll find everything *changes.*

I tip my head back. The stars are snuffed out. We'd be walking in the dark if not for the motley assortment of flashlights the men wield, all stolen from unsuspecting campers. Jeremy took my radio from me, proclaiming it was another for their collection, but Kyle, cautious Voice Three, points out that they won't need to bother with the theater of special effects ever again. They hung on to my radio anyway.

I think about the abandoned tent that Tayla and I found, how the cigarettes and food were left behind but not the flashlights. Not the lighter that would have accompanied the cigarettes. No, those things were taken after these guys terrorized folks for supplies.

But if these guys have been here since they killed Aurora's fiancé . . . how long have they been lost in these woods? Seven years at least. Clearly they've resorted to theft and maybe even worse, given the way Tayla and I overheard them talking. Given what they've done to their own friend.

Until my dying breath, I think I will be haunted by the scraps of Mickey's remains, the mockery with which they talked about him and how they dangled him so disrespectfully as a prop to frighten us.

Thinking back on all the things that have gone missing, I still don't get why they didn't steal our food, too. Evan's poncho repaired their shabby clothing, and Keiffer's batteries powered the radios they needed for their elaborate forest surround sound. With a flash, I remember Tayla's lip balm. For all I know, they palmed that, too. But not the food. I keep coming back to that.

Change your perspective.

I glance up at the bird glinting above for a clue. This is the third one we've passed, and I've kept its existence secret so far. These men seem to think that I have some insider knowledge passed down from my dad, and I *suppose* it's possible they've overheard Radhika talking about our storied ancestor, but while I don't doubt their ruthlessness, something about Jeremy and the others isn't adding up.

I just haven't figured it out yet.

Biting my lip, I dare to ask, "How do you know my dad?"

Jeremy's silent for so long that I'm convinced he won't answer, but finally, each word dragged out slowly, he says, "Used to run into him. He knows the forest like the back of his hand." He looks at me from the corner of his eye. "Was proud of his daughter."

Knows? My brow furrows. He talks like Dad is still alive. Something in my chest soars at the thought. Because if they've lasted in here this long, so could he.

Jeremy jerks his head to indicate Radhika, who's walking right behind us with Tayla, Evan, and Colin, leaving Keiffer and Kiara to make their way, slower, with Gary and Kyle bringing up the rear. For our protection, Jeremy claims, but the truth is, they're just ensuring that none of us run.

Click, click, click. This time I twist around.

It's Colin, opening and closing a lighter. Every time he snaps it, I feel a scream building in my throat. *Click.*

The lighter is shiny silver. There's an *A* engraved on it. None of these men have a name that starts with *A*. So this is stolen, too.

With a start, I remember the group I'd met coming out of the Longing Woods almost a week ago. Aaliyah and her brother Ahsan, who had lost his much-needed lighter, forcing them to end their trip early.

"Heard that one brag about being a Prior descendant, so we figured she'd know the way," Jeremy says. "If we knew that when we first ran into her and her boyfriend . . ." His smile is all teeth. "We wouldn't have let them go."

Fear scrapes against my bones. "So why did you?"

"Figured it wouldn't matter. We'd come across them soon enough, take what we need then. People don't tend to leave here."

That's why they have all the backpacks. I repress a shudder.

They're desperate for the wishing well, but why? I doubt they regret what they did to Mickey, even though it led to their imprisonment here . . . so what are they trying to undo?

Surreptitiously, I slide my gaze up to the treetops. We're approaching the next silver bird.

The first time it struck me as surreal. But now I marvel at its beauty. The seamless way it blends into the night sky until you look up at the exact moment it's illuminated by moonbeams. And then you see it for what it truly is: a sign of wonderment. How can it be anything else when nature and magic have worked in such graceful unison? The leafy canopy has formed in such a way as to create the outline of a bird, the shape cut out so the moonlight can punch through. And something tells me that if we follow it, we'll find the wishing well.

It's what's going to happen to us once we get there that terrifies me.

"Hey!" an outraged voice cries from behind.

We all turn, Gary and Kyle shining their flashlights directly at the intruders.

"Brian?" asks Tayla, squinting at their shadowy figures. "Emily?"

Kiara's gasp says it all: she recognizes Brian, too.

"You know each other?" Jeremy laughs. "No need for introductions."

"You promised you'd take us with you," says Emily, not making eye contact with any of us.

Jeremy shrugs. "*If* you followed through."

"We found the girl," Emily snaps. "We spent all day looking. We tied her up and left her for you."

"Yes, but it wasn't the right girl. We only wanted the blond." He jerks his head toward me then smirks at her. "Our deal is null and void."

For the first time, Emily seems to register our presence. She swears under her breath. "You never said she was blond! We almost had her! You didn't think that was helpful for us to know?"

"Not my problem." Jeremy hums under his breath. "Which means you two are still in the red."

"C'mon, man, that's not fair." Brian kicks at the ground. "We've been doing this too long."

That's it, I realize. *Too long.* That's the connective tissue between all the strangers we've met. Their clothing, the haunted look in their eyes, the way Brian and Emily didn't know the latest iPhone model . . . they've been out here too long. They've *lived* for too long.

"Your debt would be closer to being paid if you hadn't tried to hide resources from me."

"We need to survive, too," says Emily.

"Yes, but for how much longer, I wonder?" Jeremy taps his chin and smiles coolly.

In the daggered silence that follows, I run my fingers over the aventurine bracelet Petra gave me. It's kept me safe so far, hasn't it?

"You never lost your backpacks, did you?" I ask. "You were hoping to rob us."

Tayla seizes upon what I said. "I *knew* there wasn't something right about you two."

"Want to warn us about more bears?" Emily says sweetly.

Tayla scoffs and rolls her eyes.

It's dark, but my eyes have adjusted enough to catch some black butterflies darting between the trees, following us. They're keeping Kiara in their sights, but for what? How can they help?

A plan begins to form, but if it works, it'll officially make me worse than Tayla. I take a deep breath. It'll be worth it, though.

"You didn't want to hurt us, though, did you, Brian?"

Emily goes still. Brian's eyes implore me for silence.

"What's that?" Jeremy's interest is piqued.

Perfect. Exactly what I was hoping for.

"You wanted Emily to let us go. I remember what you said," I say quietly. "You said you were tired of all this. You meant tired of stealing from innocent people, right? Leaving them without any supplies to survive out here, to make it out of the forest. Because you needed to survive more than you wanted to let them live."

"Shut up!" he bursts out, but his eyes are wide, his forehead sweaty.

"It was just one moment of weakness," Emily says quickly. "He would have. I know he would have." She throws me a hateful look, like she regrets not making her move when she first ran across us.

"*They*"—Brian points to the four men—"demand tithe from *everyone*. Anyone who doesn't pay up gets terrorized until they do. Just half of everything, right? How are we supposed to live on crumbs?"

My heart is going a hundred miles a minute. "You're right, that is really unfair."

Tayla throws me a *What are you doing?* look, and the others are likewise confused, too rattled to think about what's being said.

But not me. My mind is clear, like I've scaled a mountain peak and am getting my first taste of fresh air, a 360-degree view of everything around me. I can see for miles. And what I've pieced together . . . there's no way, but after everything else we've seen, this is the only conclusion that makes sense.

The collection of packs in the glade. The old, old everything. The battered clothing, the styles that are straight out of another generation. Why they have never shown even the remotest of interest in stealing our food when they've had no compunction stealing other conveniences.

They're dead.

They're all dead.

And walking around are their ghosts.

Corporeal, malevolent, desperate ghosts.

28

It all ends with the butterflies. At the exact moment I piece it together, the butterflies flood us from all angles. Hundreds. Thousands. As though every single one in the entire forest has rallied here to help us. They paper themselves to the eyes of the men, Brian, and Emily. Their delicate bodies block the glow from the wildly swinging flashlights.

The confused shouting is immediate.

"Run!" Keiffer bellows, scooping Kiara into his arms.

No one needs to be told twice. We have only this one slim window of opportunity.

"This way!" With one hand I steal my radio back and with the other I grab Evan's hand. They take Tayla's, the one not currently gripping the flashlight she had the presence of mind to snatch in the panic. She shines it behind us to guide Radhika and Keiffer, making sure to keep it close and low to minimize chances of being followed.

The forest floor isn't brambly here at the lowest elevation, so there's mercifully nothing for us to trip on. Nothing to grab and rip and tear. But we run like there is.

Like there are predators hovering just out of our eyeline. Like our lives depend on it. Like the full moon is almost at its peak. Something in the trees keeps pace with us, a shadow that has the shape of a human, moves like a human, and at one point, even looks at me with the whites of its eyes like a human, but the shape is too dark and too fast to see properly. Before I can focus on it, it streaks away like it was never there.

"Nova?" Evan calls, bringing me back. "What is it? What do you see?"

I don't have an answer.

We run, and we run, and we run until the cries of agitation grow fainter and fainter behind us.

My lungs are on fire by the time the wishing well comes into view. It's only a couple of feet high, more of a circular wall than any of the cutesy fairy-tale wishing wells from childhood stories. The final bird shines directly above it, the radius around the crumbling stone shimmering misty white. There are words scratched into the face of the stone, so weathered and smudged that they're almost illegible.

Evan presses a hand against their heart, mouth open.

Radhika's voice is giddy as she crows, "I *knew* I'd find it!"

A laugh bursts out of me, wild and wonderous.

We're here. We're actually really truly *here,* and it isn't until this exact moment that I realize that a part of me never expected to find the wishing well after all. Never thought I was special enough or deserving enough or repentant enough to be *here*, the one place in all the world that could undo the worst thing I've ever done.

I'm here, Dad. I'm going to get you back.

"What do we do, what do we do?" Radhika dances in place.

Keiffer gently lowers Kiara to the ground. "Someone make the wish."

Kiara leans against him as she finds her center of gravity again. "I think my ankle is worse."

"Someone do something," Radhika insists shrilly. She shows us her watch. "Twenty minutes until midnight!"

Evan rests their elbows on the well and leans in. "I wish Kiara was no longer cursed."

We all look expectantly at Kiara. She shakes her head.

"You have to throw a coin in!" Tayla hip checks Evan. "Does anyone have a—oh, thanks, Keiffer."

"No problem. I always pick up random parking lot change if I spot it and collect enough to make a donation with," he says. "Do you think this oxidized green one is luckier than a shiny penny? Older is better kind of thing?"

"I'm sure it doesn't matter." I snatch the gleaming coin from between Tayla's fingers, give her a dirty look, and throw it into the well. For a pregnant pause, there's nothing, not even the tinkle of it hitting stone on the way down. Then, finally, I hear the soft splash of it hitting water. "I wish Kiara to no longer be cursed," I say.

Nothing happens.

Evan blinks. "Well, that was anticlimactic."

"I don't feel any different," says Kiara. She holds her arms out, wiggles them a bit. "Should I?"

"Let's do the gunky green one, then," says Radhika, plucking it away from Keiffer. "And maybe more gravitas this time. No offense, Nova, but you sounded a bit demanding. The well probably wants more respect than that."

Demanding, huh? I want to laugh. "What does the book say about it?" I ask, voice steely.

"You don't know?" Evan seems surprised.

"Never read it. Dad had a copy, but . . ." I shrug then look at Radhika head-on. Now that we're out of imminent danger, it's time for her to admit what she's doing with Dad's book. "Let me take a look at it."

"I know what it says by heart," she says. "It went something like . . . um . . ."

"You know, I'd really like to read it for myself." I hold out my hand.

"Nova, I know you want answers, but do this *later*," says Tayla. "We're running out of time."

Kiara frowns, clearly perturbed by the fact that Tayla and I know something she doesn't. "What's going on?"

"Nova," says Evan. They nod up at the full moon. "Endings. New beginnings."

"Whatever we're doing, we have to do it *now*," insists Radhika. "We're down to fifteen minutes."

With a huff, Kiara takes the coin from Radhika and says, "Please, magic of the well, accept this humble offering and return to me my good luck before anything worse happens." She touches it to her lips then lets it fall. After an eternity, it meets the water.

"You aren't supposed to ask for your luck back!" Radhika exclaims. "You have to undo the bad luck."

"Um, I have another coin somewhere." Keiffer begins to pat down the pockets of his cargo pants.

We need to go faster than this. I throw a despairing glance to the full moon then reach for my back pocket. "I have one."

Tayla glances at it, a frown creasing her forehead. "This is a . . . a two-cent piece. Is this fake?"

"It doesn't matter," Radhika says impatiently. "Just throw it in!"

"It's not fake," I say. "So it won't, like, offend the well, if that's what you're worried about."

"Hold up. Aren't rare coins supposed to be lucky?" asks Tayla.

"Yeah," Keiffer says. "I've never even seen one. But here's the penny I found at the trailhead. Toss one of them in and make the wish, Tayla."

But she's preoccupied by something else. "So how did you just *happen* to have a rare coin, Nova?"

My heart stress ball–squeezes. I should have just let Keiffer keep hunting for a coin, but *nooooo*, I just had to expedite matters, didn't I?

I meet Tayla's suspicious gaze and evenly say, "I don't know. I don't look at my change when I get it back. I've got some Canadian coins, too, if you want to interrogate me about that."

Keiffer puts a hand on my shoulder. I glance up to see

steadfast support etched into his face, including the worry lines I'm pretty sure weren't there a week ago. It makes me second-guess the way I'm going about this. Damn it.

"Before we took off, I stopped by Petra's to grab some lucky charms to help Kiara," I mumble. "The acorn was one of them. The two-cent coin was another." I leave out everything else so I don't look like a *complete* weirdo, but I think that ship may have sailed.

"I knew it!" says Tayla. "That acorn was way too pristine."

"Oh, Nova," says Kiara. "That's sweet. Why wouldn't you want me to know that?"

Evan grabs Radhika's hand and squints at her watch. "Twelve minutes," they warn.

"Why didn't you just tell us the truth?" asks Radhika.

I snort. "Seriously? Coming from you?"

"What is *that* supposed to—"

"I just gave you an opportunity to be real with me and—"

"Don't turn this around on me! I'm not the one hiding things, Nova."

"Oh, for the love of—" Keiffer shakes his head. "I'm sick to death of all these secrets. Radhika, I love you, but don't you think that's a little hypocritical?"

"Keiffer," she says. Her eyes flick to me. "Not now."

His exhale is rough, frustrated. "Then when? You had this whole trip to tell Nova you found her dad's copy of *The Way of the Wish* in the woods a few weeks ago, and you didn't!"

"Keiffer!"

"No, he's right," Evan says. "You think I don't know that you're only here for *material*? Fodder for your college admissions essay. You've been making a meal of this Henry Prior thing for years, and you thought if you found the wishing well, you could prove the legend was true and get the credit. I'm not saying you didn't want to save Kiara, too, but don't pretend that your own motivations were totally selfless."

Radhika flushes. Biting her lip, she says to me, "Nova, I did try . . ."

"And you, Tayla." Evan scowls at her. She fidgets with her necklace under their scrutiny. "You've been impossible this whole trip because you want Kiara back, and you think Nova being here will keep that from happening. You've been undermining her and, frankly, pouncing the second you think she's acting suspicious."

"Because she *is* suspicious!"

Keiffer sighs with gusto. "Tayla."

"Can I see the book or not?" I ask Radhika.

She gives it to me. "It's yours. Keep it. I'm so sorry I didn't tell you when I found it. I just . . ."

"Wanted it too much," I say. "I don't forgive you for keeping it from me, but I can understand that."

The paperback is soft. The pages rounded from reading. I picture Dad's fingers flipping from front to back, red pen poised to attack. I brush my thumb over the yellowed edge, let the cover buckle as I reach the end of the slim volume.

Then and only then do I turn to the first page.

29

I read the foreword for the first time in my life and then the rhyme that follows:

For the well to undo
Prior woe for you
A gift you must bring
A coin offering
For only one will you get
To prevent your regret
These woods are the bridge
To all that you wish
Your hurts we will stitch
But should you break faith
Beware the wraiths
Until you are ready for me
To diminish

I think I understand why neither my wish nor Kiara's worked. It had nothing to do with the coins or showing the well the proper reverence. Kiara wasn't the one to do the hexing, so she can't be the one to undo it.

It's that simple. The same words etched onto the well are here in the book, spelling it out.

Even if others had found the well, they wouldn't have been able to *use* it unless they knew how. You can only undo your *own* regret, not someone else's. You can only undo something that you *chose* to do, that you *caused* to happen.

It's why Shane knew he could undo his infidelity and why my dad talked Tayla's mom out of the trip to the wishing well to wish away Tayla's dad's illness. You couldn't simply wish something away because you wanted it gone, no matter how worthy the wish. Shane's regret was a result of his own actions, whereas neither Tayla's mom nor dad had done anything to cause his diagnosis.

But someone in the past made the mistake of thinking more than one wish was possible, tried to cheat the wishing well, didn't think twice about exploiting the forest. Henry Prior was a man so undeniably flawed that he would have plenty to regret, plenty to undo.

"Have you read this?" I ask the others. "What do you make of it?"

"I interpret it as one wish per charm," says Evan. "But no clue about 'breaking faith.'"

"Well," I say. "See this part about wraiths? I think it means *them*." I jut my chin in the direction we came. "People who perish in these woods are stuck here forever because the forest's magic is punishing all humans because . . . well, I guess because

Henry Prior tried to cheat the well into undoing all his regrets so he could have the life he wanted, even though he read this warning. Those guys, they got lost and never made it out. Their bodies don't seem to need food, but for everything else, they need to steal in order to make living bearable. If the wishing well can undo their mistake in coming here, in leaving their friend for dead, they might be saved. But they don't truly regret it, do they? They'll probably just wish to not be dead anymore, so the magic won't work."

If the foreword is accurate, then Henry Prior—the man who had the foresight to conceal the wishing well's location and shroud it in mystery—was the one to abuse its power first. All of this leads back to his actions. His greed.

And I am his descendant.

I look down into the depths of the well. I am guilty twice over.

I can choose to undo what I did to my father . . . or Kiara.

But only one. And only once.

For only one will you get to prevent your regret.

"Nova?" says Keiffer. "What are you thinking?"

In my mind, I answer: I'm thinking that I came here to save her without anyone finding out I was the reason she needed to be saved. I'm thinking that I am my dad's only hope, whether he's alive or dead. I came here thinking I could save them both. Making a choice between them was never a possibility I'd considered.

Before.

I see now that I am in another one of those moments that will forever be split into a Before and an After. That this crack in my heart will never be healed. That forgiveness isn't on the table.

The wishing didn't work because in order to *undo* something, first I would have to admit what had been *done*. The thing I need to do is the very last thing I want to do.

Dad's face flashes before my eyes.

Radhika's words echo in my memory: *The wishing well can undo any curse. Upon his discovery of the wishing well, Henry Prior founded the town of Prior's End, where everything prior could be undone if one only asked for it.*

I am Henry Prior's descendant, and I will not make his mistakes.

"I wish that the curse of bad luck I caused Kiara is ended because she's a good person and never deserved it," I say softly.

Someone gasps. I don't know who.

"You did what?" Tayla looks stricken, betrayed. "You? It wasn't Aurora?"

"I—"

What can I say? What words can possibly redeem me?

"I didn't think it would actually happen. I was just trying to expose Aurora for a fraud. I was going to entrap her into giving me a ludicrous fortune so Mom would finally see that Aurora's advice about declaring Dad dead was wrong, too. But then Kiara walked in, and I was just having a bit of fun. They were just words. I didn't think they had any actual power." A half truth. It tastes like ash in my mouth.

"Fun," Tayla says flatly.

"Guys, I think my ankle is actually . . ." Kiara tests it, twisting it back and forth. "It's better."

"Nova, you had all this time to tell us," Radhika says, sounding hurt. "Literally. You could have opened your mouth and—"

"Come on, guys. No one would have trusted her after that," says Evan. They're defending me, even though I don't deserve it.

Tayla takes a step closer to Kiara as if to underscore she's always on Kiara's side and I'm not. "Yeah, and? That's what happens when you're untrustworthy."

"She told us now," says Keiffer. "When it really mattered. Just . . . let that be an end to it."

"Why is no one else mad about this?" Tayla's cheeks are red. "Why am I the only one?"

"Will all of you shut the fuck up and listen to me?" Kiara's voice sails over the rest of us. "I said my ankle is feeling *better*! I think everything that was caused by my bad luck is fixing itself." She takes a deep breath and hobbles over to me. "Nova . . ."

I wait for her to lay into me. Really let me have it.

Instead, she cups my face in her hands and stares into my eyes. It goes on forever, and I hope she can see my genuine regret, and maybe she does because she releases me with a firm nod, as though she's come to a conclusion she suspected all along.

Maybe she's remembering what I told her about my dad,

how the last things I'd ever said to him were hurtful and how I hadn't meant them and they'd come true anyway.

"She didn't have to say anything," Kiara says. "She could have kept silent, but she saved me. She spoke up, even when it meant we'd hate her for it. And she was right! You *are* condemning her, Tayla! Even if she never got us here in time to undo the bad luck, she's *more* than redeemed herself just by going with us to the end."

"Kiara," Tayla starts to say.

"No," Kiara says sharply. "This is the end of the matter. Yes, this has all sucked ass, but none of us are allowed to beat Nova up over a mistake that she has more than made up for. *I'm* the one who was affected, and *I'm* saying it doesn't matter."

"So let's just draw a line under it and leave it here," says Keiffer, looking relieved.

"Wait," says Evan. They point at the full moon. "I mean, as long as it's still at full power . . . ?"

"There's nothing I want to undo," says Radhika. Keiffer nods his agreement.

I can't bring myself to turn away. To turn my back on my last chance to get Dad back. I made the right choice. I know that. Mom is ready to move on, and even though she will always love him, she's made her peace with never having answers. I don't know if he's dead or alive, but Kiara is warm flesh and blood, and she needed me. She is the Now.

Even if she never speaks to me again after this, after the

magnanimity of her forgiveness wears off, it will still have been the right choice to make.

Maybe I could still try to make another wish. Henry Prior had done it, allegedly. Why not me? Part of me wants to try. To my shame, a pretty big part of me.

I yearn for Dad's voice now. To give me one last lesson.

But I don't need it. I don't need him to tell me what to do. I know what he would want.

When he speaks, it's with my voice: *Don't mess with nature, Nova. Leave things be.*

"Nova?" Kiara touches my arm. It's soft as a butterfly wing, there and gone again.

I know they're all watching me. I can feel their eyes.

Wondering what *else* I've done that I need to undo.

I have to do this. I have to let him go.

With a soft cry, I turn away.

"Nova." Kiara takes my hand in hers. Her face softens with understanding.

Holding my hand in hers, she turns to face the well and closes her eyes. "I wish," she says quietly, "that the wishing well undoes itself and whatever tether is holding those lost souls here, that they find the right path to wherever it is they need to be. All of them." She hesitates, opening her eyes to look at me. "Even if it means undoing the wish you just gave me."

"No!" yelps Tayla.

"It's okay," says Kiara. She's telling Tayla, but her eyes stay on me. They're surprisingly gentle. More gentle than I think I deserve. "It's okay. I know what I'm doing."

The ground beneath us shakes. Her hand squeezes mine. And while we all watch, the wishing well collapses in on itself in a raucous crash. It looks so small now. Not magical at all. Just a ruin of rock.

To think that searching for it all these years caused all this pain. All those missing people. All those looted backpacks. I'll never know if the ghosts stole from Shane and Jules, too. If among those blue backpacks is one with a folded picture of me and Mom and Dad together, a tube of Carmex, a radio that matches mine.

Do I even want to know?

"Remember what the inscription says." Kiara points to a dull gray stone with the word *diminish*. "'Beware the wraiths until you're ready for me to diminish.' The woods will forever be haunted by them—the ones who cause harm to survive *and* the innocents who found their final resting place here—until the well is destroyed."

"They're killers. They didn't deserve to find pea—" I start to say.

Kiara smiles and places a finger to my lips. "I said 'wherever it is they need to be.' That's not for us to decide."

I stare at her a moment longer, nodding.

Tayla surprises me by asking, somewhat begrudgingly, "Do you want to go back to the glade? See if you find anything that belonged to—well, see if any of us recognize anything."

I can't bring myself to answer. The others wait me out, hold space for me to come to a conclusion. I know without being told that they'll abide by whatever I decide.

You were right, Dad. Trust your team. Your partners are your best rescuers in case of any injury, misfortune, or calamity.

Thank you for teaching me everything you probably hoped I would never need to know. Thank you for making sure I knew anyway. You probably didn't think the Fellowship of the Fling would be a thing, I know, but as unexpected a journey as this was, I did find you again. And I'll learn how to be okay again.

I was wrong in thinking it was the forest bringing me closer to you. It was never your voice or your old gear that I needed. Your words have always been with me, protecting me. The memories I didn't let myself remember for all these years because they hurt too much . . . well, they still hurt, but now I feel your love in every single one. Your presence is in every lesson. In every bird.

I may not remember your voice, but you've never spoken to me as clearly as you have here, in this place you loved so much.

I hope you find the peace Kiara wished for. I hope I hope I hope—

"I can't go back to the glade. Not now," I say. I swallow hard. Once, twice. "I don't think I could bear it if . . . I don't want to know. Not for definite. Not right now. First, um, I think there's something I need to tell Aurora."

"Okay," Kiara says simply. "Let's go home."

She doesn't let go of my hand as she pulls me away.

The others fall in line behind us.

30

Not a single ghost bothers us on the way home.

In their absence, the rhythm of the woods returns, like new spring buds after the last of the winter frost. Birds softly trill, joined by a cricket symphony and rustles that could come from any number of animals, but for once, I don't feel threatened by not knowing. There's a whole nightlife going on all around us, a welcome contrast to the hush and gloom that cast such a long shadow over this place. I breathe in a lungful of crisp, clean air. All the spite and cobwebs that choked the Longing Woods has been swept away.

Dad's voice is with me, stronger than ever. Before, it was fuzzy, like a half-remembered memory or a low muffled voice speaking in another room. But now I have clarity.

Jules Marwood is everywhere my eyes land on, my fingers touch, and my lungs breathe. Every blade of grass and dirt-caked pebble. My dad's presence is all around me.

He's always with me. He always has been.

By unspoken agreement, the Fellowship wants to put as much distance between ourselves and the well as possible. Far from any bachelor party bros or nineties teens with axes to grind. No one even thinks about stopping until it's almost three in the morning and a bleary-eyed Evan trips, flailing forward. They would have fallen flat on their face if not for Tayla steadying them just in time.

There's a stricken look on her face as she releases them.

"You good?" Keiffer asks. "You look like you've seen a ghost."

We all freeze, as though the word itself will summon them. Kiara is the first to relax, huffing out a laugh. "If I never hear the word ghost again, it'll be too soon."

My heart tells me that our way home will be unencumbered by any malicious spirits, and I want to tell them this, but the words don't emerge. It's like a dam has broken and all the *wonder* of the world has come spilling out. My senses buzz. There's the brush of wind against the cooling sweat on my neck, the blaze of crimson and rust-colored leaves whispering overhead, the nuttiness of the furry brown hen-of-the-woods mushrooms growing at the roots of dead oak trees. It isn't the same offensive odor of decay that followed Tayla and me for the past couple of days. This is more like raindrops purging the putrescence from the soil, rinsing away the ruination. Setting everything right again.

Tayla rearranges her expression, but it's still far from normal. "How's your ankle?"

"Fine," says Kiara. Her eyes find mine and linger. "Doesn't hurt. But it's not like we're going to make it home tonight anyway, so we may as well get some sleep. When we find a good place, let's stop."

After a mile of sleepy, stumbling walking, we find a clearing encircled by Queen Anne's lace and spiky green balls of angelica and goldenrod. It's an idyllic place that would be perfect for a picnic, but no one even thinks about eating. We pick our way through the wild blooms until we reach the center, where there's just enough space for three tents to cluster together.

Under the moonlight, we get the tents up and crawl inside.

It occurs to me that I haven't said a word ever since Kiara said *Let's go home*. As we unroll our sleeping bags, glimpses of the last few hours come back to me: Everyone's glances subtly checking to make sure I'm okay. The worried looks passed between them the longer I stay in my own little world. Evan and Radhika whispering about *disassociation*.

Guilt rears its head, and I want to say goodnight to Kiara, but the second I'm inside my warm cocoon, I fall fast asleep.

When I wake, it's to the chattering of birds and the soft rustles of Kiara tidying away her sleeping bag. Dawn brings with it my ability to speak. "Good morning."

She startles then smiles. "Morning. I was going to get breakfast started. You can sleep for a few more minutes if you—"

"I'll help," I say.

We slice Granny Smith apple rounds, slather them in a thick layer of peanut butter, and shower them with crunchy granola. Tayla eats her apple rounds plain, but the rest of us eat the toppings with relish.

The sun is poking out behind the gray clouds when we're

ready to be on our way. I want to check in with my friends back home, but even though I shake out the contents of my backpack, I can't find the radio. "I had it in my hand when we escaped," I say in frustration. "Where did it *go*?"

"Must have dropped it when we took off running," Keiffer says with sympathy, helping me repack.

Radhika bites her lip, crouching half in, half out of the tent to help fold one of my sweatshirts. "Should we go back for it? It's our only lifeline to the real world."

No one jumps to agree or disagree, so I make the call. "We can't even be sure where it is. Besides, thanks to Kiara, the forest is exorcised. I think the way back will be faster than our route in. Right, Tayla?"

"What?" She looks surprised to be addressed, pausing her neck stretch. "Oh, um. Yeah. Maybe. Time seems to be passing like normal again." She resumes tilting her head from side to side.

"Are you . . . okay?" Evan asks.

"I wasn't made for sleeping on a forest floor," says Tayla. "Can't wait to get home and sleep in my own bed."

That's a sentiment we can all get behind. It doesn't take long to dismantle the tents and head back for the trail. None of us got enough sleep, but our footsteps are light and eager as we walk without stopping until my stomach lets out the grizzliest rumble of my life. We break at the map board only long enough to peel squashed clementines and eat the last of our energy bars, throw away our trash, and dig a few latrine holes.

The sun is starting to dip by the time our surroundings start to feel recognizable again, though how, when all the trees look like every other tree, I'm not sure. It's just a feeling, and I've learned to trust those.

I fill my lungs with a deep inhale. The earthiness of soil and shrub has replaced the malignant odor of rot. Even the strong fungal scent of the frond-like yellow chicken-of-the-woods mushroom isn't offensive. Dad's voice is with me, not out of a memory but so achingly familiar it's as though he's next to me. Bending to show me the bright yellow meat of the mushroom, explaining that these are good to eat and reminding me once again that the warty white-and-red ones are not. The memory brings with it a sweet, bearable ache.

Kiara sidles up to me, sliding her palm against mine until I interlock our fingers and hold on tight. "How are you?" she asks, quiet enough that the others, walking a few steps behind, won't hear.

It's a hard question to answer and not one I can wholly reconcile just yet. In one version, I came here for my dad, and I let him go instead. In the other, I came here for my dad, and I found him again. Both are true, and while I'm grateful that I see and hear my father in the presence of all the small wonders around me, it's not the same as having him back as flesh and blood.

But I don't regret using my one wish on Kiara, either. I can be sad while at the same time knowing I made the right decision. The choice Dad would have made and a man like Henry Prior probably never could.

"Alive," I tell Kiara. "I'm alive."

And life, I think, is a gift that means we're always moving forward. We move on. Grief is the price we pay for loving and losing someone in this world.

Her hand squeezes mine. I put one foot in front of the other, and together we move on.

The Fellowship chatters freely even as the sun goes down. No one jumps when a twig snaps, when something stirs beyond the shrubbery. The wildlife is plentiful and more willing to show its face now that the woods belong to them once more.

"I think we're close to where we stopped on our first night," I say when Keiffer suggests we take a break to rest and eat dinner.

"Really?" Tayla looks stricken. Her dainty shoulders tense.

"What's wrong?" asks Evan.

"Nothing," she says quickly. "I just . . . got a bad feeling."

"About stopping here?" Radhika surveys our surroundings, as though something or someone could pop out at any second, then closes the gap between her and Keiffer.

"If we eat fast and push on, maybe we'll make it home tonight," says Kiara.

Evan's got the knack for making fires, and Radhika whisks up the last of the powdered eggs, and together they make us egg-tortilla wraps. It's a basic omelet fried with a flour tortilla right on top, flipped, drizzled with hot sauce down the middle, and rolled up nice and tight. I blink in amazement, not even daring to question whose pack *tortillas*, of all things, have come from. They really did overpack.

While we wait our turn, Kiara tugs me a little away.

She doesn't let go of my hand. "Nova, before we see our families, I just wanted to say . . ."

"Yes?"

"When you pretended to be Madame Aurora, you said something."

I cast my gaze at my scuffed boots, ashamed.

"You said," says Kiara, "that I'd have to sacrifice my heart's desire in order to break the curse."

"It was bullshit. I have no idea if it would or wouldn't."

"Yeah, maybe. But I didn't want to take that chance. You once wanted me to know how it felt to be obsessed with someone. Well, I was. All this time." My eyes fly to hers. "It's you, Nova. It's always been you. I would have taken my chances with the bad luck if it meant I still had a shot with you."

I can't believe what I'm hearing. "N-no," I stammer. "So all this time, we could have been . . . ?"

She laughs. "Yes."

I swoop in to capture her lips. We both taste like grit and sweat, but the kiss is sweet and giddy and makes my stomach somersault. It's far from the perfect kiss I'd imagined, but I don't even care because I'm kissing Kiara Mistry, and she's kissing me back.

She breaks the kiss and pulls back just enough so I can see her exuberant smile. In that moment all I can think is that she has a mouth made for smiling, and the unbrushed hair and tired eyes and swipe of dirt across her cheek only accentuates how radiant it is.

"I want to eat cotton candy with you on the last day of the Fall Festival," she mumbles against my lips. "I want a date. And I want a shower. Not in that order."

"Okay," I say. "Whatever you want."

"Whatever I want? Even you?" Her smile is impish.

"What about Tayla?" Maybe I shouldn't be asking about another contender for Kiara's heart when I've finally, *finally* gotten the girl, but the part of me that's insecure about where I stand among the Fellowship of the Fling demands concrete answers about what's going to happen once we're home.

She raises an eyebrow, lips twitching as if she's amused. "Nova, I'm kissing *you*."

Flustered, I say, "I know that, but—"

She presses a finger to my lips, smiles a smile of pure sunshine, and replaces it with her mouth. It's a soft peck at first, delicate as the wings of a dragonfly, then it gradually builds to firm, demanding pressure that pulses down my legs and makes my toes curl. I can feel my heartbeat in my fingertips. I raise my hands to her face, cradle it gently, tilting her so I'm the one taking over. I match the hungry want of her mouth, the desire that's been building since our moment in the tent but, in truth, a lot longer than that.

When we part for air, she slides her hands, which were loosely holding my waist, up to my neck. She noses against the shivery place where my neck and ear meet until I giggle, and then she laughs and says, "You give me butterfly flutters, Nova Marwood."

"Rabble," I say nonsensically.

"What?"

"When the butterflies are disorderly. Chaotic. Flapping about like a herd of cats." I clear my throat at the befuddled then bemused way she simply looks back at me. "Never mind. It's something I heard once."

She goes in for another peck, like she can't help herself. "Uh-huh."

"Guys!" Evan hollers. "Stop kissing and come eat! This is the *second* time I've tried to get your attention!"

"Sorry, Evan. We didn't even hear you," says Kiara as we head back to the others hand in hand.

"That was obvious," they say dryly.

Tayla doesn't make eye contact with me as we eat. She doesn't look like she enjoys her wrap, but then I don't think I've ever seen her truly happy about anything on this quest, really.

It's not just me she's avoiding. Or Kiara. She seems off. Quiet and withdrawn, willing to let me lead. She didn't offer any input about which direction to take or when to stop, and she hasn't tried to monopolize Kiara's attention even once.

Is her ego bruised because she thinks she has lost to me? No, that's not the Tayla I know and have grown to grudgingly like. That Tayla would never give up. She wouldn't hunch her shoulders like that or hide her feelings. Even when she down-played her fear and unease, she still had plenty of attitude about it. *It can't be about me and Kiara kissing. Even Tayla wouldn't be that petty.*

"Let's move on," Radhika declares the second Tayla takes her last swallow.

We've found our rhythm. We eat, clean up, shoulder our packs, and keep moving. We talk to remind each other we're still here, but even the quiet moments don't feel lonely. If a moment comes that I wonder if I am, I reach for Kiara's hand instead.

More leaves have fallen since we first came this way. The brittle clumps softly crunch under our boots. The sounds of small animals skittering and scurrying around us is oddly comforting, even though Evan declares squirrels freak them out, and the haunting hoot of an owl sounds like it comes from just a stone's throw away. The sky is a dark pewter, smudged with graphite, with the brilliance of a glowing moon just be-hind the treetops turning the forest to silver glass.

We hear the gurgle of running water before we see it. "Nova, you were right! We're close to our old campsite!" says Radhika. "Tayla, do you think you can find that stream again?"

Tayla shakes her head, but Keiffer's already bounding off in the direction of the gentle trickles with his water bottle out. We're all running low, so I don't blame his excitement. I'm on my last few drops, too, and if I don't hydrate soon, I risk the onset of a headache. We all traipse after him, eager to quench our thirst and refill our bottles.

Tayla suddenly picks up speed to match Keiffer's stride. "*Wait*," she says.

She throws out her arm to stop him like a parent trying to protect their child in the front passenger seat. There's a sudden urgency in her tone, but her voice is a croak, and I suddenly realize I don't remember the last time she spoke.

We all come to a halt, casting around worried gazes, but can't find a reason for her agitation.

"It's uneven here," Tayla says, kicking at the ground to illustrate. Dirt and twigs and stones fall away, crumbling down an incline that, now that I see it, is steeper than I'd thought. As the pebbles patter down, she takes a sharp inhale that the others miss, but I don't.

"Could have been a nasty fall. Thanks for the warning," says Keiffer, shooting her a grateful smile.

She doesn't return it. She doesn't even see it.

She's too focused on the stream below, at the displaced stones and soil.

"Let's just keep going," Tayla says, and nobody objects, even though Keiffer gives a dismayed little look at his empty water bottle.

Kiara wordlessly hands him what's left of hers, and together they turn back. With a shrug, Radhika follows. I watch Tayla, and even Evan hesitates, waiting for us. "Coming?" they ask.

It takes Tayla a beat to respond. "Yeah," she says, finally tearing her gaze away.

"What are you even looking at?" I ask, brow furrowed. I keep an eye on the ground as I approach, mindful of the erosion, but she gets in my way.

"Nothing. Just thinking how long it's been since I was here. It feels like an age." Tayla walks forward until I'm forced to take a step back. "We're holding everyone up, Nova," she says, the words so final that Evan and I both understand it's the end of the matter. She's not going to discuss it further.

Tayla links her arms through mine and Evan's, dragging us away.

"No distractions," she repeats. "Let's just get Kiara out of here first and worry about the rest later."

The rest? Evan and I exchange confused glances. *What else is there to worry about?*

31

Flashing blue-and-red lights greet us as we approach the tree line. The relief of returning to Prior's End is now dimmed by the worry about what waits for us at home. Exhausted, we straggle toward the sounds of civilization, eager to see our families, take a hot shower, and fall asleep in our own beds.

"Wait."

Tayla says it the way she did the first time. We all realize it and come to a standstill.

"I . . ." She presses her lips together like she's trying not to cry. Her nostrils flare with the effort it takes for her to speak. "I can't . . ." Her gulp is a wretched thing. "I can't go home."

"What are you talking about?" Radhika frowns, impatient. She points to the flashing lights. "We're already here."

"You don't understand." Tayla's endlessly blue eyes glisten. Her hand finds its way to her neck, and she grasps it, making a soft whine of distress. "I think this is as far as I can go. What happened . . . it's started coming back to me. In fragments. I knew that when we returned, I'd have to tell you. I knew what I'd have to do, but . . . I'm afraid of doing it."

"You're scaring me," Kiara whispers.

"Tayla." I move past the others to stand directly in front of her. "What's going on?"

She swallows and doesn't respond.

And in my heart, I begin to understand.

Why the food never met with her satisfaction. Why she's let everyone else take the lead on the journey home, as though she wouldn't be able to find her way out without me.

Why she returned from filling our water bottles on that first night with leaves in her hair, stray crimson strands coming loose from her ponytail. Why she lingered at the stream with that faraway look in her eye, like she was remembering something she'd forgotten.

Why she grasps her throat with that wild look in her eyes like she doesn't want it to be true. Why every time she touched her neck, I assumed she was nervously fiddling with her necklace.

"No," I whisper.

"Nova, what is it?" Keiffer looms over me, blocking the moonlight and casting Tayla in darkness. All I can see are her pale cheeks with two solitary tear tracks. How they dangle at her jawline then drop somewhere on the earth below.

"If we'd come across that stream a few hours earlier when the sun was still up, you would have seen the body," says Tayla. She releases her hold on her throat, lets her hand fall limp at her side.

"Body?" Kiara says it like the word has a secret meaning she doesn't understand.

"I broke my neck in the fall," says Tayla. "Days ago."

We all stare at her neck, but it's the same column of smooth, unblemished white skin as it's always been.

"What?" Keiffer asks, voice hoarse.

Radhika makes a sound like a choked gasp. My own heart stutters erratically, a feeling like a knife's edge scraping at my chest. Evan's eyes are wide and unblinking; they're robbed of the ability to say anything. They can only stare at Tayla with dawning horror, tears spilling over.

"I thought I got up again," says Tayla. "I remembered falling, the soreness in my neck and body afterward. But I didn't remember dyi—" She swallows. "Didn't remember anything else."

"No," Kiara says forcefully, like that alone can deny what Tayla's saying. "No."

"I'm so sorry," says Tayla. "I didn't think it would end this way."

Kiara grabs Tayla's face in her hands. "No, your journey does *not* end here."

"It's okay, babe." Tayla's smile is watery. "It was worth it."

"No," Kiara repeats, shoving Tayla toward the tree line. "You are walking out of here with us."

But it's as though an invisible wall sprang up to block their path.

Kiara can progress beyond it, but Tayla physically can't, not even when Keiffer bodily lifts her and tries to carry her across. Radhika and Evan each take one arm and pull. Seeing their desperation makes grief rise in my throat. If her revelation affects me, who barely knows her, I can't imagine what it's doing to Kiara, who was so afraid of being the reason one of her friends got hurt.

Kiara keeps pulling at Tayla's limbs. She refuses to let go, not even when Tayla yelps and rubs at her shoulders. "Stop!" Tayla finally cries. "You're going to dislocate my arm."

"So what?" Kiara throws back, her protest ending on a sob. "Better your arm than leaving you behind."

"Babe, it's okay." Tayla wipes away Kiara's tears with both thumbs. "Remember what you wished for? That everyone would go where they needed to be? I guess the wishing well let me come back this far. I know you'll be okay now."

"Stop it!" says Radhika, shrill. "We're all getting out of here right the fuck now." She makes as if to haul her again, but the redhead evades her.

"*Enough*," says Tayla, a hint of her attitude returning in the way she says that one word.

"Let me try a fireman carry," says Keiffer. "If she's pressed up against my back, then maybe it won't recognize that she's a separate person."

That doesn't work either.

Something tells me nothing will.

Tayla meets my sorrowful eyes over Kiara's shoulder. "I wish I could have gone with you right until the very end. Seen how it all worked out."

"You did," I say, uselessly adding, "You will."

"Go," says Tayla, nodding to the lights.

"What's going to happen to you?" asks Evan.

She shakes her head. "I don't know. Maybe I'll fade away. It's probably what happened to the others."

"No," Kiara whispers again, but this time there's resignation to it.

"My body—" Tayla starts to say, but I stop her.

"We'll bring you back," I promise. The thought of her broken body lying there makes my throat tighten, but I don't let myself cry. I don't have that right. The rest of the Fellowship does.

They all take turns hugging her, even me. Her friends brokenly whisper things that make Tayla smile, then cry, then smile some more. Is she putting on a brave face for the sake of her friends? Or has she truly made her peace with it? No, how can she? She's only seventeen after all.

I squeeze her hard, which comes as a surprise to both of us, I think, but she hugs me back. I wait for a threat to manifest, some warning of how hard she's going to haunt my ass if I fuck things up with Kiara, but it never comes. In the end, we just nod at each other. Stoic. We spent too long disliking each other for sweet words now. It would only cheapen the solemnity of the moment.

Leaving her behind is hard. Maybe the hardest thing any of them have had to do.

This time it's my turn to take Kiara by the hand and lead her forward.

The Fellowship of the Fling is ended.

32

After leaving Tayla, I'm the first to break the silence. "We can never tell anyone the wishing well is real," I say. I look at Radhika. "Absolutely no one. We have to protect it. We have to do what Henry Prior should have done from the start: left it alone."

Kiara surprises me when she says, "I destroyed it. It should stay that way."

"But it's part of our history," Radhika protests. "Nova . . ."

"And how many more have to die or go missing?" asks Evan. "Better to keep it a secret."

Radhika falls silent. Keiffer puts an arm around her shoulder. "They're right. We have to keep people safe from *it* and *it* safe from people. If people know we undid Kiara's bad luck, they'll never stop looking for it. Maybe they'll even try to rebuild it. It's a myth, it's a legend, and one day it won't even be history anymore. It'll just be forgotten."

She gives a jerky nod, but I don't know how much she believes it.

"It's the right thing to do," I tell her, and if she believes nothing else, I hope she believes *me*. "In your heart of hearts, you know it, too."

When we emerge from the woods, there's so much activity bustling everywhere around us that it takes me a moment to acclimate myself. It seems like half the town is here, but how? Why?

Austin and Caroline stand with their parents and ours. Aurora is twisting her ring round and round her finger as she hovers by an ambulance. She seems oblivious to everything going on around her, wholly focused on the trees, like she's waiting for someone. Her whole face is naked with longing, a heartbreaking mix of hopeful and desperate. Otto and Petra are pouring drinks for the gathering crowd. The scent of hot chocolate wafts over to us.

Evan gnaws at their lower lip. "You don't think they're here for us, do you?"

"What do you think is going on?" Kiara whispers. We're still holding hands.

"I don't know," I whisper back.

I turn around, half expecting to see Tayla hovering just out of sight. But she's already gone. Heart heavy, I step out into the glow of dozens of headlights.

Caroline audibly gasps and tugs at my mother's arm, pointing to all of us illuminated there against the darkness. All the other parents start scanning our Fellowship for their child, too.

Mom sees me first. "Nova!" she screams. She abandons the bearded man with a blanket draped over his shoulders and a paramedic checking his eyesight.

She barrels right into me, sobbing into my neck, which I'm

sure smells horrifying after the past four days, but she takes a deep inhale as though none of it matters. As though I'm not totally grounded for infinity after this. But honestly, if she never lets me leave her sight again, I think I might be okay with that. I cling to my mom, which is a little tough with Kiara's hand still tangled between us. With a teary smile, she extricates herself from the awkward embrace.

And then Austin and Caroline and Otto and Petra are there, hugging and kissing and love-scolding until we're all a giant blubbering mess.

"We wouldn't have survived without him," a man says to Petra as he accepts his drink. Wrapping both scarred hands around the cup, he nods to the bearded man. "The other men tried to rule like kings, but we refused to live like they did. We mostly stuck to the caves. Made our home there. He knows about foraging and medicinal plants. No one knows the forest better than him. He never let us give up on our humanity, even those of us who had already lost our lives."

"And he was one of the few who managed to stay alive," a woman adds. Her face is weathered, and she's gray before her time, but there's joy in her voice when she says, "He said he had to, for his little girl."

A woman a little younger than her with the same blue eyes and thin lips, says, "We already told the police how we all tried to leave, but we kept getting turned around every time. No one tried more than him. Especially after his friend ate those poisoned mushrooms and died so horribly . . ." She shudders. "I don't know how it happened, but suddenly, whatever was stopping him from finding his way out? It didn't exist anymore. He remembered how to leave and took us with him. He saved us."

I hear all the conversations going on around us, but when Mom opens her mouth, it all fades to white noise.

"Nova," Mom repeats again, then again and again. As though my name is her lodestone. She laughs through tears. She withdraws but only enough so she can look at my face, caress my cheek, and hold her forehead against mine. "Our North Star," she breathes.

My head jerks. What did she just say? I haven't heard that in—

"Sweetheart," says Mom. "You won't believe who's come home."

My eyes fly to the man waiting for her. For us. He's older now. There are abrasions on his face. Tiny white scars, too, that stand out starkly against his dirty skin. Nothing about him is familiar.

Until he raises his hand to greet me and I see what's tattooed on his skin.

My eyes meet Kiara's, who's squished between her parents. They keep alternating between hugging and sobbing. Sometimes both at once. We break eye contact only when her parents drag her to get checked out by the paramedic. A middle-aged couple with ginger hair and piercing blue eyes rake their eyes through the crowd, and then, having come to some sort of realization, hasten after Kiara.

I don't know whether tomorrow will bring her good luck or bad luck. But we saved her. We did some good for those who were left behind. We'll give the police directions to go back out there and see what remains they can find. Some closure for the families. For Aurora, who will finally know the truth: her fiancé never abandoned her. I like to think that he loved her until his last breath.

But I don't want to think about that now. We just made it out of there; even in my own head, I don't want the forest to claim me as it so very nearly did.

"Dad," I say.

"My Super Nova," he says with a tenderness I still don't think I deserve but I desperately need.

I don't know who reaches for who first, who starts crying first, whose legs buckle until we're both huddled on the ground.

"I'm so sorry, Daddy," I say into his neck. His shirt is stained, woodsmoke saturating the entire fabric. Holes on the sleeves, threads hanging loose on his collar. He's sweaty and grimy, but he's still my dad, and his arms are around me, and the only thought in my head is that *everything is going to be okay*.

"Shhh," he says, pressing a kiss to my hair.

I cry harder. "It was my fault. I should never have said those things. Never have told you to go."

"You were a child." His voice breaks. "It was never your fault."

"But I—"

Dad doesn't let me finish. "It was never your fault," he says firmly.

"Oh, Nova." Mom joins us on the ground, face splotchy. "You carried that all this time?"

"I said the words." My voice shakes. "Me."

Fine! Go, then! If you love the woods so much, stay there forever! I hope you never come back!

Even now, the words are suspended between us. I don't repeat them for fear of what they'll do.

But Dad must have explained this to Mom because her face softens, the worry lines on her face easing. She goes on to explain that when hordes of people started staggering through the woods, most dazed and disassociated and dirt-stained, Austin and Caroline had tried to radio me. When they couldn't get through, they ran to the town for help. Apparently Austin had panicked at first, thinking it was the start of the zombie apocalypse (because *of course* he did). And when all our parents got there, he explained what we were really doing in the woods.

"You're not mad?" I ask.

"Of course I'm mad," says Mom. "I'm furious."

"Oh."

"But I'm also proud of my baby girl."

I jerk my head up and stare. She smiles and chucks me under the chin.

"Your words matter, Nova," says Dad. The deep grooves on his forehead and the little scars marring his face and knuckles are a testament to his time away from us. A reminder of my guilt. "But so do your actions. I know you'll choose your words with more care in the future, and I also know you'll do your best to set things right when you don't. I'm grateful to be back here with my family, but more than that, I'm grateful you stayed full of wonder. You were so young . . . I was afraid that the world would try and take it from you."

I'm about to tell him that he's wrong, that the world did take it, and then I realize that I clawed it back. I might have let my wonder waver, but it was still mine. It returned to me. The wonder is part of me, just like Dad and the Longing Woods and the *occasional* magic of Prior's End.

"Never," I say, the word bubbling out through a laugh-sob, and it's the truth.

The stars are alight in the sky, Kiara is saved, and Dad is back. A little older, a little more battered, but *back*. Dad was right in what he said all those years ago about being responsible for our friends. The Fellowship isn't broken. We will not forsake Tayla to her fate. We don't need the wishing well.

We are bound by this quest and by each other and by those we've left behind. By the secret we keep and will always keep. Even without the wishing well, we will find another way. There is, after all, still some magic left in this world.

"Let's go home," says Mom. We all struggle to our feet, Mom letting Dad lean on her for support. He's lost weight, but there's quiet strength in his face.

I see that same strength in Kiara's face when I seek her out in the crowd.

In Evan's face. In Radhika's. In Keiffer's. In Austin's. In Caroline's.

And then I land on Aurora. She approaches us, looking more haggard than I've ever seen her. Older than Mom. Every bit of her sparkle is gone. My anger toward her has deflated, and all I'm left with is a sadness that she's lived with her grief this long.

My breath catches. "Aurora . . ."

"They're saying Austin's father is dead," she says.

"He is," says Dad, and I can hear how the words cost him. "Not long ago. He ate some poisonous mushrooms. We don't know how it happened. Or what happened to him after."

"I was waiting for my Mickey." Her eyes land on me. She picks at her fingernails, which I see now are bloodied. "It would have been two decades this year. I always thought if I kept coming back here, maybe one day he'd be the one waiting for me." Her eyes glitter with unshed tears as she waits for me to confirm something I think she already suspects.

"I'm sorry," I say. "His friends weren't his friends."

"I'm sorry, Nova. I know you've never liked me, but I tried to be a good friend to your mom. We both lost the men we loved." I see her smile at my parents, a genuine smile that's so full of love and grief that my own heart pinches. I know it must hurt that Mickey wasn't one of the ones to survive, to make it back to her. Suddenly, the hope she imbued in Mom over the past seven years makes sense. Aurora never gave up on her fiancé, either.

I glance at my parents. Mom gives me a tiny nod. "Would you like to come back home with us?" I ask. Maybe it's unfair of me, but I can't chance telling her about the well. Can't risk that she'll try to make the trip and rebuild something we've all agreed is best left as ruins.

But I can give her this. "I . . . I don't know if it will bring you any measure of peace, but I can tell you where his body is. And what happened."

And at some point, the authorities will go to the glade and recover all the backpacks and identify the ones who did not make it out of the forest. Hold a memorial. Honor the dead.

But tonight and tomorrow and maybe even the day after that is for my family. Mine. Whole at long last. I toss one last glance at the woods before following Mom to our car.

But after that, I think it might be time for another adventure. Time to save another friend.

Wish us luck.

Epilogue

She's never liked being alone. But here, for the first time in a month, she doesn't feel the sting of it quite so keenly. Like a wound from a blade that never healed.

The girl steps into the clearing, and the light of the full moon sets her hair ablaze. She's been here many times as the moon waned and waxed, finally whole again. Her fingertips are calloused, her nails dirty and ragged. She's bitten them to the quick. But none of that matters.

She knows exactly where she's going, and she walks there with the confidence she always had in life. She passes a forgotten radio on the ground, the battery long dead, but sometimes she thinks she can still hear phantom crackles in the woods of other radios far out of range.

A man stealthily follows behind her. He wears the same grim determination on his face as she does. In the time since his death, he has learned how to go unseen if he wishes.

He has made use of the cloak of darkness to disappear entirely, though there were a few times when he was almost caught by a girl he once knew. A girl now ten years older than when he saw her last. His suntanned skin is older and more lined, but she would know him. He couldn't face her, not as he was now, not with the sour taste of death on his lips.

The wishing well is demolished. So much abandoned power. The girl doesn't hesitate. After all, why should she? She's only seventeen. She has much more life to live. She just has to undo a death first.

The girl is unaware of the man. She is set wholly on her task. There are, after all, only a few hours until midnight. She stoops to pick up a stone. And then another and another.

Finally, it's time. Time for the last stone.

She doesn't hesitate.

She slots it into place.

Maneuvers and adjusts.

The stone grinds against the others.

One side of it is engraved with a word.

She traces her finger over that word, brow scrunched, and fervently prays. Will it work? The well can undo a regret, yes, but can it undo an unintended accident? Well, she'll soon find out.

She takes a step back and waits, blue eyes focused on that one word. Tries to quell the fear and doubt. Such a strange fate for her life to depend on this one little stone. This one word.

Diminish.

Acknowledgments

*N*o matter how many books I've written, there always comes a point in the journey that feels like taking the long road to Mount Doom—without a map! Writing a book is much like the agonies of travel that way. No matter how painstakingly you've plotted and planned, there are always surprises along the way. Unexpected journeys, if you will. As anyone who's been on a quest of their own will know, there are times you'll question whether you've taken a wrong turn somewhere. Do you reorient yourself with your surroundings and pivot? Or do you find your way back to the path? Do you find the strength to forge ahead, whatever may come?

I don't think one decision is more correct than the others. If you believe in the story you want to tell, the story in your heart, you will find your way. Eventually, of course, all the right paths converge. Everything aligns the way it was always meant to. Your perseverance and grit pay off. You trusted in the journey and made it through (what feels like) the harrowing long dark of Moria, the ghastly Dead Marshes, the formidable Black Gate, and the ultimate moment when the Eye is finally upon you. Just as Nova and the rest of the Fellowship of the Fling undergo their own trials and metamorphoses, *Hit Me with Your Best Charm* is the book that made me a stronger storyteller. Without this book, I wouldn't have the trust in my inner guidance system that I do today.

While much of the writing process is solitary, when it comes to the path to publication, there are many people who help share the load. I am grateful as ever to those who made the journey a little lighter—including and especially my editor, Dana Leydig—and the rest of the team at Viking Children's Books, who transformed a story into a published book. I don't take for granted how fortunate I am to work on a second book with such a forward-thinking editor, and I'm eternally appreciative that I'm able to collaborate every step of the way. My agent, Jessica Watterson, has a magic all her own in making authors' dreams come true, and bringing *Charm* to readers is certainly one of mine! I am lucky to count such steadfast champions in my corner, including production editor Sola Akinlana, publicist Sierra Pregosin, and marketer Felicity Vallence. Publishing *Charm* with you all feels like some kind of magic.

I am immeasurably thankful for everyone who read, reviewed, loved, and blurbed this book. For anyone who has good things to say, now and in the future, wherever you share those words, thank you from the bottom of my heart. You and the fantastic folks at Penguin help so much in getting my books into the hands of readers all over the world. Thanks also go to Jillian Goeler, whose illustration conjured the perfect blend of pretty and sinister I had in my mind to craft the cover of my dreams, and book designer Kaitlin Yang and art director Theresa Evangelista. And to those who remind me that I have, in fact, not forgotten how to write a book: Thank you to Daniel, Rachael, Sue, Rachel, Emily, and the countless other authors, bookstagrammers, librarians, booksellers, and other creatives who have—in ways both big and small—been part of my journey. I will never know all your names, but know that I appreciate your passion from the bottom of my heart.

No acknowledgment would be complete without my deepest love and gratitude for my parents, who have done more for me than I can ever possibly articulate. Because of you, I've had unyielding support, the best adventures, and more imagination than I know what to do with. I've been lucky to share that imagination and camaraderie with my best and oldest friend, through all the good and bad, through all six of my books, and through all the stories that are yet to come. Kate: The world is ahead!

Charm isn't just an ode to *The Lord of the Rings* (although anyone who knows me will attest that I can't resist leaving little sprinkles of my *LOTR*-loving heart in all my books). *Charm* is—in equal measure—about guilt and grief, strength and salvation. It's about getting so mired in your own thorns that you can't find your way out again. And it's about the determined people who hack away at those thorny defenses and pull you to the other side. It has never been more apparent to me that friendship, courage, and empathy are the brightest and most inexhaustible flames we must kindle during our darkest times. At the Council of Elrond, Frodo said he would undertake the journey but did not know the way. So too did Nova set off on a quest of her own without much else to go on but hope. Both of them left home with little more than inner courage and the courage of their friends. And in the end, after much hardship, two rather unlikely people changed the course of the future. More than ever, this message carries power and inspires me as both a writer and human.

The final thanks are for you, reader. Your time is precious, and if you have spent yours reading this book, I hope the journey was worth the destination.

"If you're a fan of rivals-to-lovers, look no further!" —Aiden Thomas, *New York Times* bestselling author of *Cemetery Boys*

★ "A joyful ode to being true to yourself and finding love where you least expect it." —*Kirkus Reviews*, starred review